The Shiloh PROJECT

With the exception of recognized historical figures, the characters in this novel are fictional. Any resemblence to actual persons, living or dead, is purely coincidental.

Cover design by Mobley Art & Design

Printed in the United States of America.

ISBN 1-56322-041-5

To
Ha-Melech Laolam Vaed
(The King of Forever),
whose story it was from the beginning, and is.

The sceptre shall not depart from Judah,
nor a lawgiver from between his feet,
until Shiloh come;
and unto him the gathering of the people.
Genesis 49:10

Sudden light compressed his eyes to a red squint.

He was aware of blasting heat prickling his armpits, the grit of sand against bare skin, the stink of fear. And silence. The sound of open, empty air, broken by a woman's voice, shaking, on edge: "Mel? What…"

Rolling to his other side, half sitting, he shaded his eyes, sand adhering to his sweating forearm, crumbs of it falling on his lap.

Ruth Foster crouched there on half-buried hands and bare knees, wide eyes peering through skeins of black hair that hung to curl on the sand. Sweat trickled down the vee of her throat.

God! She looked so vulnerable, so…young. Not a bit like the smart, capable mathematician he knew she was. Like she was only minutes ago. Embarrassed, he looked away. *Another innocent in my care. God, not again.*

"What…happened to us?"

He couldn't speak, could hardly think. Tasting salt, he licked the corner of his mouth. Already he felt the sun burning his exposed skin.

Air moved behind him. Ruth's sand-encrusted hand reached past his eyes, touched his cheek, not gently turned his head. "Mel!" It was almost a shriek.

"Wait, let me think."

"Wait? I'm burning up! Why is it daylight? Where's the airport? How did we get here?"

"*Hold it!* Good God. Look, how long since you slept?"

"I think I have every right to be—"

"We dozed off, or—No! That slimy waiter slipped us a mickey. Then they kidnapped us and dumped us in the desert."

"Why?"

"How should I know? 'Cause I'm a Jew. Got a better explanation?"

"There must be one. That one stinks. No drug in the world could do that. One second we're sitting over coffee, it's midnight in Baghdad—"

"Where we had no business being in the first place."

"But at least we *know* how we got there. The next second, dumped in the sand.—*Oh, it's hot!*—Where's all our stuff?"

A light breeze caught a piece of paper and turned it over. Lunging for it, Mel now noticed their papers, pens and flight bags baking in the sand behind them. "See if everything's here."

"My luggage... My clothes..." she moaned, rummaging through her purse. "That's crazy! They left all my cash."

"Bought my theory, huh?"

"Look, let's get someplace cool. Quick. I can't think with a fried brain."

Brushing off sand, they pulled themselves to their feet.

Mel looked around. "Not so quick."

They stood on the highest point for miles, a flat sandblown rock thirty feet above the general level of a yellow-brown desert that stretched to the horizon on all sides.

What was that? Mel pointed to a dark green line on the horizon in the direction of his short shadow. "Could that be some shade?"

"We've had it, if that's the closest—"

"Ruth, it's our only chance. Come on."

Hefting her flight bag, Ruth paused. "Wait." She squatted, unzipped it.

Mel watched her pull out a cotton miniskirt and stretch the elastic waistband around her brow. Tucking a loose strand of hair back under the fabric, she anchored it with a bobby pin. "Instant burnoose."

That's more like it, he thought. "Good idea."

"You must have something."

"My miniskirts are all too big around the waist."

She grinned, a sight to gladden his heart. "Come on, let's get down off this rock. Maybe there's some shade at the base of it."

Tucking their papers into the flight bags and slinging them over their shoulders, they scuffed across the flat top of the rock toward the nearest edge. A yard from it, Ruth's foot suddenly sank into a concealed crevice. She teetered on the brink; Mel grabbed her arm; sand cascaded thirty feet straight down. "Watch it!"

"Not that way," she gasped, recovering her balance. They turned back to look toward the other side.

Something was wrong. What was he seeing?

"What's the matter?" asked Ruth.

"What's wrong with this picture?" Mel could see the scuff marks of their progress through smooth sand. Apparently there wasn't much wind between sandstorms. A land of extremes. Great.

"It's blurry, too much sweat in my eyes." Wiping her brow with the edge of her headdress, Ruth glanced at Mel. "Is that it? Too humid for a des — Tracks!"

He nodded. "You've got it. Where are their tracks?"

"They must have brought us here by helicopter."

She'd accepted his explanation, but… "Ruth, a helicopter would have scoured this rock clean."

"Maybe more sand came."

"If we were here that long we'd be dead now."

"Okay, it's a mystery how we got here. But right now I'm more interested in how we're gonna get back. Come on." They trudged across the rock toward the other side, which faced the short line of dark green in the distance.

The high sun poured heat down the sloping side of the rock. The side that should have been in shadow.

"Just our luck. No shade here, either."

"At least we can climb it." Ruth stepped gingerly over the edge.

"Easy, don't twist an ankle. Looks like a talus slope down below."

"Sand-frosted boulders. Just like the Appalachian Trail, no?"

Choosing each step with care, they descended onto buried blocks of stone, shoulder-bags swinging awkwardly.

"Carry your bags, ma'am?"

"Why thank you, sir. That's okay."

She didn't look okay, with that purse dangling from her neck. But her attitude had improved. Maybe they'd get out of this alive. Lucky they'd arrived on a high point, where they could see—

"Don't stop." Ruth frowned at him. "Dynamic balance is the only—"

"Take a look." His hand swept the horizon.

The dark green line was gone.

In the end Ruth had to climb back up the rock to where she could again see their goal, while Mel proceeded out into the featureless plain in the direction she pointed, depositing first her bag and then his own in a straight line toward the oasis. He returned to the first marker and waited while she climbed down to join him, pick up her bag, and carry it ahead to mark the next position. Taking turns in this way, they hoped to maintain a straight path toward the unseen target. But their progress was maddeningly slow.

Soon they saw that their trail remained visible for a good distance pointing straight back toward the rock. Using it as reference they could avoid setting markers, and thereafter made better time. Still, the sun was low over their right shoulders when the tree line finally reappeared—forty degrees off their course.

"Is that it? Way over there?" Ruth collapsed to the ground. "Oh, God. We almost missed it."

Mel sank down beside her. "Rest, but not too long. We have to get there before dark, or we still could miss it."

"How much farther?"

"Two or three miles. Should go pretty fast now. The ground's firm here."

"Good."

She wasn't mentioning the one thing on both their minds. Water. There had to be water there. Trees meant water. They couldn't go another hour without it. If they could get up again.

"Mel." Ruth licked her cracked lips. "There's bound to be...people there, isn't there?"

"Bound to be." Groaning, he rose and stretched. "Time to go," he said, offering her his hand.

"Just one more minute." She lay flat, arms cradling her head.

"No!" Panic rose in him. He fought it down. "Ruth, it's in sight. The end is in sight!"

She mumbled something.

"What?" He leaned close. This time he heard the whispered word. He wished he hadn't.

"Mirage."

It can't be! Please, not a mirage.

"Ruth, get up. That's no mirage." He tugged at her arm. "We would have seen it straight ahead, where we expected it, not off to the left." Was that true?

"You're lying." But slowly she drew her arm in to lift herself to one elbow. "I guess I have to try, don't I? What if it is real?"

"It's real. Here." He crouched, supported her under one arm, and lifted. She stumbled to her feet. He took her purse and flight bag.

One step at a time, they lurched toward the apparent oasis. But not as fast as before, Mel realized. That rest hadn't done them any good.

Her weight was a nylon cable tethering his shoulder to the ground. She was asleep, he thought. Her feet were dragging.

His tongue was thick...Getting hard to breathe...Need water. His breath rasped loud in his ears. Water.

His breath. Where was Ruth's? Adrenaline spiked his blood. His heart raced. "Ruth!" With a surge of strength he yanked her around to face him. Her eyelids were grit-grouted shut, lifeless. "Ruth!"

Ear to her lips, he held his breath, listened. Faint, shallow, but thank God! She was still breathing.

How far now? Lifting his eyes, he could see individual palm trees. And, under them, square shapes. Buildings. People. Buildings meant people. And help. Another half mile. Come *on*, Ruth. "Come on! People! Water!"

Miraculously, one leg swung forward. Then the other. She was walking!

They made it fifty more yards.

But the trees were too far…too thirsty far.

They fell.

Is this the end? he wondered. No! So much to do… Shoshana…

But he couldn't move. Couldn't even breathe.

From his military training Mel knew the stages of dehydration: his mucous membranes were already drying up, thickening; next his alveoli would wither, the essential blood-ventilating lung lining; then oxygen starvation and blackout, and finally death.

His mind wandered, playing its own tricks. He saw Shana standing beautiful in the patch of sunlight, swinging her clipboard.

Her life, too, was over.

"No!" In a last dying spasm he flung his arm out to reach, to save…It fell in a ditch, limp, useless.

Death. Release into oblivion.

Finally, an end to the struggle to salvage the wreck of his career. An end to the nightmare, to the hell his life had turned into…so suddenly. Without notice.

All in the golden afternoon.

0
Prerequisites

It began at the Wednesday faculty meeting. Assistant professor Melvin Schwartz actually liked meetings. Most of his colleagues hated them, grudging time stolen from research, but Mel viewed office politics as an entertaining and instructive show.

At this particular meeting even the agenda was modestly interesting. After a heated debate over the necessity of a physics requirement for math majors (during which the department chairman, Morris T. Imbray, repeated a joke he had told only the day before in much the same company but was nevertheless rewarded with interest by the appreciative laughter of assistant professor Schmuyle Goldenberg, who was angling for promotion, but who didn't roll on the floor this time), and the appointment of a reluctant committee to evaluate textbooks for next year's freshman calculus course, Morris announced a forthcoming conference, with small result.

"You're sure, Adam? Very well, since no one seems interested in attending the Kovalevskaya Centennial Conference, we'll leave that. Next on the agenda..." Morris picked a slim folder off the pile on his desk.

Associate Professor Irving Kampf tipped his chair back to catch Mel's ear. "What, no takers for Moscow in winter? I'm staggered."

"Quiet, Irv. I want to hear this." Mel read the cryptic item with curiosity:

4. Special admission of S. Rabin.

"...the S. Rabin item," Morris continued. "I haven't yet interviewed this child, but the case looks strong. The principal was...unrestrained...in his recommendation. We may have another Gauss here, even a Milnor."

"Why?" Schmuyle, seated halfway around the ragged circle of chairs, grinned nastily. "What has this Rabin published?"

"I am given to understand that Rabin has written two papers of good quality, which were submitted to *Acta Mathematica* and the *I.H.E.S. Journal* and critically refereed. They were not accepted for publication—"

"Aha!"

"Ramanujan syndrome, I bet," said Mel half to himself. Morris heard.

"Correct. Prior publication." The chairman leaned back in his padded office chair. "But recent."

There was a silence.

"Of course his teachers knew nothing of it." Schmuyle sneered.

This disdain for schoolteachers was fairly typical of research mathematicians. Mel himself loved to teach, especially freshmen. And his students did well. Not that that earned him any points toward promotion, rather the reverse.

"Her teachers," Morris corrected. "Miss Rabin is a girl. Eleven years old. No, she is already beyond them. That, of course, is why they thought of us here at the Technion." The Haifa university was known throughout Israel, and far beyond.

Sammy looks worried, thought Mel. His paranoia is showing: a new rival! Why doesn't he relax? The world can always use another genius like Gauss.

Sure enough, Schmuyle was first to speak. "Who's going to nursemaid her?" He glanced toward Mel. All eyes followed.

They don't want any more teaching hours, Mel thought. They already begrudge the standard six.

"It is felt, and I concur," Morris answered, "that Rabin should be given the opportunity to advance at her best speed—in mathematics. In other subjects she is progressing at a more usual pace. Therefore, and for the sake of her normal socialization, she will not yet be admitted as a full-time student. She is to be released from her sixth-grade classes early each afternoon—"

A groan arose from his audience. "Five days a week…"

"—to be privately tutored by certain of us here." Morris too looked over at Mel. "I have decided to ask Professor Schwartz to take charge of arranging her schedule. Mel?"

"I'll be delighted." Now it was Mel's turn to survey the group gathered in the chairman's office, while his colleagues cringed. "I'd like a copy of the weekly schedule of each of you." He addressed Morris. "How soon does this start?"

"No need for precipitate haste. Can you be ready by Monday?"

Mel swallowed. "Sure. Then I'll need those schedules this afternoon, please."

"I'm confident you will all extend Mel your fullest cooperation. On to Item Five: Observance of Secretaries' Day."

As the faculty filed out after adjournment, the chairman said, "Mel, may I speak with you a moment? Please close the door. Have a seat. Mel, I'll come right to the point."

Oh-oh. My publication list, Mel thought.

Morris took his seat behind the desk. "Your published papers have been few and far between...numbering, I believe, four?...in your three years here."

This is it. I'm history, Mel thought. Finish out the year and I'm canned.

"As you know, our budget next year allows for only one new associate professorship. Tenured positions are coming under increasing scrutiny by the Dean's Committee."

Mel squirmed in his chair. What could he have done differently? Those four papers took a long time. They were good, too. They'd already been cited nine times, by well-known people. Should he have padded his list, like Sammy?

"Schmuyle—"

No!

"—on the other hand has a record of scholarship that is unsurpassed in our department."

Numerically. Twenty feeble notices, one pretty good result. Why was Morris smiling?

Hope flickered. Briefly. Morris was looking down now, at an envelope on the desk, not meeting Mel's eyes.

"You are also familiar with our department's long-standing policy which finds it inadvisable to retain faculty at the Assistant Professor level past the third year. Therefore I thought it incumbent upon me to inform you early, in the expectation that you would—"

—be able to start looking. In the teachers' colleges, Mel finished silently. That's why Morris is giving me S. Rabin. He considers tutoring her schlock, just like the others do, and he doesn't need to keep me happy anymore. Funny, I thought he was enthusiastic about her. I certainly am! What an opportunity! A parting gift.

But Morris was still speaking.

"—in taking these factors into consideration, and naturally expecting the promotion to go to Schmuyle, who, it must be admitted, is deemed highly qualified and deserving by the Dean—"

What's this? Who else is in the running?

"—soon start, as they say, 'looking.'"

"Thank you, sir; I appreciate the warning."

"Don't."

"But I do."

"Don't start looking; I mean for you to have the post."

"Me?" Do I look as dim as I feel? Me!

"You. Sammy's list is padded, and the Dean is a fool. Trust me to go to bat for you. Those papers of yours are sterling in quality. They impressed Mortimer Rubel sufficiently that he wrote me this letter."

The chairman handed Mel the envelope. Opening it, Mel read:

> My dear Morris,
> Be careful not to lose young Schwartz. He's destined for stardom. Saunders agrees. See our citations in Trans. AMS 6/93, Comm. Math. Helv. 11/93, Annals 8/94 and Pacific J. 9/94.
>
> Best wishes,
> Mort

Mel looked up. "I—"

"Keep your nose clean and you're a shoo-in." Morris's smile was broad now. He rose and started around the desk.

"Thank you, sir."

"It's highly unusual to see a first-rate researcher who's also a born teacher. That's why I felt you were the ideal tutor for Miss Rabin. You were serious when you expressed delight, weren't you?"

"Yes."

"One day she'll put us all in the shade. Then, to have been her teacher..." Morris put his left hand on Mel's shoulder and looked down into his eyes. "You do understand that I fully expect you to bear the brunt of the actual tutorial duties personally."

"I want to, yes."

"Fine; go to it. And congratulations. My own immediate future is rather more onerous: breaking the bad news to Schmuyle." The chairman offered his hand. Mel, after a quick palm-wipe, shook it.

"Why me?" Irving Kampf frowned at his office visitor. "I thought you were my buddy."

"Look, Irv," said Mel, perching on the corner of the desk, "it's only two hours a week, and someday you'll look back and say, 'I taught Rabin.' Besides, you're one I can trust to do it right."

"Oh, great. My reputation preempts me."

Mel grinned. "And you're free those hours, when I'm not."

"Now we come down to it. I knew I should have doctored my schedule like Sammy.

"See? That's what I mean. Integrity."

The chair springs creaked as Irv leaned back to rest his head on the whiteboard. "Mel, you owe me one."

"Thanks, Irv. You're gonna love this."

"Maybe." Kampf's bland round face relaxed. "At least it won't interfere with my square dancing."

"What level are you up to now, Irv?"

"Challenge. In fact, Sadie and I just started a C1 class." Irv's eyes lighted in recalled pleasure. "Another hundred-fifty calls to memorize, like *Zing:* 'From any formation of boxes, leaders do a three-quarter zoom while trailers step forward and quarter in.' Plus phantoms. You ought to sign up; we love it."

"What's a zoom? No, never mind, I don't want to get you started. I'd need a partner, anyway. And I just don't see the fascination."

"Mel, you wouldn't believe how it takes your mind off your troubles. One blip in your concentration and you bust the whole square. Ruin it for seven other people."

"Sounds too intense for me. Anyway, what is it? Close-order drill set to music. I get enough of that in the IDF." He was now a reserve first lieutenant in the Israeli Defense Force. And actually, he hadn't had to do any drilling since he was commissioned. But it was bad enough watching the grunts do it.

"Music?" Irv grinned. "I didn't know they had harmonicas in the Shavetail Symphony."

"Congratulations on your second bar, Captain Kampf." Mel extended his hand, leaning across the desk.

"Thanks." Irv shook it. "You're up for promotion soon, too, aren't you?"

"Guess it'll depend on whether I make associate professor here."

"No problem. Who's your competition, Schmuyle? I'm rooting for you, what more do you want?"

"What more could anyone want?" Mel stood, then paused. "You know, Irv, I guess that's about right. I can't remember when I've had a better feeling about the future, when I've ever been happier."

On Monday afternoon Morris Imbray once again summoned Mel into his office. This time a third person was present.

"Professor Schwartz, may I present Miss Shoshana Rabin."

The girl arose like the sun from her perch on the edge of her chair. Wings of bright gold hair swung, brushing the neckstrap of a short blue sundress, as she advanced on white laced sandals. Extending a tanned arm, she smiled up at Mel from the level of his chest.

Mel shook hands. Shoshana, he thought. That's a pretty name. "Welcome to the Technion, Miss Rabin." For the first time that day, Mel noticed the weather. Through the office window the day seemed unseasonably warm for the ninth of Heshvan, late October. It reminded him of southern California Indian summer, warm Santa Ana winds bending the palm trees… Her light voice drew him out of his sudden reverie.

"…looking forward to our classes together, Professor Schwartz."

"Are you ready to start? Perhaps you'd like to see the campus?"

"I've seen it. I've used the library here a couple of times."

"Oh, yes, your papers. I've looked them over, and I'm impressed. You show amazing insight and mathematical maturity—"

"For someone so young?"

She had a dimple! "For one so young, yes." He grinned back. "Well then, let's adjourn to my office, and let the fun begin."

"Yes!" Her skirt flounced as she spun back to retrieve a pen and clipboard from the corner of Morris's desk.

On their way out, the chairman drew Mel aside. "Have you heard from Schmuyle lately? I want to give him some suggestions concerning outplacement, but I haven't seen him since last Wednesday."

Mel shook his head. "Neither have I. I thought he was sick."

"He hasn't called in, according to Honey." Honey Kusch, the new department secretary, had in Morris's phrase "boarded a moving train and become the conductor." Her beauty equaled only by her brains, she would not have mislaid a message from Sammy, Mel knew.

"Maybe he's on a bender."

"He did take it hard. He was so sure of himself." The chairman sighed and leaned on his hands on the desk.

"He'll be okay, he's a survivor type." Mel shrugged. "Still, I know how I felt when I thought you were giving me the sack. I'll see what I can do."

"Thank you. Now go meet your new class of one, with my blessing."

Shoshana had found a patch of sunlight a few yards away and was basking in it, eyes shut in her upturned face, honey-tan shoulders glowing as the warm breeze played with her hair. Her arms hung relaxed at her sides, one child's-hand nevertheless firmly gripping the clipboard.

What an honor, Mel thought watching her. He shook his head and walked to her side. "Okay, Miss Rabin. Ready to go."

"Okay. And you can call me Shana if you want. It's quicker."

"Fine, and you can call me Professor Schwartz."

She grinned and swung her clipboard, spinning around on her toes. "You're funny, Professor Schwartz."

"Thanks, I think. Let's go."

"What!" Mel stared across his office desk at Schmuyle.The missing professor had turned up in Mel's office with a proposal.

"I said, could I persuade you to take up your career elsewhere? There are better schools than the Technion. A few. Princeton has a lot more going on in algebraic topology than here; this is almost a straight algebra department."

"Princeton! I'm from California. I could never live in New Jersey." Mel shook his head. "Sammy, I can't believe I'm having this conversation. If I looked up 'chutzpah' in the dictionary, would I find 'See Schmuyle Goldenberg'?"

"It was worth a try." Schmuyle slouched against the arm of Mel's guest chair and stuck his hands in his pockets.

"Why don't you apply to those other places yourself? Like Princeton? You've got a good number of papers published."

"It's a lot easier to get a job when you have a job. Besides, those places want a track record that's a little more...substantial, shall we say?"

I'll say they do, Mel thought. He tried to change the subject. "Have you talked to Morris since you came back? We missed you here, by the way."

"I'll bet you did, filling in for me while I was indisposed. No, I don't want to talk to that two-timing bastard. After all the effort I put in sucking up to him! He'll just point me toward a roach motel."

"Teachers' colleges aren't that bad."

"So why don't you go to one? You like students so much, especially that Rabin chiclet." With a visible effort, Schmuyle grinned. "And you're sure in my way here."

"The breaks, Sammy. It's this austerity budget. If Israel was still getting eight billion a year from the U.S., we'd both be promoted."

"If's don't fill the gas tank. Well, I can see I'm wasting my time with you." Schmuyle slammed the office door on his way out.

Mel rose from his desk, walked to the door, and opened it. Why, he wondered, didn't Sammy try something a little more constructive than just asking him to step aside? What does he think I am? Well, I did promise Morris.

Returning to his desk, he pondered for some minutes, then wrote:

> Dear ——:
>
> This is to recommend my colleague Schmuyle Goldenberg for the post of associate professor at your institution. A prolific researcher, he is best known among logicians for his result on the metasyntax of well-formed formulae.
>
> Dean Willard Trump regards professor Goldenberg most highly, and only unfortunate budgetary constraints prevent his retention and promotion to tenure in our department.
>
> I would appreciate it if you would look with favor on professor Goldenberg's application.
>
> Sincerely,
> Melvin Schwartz

There. He might not be off the hook entirely, but it was a start.

Rising from his desk, Mel left the office and walked down the hall to the secretary's cove, where Honey Kusch sat poking at a terminal.

"Hi, Honey."

"Professor Schwartz, how may I assist you?"

"Would you please type this? Leave the name blank, just get it into my VAPID file and give me a hard copy for Sammy."

Not for the first time, Mel wondered why such a gorgeous nineteen-year-old girl chose to work as a mathematics secretary. They should count their blessings. She certainly made the department hum.

"Right away, sir."

Mel knew the truth of that. In fifteen minutes, tops, the letter would be spell-checked and waiting at his terminal, with a copy laser-printed on departmental letterhead sitting on his desk. "Thanks."

Honey's fingers were already flying. As Mel turned to go, though, they paused in their dance.

"Oh, Professor Schwartz? Miss Rabin called to say she can't make it to class this afternoon; she's under the weather. I left you an e-mail message."

"Thank you, Honey." Why was bad news always so prompt? Darn, now he wouldn't see her 'til Monday. Irv had her tomorrow. He hoped she was all right. Well, he could use the time to catch up on his grading.

Mel had expected to enjoy tutoring such an able student, but Shoshana had exceeded his fondest hopes: leaping ahead to grasp the subtlest concepts intuitively when barely introduced to them; cracking, laserlike, through to the kernel of the toughest proofs; sometimes even shooting out whole new lines of research like a Roman candle. And with all this she was simply a delighted child, clapping hands in joy at an elegant result, laughing happily over the unexpected turn of an argument, in her exuberance pushing his arm aside when she saw a shortcut in some reasoning he was pursuing at the whiteboard.

"You don't need all that, sil—Professor Schwartz; see, you can just take out this, and cut right to here."

Demonstrative. Lovely. Happy. Above all, smart. And never absent, until today.

Mel was almost sorry he'd let Irv have a couple of hours of her time each week. Guiding her through mathematics was now the peak of his day. She was a teacher's dream come true. While it lasted. In less than a year, he could see, Shoshana wouldn't need him any more. She'd be on her own, a full-fledged research mathematician at home in the current literature, then far surpassing it. Even now he sometimes felt superfluous, but she was still learning in the arena of graduate textbooks, still in the mode of preparing for her "prelims," and there were too many books. She couldn't read them all. Mel and Irv could guide her to the best ones. Her tutors were still needed. But only just.

She'd already read voraciously if indiscriminately, causing a minor problem of unexpected gaps in her background. It always amused him to come across these reminders that she was after all a child.

One such gap became evident a few days after Shoshana was back in class, looking perfectly fine again after her brief touch of flu.

"How could you have missed the exponential function?" Mel asked her. "It's the most important function in all mathematics."

"I'm sorry."

"Hey, come on, Shana, I was just kidding. Cheer up."

"I do know some of it."

"Sure you do, you just didn't learn the right definitions. Like the logarithm, you know all about that."

"It's the inverse of exp."

"Yes, but if you define it another way, the right way, you can get more mileage. Watch. You're gonna love this." Mel waved to a colleague passing in the hall as he stepped to the whiteboard. Shoshana came to stand beside him and watch closely as usual. So he couldn't put one over on her. What a kid! Mel quickly scrawled the complex contour integral definition of log z on the board.

"*That's* the logarithm? How funny. What's gamma?"

"Any path in the plane. If it loops around zero, you get different values for the log. You knew about that, didn't you?"

"I heard the log was multi-valued, but I didn't understand it."

"Shoshana! I find that hard to believe."

"I was only eight, and I never needed to get back to it. How do you prove this is really the log, the inverse of exp?"

"That's the beautiful part. It's a purely formula proof, no intuition required." He put up another function.

"Ugh!" Shoshana grimaced prettily. "Where'd that come from? Oh, I know. You cooked it up to make things come out right."

"Exactly, only it wasn't me." He wrote down the few lines of the proof. "See?"

"It works!" She beamed. Then, hopping up and down as another thought struck her, "And look! This way you can take logs of negative numbers!"

"Right. Most of 'em."

"My teachers all said you couldn't do that!" Clapping her hands, she leaped into the air and came down dancing. "This opens up a whole new world!" She threw her arms around Mel's waist.

Understanding! The teacher's miracle! He hugged her back in sublime joy.

The door burst open.

"Aha!" It was Schmuyle Goldenberg.

Morris pushed past him into the office. "Mel!"

Mel released Shoshana and stepped back, puzzled and slightly annoyed at the interruption. "Yes?" He could see Shana was a little curious, too.

"I'd like to speak to you, please. Would you step outside? Miss Rabin, kindly wait here. It won't be long."

"Yes, sir." She took a seat and bent over her clipboard to take notes.

"What brings you two to my door?" asked Mel once they were down the hall. Morris had led them into a deserted classroom and shut the door.

Door! Why was that important? What was it about doors?

"Mel," the chairman said quietly, "child molestation is a serious matter."

"He was French-kissing her," Schmuyle said before Mel could react, "and groping under her skirt."

As it sank in that these incredible words were meant to apply to *him*, Mel gasped at the reckless virulence of Schmuyle's accusation, the depth of evil plumbed here. He's really doing this! He really means it! "You son of a bitch!" Mel reacted without thought. The next moment, through a red haze, he saw Schmuyle sprawled on the floor, rubbing his jaw.

"I saw what I saw." Blood trickled from the corner of his mouth.

"That's a damned lie!"

"And I saw enough," Morris added. "And you did have your door closed. Mel, how could you?"

That's it! The door! I left it open! Didn't I? Mel was suddenly faint. "I left it open! I always do. I'm sure I did!"

"Mel, you can't deny facts."

Through his growing panic Mel saw actual tears glistening in the chairman's eyes. He believed this! He couldn't! "Morris. You know me! I would never do this. Especially to Shoshana."

"Aha," said Schmuyle again, rising to his feet.

Mel knew he'd made a tactical error. "I mean she's extra special. A precious national resource..." He shut up, realizing he was only digging himself in deeper.

"Every child is precious, Mel. Schmuyle, I'd like to talk privately to Mel. Please excuse us. Get out. Now."

Schmuyle bounced out the door without a word.

After a minute of silence Morris said, "Come to my office."

Mel was embarrassed—*as if I were guilty!*—to find Naomi Imbray, Morris's wife, waiting in the chairman's office. He looked at her feet as he mumbled a greeting.

Morris seemed nearly as disconcerted. "Hello, dear. I'll join you for tea in just a few minutes. Would you mind going ahead without me?"

"Certainly. Sorry I interrupted."

When she was gone Morris said, "I don't know what to say. This all seems unreal."

It was almost better when Morris avoided his eyes. That look of disgust... "It is unreal. It's not true. I never molested Shoshana, or anybody else. Never would. Sammy's motive is clear."

"Mel, I saw it with my own eyes!" The chairman sank into his seat with an air of infinite lethargy. Mel remained standing.

"You saw an innocent hug." Wisdom told him not to add, "She started it."

"But why even a hug? And your door was firmly closed. In fact, that's why I came. Schmuyle told me you were in your office with a girl with the door closed. And he was right."

"Look, I can't explain the door. Obviously it was closed, I saw you two open it. But I never close my office door. I know the policy, it's a wise policy, and besides I never bother. In fact," He paused, remembering. "Sammy slammed it the other day when he left, and I was annoyed to have to open it. What day was... oh, yeah, it was the day Shoshana was absent. Honey would know. I always leave it open; I like it that way. Why would I close it?"

"Why indeed." Morris shuddered.

"No, now, come on. All right, so maybe I had a lapse—Wait!" Mel's fist thumped the air. "I know it was open! Not ten minutes before you came! I know because I saw somebody in the hall. I waved at him. You can't do that through a closed office door."

"Who was it?"

"I'm trying to remember. My mind was on the mathematics, but I know it wasn't one of the women. I'd like his corroboration, but I don't know if he waved back or even saw me."

"If you could come up with his name, it still might help: he might recall the door's being open. But then how did it get closed? No breeze did it. The windows are sealed shut because of the air conditioning. Mel, even if this is true, and I admit you've raised a reasonable doubt in my mind...easy to do, since I don't want to believe this...why the hug?"

"Spontaneous excitement about the math. Wait." Mel held up his hand, trying to think of how to frame this so Morris would believe. The one thing that must not happen, the one thing that could save him, was to ask Shoshana about it or involve her in any way. He'd rather die, and that was a plain fact. "Look, you're not going to so much as hint about this to Shoshana, are you?"

"Of course not. What kind of a fool do you think I am?"

"Let me tell you exactly what happened. I defined log z for her using the contour integral. She was tickled pink. She said, let's see, that meant you could take logs of negative numbers. She was really excited. She said her teachers had told her that was impossible."

Morris was paying attention. Mel hoped he was getting the sense of how it had been. "She danced up and down, said, 'This opens up a whole new world!' and gave me a hug. That's it. Wasn't the hug you saw that kind of a hug?"

"Well, but groping! Kissing!"

"Did you see any of that? You were in the doorway less than one second after Sammy. Did you even see me straightening up? Shoshana's short."

"You're short too."

"Not that short. Think about it. If you boot me because of this, who will get the promotion?"

"That is certainly a consider—Would he do that? Would he stoop so low?"

"Remember, he's a survivor type. I don't know if he'd drag down Shoshana; surely he's not that vile. But me, certainly. "

There was a pause.

"Mel, the department cannot afford even a breath of scandal at this juncture. And I cannot have an accused child-molester teaching my students. I must consider the possibility that Schmuyle may be telling the truth and you lying. That door was closed. You were in a clinch. How long had that been going on? What were the odds against our happening to open the door exactly at the instant of a momentary, as you claim, hug?"

"Long odds. Rotten luck."

"This case must be cleared up, one way or the other, and soon. Until then you must be isolated from any contact with students." Morris straightened in his chair. "Mel, I'm sending you to Moscow."

"Moscow? The conference. But how can I clear my name in Moscow?"

"It's the only way. It absents you with excuse, and that's imperative. Schmuyle and I shall conduct an extremely discreet investigation. No one else will be brought in."

"One too many already. Morris, if he leaks...if it gets back to Sho—"

"I'll make the consequences to him clear. From her reaction just now, Shoshana does not realize the enormity of what has happened—"

Mel stepped to the desk, leaning his knuckles on it. "Nothing happened!"

"So you say." Morris held his ground. "Even if it did, she can still be spared some of the trauma of it, and that will be my chief goal. I contemplate no legal action, to protect her; but I shall expect your immediate resignation. And Mel."

"Yes?"

"I'll see that you never teach again."

[illegible] come up short too.

[illegible] danger. Think about it. [illegible] better [illegible] the way [illegible] affect the promotion.

That's certainly a consider[illegible] Would [illegible]

[illegible] survey [illegible]

[illegible] the same [illegible] showed [illegible]

[illegible]

M[illegible] department [illegible] and [illegible] friends, at the [illegible]

[illegible] What [illegible] against [illegible] to operate [illegible] documentary, as you think [illegible]

[illegible]

[illegible] one way or the other [illegible] soon. Until then [illegible]

[illegible] and that [illegible]

[illegible] Morris, if [illegible]

[illegible] the question [illegible]

[illegible]

[illegible]

[illegible]

BOOK I

Traveling Light

1
The Lost Paper

Melvin Schwartz knew he needed to respond, and strongly; but he was helplessly on his way to Moscow. On top of his fierce anxiety, frustration was driving him to a frenzy.

He'd just turn around and go back. Morris couldn't stop him. But Morris could fire him. With extreme prejudice.

It had been two days! What was happening to Shoshana? What must she be thinking? God, don't let her find out. Please! Keep Schmuyle's mouth shut. In fact You should strike him dead for his lie. Ambition is one thing, but this! He'd never in a million years risk this, unless he was very sure he'd get away with it. Well, I have to make sure he doesn't.

But how? How do you prove your innocence of such a thing anyway? And to a mathematician, never mind in court, God forbid.

Here he went again, round and round. He was stuck in London overnight because Morris couldn't wait to get him on a direct flight. Stuck going to this conference for a whole week while Schmuyle had a clear field to cook up whatever evidence he wanted.

And who was it he'd seen outside his door? According to the schedules they'd given him, nobody else was free that period.

What difference did it make? So he saw the door open. So what? It had been shut when Morris arrived, that was damning enough.

At least Mel knew he hadn't shut it. He knew he was innocent. And so did Shoshana, of course. God protect her! May the question never be put to her! God, if there is a God, he thought, you know I don't care what happens to me. Only save Shoshana.

But if he didn't clear his name, clear it beyond all doubt, the lie was sure to leak out. And there went her life. As well as his own.

This conference was already a feeble enough excuse for his absence. It wasn't in his field, not nearly. And why such a sudden departure? Without saying goodbye?

She was sure to see through that cock-and-bull story Morris was going to give her, to have already seen through it! My God, he kept forgetting it had been two days! Two days of doubt and suspicion. He had to get back.

BEEEP!

Now what?

"Do you have a bunch of keys in your pocket?"

"Oh, yeah...here." Mel handed them to the Heathrow security agent and passed under the arch again. This time it didn't beep. Retrieving his flight bag from the x-ray belt, he walked into a wide concourse of gate lounges, coffee shops, bars, and souvenir stores, toward Gate 7B and his rendezvous with British Airways flight 17, departing at eleven o'clock GMT for Moscow.

His watch, already set to London time, read 9:58. An hour to wait. He'd better check in right away, before he lost it completely.

The counter at the gate was unattended, but there was a cafeteria across the way. Mel entered, selected coffee and mince pie, and sat down at a window booth. He opened his flight bag and drew out a stack of papers. Some of the sheets were stapled photocopies of journal pages; others were covered with scribbled notes. Unclipping a pen from his shirt pocket, he turned to the middle of an article from the 1889 volume of *Acta Mathematica.*

But it wasn't the sort of thing that was easy to put out of his mind. He managed a rueful grin. Not even square dancing would do it, Irv.

Still he had to try. He had to know something about Kovalevskaya's work, or it was sure to come out at the conference that he had no business being there. It would get back to Adam Harrod. It was Harrod's specialty after all. Mel was just lucky Adam didn't want to bother attending, and add fire to the smoke.

For Shana's sake, he had to do his best to make it pretty convincing, in fact.

Well, he could do it. There was bound to be some crumb of research he could latch on to. Madame K. didn't know about categories and functors, for instance. Maybe his generalization that he started thinking about last night in the hotel room would work out.

He read for forty minutes, drawing cryptic symbols on a scribble sheet. Finally he reached an impasse, staring at the last expression he had written:

$$\int \frac{\sum_{j=m}^{n} (j+6)P'_{mn}(t-i-j)}{P_{mn}(t)}\, dt$$

Here was the same sticky part again. Now what? He had no more insight than before. He laid down the pen, stroked his mustache, and stared out the window, then at the adjacent wall, then at the clock on the wall, which said 10:55.

As this registered, the roaring in his ears resolved into: "Last call for boarding British Airways flight 17 through gate 7B, departing at eleven o'clock for Moscow."

Mel quickly stuffed the papers back into his flight bag and dashed across the concourse, where a steward was standing alone by the open gate. He fumbled for his tickets.

"Boarding pass, please."

Mel looked toward the check-in counter, again unattended.

"Sir? Please?" The steward extracted a wad from Mel's tickets and handed the rest back, opened to his boarding pass. "You're pre-boarded, Dr. Schwartz: seat 34B. Thank you. Right through there."

Seat 34A, the window seat, was occupied by a thin young man in a windbreaker, already typing on a laptop computer. He didn't look up as Mel sat down.

A steward at the cabin door began to close it. Mel saw the more experienced passengers scanning for vacant seats they might prefer. The aisle seat, 34C, was still vacant.

Suddenly the steward opened the door to admit a woman with an envelope in her teeth, trying to zip her purse while clenching her flight bag with an elbow. The zipper moved; her long black hair swayed as she transferred the envelope to one hand, then made a beeline for 34C. She plopped down into it, with a flounce of her beet-red skirt and a ragged sigh.

"The plane from New York was late." Tucking in a loose tail of her white blouse, she grinned shyly at Mel.

After one glance into her brilliant blue eyes, Mel was afraid to look at her. She was too beautiful, and he was in enough trouble.

The seat belt announcement prompted Mel and the girl to strap in. The thin young man switched off his laptop and shut it with a click. "Aardvarks dark," he mumbled, barely loud enough for Mel to hear.

"I beg your pardon?"

"Aardvarks *dark*, I said!" Heads turned at his sharp answer.

"Oh." Mel busied himself with his breeze control. Strapped in between Beauty and the beast, he thought. Hope we have a fast tail wind.

The plane taxied, poised at runway's end, roared. Acceleration crushed Mel exhilaratingly into his backrest.

As soon as the seat belt light went out, the three reached simultaneously for their cases under the seats in front. For a moment, they stared at each other.

"Workaholics!" the girl said. Suddenly they were all laughing.

Didn't know I had any laughs left in me, Mel thought. He glanced over as the boy switched on his laptop and hunched over it. It seemed to be booting from the hard disk and coming up in the edit window of an integrated program development environment—

And was the boy also mumbling something like "Aardvarks bright"? Mel didn't want to know. He turned to his own work, glancing at the girl.

From her carry-on she withdrew a stack of paper. Some of the sheets were stapled and looked like photocopies of journal pages.

Trouble! But he couldn't resist. Besides, he rationalized, maybe he'd learn something. Something he was already supposed to know.

"Going to the conference?" he asked.

"The Sophia Centennial, yes. I've always been a big fan of Mme. Kovalevskaya's."

"So have I," Mel lied.

"Even her novels?"

"Her laundry lists. Whatever."

"I was twelve when I read *A Russian Childhood*. I read it three times. She changed my life. What are you working on?"

"A homological generalization of her result on rigid bodies—"

"—moving about a fixed point. Neat. I'm going to the Soviet Academy of Sciences to see if I can turn up her lost paper."

Mel nodded. Good, something he'd happened to come across in a footnote. "The one she wrote Mittag-Leffler about. Wouldn't that be in Stockholm? Assuming it still exists."

"Her papers tend to drift toward Moscow." She sighed. "Letters, for example. Nothing in Stockholm, or Berlin, or Paris. I looked there last summer."

The boy's fingers clicked quietly, rapidly, on the keys.

"There should be someone at the conference who knows something about what became of her missing paper," said Mel.

"I hope so. Anyway, I'm presenting the results of my conjectures about it. I think I've found a line on what it was about, and managed to pursue it a little."

"You're ahead of me," Mel began. "Maybe you could help—"

"I have the missing paper," said the boy.

The interior of the plane blurred as their heads whipped around. "What!"

"I have it; I have the so-called lost paper of Sophia Kovalevskaya; I watched her hide it, but you're not going to get it! This plane is going to Baghdad!"

"No, it's going to Moscow," Mel objected automatically.

"That's what you think. Steward!"

Hijack! I'm sitting next to him; I have to do something, Mel thought. Where's his gun? Can I distract him?

The boy drew back as Mel reached for his thin shoulder. "Say, about that paper…what's your name, anyway?"

"Chazz."

"Mel."

"Pleased."

Polite, Mel noted. Not a street tough, then; I can take him.

The girl leaned around Mel. "Ruth. What did you mean about finding the paper? I've been looking for it for a year."

"Aha. It would, you think, make mathematical history. It would bring fame. But no! The paper is much more important than that. You see, I have discovered Sophia's secret," his voice dropped into a whisper, "and it enables—"

"You called, sir?"

"Ah, yes, steward. Please tell the pilot to change course to Baghdad."

"And if he refuse?"

"Subjunctive mood! How quaint; how British. If he refuse, I shall...but look here."

The steward leaned over. On the computer screen, Mel saw the words:

**** HIJACK BOMB PROGRAM ****
*** MAIN MENU ***
Ready to arm bomb? Y
Ready to detonate bomb? Y
Are you sure? Y
HIT ANY KEY TO CONTINUE.

"As you see," Chazz explained, "I need but hit any key to continue, and this computer will transmit a certain coded message to the baggage compartment, where my bomb is. It transmits at only twenty-four hundred baud, but that should suffice."

"I shall convey your message, sir."

Hit any key! Mel despaired.I can't stop that. He's got us. If I could grab the thing, or cut the power switch. Too risky. Wait for him to let down his guard. "Now, where were we?"

"You were trying to worm Madame K.'s secret out of me, but you won't," Chazz replied. "Never. And do you know why? Because of that silly mustache."

"Then tell me," urged Ruth.

"You're with him! You're with him!"

In the meantime, the security agents, stewards, and other passengers were abuzz: "Do it!" "No, don't! If he hits a key—" "He's bluffing. Take him!" "No, don't!"

Mel only half heard, as he considered what might have an effect. "Excuse me," he said. Ruth got up and stepped into the aisle to let him out. "Back in a minute." He departed aft with his flight bag.

"Fear does that sometimes," Ruth murmured, resuming her seat as the steward returned from the cockpit.

"The captain has—" he began.

"Attention," the voice over the loudspeaker interrupted. "This is your captain speaking. We're currently flying at an altitude of fifty thousand feet.

The temperature outside the cabin is forty degrees below zero and our ground speed is five hundred fifty miles per hour. We are experiencing a slight delay in our arrival at Sheremetyevo airport in Moscow. Passengers on the right side of the cabin: If you look out your window, you will see a magnificent view of the Hook of Holland as we bank for a course correction."

The announcement was repeated in Russian and French.

"The captain has agreed to your terms," the steward said. "Whatever they might be. What are they, if one may be so bold?"

"I have only two: land me safely in Baghdad, and let me get away."

"No imprisoned terrorists to release? No prime time?"

"No."

"Very well, sir."

Mel returned from aft. "Excuse me."

Ruth stepped into the aisle to let him in. "Feel bet—You shaved it off!"

"Mathematics is my life." He turned to the hijacker. "Chazz, the Iraqis will never let us land. They'll blow us—"

"Quiet. I'm concentrating on not hitting any key."

"Maybe he really has got a bomb in his luggage," said Ruth. "Let's let him concentrate."

And so for hours they sat, dozing fitfully, while the plane droned through the darkening skies over the ancient road to Baghdad.

At Saddam International Airport, the SWAT team consulted with the airport officials and decided that before they struck they would give the skyjacker a car and let him get far enough away from the airport that his computer-generated commands wouldn't work. As he drove away into the night, the plane was evacuated and searched.

In the airport coffee shop, Mel and Ruth tentatively sipped the local coffee while their waiter hovered suspiciously.

"Think he suspects I'm a Jew?" whispered Mel. "My life's not worth a plugged shekel if—"

"I'll never tell," Ruth reassured him. "Hey, relax. You look like a cat on skates."

"That graceful?" He grinned. "All right, let's change the subject. What did Chazz mean? How could it make sense?"

"How much did he really know?" Ruth set down her tiny cup. "Whoo-eee, this stuff is strong."

"An acquired taste," Mel agreed. "That's a good point. Did he say anything he couldn't have learned about just from listening to us?"

Ruth considered a moment. "I guess not."

"I don't even think he's a mathematician. Just a nut. I shaved in vain."

"It'll grow back. You know, I don't usually like mustaches, but I thought that one was kinda cute."

"Thanks. But why did he hijack this flight instead of just buying a ticket to Baghdad?"

"Maybe he found a ticket to Moscow in the street? Or stole one? Muggers can't be choosers."

Mel shook his head. "Money, that's it. Maybe he's a mathematics student. Whiz kid type. Got into college early, did great work early, like John Milnor. Maybe his department paid for his ticket to the conference."

"But he wanted to go to Baghdad..." Ruth began.

"...so urgently that he was willing to hijack a plane to do it."

"What's in Baghdad?"

Mel shrugged. "Miles and miles of nothing but miles and miles."

"Of nothing."

"On the other hand, I could be wrong. I was a math major. The only thing I liked about geography was that the book was big enough to hide my comics."

"Not my subject either," Ruth agreed. "After all, geography is just...there. Nothing to prove."

"Memorization."

"Right," she said.

"Now I wish I had done some memorization, at least about Baghdad. What are its exports?"

"Sand and camels? Don't laugh; the principal exports of Paradox, Colorado, are wood and horses."

"Wooden horses?"

"Horses and wood. They raise Arabians around there, and they have a sawmill."

"I never heard of Paradox, Colorado," Mel admitted.

"The name intrigued me, so I went there. Once."

The waiter returned to their table. "More coffee? How about a piece of mince pie?"

"Yeah, I'd like some," said Mel, anxious to please. There was a sinister look about this guy, despite his jolly veneer. "Both. Ruth?"

"Do you have American coffee?"

"Only Kona and Folger's."

"I'd like a cup of Kona, please. No pie," Ruth ordered. "How come you have mince pie here? I thought only Vermont farmers ate that."

"For breakfast," agreed the waiter. "That's the definition of a Yankee, and we get a lot of Yankee tourists here now. Maybe six a year." He departed.

"Probably all hostages," Mel muttered.

"Yeah, look at us: Yankee hostages."

"Sorta."

"Hm?"

"I'm an ex-Yank. Recently emigrated to Israel. I'm at the Technion. Don't tell the waiter."

"Did you mention Israel?" asked the waiter, arriving with the pie and coffee. "We occasionally see Israelis here. We take their money, and they leave. Quickly."

"As for us, we're stuck here until they de-bomb our plane."

"Haven't you heard? The hijacker's luggage went to Tokyo. They're searching that plane now. Yours is being refueled. Boarding in twenty minutes."

"Waiters hear a lot," Ruth said.

"Also," added the waiter, "they found the guy's rental car out in the desert, empty. No computer, no nothing."

"Who was he, anyway?" Mel asked.

"A math student at Uppsala, Sweden, named Caspar Lundquist."

"I thought Chazz stood for Charles," said Ruth.

"Chazz was a pet name his maternal grandmother Helga—"

"Now cut that out!"

"Just kidding, the police radio didn't mention that. Will there be anything else? Dessert? We have—"

"Just the check, please."

"So, he was a mathematician," Ruth said as the waiter left.

"Assuming you can trust the waiter."

"Everybody trusts waiters. They have to."

Mel disagreed, but said only, "If he was a mathematician, he must have been telling the truth."

"Right, because he never said, 'I lied.'"

"But then that's fantastic. There really is a secret, that 'enables'..."

"Enables what? Easy prime factorization?" guessed Ruth. "That would be worth something nowadays."

"We'll never know."

"Right. And he says he saw Sophia hide her paper. But how? He's a kid; she died in 1891."

"Maybe he just meant he saw where she had hidden it. He found it."

"Must have. Anyway, if he's got it, I certainly won't find it in Moscow." She sighed. "That shoots this trip."

"You're still going to give your talk, aren't you? I'm really excited about that stuff. It's so close to mine, but from a different direction."

"Oh, yeah. Where I try to reconstruct what she did. I hit a snag, though. I get just so far and no farther."

"Let's look at it now. We have fifteen minutes. Maybe I hit a different snag. Anyway, you're way ahead. At least you'll help me."

"Okay." She opened her bag. "Just so we don't miss the boarding call."

"Right, when I'm involved in her stuff I tend to lose track of time."

They hauled out their papers, a mathematician's working tools: brightly highlighted photocopies of published articles; varicolored pens; scribbled scraps of argument, diagram, and conjecture, on odd sheets of paper. Soon they were engrossed to the point of oblivion, working together toward a shared discovery. Mel barely noticed the waiter leave the check, then duck out a side door.

"Now right here," said Ruth, "is where the complex time idea is used to integrate this fourth equation of motion. After that, my conjecture is that Sophia tried to see if the same trick would work on other problems."

"Wait a minute. This form you have here looks like a generalization of

$$\int \frac{\sum_{j=m}^{n} (j+6)P'_{mn}(t-i-j)}{P_{mn}(t)}\, dt$$

which is where I'm stuck."

"Let me see...yes, it is. But where'd you get that? How did you think of restricting to imaginary time?"

"It seemed the symmetric thing to do," Mel said. "But then I couldn't integrate it."

"This thing probably doesn't have any closed form antiderivative. Of course, for any particular case, you could get a quadrature by numerical integration; do you have access to a computer? Silly question! Who doesn't, these days? Any kid—"

They looked at each other.

"Is *that* what he was up to?" asked Ruth.

"I don't know. Anyway, we don't have a computer here; let's try and think by hand."

"Well, to do the similar thing with real time, you'd extend it to complex time. What's the analogy?"

"Maybe conjugate first? Let's see: if I put t bar for t in your form, and subtract, that would cancel out real time." Mel scribbled. "Here's what I get."

"But look!" cried Ruth. "These terms can be individually done by residues; see, here, these two poles will cancel…in fact, all the non-imaginary singularities cancel."

"That's right! That leaves only this imaginary simple pole…hey, I can read off the answer now! It's—"

Simultaneously Ruth said, "By the residue theorem, it's—"

"$2\pi i\,[\,(n - m + 1)\,(m + 6) + 1/2\,(m + n)\,(n - m + 1)]$," they said in unison.

Suddenly the coffee shop was gone; the airport, all Baghdad was gone. In its place was desert, under a blazing sun.

2
The Rabbi

What's that? Mel lay near delirium, sprawled on the ground, one arm outflung and lying in a ditch, trying to concentrate, trying to think what had caught his attention.

It came to him. It was his arm. Something about his arm…no, the hand at the end of his arm. It was cool.

Must be the only part of him that was cool. Cool hand Mel.…

It was wet. Water! His hand was lying in water! A puddle, in the desert?

Mel performed what seemed a superhuman feat of strength: he raised his hand to his parched lips. Drops of water trickled into his mouth.

They spurred him to worm closer to their source. Cupping his hand, he brought a whole thimbleful of water to his tongue. He could almost hear it hiss as it coursed through the hot, thick, dusty coating of his throat. The water of life.

Not the end, then. Not over yet, by God! He drank. Carefully.

Ruth! he thought at last, ashamed. God, don't let it be too late…With trembling fingers he sprinkled her face. Her eyelids fluttered.

Thank you. Cradling her head in the crook of his arm, he administered the life-giving fluid.

Eventually she could sit up. "A miracle…"

"We can make it, now."

"Yes…Look, Mel. What's that? A garden?"

He turned to follow her gaze. A few yards ahead lay a field of blue flowers in orderly rows. They had almost reached them.

He'd never seen those. He'd only been looking at the next step.

Out from among the flowers extended the miracle-ditch. Now Mel saw others parallel to it. "A crop of some kind. Irrigation ditches."

"They saved our lives."

As they waded through the last rank of blue flowers and entered the village between low vine-draped blockhouses, the temperature increased and the breeze diminished to nothing.

"What's that smell?" asked Ruth.

"Open plumbing. This your first time in the Third World?"

"I guess *so*."

"You get used to it after a while."

"I don't plan to stick around that long."

They walked down a dirt street between stucco dwellings. A ribbon of brightness ahead indicated a stream. Tree-lined, it was parklike and inviting.

"Shade," Ruth breathed. "At last."

"It must be Thursday already."

"I've been flying since Tuesday night." They sank gratefully to the grass under a date palm. "Where are all the people?"

"I was wondering about that myself. You don't suppose..." Mel bit his tongue. Too late.

"What?"

"Nothing."

"Don't do that to me, Mel. Let's hear the discouraging word."

"Ghost town."

"Can't be. Smells too ripe."

"I hate to say this, Ruth, but that smell can linger for weeks."

"What are we going to do?"

Mel had no answer. They lay by the stream in despair while the sun sank.

He was crouched on a giant keyboard in front of a supertwist screen:

**** SOPHIA KOVALEVSKAYA ****
*** MAIN MENU ***

1. Novels
2. Published Papers
3. Biography
4. Relationship with Weierstrass
5. Disposition of secret or 'lost' paper, that enables

HIT ANY KEY TO CONTINUE—

He wanted to continue, but found he could only hop. Looking down, he saw to his horror that he had been transformed into a cockroach. He hopped in desperation and landed as hard as he could, on the "T" key. Unfortunately the keyboard action was rather stiff and the key didn't depress. Trying again, he landed this time on the "I" key, on his head. Nothing happened. He hopped again and again; the whole keyboard was shaking…

Someone was shaking his shoulder and saying, "Ho! Ho!" Mel opened one eye. A long white beard. Santa Claus! But he had been de-colorized; he wore gray, not red. "Ho!…Ah!" Seeing Mel wake, the man stepped back.

Now that he wasn't saying "Ho! Ho!", Mel saw that he looked more like a Hasidic rabbi. Half a dozen villagers stood well behind him.

Beside Mel, Ruth stirred and sat up, yawning. "What's going on?"

"Speak English?" asked Mel, rising stiffly to his feet.

The group drew back. The rabbi said something Mel didn't catch.

"Salaam," Mel ventured; he had picked up basic Arabic since his emigration.

The rabbi's eyes widened. "Shalom." He bent his head and touched fingertips.

"You speak Hebrew?" Perhaps the man was a scholar.

"A Jew!" The rabbi beamed in delight. "Yes, but poorly, having learned late in life. How came you here? Is that magician's garb?"

Ruth stood and brushed a crumb of dried mud off her skirt. "What's he saying?"

"He speaks Hebrew. Wants to know how we got here."

"Hebrew, in Iraq?"

Mel addressed the elder in Hebrew. "We do not know how we came here. We were hoping you could tell us. We are not magicians, certainly. Where is the airport?"

"What is an airport?"

Mel looked at Ruth. "I think we're gonna miss our plane."

He turned back to the rabbi. "Which way is Baghdad?"

"I know not this Baghdad. Is it a spirit city? Two days yonder lies Babylon," he pointed, "but—"

"Babylon! Ruins interest us not. And we're not spirits; we're flesh and blood, as you are. Have you a telephone?"

"Telephone?"

"Getting nowhere," Mel sighed to Ruth. "He doesn't know…wait." He turned back to the rabbi. "Sir, what place is this?"

"Opis," answered the rabbi. "A mere village, but we have a minyan."

"Did he say minion? We're nobody's—" Ruth began.

"No, a 'minyan.' Enough men for a synagogue. Look, I know how frustrating it is not understanding a word. But you're not missing much. I have only negative results. This guy never heard of airports, telephones, or Baghdad. We can't call a taxi. We're stuck here in Opis, have to trek out. Ever do any hiking?"

"I'm not in the mood, Mel."

"This time we need supplies. Tents, stilsuits, canteens. Food. Maybe we can buy some."

"Doesn't look like Abercrombie & Fitch country, but ask him."

"Kind master," Mel said (it came out *rabboni*, but the rabbi didn't seem to mind), "we are lost. We are hungry. We need proper attire. We would like to purchase these things."

"Ah! Forgive my oversight," said the rabbi. "Your money is worthless here. Most certainly you must break bread with my humble household. All I have is yours. Come."

"Let's go, Ruth. He's gonna feed us."

"That's for me! Love this Arab hospitality."

"Yeah. Kosher, in this case, I suspect."

The rabbi's name was Nab, and he really was a rabbi, the spiritual leader of a small group of other native converts and a few Jewish immigrants residing in Opis. What seemed like his entire flock joined him and his family at dinner. Curious as they were, they only traded small talk until all the prayers, blessings, and amenities were done with and the first course (soup) served, by Nab's twin seven-year-old granddaughters.

"Isn't this wonderful?" asked Ruth. "These people haven't changed their way of life in a thousand years."

"Completely untouched by modern civilization," Mel agreed. "Too bad for us, though. We must be really out in the boonies."

"I hope you will not think me rude," said Rabbi Nab at last, "if I now respectfully request that you kindly enlighten us as to whence you and your wife came and why. And why you wear such strange garb? You terrified the whole village into hiding."

"Excuse me just a minute." He turned to Ruth. "Ah, he thinks you're my wife. We have to let him, otherwise you're a serious anomaly in backwoods Iraq." That frown. He didn't like it one bit. But what choice did he have? Anyway, it couldn't do any harm. "Now he wants the whole story."

He turned back to the rabbi. "Most gracious host, we come from a far land, where we were journeying when an evil person diverted our…caravan…by the use of arcane powers. We fell into a slumber and were separated from our party, we know not how. We awoke on yon distant rock."

"Then you sought shade, and slept again. I blame you not. Travel does weary, even when not…'diverted.' And fear and panic exhaust. But you are safe here, at least for the moment." He touched the sleeve of Ruth's white blouse fastened with Velcro. "This garb is the fashion in your land?" Understanding, she nodded. "Wondrous stuff. Now I suppose you would rejoin your party."

"As soon as possible, kind teacher."

"But first you must rest. Restore your spent energies. Please accept my humble hospitality for this night. There is plenty of room. On the morrow we shall outfit you for your expedition."

Morrow? "Expedition?"

"To Babylon, center of learning. The best hope for a solution to your problem."

Mel looked at Ruth, not meeting her eyes. He wiped his brow. "He's offered to grubstake us to 'Babylon' tomorrow. Probably means Al Hillah; they must still use the ancient name for it here. Though I never heard it called a center of learning."

"Well, they must at least have a phone there—'tomorrow'?"

How could it get any worse? "We're invited to spend the night. Get some rest. Look, I won't bother you. These are exceptional circumstances."

"I..." Ruth paused. "I suppose it's kind of like camping out, isn't it?"

"It's only for two or three nights. Hey, I'm really sorry. I didn't know we'd be here overnight. Now we're stuck."

"I guess it's necessary. No monkey business?"

"No." He had no difficulty promising this, after his recent experience with Shoshana. Was he going to be turned off for life?

"Okay. Accept."

Mel let out a long breath. "Friend Nab, we accept with heartfelt thanks."

"Excellent! Done! Now, if you will excuse me for a few moments, I shall give my wife Isla the good news. She knows little Hebrew." He turned and began to address the rest of the company in his guttural but mellifluous native tongue.

Watching their open faces, Mel could guess what they heard: their eyes grew wide at the idea of a person so wicked as to divert an entire caravan; they gasped to hear of arcane powers; their lips pursed in sympathy for the weary travelers, separated from their party; by the end, they were beaming at the opportunity to treat strangers as the patriarch Abraham had when he entertained angels unaware.

"Funny: I thought I'd recognize at least a couple of words, but it's all gibberish," he told Ruth.

"Eavesdropping is the hardest job in a language you're weak in," Ruth observed. "When I was in Sweden—"

"There is just one other thing," said Nab. "But I will consult with those wiser than I in such matters, and I am sure we can resolve the problem."

"Good sir," Mel asked, "what is this problem?"

"Babylon is under siege. Cyrus has sealed it tight as a timbrel. None can go in or out."

3
The Village

"Cyrus?" asked Mel after a pause. "The Mede?"

"The Persian. You must refer to his general, Darius."

Mel glanced at Ruth. His panic must have shown on his face. "Trouble?" she asked.

"Not sure. He says Cyrus the Persian has Babylon under siege. Wasn't that long ago?"

"B.C., I'm positive. Bet they're making a movie!" Her eyes glowed with excitement.

Mel cleared his throat. "That's not how it sounded."

"See if he knows anything about Israel. Wait! First see if he knows he's in Iraq."

"Wish I could just ask 'What year is it?' and get an answer I could understand."

"You don't seriously think—"

"Nah! Just a wild hypothesis. Let's test it. Please, sir," he said, switching languages again, "what is the year?"

"The year seventeen of the reign of good King Nabonidas."

"See, I knew—"

"Also the sixty-eighth year of captivity of my Judean friends."

"Captivity!"

"We keep close track of that, for it is written that this captivity should last seventy years."

"Ruth! My God! We've gone back in time! We're in the Babylonian Captivity period."

"That's sunstroke talking."

"Maybe, but I'd like to see just one light bulb. Or Tootsie Roll."

"Come on." She caught his face, not too smartly, between her palms. "Snap out of it. We're only in a local pocket of primitivism, that's all. Landsat Five probably has us in its little orbiting lens right now."

"Wave!"

Rabbi Nab looked wide-eyed at Ruth, but said only: "You are perturbed, friend Mel. Have I offended you in some way?"

"Not in the slightest. But we may be farther from home than we first thought."

"All the more reason for patience. Relax. Rest, in preparation for your expedition. Here, have some veal kebab. Was the soup to your liking?"

"Delicious. Thank you." He turned to Ruth. "Okay, you're right. It's only hearsay so far. But let's go along with these people until we get some hard evidence."

"We were going to trek out of here in any case. Might as well see what our host means by 'Babylon.'"

"Relax and enjoy it, for now. This is the best I've eaten since I left the kibbutz. Nothing like raising your own food."

After dinner Ruth told Mel she'd help the women clean up. "These guys wouldn't appreciate it if a woman sat in on a council of war, and I can't understand them anyway."

"I wish you could. You get good ideas."

"I get the best ones doing dishes. Fill me in later."

"Maybe some Hebrew lessons, too. See you back at the room."

Nab had gathered a small group of tough-looking men—for brandy and cigars, he thought. They sat on cushions around a flat circle of packed sand in the middle of a room lit with oil lamps, as dusk fell. The rabbi handed a stick to a grizzled, aquiline man. "This is Sergeant Zaran," he told Mel, "one of my better Hebrew language students. He is a veteran of the Battle of the Eclipse."

"I am honored."

"So," Zaran said, drawing two roughly parallel but wiggly vertical lines in the sand. "You are here, on Tigris." He punched a dot into the top of the right-hand line. "Babylon is here, on Euphrates." Another dot at the bottom of the left-hand line. "Army of Cyrus. General Gobryas, good man, has command. I do not know if Cyrus is there." He drew a contour around Babylon. It reached almost a fifth of the way to the top dot.

"Is that to scale?"

"No, a figure. Here." He scuffed out the picture and drew a square, with a wiggly line running down through it. "Babylon's wall. The army of Cyrus surrounds it, just out of bowshot." He drew a careful contour. "Camps on four sides." Four dots. "Patrols out to a Sabbath-journey from wall. Tight guard near wall, all around."

"What about the terrain?"

"Flat, river valley. Some low hills about here."

"How tough is that wall?"

"Biggest wall ever," Zaran said in admiration. "Two hundred cubits high, sixty thick. They race chariots on top. Gobryas will never get through."

"Well, what does he hope to gain? Starve them out? What is he doing now?"

"Too long to starve out; storehouses full, farms inside wall. Army can't live long off land, crops not ripe for months yet. City has plenty of water. Euphrates runs right through. Some activity by army up river. Do not know what."

"How can we sneak in? I sure don't want to wait until the siege is lifted; it might be months. Hey, can these people swim?"

"Ho! Excellent swimmers. Army trains them. You swim? We race sometime."

"Then we can't just swim in, or Gobryas would have done that."

"Even if we got past the grate, the river runs far under the wall. Too far for anyone to hold breath."

"I had thought," Nab put in, "that a less direct method might work. Perhaps we might try stealth or disguise, as the lion blends into the sand. Is there no coming and going at all? Are there no exceptions?"

"A city under siege might as well not be there," said Zaran. "Even if we get past army, then what? Babylonians never admit us. They suspect trick no matter what we say. Especially if Cyrus lets us through. It is usual paradox of siege."

Paradox, Colorado, flashed through Mel's mind. "What if we build an enormous wooden horse—"

"That trick is only good once. Besides, Chaldeans are not curious like Trojans. Always a festival."

"Then how about an enormous wooden gopher…" Mel shook his head. Sunstroke indeed. Or fatigue. "Never mind. What do you suggest?"

"It is impossible. You and your wife must enter Babylon?"

"Uh—" It's not my idea!

"The Persian," Nab pointed out, "will soon turn his attention to our village Opis. He means to subdue all Mesopotamia. When he does, you had best be gone; he would surely detain you."

"Just wait out siege. Cyrus will tire and leave in due time. Then the city will welcome visitors."

"I would not risk waiting," advised Nab. "At any moment Cyrus may invest us."

Mel didn't remember enough history to know what had happened at the siege of Babylon. Hadn't Cyrus pulled some trick?

"Come, my friends." Nab stroked his long beard. "The sun rises early over the two rivers. Often answers befall while we sleep." He began a brief translation into Akkadian. Enlightenment spread across the faces of the men who hadn't followed the Hebrew.

When he finished there was silence; then a man (an ugly brute, Mel thought: look at that scar!) spoke shyly. Zaran replied. The rabbi and another warrior, even more piratical, joined in. Soon there was an animated discussion.

"Well, that is worth some consideration," Nab said to Mel when it was over. "It has been suggested that something might be done under cover of darkness. In a boat, you might silently float down to the very wall of the city, past the army."

"Then the problem is reduced to scaling the wall."

"No easy task, in the dark. A two-hundred-cubit ladder? Formidable."

"But perhaps not insurmountable."

"Why does Gobryas not think of that? Maybe knows something we do not," Zaran said.

"We need more information," Mel said. "Is there any way we could get a closer look, undetected? Spy out the lay of the land?"

"Well, we can easily penetrate the fringe of the army," replied Nab. "As yet the troops haven't had the necessity of raiding civilian henhouses. Mutual toleration still obtains."

"Cyrus is politician," Zaran put in. "He wants popular support when eventually he rules Shinar. It is said the people of Nineveh welcomed his army as liberators when city fell. He goes easy."

"There is commerce with the army as well," added Nab. "To my humiliation I must tell you that the gold and glamor of the warriors have beguiled many of our women. The troops can be approached."

"Very well, we seem to have a plan." Mel yawned. "Now I must sleep. Please excuse me; I have been up a long time."

"Certainly." The men retired. Nab lit Mel's way to his room with an oil lamp. "Sleep well. God guard your dreams."

"I thank you; yours also."

Ruth sat waiting on the bed by another lamp. "Hi," she greeted him. "How'd it go?"

"A capsule summary is that we don't have enough information, so we're gonna scout the territory."

"What does that entail? Hiking there, looking around, hiking back, then coming up with a plan, and hiking back down there again?"

"Well, floating—"

"Nonsense! We'll fly in."

Mel stared.

"Men," she muttered. "You must be sleepy to settle for a program like that." She smoothed the linen bedsheet next to her. Mel sat. "When we washed the dishes I saw a fishnet lying by the stream."

"That clears that up."

"Wait. Remember I said I get my best ideas doing dishes? This time it was while I was making the bed here, that's fairly mindless too. Thinking of the problem of getting past Cyrus and the city wall, I had a mental picture of Babylon and the army around it."

"I have one too. This sergeant—"

"An aerial view. Then when I shook out the sheet, it sort of ballooned up."

"Ruth, you're a genius!" He hugged her enthusiastically. "That fishnet—"

"It was a purse seine." She shaped an elongated globe with her hands. "Looked real light, about eighty feet long."

"Will they lend it to us?"

"Maybe we have some gadgets we could trade for it. It needs to be lined, too. With linen. That's a lot of labor—"

"And a lot of linen; let's see, a cylinder eighty feet long, say forty across, that's..." He poked buttons on his calculator watch. "Thirty-two hundred pi: that's ten thousand square feet. Plus twelve-fifty for the top. They'll never come up with that much linen. That'd clothe this whole village."

"Know what crop that was growing in the field we walked through this afternoon?"

"What cr—"

"Flax. And I saw big looms. This place is the linen center of Mesopotamia. They have warehouses full of it."

"Fantastic! Wait, will this hold air?" Lifting a corner of the sheet, he blew through it. It puffed out.

"Maybe for long enough. I thought of coating it with wax, or oil."

"Too heavy. Wish we had some sheet plastic."

"I have a ground cloth in my bag. Not very big, though."

"May not need it. How's this? We'll make the balloon here, and float down the rivers with it. Then, if we need it, we'll have it."

"And fly with it. Hope it doesn't come to that. Sounds dangerous. Oh, Mel!"

He was scared himself. He put his arm around her shoulders. "It'll work out."

"But I'm starting to believe this...that we're stuck here, millennia before we're born, in this awful *history*! What can we do?"

"Just go with the flow." Mel wished he could come up with a less inane suggestion, but he was starting to believe it too. With the belief, a desperate feeling of being trapped, helpless, crept upon him. "Try our best."

"We could pray, I guess. Do you believe in God?"

"No. Do you?"

"I don't know," she said. "But I never needed Him so much."

"It couldn't hurt. Uh, how do you pray? I only know some Jewish blessings by rote."

She looked up at the tiles and timber of the roof. "God, help us! Please!"

"Sounds right to me. God, if you're there, help us, please!"

"Mel, listen. This just came to me. How do you think we got here?"

"The stork?"

"Stop joking; I refuse to be cheered up."

"Well, we were going through—"

"'Going through' is right!" Twisting to face him, she seized his upper arms with both hands. "We made a breakthrough, going through Sophia's paper together—"

"—using complex time! Right! And if time is a plane, instead of a line, then you could…wander…"

"Stop right there!" she cried. "It'll happen again!"

"Okay, you're right. Let's talk of something utterly carefree and exuberant. What news of the war?"

"What war? What's carefree about war? What are you talking about?"

"Just trying to change the subject. Hey, something puzzles me."

"Only one thing?"

"One in particular. Nab said Cyrus's general was Darius the Mede, but Zaran kept calling him 'Gobryas.'"

"So Cyrus has two generals. Big army. Who's Zaran?"

"This wiry old sergeant I met. Real keen bird. He even speaks Hebrew pretty well."

"That reminds me. Could you really teach me Hebrew? This family...the women are awfully sweet, but it was hard making conversation. The young ones speak Hebrew. I picked up a few words. 'Shalom' means 'peace,' 'abba' is 'father,' 'mayim' is 'water.'"

"That's great! You're a quick study! I'll be glad to teach you Hebrew. When I emigrated, the Israeli government put me through this five-month language course."

"I'm usually pretty quick with languages. Swedish, French—"

"I can at least get you started. But not tonight, please. I'm beat." And he had to psych himself up to teaching another innocent girl. Would he ever get back? And even if he did…

"Me too, exhausted. Let's hit the sack. Turn your head." He complied. Shortly she was lying in bed covered to the chin. "Okay, your turn." She faced the wall.

Mel changed into pajamas from his carry-on and crawled under the sheet on his side. "Good thing we're short. This bed was built for Napoleon."

"Or us. If we were much taller, we'd be conspicuous here. All these people are short."

"Except the kings and generals, I bet."

"Mmm. Turn out the light, please."

Mel reached over, picked up the clay lamp, blew it out, and put it back down. "Good night," he said. But Ruth was already asleep.

Mel slept soundly and without dreams, but not for long.

Humid, oppressive heat woke him in the middle of the night. The linen sheet was thin, almost sheer, but still too—*Yipe!*

He was forcibly reminded where he was. Ruth's leg lay over his thigh, and her arm was draped around his chest. She blew a gentle snore onto the back of his neck. Dark as it was, he had little doubt about what she was wearing.

Not fair! He'd stayed on his side of the bed...

And his sleeping body had betrayed him.

No no no! His desire evaporated in panic. Sweating, he eased out from under her, slid off the bed, and tiptoed around to the other side. *Don't wake up.*

Removing his sodden pajama shirt, he dropped it on the floor and lay down carefully on top of the sheet.

Ruth stirred. He froze.

She snorted, rolled onto her back. He lay still and waited, rigid with tense fear. After an eternity, she resumed snoring. He let out his breath without a sound.

The sleep of the just. She really was an innocent. He'd better be a lot more careful.

At last his tension calmed, his thoughts began their customary jumble at the borderland of sleep. That's all he needed...lust in the dust...

"Wake up, sleepyhead!"

The sun shone brightly through the open window. Ruth was standing over him, arms akimbo. "It's almost time for breakfast. Get up now; Isla wants to talk to us."

"She doesn't speak much Hebrew." He swung his legs out of bed. Ruth turned her back so he could get dressed. She'd slept right through it. Good.

"Nab can translate. She's looked over my trade goods, likes some things. Now we want to see what you've got."

"Here's my bag." He handed it to her. She dumped it out on the bed. "Hey! I'll never get that packed again. It was crammed."

"I'll repack it, little camper. A Swiss army knife!"

"We might need that," he protested.

"What for? A new shirt, in cellophane!"

"Give me that," he said. "I want to save the cardboard out of it before I forget."

"Here. Razor, socks, underwear, deodorant, shave cream: not very—"

"Ouch!"

She glanced over at him. "What happened?"

"Pin got me. Why do they use so many pins in these shirts?"

"Pins! How many?"

"Fourteen, if experience is any guide. Thirteen that you can find without putting it on."

"They'll rave! They're weavers!"

"I have something they'll like better." He opened a black leather box and, withdrawing his harmonica, began playing "The Sailor's Hornpipe."

"I didn't know you—" The curtain to their room was flung aside and the twins, Kona and Mona, ran in squealing with delight. With smiles and gestures and giggles they made their meaning clear: "What is that?" and "Play it again!"

Mel played "Turkey in the Straw." The girls skipped and leaped in time, whirling and jumping and clapping hands. With a pang, Mel remembered Shoshana dancing on that golden afternoon. How was he ever going to get back there?

His tune souring, he stopped.

"We want more!" said Mona. "But now, break fast!"

"Coming. You speak good Hebrew." Mona blushed and smiled at the floor. The twins turned and scampered away, laughing. "Come on, Ruth. Breakfast."

Good smells drew them to a bright room with slatted roof, two walls open to the sunny morning. The family gathered around a linen cloth spread on the floor, laden with jugs and dishes full of steaming food: eggs, chicken, rolls and butter, juice, something resembling granola, milk, muffins, dates, preserves, and other delicacies. No mince pie.

On bright embroidered rugs they settled down between the rabbi and his wife.

When everyone was ready a silence fell. Nab prayed: "Blessed be thou, O Lord our God, King of the universe, who bringeth forth bread from the ground." He picked up a roll and broke it. Then he winked at Ruth, sitting on his right. "Eat. Enjoy."

She broke a roll of her own, trapping scrambled eggs between the halves. Mel reached for the pastrami. Passing him the mustard, Isla said, "So, you like...here? Us?" She waved to include the company and the world.

"I love it here, you're beautiful. But..."

"I understand."

"So tell me, please, Madam, what interests you the most of all Ruth's trinkets." She looked blank. "What thing do you like best?"

"Oh! Mirror. Little powdery mirror. Like magic, so clear!"

"What do you think of this?" He drew forth a pin about an inch long, with a shiny spherical head.

"So bright!" She tested the point. "Sharp!" She clearly knew all about pins. "Could use four hundred of these!"

"Sorry, we only have a dozen," Mel said. "You're welcome to them, though."

"Every little bit—"

Across the table, Kona shrieked.

"Kona!" her father scolded.

"Mona! Mona!" the little girl cried, adding something in her native language. She pointed at her twin.

Mona was perfectly still, and blue.

Throwing aside his dish, Mel scrambled up and across the spread. He reached down and hauled Mona to her feet. She was not breathing. He spun her around and embraced her from behind. Clasping one fist in the other hand, he pulled sharply inward, just below her rib cage.

She coughed. A piece of muffin flew out of her mouth. She gasped and wheezed.

"Breathe! Breathe!" Mel urged, still holding her.

She breathed. Gradually the blue color faded from her cheeks.

"Thank God," said Ruth at his side. They hugged the little girl.

"All right now, it's all right now." Mel handed her over to her pale mother and father.

The rabbi reached them. Mona spoke to him.

"She says it was horrible," he translated. "She could not speak, could not tell anyone she was choking. Kona noticed it. She saved Mona's life."

Kona hugged her sister. "Oh, Mona!" she sobbed.

"As also did you, of course," Nab added. "My third child died that way one evening. We watched it happening, but could not help. You must teach me this thing you did."

"It's called the Heimlich maneuver. Here, I'll show you right now. Clasp your hands together, like this." He demonstrated. "Oof! That's right, you've got it. Think you can teach the others?"

"Indeed. Immediately." The Rabbi spoke to his family in Akkadian. Each of them turned to his right, put his arms around the one next to him, and pulled. A circle of 'oofs' came from them.

"You've got the idea," said Mel.

The crowd dispersed, most having lost their appetite.

The rabbi said, "Now I am in a quandary."

"How so?" asked Mel.

"There is so little we can do for you, and nothing we could do would be sufficient to express our gratitude. You are my son. You have but to ask."

"Anyone who knew how would have done what I did. We on our part would be forever in your debt if you could lend us some old sheets and that big net you have lying out back."

"You ask too little."

4
Siege

Four days later they stood on the windswept crown of a hill overlooking the trampled plain where Cyrus's army camped outside Babylon.

"Jesus Christ," Mel breathed.

"It *is* real," said Ruth.

A myriad bronze-helmeted troops, mounted officers riding in their midst, drilled among ten thousand tents aligned in orderly rows—vermin under the walls of the city.

Over it all towered Babylon. Its wall stretched to the horizon, pennons whipping in the wind along its crest, where chariots rolled carrying supplies and relief guards for the archers who stood like cilia in the embrasures.

"It's a geometric Sierra," Mel whispered.

"We're really there. God help us."

Far behind the wall they saw the tops of buildings even more monstrous, dominated by a thousand-foot ziggurat.

"Spoke I not truly?" asked Zaran. "Biggest wall ever built. Solid brick. It extends many cubits underground."

The Euphrates River ran wide, deep and swift into the massive scarp without apparent resistance.

"I cannot believe that is a weak spot," said Ruth in Hebrew.

"Heavy iron grill there, under water," Zaran replied. "Inside, river walled off from two halves of city, guarded, crossed by ferries, drawbridge—even tunnel."

"Tunnel! Under the river?"

"Many collapsed or died, digging. Now is perfectly safe, not even damp."

"Where are the gates?"

"Hundred gates of brass. See there? And there?" They could just make out the two nearest. "All heavily guarded."

"Still, a determined assault—" began Mel.

"You can not see half." Zaran smiled. "Inside is moat; inside that, another wall just like this. Then more walls."

"Start digging."

By dusk they had laid a huge bonfire in the bottom of a ten-foot pit in the hilltop. Stretched out next to it lay the great balloon, half a dozen villagers lashing its mouth to poles. A mesh harness hung from its neck. With dark, the wind had shifted. It now blew from the northwest, as Zaran had predicted, straight toward the city.

"Let's light the fire now," Mel said. "By the time it gets hot, it'll be good and dark." He lowered himself into the pit, torch in hand, and walked around the base of the bonfire, igniting well-placed sticks of tinder. He clambered out.

"Is this going to work?" Ruth asked.

"You checked the calculations. Half a ton of lift, even allowing for leakage. We should go up like a rocket."

"Some rockets don't come down," she pointed out.

"See that smoke?" They could just make it out in the dim sky. It rose at an angle to about a thousand feet, then sheared off. "Winds aloft are stronger. We should sail well into the city, then come down when our air cools. It's cold up there."

"I'm cold down here. Glad we had jackets in our flight bags." They were wearing them under the local robes. "Even if we do look like Arab quarterbacks."

"The net is plenty strong," said Zaran. "Linen…maybe."

"Zaran, for the last time: are you sure you want to come along to translate?" Ruth asked. "You've already gone above and beyond—"

"What have I to lose? One last adventure. Besides, I have friends in the city, not seen for one year. Wait until they hear I fly over wall! They must believe, too, for there I will be, in the city."

"I wouldn't count on it," said Mel. "Sometimes no amount of evidence will change a mind."

"Even in mathematics, where you can prove—" Ruth began.

"Fire is getting high!" called a voice. "Best go soon!"

"Thanks, Sarb. All right, folks, now we unfold the neck over the pit. Don't let go! Agom, are those stakes in tight?"

"Tight as timbrel, boss."

The body of the balloon, lying upwind of the pit, began to stir as hot air forced its way up into it through the neck.

"Hold that top down!" called Mel. "Don't let it swing around! Okay, fellow voyagers. All aboard. Lash in tight." He saw to Ruth's harness, then checked Zaran's. The long tube, fluttering noisily in the wind, now arched half-inflated between the fire and the top. Smoke had a clear passage into the arch. The fire shot up sparks, most dying before entering the balloon's long body. Hot air started to leak away as the pressure in the bag increased.

Mel lashed himself into the harness. "Let go the top!" he called. "Agom, you hang on tight." The top of the balloon rose, like a scared ghost, into an upright position overhead. More smoke was trapped; the bag swelled grossly. A rope parted.

"Agom! Everybody! Let go—cut the ropes!" The crew sawed frantically. Sarb and Agom hammered sideways to loosen the stakes. Two pulled out; another rope, part sawn through, snapped; then everything broke loose at once and the ground dropped sickeningly away from under them. Ruth screamed.

Zaran yelled, "What?"

"I said, 'Wheee!' "

"Quiet!" Mel hissed. "Cyrus can hear you all the way from Egypt."

They rose swiftly over the army encampment. Now that the wind had them, silence closed in. The mighty wall swung downward and toward them. Stars blazed above.

"Glory to God of Abraham, Isaac, Jacob! What a sight," Zaran whispered. "All Babylon—*beneath* us!"

Now the outer wall was far below. On it watchfires sparkled, outlining its double structure and throwing shadows on rubble filling the gap. Ahead was the moat, and the inner wall.

The fabric groaned, netting creaked. "Hang on tight!" Mel warned, as the great tube leaned far over toward the horizontal and accelerated. The passengers swung out behind, then pendulumed under the bag for a few wild seconds until they stabilized.

"Talk about an 'E' ticket," Ruth gasped.

They were past the inner wall and dropping. Their ground speed slacked off as they descended below the wind shear zone.

"We're coming down too fast!" shouted Mel. "Cut the ballast!" A great gray roof rose under them.

The balloon lurched. "Mine gone!" Zaran called.

"Mine too!" yelled Ruth.

Mel's knot was stuck. His fingers were freezing and stiff. *Cut it!* He fumbled under his robe as the roof rushed up at him. Somehow he got the big blade of his Swiss army knife in his teeth, opened it, and cut. His ballast fell away. The harness dug into his crotch and armpits as the balloon lurched. From somewhere above him came a tearing, ripping sound. They were twenty feet above the vast roof, descending more slowly now, but its edge rushed toward them, and beyond was only blackness.

"The bag is collapsing!" screamed Ruth.

"Jump!" Mel shouted. "Quick release!"

Three sets of knots unraveled and the travelers tumbled to the roof as the balloon blew over the edge. They lay there, stunned and breathless, for moments.

"Ruth? Zaran?"

"I'm okay," Ruth managed. "Nothing broken."

"I am not dead," called Zaran. "But do not care, after that ride."

"Where are we, anyhow?" asked Mel.

"Roof of the Grand Palace of Nebuchadnezzar. Too near the edge." They stood up, moved away from the void.

"So!" Mel sighed. "A good landing."

Zaran frowned. "Good?"

"He means it's a landing we can walk away from."

Starlight disclosed a lake-sized expanse of roof encrusted with vent hoods, trees, water tanks, and other structures.

"I served in palace guard," said Zaran. "Should be patrols on roof." They snuck toward a shadowy shed that sheltered a stairwell. "Strange we do not see."

"Maybe they're off defending the outer wall," Ruth suggested.

"Must be. Let's take advantage of it." They reached the door of the shed. It opened easily. Stairs descended into blackness.

"Hold it; I have a light." Ruth rummaged in the purse lashed to her waist and withdrew a small key-ring. A tiny penlight hung from it. They entered the shed. "Close the door." She switched on the light. Piercing the darkness, its beam elicited a startled grunt from Zaran. It lit the stairs down to a landing twenty feet below, where there was a door.

"Stay near side of stairs so they do not creak," said Zaran.

They went down, listened at the door. Nothing.

"Turn off the light a minute," Mel said; Ruth complied. The dark seemed absolute, but in a minute his eyes adjusted enough to see a dim bar of light under the door. "What's out there?"

"Palace attic. Storerooms, armory, museum, guardhouse. Servants' rooms on the floor below. Below that, clerks' housing, then offices, then royal quarters, grand ballroom, throne room, audience chambers—"

"How many floors has this place got, anyway?" asked Mel.

"Museum?" asked Ruth simultaneously.

"Eight, counting dungeons. Nebuchadnezzar started the museum to show off special spoils of war. Rare things from nations he destroys."

"Let's go there!" Ruth said. "Mel, this Mitchell you've got a letter—"

"Mishael."

"This Mishael you've got a letter of introduction to. He's a clerk of the palace, right?"

Mel smiled. "Administrative Magician Emeritus of the Court."

"He has offices here?"

"So I'm told."

"Well, he won't be in them now; it's late. We'll have to wait for him. If we leave the palace, we'll never get back in. Let's wait in the museum! Think what might be there!"

"She is right," said Zaran. "No one goes there. It is good place to hide. I know Meshach's office. When morning comes, I take you to him."

They opened the door cautiously and followed Zaran down a narrow corridor toward a burning sconce at the intersection, around the corner into a wider corridor lined, at long intervals, with doors, then through one of the doors. They shut it behind them, and Ruth turned on her light. They gasped.

"Museum storage," Zaran said. "Now you know why Babylon is called 'City of Gold.'"

The room, fifteen feet high and too deep to see to the back, was lined and filled with shelves like library stacks. But these held treasures. Row upon row of golden shields, bracelets, ceremonial swords, necklaces, goblets, figurines, crowns, candlesticks, and plaques gleamed in the moving circle of light. A thin film of dust coated everything, but nothing was tarnished.

"The door wasn't even locked!" Mel said.

"Babylonians respect law," replied Zaran. "Codes of Hammurabi and Moses deal strictly with thieves. First offense, pay back ten times or lose right hand."

"What happens to trespassers?" Ruth asked.

"You do not want to know."

"Look, we have an excuse. We're refugees," Mel tried to reassure Ruth. "Extenuating circumstances. And we're not going to hurt anything—"

The door opened, light flooding in from lamps and torches held aloft by four servants and two armed guards in the corridor. Their eyes widened, mouths gaped. The guards called out and reached for their swords.

Mel, Ruth, and Zaran bolted through the stacks. The guards lunged after them as the servants cowered.

"Here!" shouted Zaran. He wrenched open a door at the back of the room. They followed him through and slammed it. Hearing shouts and running feet, Mel wedged a stone tablet against the door and looked about.

This room was brightly lighted and spacious. In its center was a curious object resembling a baby's bathtub, with two dragons mounted on its massive gold lid. Another stone tablet was propped next to it. Nothing was dusty.

"This way, out the front door," Zaran urged. They raced through the museum toward another door, which opened onto a dim corridor. "Quiet," he whispered. Voices called to each other down the corridor. Across it, in the direction of the voices, was another door. "There." They sprinted through it.

"Did they see us?" Ruth gasped. Her penlight revealed a large room piled with dusty chests, cabinets, chairs, sofas, and tables, broken and worn.

"Now, one more thing," Zaran whispered. "The back door of this room is near main stairway. Downstairs, where people are, we can blend in. Come."

They crept through the attic toward a door. As they reached it, the voices grew louder and the door behind them opened. They were still concealed by the old furniture.

"No choice," Zaran said. "We go." He opened the door and they went through as quickly and softly as they could, closing it gently behind them. A broad stairway lay three yards to the right, down a main corridor.

"Home free," Mel whispered—

A door burst open across the corridor. Six guards sprang out and surrounded them. The door behind them opened and disgorged the original two guards. "Zaran!" cried one.

"You're right, Zaran," Ruth said. "I really don't want to know what happens to trespassers."

Zaran spoke to the guard he knew, who replied briefly.

"Not good ," said Zaran. "King Nabonidas is in Arabia again. Very bad."

"Why, who's in charge?" Ruth asked.

"Belshazzar."

The corporal of the guard arrived around the corner. He spoke; the troops replied. He turned to the original pair. The one Zaran knew spoke at length. The corporal regarded Zaran critically, reached toward Ruth and pulled back her cowl. Some of the company grunted in surprise.

The corporal spoke to Zaran. At his reply, all the guards burst out laughing. The corporal snarled at them, shutting them up. He quizzed Zaran, who lifted both hands and one eyebrow, shrugged, uttered a brief phrase and pointed.

The corporal barked an order. Two of the guards who had come out of the armory saluted, turned, and ran off down the stairs.

Issuing another command, the corporal spun on his heel and marched back up the hall. The guards gestured for the captives to follow.

At the intersection with the wide corridor they met the four servants bearing golden vessels and goblets incised with Hebrew letters. The first two guards rejoined the party, and the six went downstairs.

"Those cups looked familiar," Mel observed.

"Sacred vessels from Solomon's Temple," said Zaran. "What do they do with them?"

They arrived in the orderly room. The corporal spoke to a sergeant, who vanished behind a door. He soon returned and led them into the inner office, where a polished, trim man with gray-streaked hair sat behind a desk.

"Captain Isaac!" Zaran said in Hebrew.

"Zaran, it is really you!" Isaac exclaimed. "What are you doing here? How did you get in? And who are these?"

"Sir, these are magicians from a faraway land, here by misadventure. He,"

Zaran pointed at Mel, "bears an urgent message for Magician Meshach. We wait for his office to open—"

"In the museum? And what's this about flying here?"

"We flew by skill, not magic. A simple craft; it blew off the roof. Your soldiers now go to bring it back; you will see. And, sir, if I had known you were in charge, I would not have tried to hide. We just wanted to avoid formalities, tedious explanations, before seeing the magician. Quick in, quick out."

"Well, I can appreciate that," said Isaac. "And I know you weren't trying to steal the King's gold. Still, you should have checked in. How did you get past the roof patrols?"

"No patrols."

"I'll have their stripes!" Isaac called out something in Akkadian. The orderly sergeant appeared instantaneously and saluted. The captain asked a question. The sergeant answered. The captain spoke to the sergeant loudly for ninety seconds while the sergeant grew red around the whiskers. Then the sergeant saluted and vanished.

The captain drew a breath. "Now, where were we?"

"The letter for the magician," Zaran reminded him. As Mel drew it from his jacket pocket, the guard who had recognized Zaran appeared in the doorway, clicked to attention, and saluted.

Captain Isaac asked him something. The guard began to explain.

"What's he saying?" Mel asked Zaran in a low voice.

"They found the balloon. Most of it. Dorfu left a guard, came back for men to fetch it. Ruth, Captain Isaac is a good Jew. He knows me. Do not worry."

"Whew!" breathed Ruth. "What a break!"

Private Dorfu finished his report. Isaac turned to them. "Well, this puts a rather different complexion on the matter," he said. "I'm afraid, Zaran, that I have no choice but to report this incident. Come."

"Report?"

"We must interrupt the King at his revels. Immediately."

Ruth shook herself as if trying to overcome fear. "Captain," she began.

"You speak Hebrew!"

"But poorly, having just learned. Captain, is it not so that guards search the person of anyone seeking audience with the king?"

"Yes, as a matter of caution."

"Good thinking, Ruth," said Mel. "Sir, we have a lot of baggage. Can we just leave it here? Fetch it later?"

"Very well," Isaac agreed. "That will expedite things downstairs."

"I was getting hot in this jacket," Ruth confessed to Mel in English.

"You sure acted cool." Doffing their robes, the fliers untied their bags, purse, and pack. Mel and Ruth removed their Moscow jackets. Mel stuffed the letter in his pants pocket.

"What a relief." Ruth wiped her brow. "It certainly is hot in here."

"The palace is famous for its furnaces," said Zaran.

"Yes, it's a well-designed heating system," Isaac observed. "Safety factor of seven. You can leave your things behind my desk. No one will touch them. Now we must go." They put their robes back on over their "magicians' garb" and started out. Isaac spoke as they passed through the orderly room and two guards joined them.

As they descended the fourth flight of stairs, sounds of laughter, music, and shrieks growing louder, a woman appeared on the landing below. Short but not bent, eyes flashing in a nest of wrinkles, she was the oldest woman Mel had ever seen. Her robe was plain, dyed a rich purple. Two maids flanked her.

Captain Isaac braked to a halt, made a deep obeisance, and spoke to her.

"Bow, quick," urged Zaran softly. "The Queen Mother." They bowed.

She looked sharply at Mel and Ruth, and spoke to Isaac. He replied.

"Now, that is interesting," she said. "How does it happen that persons from such a distant land know the Hebrew tongue?"

"I have sojourned in Is—in Judah, my Queen," answered Mel.

"Judah is a howling rubble," said the queen. "It has been sixty years since my King subdued it. Israel is even worse. You are but a boy. Tell me the truth." She held his eyes with her own.

"I speak truth," said Mel. "By some magic I have been brought from...another century."

Zaran gasped.

The queen did not blink. "I cannot help you directly," she said. "I have little authority here. But I shall pray. And there is one whom you must meet. Come to see me tomorrow; I shall introduce you. He is good at puzzles." She turned to Ruth. "Do not worry, my dear; all will be well. You shall return to your future and your land." She bade them good night and swept off with her retinue.

"Most curious," mused Isaac. "Come, my friends. On to Belshazzar's feast. And let me do the talking."

5
Dropping in for Dinner

The guard at the great doorway touched his helmet and spoke to the captain. The captain spoke a few words with him and they went in.

"It's as bad as a disco!" Ruth said.

"What?" asked Mel. She shook her head.

The great white-plastered room was packed with people, and was stiflingly hot. Most in the crowd were nearly naked; it was easy for the captain to plow through them in his iron armor. Flaming chandeliers and wall sconces filled the air with smoke, and brightly illuminated couples dancing, drinking, and reclining. On a raised stage at one end of the room, musicians played sackbuts, timbrels, lyres, and dulcimers but their music was drowned in the noise. Nearby, at the high table, sat the king-regent Belshazzar among his concubines and courtiers. His arm encircled the woman on his right, with whom he was in earnest conversation; in his left hand something ornate glittered in the flickering light.

Ruth saw. "Sacrilege!"

The king pressed the sacred goblet to the woman's lips; wine dribbled down her chin.

Captain Isaac's mouth tightened into a thin line. He approached the king. "Sire," he said in Akkadian.

"Ah, Isaac!" the king cried. "Companions, observe General Jew!" He waved his hand, slopping wine out of the goblet. "Do you think my revel good, General? What brings you here?"

"Sire, an urgent—"

"General my Jew, an idea occurs. Why don' you go get some of your Jew compatriots and sing for us? Wouldn' that be a good idea?" He addressed his nobles. "Would you like that?" They nodded. "Sing us one of the songs of Zion. Some lively tune."

"Just as you command, sire. In fact, I have something even more entertaining for you here. See these people: are they not queer? They came into the city by flying! Perhaps Cyrus could also—"

"Nah, nah," said the king. At least he was finally paying attention. "Don' worry about ol' Cyrus. Don' give it 'nother thought. He'll never enter this city. Babylon's impregnable!" He turned to his concubine. "But you're not, eh, woman? Why should we not found a dynasty?"

"Your highness!" shouted Isaac. "We are in danger! While searching for the ball—while searching outside, my guards noticed that the river is unusually low. Something is amiss."

"The river? The Euphrates?"

"That's the one."

Belshazzar scowled. "Who did it? Who are these people?" He squinted at Zaran. "I've seen you before. Haven' I?" Zaran opened his mouth, but the king had noticed Ruth. "Wait. What have we here?" Leering, he set down the sacred vessel. "Hail, n'chanting one!" He reached toward her breast.

Mel slapped his hand away.

A gasp went round the table. The king's eyes bulged. He reddened and struggled for breath. "You dare!" he croaked. "I am the king! Guards!"

The guards snapped to attention. Guests seated nearby ceased their babble. The music stopped. Perfect silence fell on the hall.

"Take this one and skin—"

A table crashed over, scattering dishes as the diners scrambled away from the wall. Mel, and everyone else, turned to look.

Something was moving up there by the sconce. A huge spider? No, a hand! A man's hand! It held a stylus and appeared to be writing. It was the most convincing hologram he'd ever seen. Except—

Words were appearing on the wall under the fingers.

Mel shivered. The entire great hall was wrapped in silence, watching the fingers silently write. A sour odor came from the king. Sweat streamed down his face.

The hand finished writing and disappeared, but the words remained, glowing red, stark against the white wall.

Mel couldn't read them. "What does that say?" he whispered to Zaran.

"Money. It's just some coins…names of coins. A mina, a shekel…" Across the expanse of the ballroom, other murmurs arose.

"Mel." Ruth grasped his arm.

"Yes?"

"You're crazy for sure! But thanks," she whispered. "Mel, do you know what that is? That's the handwriting on the wall."

"I see that—what!" His skin prickled. His back hairs lifted. "But that's just a story. A myth."

"A miracle," she said softly.

The king was stone sober now. "Silence!" he shouted. "Captain, send for my magicians. Bring the sorcerers and soothsayers, too; the astrologers and Chaldeans; all my wise men. Roust them all out of bed." Isaac spoke to one of the guards, who took off at a trot. The king raised his voice. "What does this mean? Who can tell me?"

Nobody spoke for a long moment.

"Perhaps the king is coming into some money?" ventured a prince seated at the high table.

"I don't want guesses. This is not a happy message." The king trembled. "My magi will interpret it. We'll wait for them."

All waited in silence and dread. The words glowed mockingly.

Finally there was a stir at the door. Twenty-four magicians bustled across the room, stifling yawns. They wore full curly beards, long black robes, and tall pointed hats. Seeing the glowing words, they stopped abruptly. One stepped forward.

"O king, live forever," he said. "What is your pleasure?"

"What do you think, idiot? Interpret those words for me."

"Why, who wrote them? Ask him—" the sorcerer began. A man at his side whispered in his ear. "What! Really? A hand you say. Sorry I missed it."

"Get on with it," growled the king.

"Just so. Let me see. '*Mene, mene, tekel, upharsin.*' Coins. Simple."

"But what does it mean?" the king raged. "What is the message?"

"I haven't the foggiest." The mage turned to his colleagues. "Anyone?" They shook their heads. "No." "Beyond me." "Seems to be some money."

"You pretenders are useless!" screamed the king. "In the olden days, Nebuchadnezzar would have had you cut to pieces." He turned to include everyone in the grand ballroom. "Hear my offer: if anyone can interpret this message for me, I will clothe him in scarlet and...and give him a gold chain to wear around his neck." He waited. "And make him third ruler in the kingdom!"

"Well, in that case..." the chief astrologer muttered. He raised his voice. "O king, if we could have but a little time to ponder this saying, do some fast research, consult our library?"

"All right," granted the king, "but be quick."

The seers went into a huddle. Baleful actinic light flashed from the group. Puffs of purple smoke arose. Four sorcerers began to chant. Something resembling a glowing orrery appeared in midair. Someone had conjured up a lectern bearing a volume massive as Webster's Unabridged; he riffled through its pages. Tiny explosions smote the air. After a few minutes the smoke dissipated and the chief astrologer turned to the king.

"O king, we have made progress. Some of these words have alternate, archaic meanings. 'Mene,' for example, can mean 'number' as well as a unit of money.

A shekel is a unit of weight as well as a coin. Beyond that, observe that a upharsin is exactly half a sheckel. In light of these findings, we conclude…"

"Yes?" urged the king.

"Yes, tell us!" "What is it?" "What does it mean?" The cries came from all around the ballroom.

The seer waited patiently for quiet. "Thy kingdom, Highness, is fated to convert to a new mathematic system based on binary numbers."

Screams of rage filled the room. Belshazzar wailed in dismay. The mob surged forward. As they began to savage the Chaldeans, a small figure clothed in royal purple appeared in the doorway. The mob drew back, abashed. A few draped napkins over their nakedness. "The Queen! The Queen!" they whispered. Silence fell.

"O king, live for ever," the Queen said, in formal Akkadian. "Let not thy thoughts trouble thee, nor let thy countenance be changed: There is a man in thy kingdom, in whom is the spirit of the holy God; and in the days of thy father light and understanding and wisdom, like the wisdom of the gods, was found in him; whom the King Nebuchadnezzar thy father, the *King*, thy *father*, made master of the magicians, astrologers, Chaldeans, and soothsayers; forasmuch as an excellent spirit, and knowledge, and understanding, interpreting of dreams, and showing of hard sentences, and dissolving of doubts, were found in the same Daniel—"

Mel gasped at the name.

"—whom the King named Belteshazzar; now let Daniel be called, and he will show the interpretation."

"Did she mention Daniel?" Mel asked Zaran. "*The* Daniel?"

"Judean prince, captured by Nebuchadnezzar. He is retired now."

The king ordered Daniel summoned. A hubbub grew as some of the older lords began to tell the young nobles whatever they could remember about Belteshazzar and his exploits.

"If anyone can solve this riddle, Belteshazzar can. I remember my dad telling me about one time the King…the real King, Nebuchadnezzar—"

"Say, did you hear Queen Amytis put Belshazzar in his place? 'The King, thy father,' she says."

"—had this dream, well, these astrologers think nothing of interpreting dreams, and who can tell when they're wrong? But this time—"

"Dreams are one thing, but my dad said there was some action involving Belteshazzar's friends being burned alive."

"—the King was too smart for 'em. 'You tell me what I dreamed,' he says. 'I forget. I'm sure I'll remember it when I hear it, though.' And then he comes up with this incentive plan—"

"Nah, they weren't burned, just thrown in the big furnace."

"Same thing."

Daniel arrived.

He was a big man with long white hair, skin smooth as a baby's except for a pure white beard that hung halfway down his robe. Bearing himself erect with the aid of a stout staff, he advanced to the Queen's side as the crowd made way under his piercing gaze.

His eyes met Mel's. Was that the faintest glimmer of a smile?

Belshazzar addressed Daniel in Akkadian. Daniel answered at length.

"What's he saying?" asked Ruth.

"Belshazzar offers him third place in the kingdom," Zaran whispered. "Daniel says no. He chides the king. Says Nebuchadnezzar learned from mistakes, but Belshazzar does not. Playing with sacred vessels is too much for God; God sent the fingers to write on the wall."

Daniel strode over to the wall beside the bright candelabra. He indicated the first word. "*Mene*," he said.

"He interprets now," said Zaran. "'God hath numbered thy kingdom, and finished it.' Your time is up."

"*Tekel*," Daniel said.

"'Thou art weighed in the balances, and art found wanting.'"

"*Peres*."

"Is a root word: means 'divide.' 'Thy kingdom is divided, and given to the Medes and Persians'!"

"That's it!" cried Mel. "This siege...I remember what happened. The fall of Babylon. We've got to get out of here!"

"Not so fast," Captain Isaac objected. "You're still under arrest. I must hold you until the king finishes passing sentence."

"But look," urged Ruth. "The king is leaving. He's forgotten all about Mel."

"I shouldn't wonder," Isaac said. And indeed it was true. Having invested Daniel with robe, chain and office, Belshazzar was retiring with his women and trusted advisors. A throng of worried sages and lords surrounded Daniel.

"If Daniel is now third ruler in the kingdom," Mel asked, "who's second?"

"Why, Belshazzar himself," replied Isaac, "after his father Nabonidas."

"This slime is his son?"

"Do not Judge Belshazzar too harshly." The Queen had come up behind them. "He was not always thus. A weak man, he could not absorb the power thrust upon him. See how he has kept his promise even to his messenger of doom." She indicated Daniel. "Even to a Jew."

Queen Amytis turned to Captain Isaac. "Your urgent message must now be delivered to the acting regent, Daniel."

"You're right. I had forgotten Cyrus and the river." Isaac spoke swift words to his guards, then strode toward Daniel. The guards surrounded Mel.

"What does this mean?" the Queen asked Mel. "Why do they detain you?"

"Belshazzar was about to molest me," said Ruth. "Mel slapped him."

"You dared lay a hand on the royal personage?" The Queen turned. "Daniel!" she called. Daniel and Isaac were already returning. "Daniel, these are the persons I told you of. This one has uncommon courage. He struck the king in defending his lady's honor. Perhaps he will prove even better suited to your purpose than we thought."

"Peace," Daniel said. "I am happy to meet you." He spoke to the two guards in Akkadian; they departed. "I have given them something better to do than detaining you: see what's happening at the river. Captain Isaac concurs."

"Daniel has persuaded me that Belshazzar won't be in power much longer," said Isaac. "As regent, Daniel has taken over your custody. I am much relieved."

"As am I," Mel breathed.

"Belshazzar won't remember any of this tomorrow, so drunk was he," said Daniel. "Too bad. It seems to be a common human failing, to forget miracles. And this was a sorely needed warning. At any rate, he'll never recall your striking him, so there is no need to put you to death with great haste for such a noble deed. Consider your sentence commuted. Besides, there are matters I would discuss with you tonight, if you are willing."

"And we with you," Mel said. "Quite willing."

"An interview with the prophet Daniel," murmured Ruth. "Who could believe it?"

The prophet addressed the musicians, who began to play. He bade a servant gather up the sacred vessels. Mounting the stage, he made a brief announcement. A thousand chastened lords got to their feet, assisting their ladies to rise.

"The party is over," said Zaran.

The guests started filing toward the great door. Suddenly those in front cried in alarm.

Isaac's two guards had returned…at the point of Persian swords. One shouted something. Zaran translated.

"He says the river is gone. And Belshazzar is dead!"

6
Let My People Go

Darius's men seemed to know whom to seek out. Having already seized the armory, they let the unarmed guests file out under scrutiny, with instructions to return to their own homes and remain there until further notice: which notice Arxes, the Persian commander, assured them General Darius would soon provide. Then Arxes approached Daniel.

"Do I have the honor," he inquired in polite Hebrew, "of addressing the great soothsayer Daniel from Judah?"

"I am Daniel, of Jerusalem. Are you he who slew the king?"

"A most unfortunate accident involving one of my sergeants who had drawn his sword. Under my orders, I admit. We were in the king's apartments, securing them for Darius's use, when Belshazzar stumbled. The sword pierced his heart. We were anticipating no bloodshed, having met little opposition."

"How did you enter the city?" asked Isaac. "Down the river bed?"

"Some members of the resistance agreed to unlock the underwater gate for us: the same ones who had signaled us from the wall that the great feast was beginning and it was time to cut the final bank of earth between the Euphrates and its new channel."

"Collaborators!" whispered Mel. "Treachery!"

"Mel, shut up!" Ruth hissed. "You're going to get us all killed!"

The Queen heard. "You misgauge the political situation. The people have long been loyal to Nebuchadnezzar, my King, and to good King Nabonidas. But Belshazzar, though of royal blood, is viewed as the enemy. He increased taxes to finance his debaucheries, neglected the temples, and persecuted the Jews."

"Cyrus is perceived as a liberator," Daniel confirmed. "I will gladly surrender the city and the kingdom to his army of liberation and his general, Darius the Mede."

"We Persians are less cruel than the Chaldeans. As are the Medes. It is not the mode for a Median to be mean. We shall not sack this magnificent city. Note that we never once fired our siege engines against your magnificent Ishtar Gate."

"You couldn't get them close enough," muttered Captain Isaac.

"What did you say?"

"Good riddance!"

Mel could contain himself no longer. "Sir," he asked, "were there any Jews in this 'underground resistance movement'?"

Ruth's undertone was insistent: "Mel!"

"I led it," said Daniel. "In fact, it was to enlist your aid therein that I wished to talk with you this night. Now, I am glad to say, it is moot."

"There, see?" Ruth whispered urgently. "Now will you shut up?"

"You, Daniel, a holy man of God!"

"Mel," Ruth said in English, "(a.) You don't believe in God, remember? Two hours ago you didn't believe in Daniel. (b.) You just referred to Belshazzar as 'slime.' (c.) Recall a certain guy who made common cause with his sovereign's enemy France: George Washington. Q.E.D."

Mel thought about that for a minute.

"Our history is full of holy men of God who were fighters," Isaac put in. "Abraham, Joshua, David…"

"If Nabonidas had not been so retiring," said the Queen, "perhaps none of this would have been necessary. As it was, I myself sought Daniel's aid against my own grandson."

"As God led me, so I did," Daniel said.

"Mel, we're wasting these folks' time," said Ruth, again in English. "They don't have to explain their motives to us. The fact that they're being so gracious, and not simply beheading you, ought to tell you something. Now apologize and let's get on with our business. Remember that? The twentieth century? Air conditioning? Quarter pounders at McDonald's?"

"You're absolutely right. My Prince, I humbly apologize. I'm sorry I doubted. Forgive me for wasting your time, and thank you for your kind indulgence; you too, Your Highness, all of you. I have been a schlemiel."

"A 'peace of God'?" asked Ruth quietly in English.

That had come out wrong, hadn't it? "An oaf."

"Forgiven," said Daniel. "I would still dearly love to converse with you two. Perhaps soon, in my apartments. First, however, there is more pressing business. Colonel Arxes, a word with you?"

"Just as you wish. My own business is a matter of mere moments. Darius wishes your recommendations for officials of the new regime."

"I have already drawn up a list of some hundred names. It's in my chambers. Let us go there now; I have something to show you which will intrigue Cyrus also."

As they all proceeded upstairs, Daniel asked, "How old is Cyrus?"

"I'm not sure," Arxes answered. "Certainly younger than his general Darius, who is sixty-two. But I must tell you that Cyrus is not presently with this army, nor soon will be."

"I thought not," Zaran said.

"His Egyptian campaign is running into difficulties, then?" asked Daniel. "A disappointment. You will see why, presently."

"Frankly, yes. It might be a year or two before the western front is quiet. Meantime, Darius the Mede has been given the regency. He will be king here in Cyrus's stead. He has plenipotentiary authority. His word is law throughout Babylon province—the law of the Medes and Persians."

"Which cannot be revoked," Daniel said.

"Quite correct."

They arrived at a door in the west wing of the palace. Daniel ushered them in. Burning rushes provided soft illumination in a large living area which had been partially converted into an office. Doors on the left and right presumably led to kitchen, bedrooms, and other private family chambers. Cool night air ("What a relief," Ruth murmured.) entered through a picture window leading to a balcony with a view of the temple of Marduk across the river, now a ditch of aromatic mud. Fortunately an easterly breeze was blowing.

"I requested a view toward the Temple in Jerusalem," said Daniel as he lighted candles and torches. "A little irony there. Please be seated; consider yourselves at home." He rang for a servant. A middle-aged woman appeared presently. "Martha, please bring refreshments for my guests. I see you were awake. Trouble sleeping?"

"With all the ruckus going on outside, yelling and banging, who could sleep? What's happening?"

"The city is fallen. Belshazzar is dead."

"Praise the Lord." She departed.

Daniel went over to a rack near his desk and selected two scrolls. "These are my recommendations." He handed one of the scrolls to Colonel Arxes. "And this is a copy of a book written much longer than sixty-two years ago." He unrolled the other to a certain point. "Read there, if you read Hebrew."

"Thank you. 'That saith to the deep, Be dry, and I will dry up thy rivers. That saith of Cyrus—' Daniel, this passes belief!"

"Please continue."

"Cyrus, my shepherd, and shall perform all my pleasure; even saying to Jerusalem, Thou shalt be built; and to the temple, Thy foundation shall be laid—'"

"Wait a minute," Mel interrupted. "What is he reading?"

"The prophet Isaiah," Daniel replied.

"But—"

"Quiet!" whispered Ruth. "Listen!"

"'Thus saith the Lord to his anointed, to Cyrus, whose right hand I have holden, to subdue nations before him; and I will loose the loins of kings, to open before him the two leaved gates; and the gates shall not be shut; I will go before thee, and make the crooked places straight; I will break in pieces the gates of brass, and cut in sunder the bars of iron.'

"Amazing! Daniel, I must tell you something. When my scouts came to the grille in the riverbed, they expected Arioch and Melzar, who were to meet them there, to unbar the brass gates from inside. Failing that, my men had brought prying tools.

"But the grille was gone! The iron bars were broken. The gates lay in pieces on the river bed. Some flood must have rolled a boulder through them. We did not need to wait for your two. Our whole company was able to proceed along the river, hidden in the shadows of the walls, all the way to the palace. Truly your God made the crooked places straight."

"Really? What a coincidence." Daniel smiled. "Now read in this place."

"'He shall build my city, and he shall let go my captives—' So this is why you were so willing..."

"As you see, God called Cyrus his anointed; who could then resist him? I thought to avoid bloodshed."

"Now just a minute," Mel interrupted. "When was this written?"

"Over a century and a half ago," replied Daniel.

"Are you trying to tell me Isaiah knew, *that* long ago, that Babylon would fall to a man named Cyrus? Through rusted iron bars? In a dry riverbed?"

"And that Cyrus would free my people. And when it would occur."

"But how could he?"

"Mel, that's prophecy," Ruth said. "That's what prophets *do*."

"A prophet tries to tell people what the King of the Universe reveals to him. Rarely do they listen. So he writes it down."

"But they just fake it!"

"A grave accusation," reproved the Queen. "Know you not the penalty for prophesying in the name of God and being wrong? Death by stoning."

"That's why it doesn't pay a prophet to be too specific," Mel muttered.

"I heard that," protested Ruth. "What could be more specific than this? Calling Cyrus by name? Mel, straighten up."

"But look," Mel said, "to survive, a prophet would have to bat a thousand. He couldn't be wrong once."

"Right," said Ruth.

"But the Bible is full of incorrect prophecies...and contradictions."

"Name one," she challenged.

"Well, I—Look, Ruth, I thought you were an agnostic?"

"Not in this foxhole, I'm not."

Colonel Arxes had been reading silently, his lips moving. Now he spoke. "Daniel, this mentions treasure: that Cyrus will cart away some idols. Do you know anything about this? Are any of the idols valuable? And where are they?"

Without a word, Daniel pointed out the window.

"Tyrax, take a squad and see what's in that temple," Arxes said. Tyrax saluted and exited.

"There are more than one hundred temples in this city," said the Queen, "many housing idols of gold. Idols to Bel and Nebo, to Ishtar and Marduk. Take them all."

"Only leave the sacred objects that were removed from the house of God in Jerusalem," Daniel said. "They are to be returned to it."

"Perhaps you would be so kind," said Colonel Arxes, "as to appoint some knowledgeable individual to tell me which are which?"

"Captain Isaac, you know the sacred objects from the Temple, do you not?"

"Yes, and I also know where the inventory is listed."

"Then please accompany Colonel Arxes and be his guide to the treasures."

"As you wish. I'm eager to find out more about these travelers, however."

"Please come now," Arxes asked. "My troops are honest, but all that gold! And they could damage your holy objects."

Tyrax returned and saluted. "Sir, in that temple alone is so much gold we shall need a crane to remove it."

"Let's go." Isaac and Arxes departed with their men. The room seemed much more spacious and quiet.

Martha entered, pushing a brass cart laden with cakes and steaming mugs, bowls, and pitchers. "Refreshments. Tea, chicken soup, things to nosh. Help yourselves. Eat! Enjoy!"

"Thank you, Martha; we shall. You may retire now." Martha curtsied and left. The guests helped themselves.

When they were settled again, Daniel said, "Now, my friends, you shall satisfy my curiosity. Who wishes to be first?"

7
Our Fair City

"I think this may help clear things up," Mel said, reaching under his robe. "You should probably read this first, sir." He handed Daniel the letter of introduction. "As you see, it's for someone named Mishael, but—"

"Mishael!" Daniel said, looking at the superscription. He unfolded the letter. "My brother in faith! He would have wanted me to read this. You see, Mishael died in bed last Tashritu. He is now in Abraham's bosom. Who gave you this? Ah, I see: it's signed by a Pastor Nab." He began to read aloud:

18 Arahsamnu 68

Dear Mishael, my mentor, my spiritual father:

May the grace of God the mighty King be yours! How are you? The village prospers. My congregation now numbers forty-two. We have not yet had the pleasure of a visit from Cyrus, so things are fairly normal here thus far.

The bearer of this letter is Melvin Schwartz, a man ensorcelled here from a distant land with his wife Ruth. They desire and greatly need some wise counsel to help them to return. They have strange, wonderful skills and devices, but say they are not magicians.

They are mysterious but good. The man saved my granddaughter's life when she would have choked to death. You remember little Mona? She's a big girl now, and happy she is alive. As are we all. You will have my undying gratitude if you help these folk in any way you can. More: you will be fascinated by their tales (and ask Mel to play for you on his 'harmonica').

Hoping to see you when the siege is lifted. God bless you!

Yours,
Pastor Nab

P.S. Don't let Mel get away without teaching you something called the 'Heimlich maneuver.' — N.

"This certainly is a fine grade of papyrus," mused Daniel, turning the letter over in his hand. "I've never seen its like."

"Uh…it's a shirt cardboard."

"Nab will be sad to hear Meshach is dead," Zaran said.

"He lived to a ripe old age," said Daniel. "Almost ninety, like me. He had a full life, and is now with God."

"I know. But Nab will still miss him. Meshach was like a father to him."

"Of course. But consider: we have had fifty more years of his fellowship than we might have had, but for the intervention of the Lord."

"Agreed. Nab would never have known him, if he was burned as intended."

"'Burned'?" asked Ruth.

"You do not know story?"

"I'm afraid I do," Mel said under his breath.

"Meshach and two others were thrown into a furnace for not bowing down to a statue of the king. The Lord God joined them and kept them cool. They did not even smell of smoke."

"Let me guess," Ruth said. "Were the others Shadrach and Abed-Nego?"

"Hananiah and Azariah, yes," replied Daniel. "So you have heard the story. They are still strong; I will introduce you tomorrow, if you like. Good men."

"I would dearly love to meet them," Ruth said.

"So would I!" said Mel. To Ruth, "Ruth, wake me up. I'm dreaming I've been carrying a letter of introduction to Shadrach for three days. Shadrach!"

"Meshach," Ruth corrected.

"I was away when it happened," said Daniel. "Ashpenaz tried to get them off on a technicality—no dulcimer—but they confessed: 'Go ahead, throw us in the furnace,' they dared the king. 'God will save us. But even if he does not, we aren't about to bow down to a statue of you.' What faith!"

"It worked out for best, anyway," Zaran said. "They got promotions."

"I can't imagine how it felt," said Ruth with a shudder, "being tied up and dragged toward that awful fire."

"Nor can I," Mel added. "Or how you felt, Daniel, in the lions' den."

"Lions' den? Me, in a lions' den? Never. I would not go near lions. Those beasts are dangerous."

"Well, I guess not everything in the Bible is accurate," said Mel in a drowsy aside to Ruth.

Daniel replied to Ruth's implied question. "Yes, I asked Azariah the same thing. He said he felt only a cool, scented spring breeze that grew fresher even as the soldiers bearing him began to drop from the heat. Then he knew God was in control. As always."

"Ow!" cried Mel. "Why'd you do that?" he hissed.

"You were dozing off," whispered Ruth. "Have you no respect?"

The Queen spoke. "Daniel, I think our guests should retire now."

"I'm sorry, but I guess she's right," Ruth agreed. "Was it only this morning we carried the balloon up that hill?"

"And did all that digging?" added Zaran. "Could have waited one more day and just walked into city."

"What, and miss the party?" Mel grinned, his eyelids opening briefly. "Ow!" he yelped as Ruth elbowed him again.

"My humble apologies," said Daniel. "Of course, you must be exhausted. You must rest. You may stay here. I have plenty of room now."

"Our things…" Ruth began.

"I will get," offered Zaran. "Am not sleepy yet. Can exercise legs."

"Thank you, Zaran." He left. They said good night to the Queen, and she departed. Their host led them to a spare bedroom.

Inside, Ruth said, "Plumbing! ... and look, Mel! A shower!" She pushed a knob. "Hot water!"

Perversely, the short walk had revived him a little. "You go ahead," he said. "I'll wait for our stuff."

"Thanks." She tossed her robe on a chair, sat on the bed, and bent to unlace her Reeboks. "I'm not going to pass up a chance like this."

Mel flopped backward on the bed next to her, hands clasped behind his head. "What a day."

"Yes, wasn't it?" She dropped a shoe, tugged at her sock. "Oh, listen, Mel."

"Hm?"

"I never did get a chance to thank you properly for what you did. You fool. Mel, that was a *splendid* thing to do."

"Just an instinc—" She leaned over and planted a sweet kiss on his lips.

"Wow!" he said, when he could. He sat up. "I'll slap kings all the time." He reached around her for more. "Ruth—"

A knock sounded at the door.

"Just a minute," she called. Separating herself from his arms, she limped to the door and opened it.

Daniel stood there. "Your bags."

"Oh, thanks. Here, I'll take them. I'll just put them right here on this chair. Daniel, this place is fabulous. I didn't know you had plumbing back…"

"Back here in your past?" He smiled gently. "My dear, how strange and frightening all this must be for you. And you," he included Mel. "But be of good cheer. The God of Abraham, Isaac, and Jacob is the same loving Father now as he is in your future time. And he is in control. Good night, and may his Spirit guide you."

When the door was again shut, Ruth said, "Mel."

"Yes."

"Mel, I really am grateful to you. And I have warm fuzzies toward you, and I know you respect me."

"More than that."

"But—"

"I know. We almost got carried away there, didn't I?"

She laughed. "Right. Now, tomorrow, we really have to get organized, and get out of here.—Turn your back while I take off my other shoe."

They slept late. Finally Martha knocked, entered with a tray, and bustled about the room, opening the curtains and setting out dishes. "Good morning," she said as they yawned and stretched.

"That sure smells good," said Mel. "What time is it?"

"About the third hour. Daniel has already gone."

"Gone? Where?"

"Darius summoned him to the court, for consultations. He left word that he would probably be home at midday."

"Thank you. We'll get up now."

"I should hope so." Martha smiled. "Lazy bones." She left.

They sat at the breakfast table. "Well," said Mel, "that gives us a few hours to get our act together."

"Plan B."

"Right. The only plan we've got."

By the time they had finished eating and Mel had shaved (he had seen no one here wearing any sort of mustache, let alone a silly one, so didn't risk it), Martha was back with a message that Queen Amytis awaited their pleasure.

A few minutes later they joined her in her living room. "Sorry to keep Your Highness waiting," Mel said. "We just woke up."

"That's quite all right," said the Queen. "While Daniel is occupied, I thought you might like to see a little of our fair city."

"This is as close as we can get," said Queen Amytis.

They had crossed the dry river on Processional Way, over one of the twenty-eight bridges in the city. They stood at the rear of a vast enclosure in the temple of Merodach, which had been visible from their window.

At the front of the room, workmen from Darius's construction battalions swarmed over a framework erected around a huge gold idol with wide, staring eyes.

"That is Nebo," the Queen said. "Nebo and Bel together contain two thousand talents of solid gold. They are the largest idols in West Babylon."

"Most impressive," said Mel. "How much is a talent?"

"A year's wages in gold."

"I seem to remember twenty to fifty pounds," said Ruth.

"Thirty tons of gold!" Mel exclaimed. "Think what that would be worth at four hundred dollars an ounce."

"Where did they get so much gold?" asked Ruth, as they left the temple.

"More to the point, what are they going to do with it? Where is Darius taking these idols?"

"I know not. Nowhere, by the looks of it. They will probably be broken into pieces for removal, later to be melted down."

"Mel, there's no chance the secret would be kept for twenty-five hundred years anyway. Forget the gold. You don't need it."

"Right. I can make twenty thousand a year, just teaching mathematics."

The Queen's eyes had widened at Ruth's comment. "I had no idea you people were from so distant a future. You must have seen the fulfillment of many a prophecy, yet you believe not. Why?"

"I can't speak for Mel, but in the church, center of worship, I grew up in, prophecy was never mentioned. The pastor was rather a skeptic. We concentrated on ethics and social functions. And politics. Then, when I went to college, a school of higher learning, I stopped going. Except for religious holidays, like Christmas and Easter."

"Ishtar?"

"No, Easter. A festival held in the spring, with decorated eggs, and bunny rabbits, and singing—"

"Just so," said the Queen.

"But I have to admit," Ruth continued, "that what with the events of the past few days, I'm starting to question my faith...that is, to wonder whether it might not be true after all. What I was taught in Sunday school. Miracles and all." They had returned to Riverside Park, and were walking along an elevated pathway that clung to the side of the river wall. The top of the wall formed a low railing on their left. Across the river, in the middle distance ahead, rose an enormous mound of green, like a steep hill—but they could see through it in places: spots of daylight stood out brightly and twinkled as the trees swayed.

"As for me, my Queen," said Mel, "you should understand that in our time there is a body of knowledge called science—"

"In this time too," Amytis interrupted. "You must discourse with Daniel. He has been trained in all kinds of science."

"I am referring to a particular method," said Mel. "Observation, conjecture, prediction; testing, to confirm or refute the prediction; theory leading to further observation, all measured quantitatively, using mathematics."

"Resulting in the building up, over the years, of a body of tested, sure knowledge."

"Precisely."

"Like the Necronomicon, the Encyclomancia, geometry. Very familiar."

"Uh..."

"By your time, you must have added greatly to this store. Is that how you were able to fly into the city?"

"Yes. But, uh, my point is that, that when new facts are observed, that contradict a theory, then that theory, however devoutly held—"

"Must be renounced, of course!" agreed the Queen, "and its prophets executed."

"Well, we—"

"We no longer execute false prophets of science," Ruth put in, "because they do not claim to be speaking for God—"

"Just the opposite, in most cases," muttered Mel.

"—they may be sincerely mistaken. They must have the freedom to make predictions that may later be proven wrong; that's part of the method."

"Can it be, then," the Queen asked, aghast, "that your people have observed facts that contradict the theories we have so long held? Do your rulers no longer consult astrologers, for example?"

"Of course not."

"Mel, where have you been? On Mars?"

"Astrology is bunk," he continued, ignoring Ruth's comment. "At any rate, our science excludes on principle any discussion of things which cannot be observed, measured, and tested. Repeatably. By anyone."

"Any guy on the street with a superconducting supercollider."

"Then you can have no theory of origins, or miracles," the Queen pointed out, "except what has been recorded by observers, since such things are by definition inaccessible or unrepeatable."

"Uh, Darwin…"

"Let's not open that can of worms," said Ruth. "Let's enjoy the tour. O Queen, what is that great ditch ahead?"

"Since the ferries are not running, and you have already crossed a bridge, I thought to lead you through our tunnel. That is its western entrance."

"Wonderful!" Mel said. "I could hardly believe it when Zaran told us— Where is Zaran, anyway?"

"Martha said he woke up early and went to visit some of his old vet buddies," Ruth told him.

"Has he got some war stories to swap now!"

They joined the crowd descending a long, curving ramp that led into a dark rectangular opening far back from and below the level of the river wall. A chill wind blew out of it into their faces. Sheltered rushes burned along the roof corners, casting indirect light on the ceiling of the tunnel. As they entered, their steps echoed hollowly. The murmur of the throng was amplified. Farther in, their eyes grew accustomed to the dim light. The tunnel was fifteen feet high and wide enough for three idols to pass abreast. Its sides were lined with great brick pillars, half-embedded in the walls, supporting heavy wooden beams and—

"Is that reinforced concrete?" Mel gasped. The ceiling appeared ribbed in a rectangular array, like a waffle, between the beams.

"A slot was dug into the top of the face," explained the Queen. "Iron bars, cast in a grid, were laid across the beams. Concrete was poured over them, then gravel, then pitch. When all had solidified, the earth was excavated from underneath and the roadbed laid down. I watched it being built, three cubits at a time: my King often brought his bride here."

"Wasn't that dangerous?" Ruth asked.

"He was so proud of his works, of this city," replied the Queen. "He delighted in showing it to me. And he took every precaution to insure my safety, and the safety of his workmen. Yes, it was dangerous. More so than we knew, at first. You feel this wind?"

"I certainly do."

"It is from the wind-wells: giant caissons leading up above water level, with funnels that turn to face the wind up there, and force it down here. We learned to do this the hard way: several workers collapsed as their lights failed; some died before they could be rescued. A general redesign was required."

"It would seem hardly worthwhile to dig a tunnel," Mel observed.

"It was part of our defense system," explained Queen Amytis. "In the unlikely event that an invader should gain access to the river, we could close all the watergates, raise the drawbridge, and still have traffic between the two shores. Oil could be poured—"

"Oil," Mel said. "That's the principal product of Iraq."

"Shh."

"—onto the water at the northern end of the city and ignited. A clever and farsighted man, my King."

"As long as the river had water in it, a good plan."

"I trust Darius will soon repair his dike upstream. Our crops will perish if the river stays dry too long."

"What about cave-ins?" asked Mel.

"I was trapped in one," Amytis said.

"What?"

"During one of my visits to the face of the tunnel just after it had passed the west caisson, the ceiling collapsed behind us. There was air, but it took two hours to dig us out. At least we were together. Here is the place." She pointed to one side of a great grilled hole in the ceiling. A turbulent wind from it whipped their robes.

"But the water rushing in—" Mel began.

"Water? You think we tried to dig this tunnel while there was water in the river? Now, that would have been dangerous. Nebuchadnezzar diverted the Euphrates for a year, after stocking our granaries. How else could we pave the river bed?"

"The river bed is paved?" asked Mel.

"It is difficult to see under all that silt, isn't it? Perhaps you have never heard of something called erosion," the Queen ventured. "Unpaved, the river would eat away at its banks, and the walls would collapse after only a few decades. This city was built to last. When all was sealed, we let the water in carefully, a little at a time. Nothing leaked. We had even finally managed to exclude the ground water."

There was a brighter light ahead. The end of the tunnel? wondered Mel. But they hadn't started up again.

It was a wide spot in mid-tunnel, lighted by elaborate candelabras and torches, with a circle of decorative tiles on the floor and an idol of Lilith standing in an alcove. Some of the passers-by had stopped to lay flowers at her taloned feet.

"Let me guess," Ruth guessed. "This is where the two tunnels almost met."

"Correct. Missed by over a cubit," admitted the Queen. "My King made a virtue of necessity."

"A cubit," said Mel appreciatively. "That's some fine surveying."

A short ramp led them up to the eastern half of the tunnel, past rumbling donkey-carts laden with sacks of grain. Finally, blinding daylight showed ahead. The wind was at their backs as they emerged and started up the long, curving ditch of the exit ramp.

Rounding the last wall, Ruth gasped.

Just ahead was a great park massed with flowers. In the park, among trees, pavilions and waterfalls, there rose dozens of enormous parabolic arches. Doors were cut into their bases; railed staircases clung to their sides, leading past balconied windows scattered in vine-covered walls. The effect drew the eye up and up, lost in perspective, to their peaks. The peaks supported a vast platform, where the stairs led. And on the platform was another great park. With more dozens of flowered arches.

Seven levels, Mel counted. Good God, seven levels. "Magnificent," he whispered.

"My love song," said Queen Amytis. "My King's wedding gift."

"Beautiful," Ruth said. "Truly, a wonder of the world."

"This makes the Taj Mahal look like a plastic toy. Who lives here?"

"Nobles of the court," replied the Queen. "Our honeymoon cottage was on the top level, by the lake."

This is a little old lady, Mel thought. Real old. Yet she has the dreamy smile of a new bride.

Ruth evidently had the same thought. "Oh, Queen Amytis," she begged, "please tell us how it was…how you met."

The Queen's eyes glistened. "We met in wartime."

8
Amytis

"It was wartime, and our fathers were allies against the Assyrians. My King, at that time an adjutant in his father Nabopolassar's army, was sent as an envoy to Ecbatana, to my father Cyaxeres' palace, to bring plans of the siege of Nineveh. Even then he was a brilliant strategist whom his father trusted to iron out the details with mine. Nabopolassar himself was occupied coordinating tactics with our other ally, Scythia.

"I was in the palace nursery, playing with my little niece Mandane, when her mother Aryenis came running in.

"'Amytis! Amytis! Come quickly!' she said, breathless. 'I have a surprise for you! We have company, and wait 'til you see him!'

"Together we crept to the door of the throne room and cautiously peeked around the arras. There before the throne stood a tall young man with curly black hair and the beginnings of a beard. He held an iron helmet in his hand. His bearing was regal, and he looked so serious! My father was speaking, and the lad was concentrating on the words: listening, I could tell, not framing his reply. Yet when my father finished, he responded immediately, in a deep pleasant voice:

"'The Khawsar will be in full spate then, and the grain harvest not yet ripe. Besides, the people are expected to rise up in revolt against their Assyrian tyrants.'

"It sounded so sensible and mature! I still remember every word. I had to meet this splendid young man who stirred my heart so.

"Next to me, Aryenis whispered, 'What did I tell you!' A few years older than I and happily married to my brother Astyages, she took a sisterly interest in my own romantic prospects. Until now I had borne it with, I hope, good-humored patience. Boys were boring. Now, however, I began to see a glimmer of what all the excitement was about.

"'How can I meet him?' I asked.

"'I'll fix it, little sister. I'll get Astyages—'

"She had spoken too loudly. 'You may as well enter, ladies,' said my father, smiling, 'and join in our discussion of tactics. This is—'

"Nebuchadnezzar's eyes met mine.

"Clang! went his helmet, on the floor.

"'A thousand pardons, Your Highness,' he said, bending to pick it up.

"'—Nebuchadnezzar, prince of Shinar,' continued Daddy. 'Prince, my son's wife Aryenis, and my daughter Amytis.'

"'I am truly charmed,' he said, bowing with a flourish. He was blushing furiously. We curtsied. My own face felt hot and my tongue tangled.

"'Welcome to Media, good sir,' said Aryenis.

"'Yes, and to Ecbatana; have you seen our gardens?' I asked, foolishly.

"'Not as yet; I have just arrived.'

"'Now, ladies, you really must excuse us,' said the king. 'We can continue this pleasant discussion at dinner. Prince, please let us move into my map room.'

"'Certainly, sire. A pleasure, my ladies. Until tonight.' He bowed again and we parted.

"At dinner that night, and for the next few days, while Nebuchadnezzar's business kept him in our town, we made many opportunities to improve our acquaintance. If that can be said of a pair so instantly smitten as we. I showed him the gardens, accompanied of course by Aryenis and sometimes my mother, and he spoke of the beauty of Babylon, and of his plans. Too soon he departed.

"I did not see him again for five years, and then it was at our wedding, arranged by our families for political reasons. He was then a general. Knowing he would soon be away campaigning in Egypt, he had constructed these hanging gardens for my abode in memory of our walks in the gardens of Ecbatana, that I might feel more at home.

"He returned when his father died, bringing Daniel with him, and after his coronation we moved into the palace. Daniel was a constant companion. The three of us used to debate religion and politics in the evenings, after dinner and sometimes very late. Daniel's God had given him not only the interpretation but the content of my husband's dream; this convinced us that his God was indeed a powerful and knowing one.

"At the fiery furnace, I became an apostate from Ishtar, Bel, and the rest: I became a believer like Daniel. The king was almost persuaded. It was not until after his illness, however, that he was totally converted."

Here the queen paused in her storytelling and smiled softly, her gaze turned inward.

"His last words to me were, 'My beauty, I know that I go to be with God, and that someday we shall walk together again, in the garden.'"

"What a beautiful love," Ruth said. "I'm glad I asked."

"I must return now," said Queen Amytis. "I am old. You, however, may stay and enjoy the gardens a little longer if you like. Here is my sigil, in case you should wish to visit our cottage above." She took from her finger a rather plain ring, a girasol set in gold; two triangles were carved into the face of the opal.

"Thank you," Mel said. "The Shield of David!"

"Yes," said the Queen. "The Shield of David." She departed toward the eastern river-walk.

They watched her out of sight. Then Mel turned to Ruth. "Want to go up?" he asked, pocketing the sigil.

"Do we have time?"

"I guess not, not unless they have an elevator. Let's just walk around the park." Their feet crunched gravel as they headed for a waterfall that plunged into a flower-banked pool. It was absolutely fantastic, Mel thought. Why didn't they build pleasure gardens like this where he lived?

Bathers were splashing, diving from rocks, basking in the sun that poured down through shafts in the levels above. Children shrieked with glee. They even had the heat and humidity licked. Wouldn't he love to…"Got a bathing suit?"

"I always pack one for a Moscow winter."

"Me neither. Looks like they don't use 'em here, anyway."

"I do." They continued on the path, farther into the interior of the park.

"Ruth, do you believe this? Are we actually here? Walking through the Hanging Gardens of Babylon?"

"I know. How can it possibly be? And how…how real it all is." She stooped to pluck a blade of grass. "And beautiful. Much lovelier than I ever imagined. Not like in the books."

"And magnificent. An extravagant wedding present. What a place for a honeymoon. Or any sort of vacation."

"Right. 'See beautiful Babylon. All-inclusive tour of the sixth century B.C.'" Suddenly, without any warning, she started to cry.

"Let's go back." He patted her shoulder gently, searching for some distraction. "Oh, look: there *is* an elevator!" He pointed to a wooden cage rising on ropes toward a cutout in the openwork platform above. A twin cage was descending. "Must be donkey powered. Want to go up?"

"I want to go *home*," she sobbed. "We don't *belong* here."

"We'll go find Daniel. Somehow I'm sure he can help."

"Not much of a Plan B, is it?" She smiled through tears.

Proceeding north along the river, they soon came to the elevated Processional Way and recognized where they were. They walked onto the palace grounds, up the steps of the main central building, and into the west wing.

Daniel was waiting for them in the cool of his living room. Seated with him was another old man, wrinkled where Daniel was smooth. "Good morning," Daniel greeted them. "You are not late; Darius let me go early. He intends few administrative changes, just some shuffling of personnel, to make Babylonia a gentler, kinder nation. I have been confirmed as third ruler in the kingdom, after Cyrus and Darius. Hananiah and Azariah will share my duties." He introduced his guest. "These are the travelers of whom I told you: Mel and Ruth. This is Jehoiachin, King of Judah."

"Your Highness!" Mel and Ruth genuflected.

"Oh, get up, get up," the king protested. "There's no call for all this folderol. Don't know why they still call me that. I was only king for three months, as a youngster. And you can call me Jeconiah. Coniah for short."

"Your Majesty," Daniel said, "you know perfectly well the people expect to see you back on your rightful throne one day."

"Well, don't wait standin' on one leg," Coniah advised. "I don't expect it. Be lucky if the Chaldeans don't slip some poison into my ration one of these days. I'm just holdin' on, livin' from day to day, wonderin' why they keep feedin' me. Hee! Hee! Speakin' o' that, Daniel, where's lunch?"

Daniel rang for Martha.

"Yes?" she called, coming through the door. "Oh, good, you're back. Lunch is about ready."

"Can we just sit here for a minute?" asked Ruth. "We've walked our feet off."

"Of course. Sit, sit. I'll bring you a drink."

They leaned back into the cushions. Mel sat up. "Before I forget," he said, reaching into his pocket, "the Queen lent us her ring so we could tour her cottage. May I return it to you? In case we don't see her soon."

Daniel refused it with a gesture. "The Queen intended that you keep it as a memento." He smiled. "I know her romantic nature."

"I had no idea! We must thank her."

"As generous as her King," said Ruth. "We ought to have realized."

9
Lunch with a King

Martha served them cups of cool, scented tea.

"What think you of my adopted city?" asked Daniel after a sip.

"Magnificent," said Mel. "If I were in captivity, this is where I would want to be captive."

"Oh, Mel…you are! We are!" Ruth's voice shook. "This is our own Babylonian Captivity!"

"And, pleasant though it be, your chief desire is to return home," Daniel said.

"Yes."

"Now you know how we have felt, for nearly seventy years. Why we have kept up our thrice daily devotions, facing west toward a Temple that no longer exists. We don't belong here, eating the king's pleasant bread. We want to go home. Soon we shall."

"What makes you so sure?"

"The first of us have now been captive sixty-eight years: since two years before the death of King Nabopolassar. And seventy years are numbered for our captivity; see, here." Daniel unrolled a scroll and indicated a line.

"'And these nations shall serve the king of Babylon seventy years,'" Mel read. He looked back at Daniel.

"Last night you heard that it would be Cyrus who would set us free," Daniel continued. "The time is almost at hand, evidently."

"Evidently," agreed Mel. "As soon as Cyrus arrives."

"When you show him that letter addressed to him from Isaiah," Ruth said, "I'd like to see the expression on his face. But not if I have to wait a year or two."

"I, too, am blessed by seeing the fulfillment of a prophecy," Daniel agreed. "One ought not, of course, need to see it; faith that if God foretells it, it will be so, should suffice. Nevertheless God graciously proves His word to us again and again, knowing our weakness: as Boaz bade his reapers leave extra handfuls of grain on purpose for Ruth."

"One of the few upbeat mother-in-law stories," commented Mel.

"And an inspiring story of redemption of one who was destitute," Daniel continued. "One might almost see in it an allegory of the love of God for his adulterous wife Israel, except that, surprisingly, Ruth was a Gentile."

"She was? So am I," Ruth said. "Perhaps God will love me too, and get me out of here."

"Uncle Matt didn't see the fulfillment of Jeremiah's prophecy about him," Coniah put in. "'Course, Ezekiel prophesied he wouldn't! Hee! Hee!"

"Your Highness, it ill becomes you to jest about the horrible fate of your unfortunate successor, King Zedekiah."

"Well you prophets make me tired with all this talk about seventy years here and a Temple that isn't there. And whose fault is that? Uncle Matt's, that's whose! If he'd only kept his nose clean, we'd still have a Temple to go home to! Got what was comin' to him, I say."

Mel caught Ruth looking to him in appeal. Guess she never heard of 'Uncle Matt'! he thought wryly. Didn't they teach these Christians anything? He shrugged and shook his head. Her guess was as good as his, he admitted. He couldn't keep track of all these Hebrew kings either.

Daniel evidently noticed the interplay, for he said, "Jeconiah, my other guests seem ignorant of the story."

"Why not? They're young, aren't they? Look here, I inherited the throne just in time to surrender to King Nebuchadnezzar. Ever hear of him?"

"Oh, yes, Your H—Jeconiah," Ruth replied.

"Nebuchadnezzar deported me here, put my uncle Mattaniah on the throne as a puppet. Renamed him Zedekiah. Well, he ruled peaceably for nine years, then the Egypt faction got to him, near as I can make out, and he revolted. Long and the short of it is, after a two year siege Nebuchadnezzar burnt the city and the temple, just as Jeremiah predicted, and put out Uncle Matt's eyes."

"Ugh!" Ruth shuddered.

"You wanted to hear the story, didn't you? Not a pretty one, for such pretty ears. Uncle Matt was brought into captivity blind, and that fulfilled Ezekiel's prophecy." He looked over at Daniel. "Got that scroll?"

Daniel produced it. Mel read: "And I will bring him to Babylon the land of the Chaldeans; yet shall he not see it, though he shall die there."

"Yep. Read the fine print. That's the moral," Coniah concluded.

"Lunch!" Martha announced. "Served on the balcony."

After lunch King Jehoiachin took his leave, pleading his need for a nap. The others sat for a while under the awning, looking over the balcony rail past the river and temple to the farmlands and clusters of dwellings, almost villages, contained within the city wall. Water was already rising in the river, sparkling in the sun.

"Daniel," Mel began, "we have a problem."

"Yes. Perhaps I can help. Please feel free to tell me all you wish. How did it begin?"

"We are mathematicians. We were en route to a conference in Moscow, when our plane was hijacked. You see why we haven't gone into detail before now."

"Certain terms are obscure, I agree. You may explain them, if you wish, or if you think they are essential to the statement of the problem."

"I think," Ruth put in, "that you may need to know that our time lies 2500 years in your future. A time of unbelief, yet with greatly advanced science."

"That distant! You must be very near to the Time of the End. Remember what we were discussing before lunch? There is one prophecy in particular that I would like to see fulfilled, but of course I was born for this day, not that! Isaiah writes of that latter day: 'the Lord shall set his hand again the second time to recover the remnant of his people...and gather together the dispersed of Judah from the four corners of the earth.' Know you anything of this?"

This sent chills up Mel's spine. He shivered. Every inch of his skin tingled. "Yes," he stammered, "yes: this happened in my lifetime. In fact, I am one of the dispersed who was regathered."

"I didn't know that was in the Bible," Ruth said.

"What great joy! Thank you, Father. 'Though Israel be not gathered, yet...my God shall be my strength.' Thank you for revealing to me through these people what my eyes shall not see."

"But Ruth," Mel lapsed into English, "that means that we're living in the end times! Or were...will be..."

"Sounds like you're starting to believe this stuff."

"Uh..." He noticed Daniel waiting patiently. "Please excuse me, sir," he said in Hebrew. "I got excited."

"You are surprised?" Daniel asked. "Have our Scriptures not endured to your age, then? A sad—"

"Oh, they have," said Ruth, "but nobody reads them."

"Well, not nobody. But we haven't read them. Just heard a few of the more colorful stories."

"The Books repay careful attention and devout study, not only in knowledge, but in joy."

"It begins to appear," Mel said, "that you're right."

"I wonder what the Books have to say about our own situation," Ruth said.

"I was wondering the same thing. Please tell me more about your situation."

"Well, we were hijacked—brought against our will—to a large city called Baghdad, which will rise roughly on the site of Opis," Mel continued.

"We assume it's the same site," put in Ruth.

"We were just sitting over coffee in...an inn...and discussing a mathematical problem. Now here it gets complicated."

"Mel, let me. There will be a wise woman named Sophia, who will hit upon an ingenious new method to solve a certain problem."

"The problem of how a rigid body moves about a fixed point."

"Mel, he doesn't need—"

"Well, it would seem to me," mused Daniel, "that the problem can be broken into two parts." He raised his right index finger. "First, consider any other point of the body. Together with the fixed point," he indicated this by thumb and finger of the other hand, "it determines a straight line," he spread his hands apart, "and the motion of any third point on this line is in lockstep with the second point." The third point was his little finger. "That is: whatever curlicue the second point traces out as it moves upon its sphere, the third point will trace out similarly upon its greater or lesser sphere." He swept them both in an arc centered on the fixed thumb and finger. "So the motion of that point is completely determined by its distance from the fixed point, and the motion of the second point."

They talked with their hands back here too! Mel grinned.

"Second, consider a third point which lies off the line. Its motion is determined by the rotations of a circle about the line, composed with the motion of the line itself. Thus is every point of the rigid body accounted for. Have I followed it accurately so far?"

Mel and Ruth looked at each other. Ruth shook her head as if to deny she'd heard this. "A geometric genius," she said. "What an intuition!"

"Dear God, he's broken it down into SU(3) x S^1. A product of Lie groups. What does this do to the mechanics?"

"Simplifies it a lot, I should think."

"May not even need complex time to solve it, now—Ruth! We haven't even told him about Sophie's 'ingenious new method'!"

"And he's probably made it unnecessary." She rocked back on her wicker chair. "But that's what got us into this mess in the first place. Better tell him."

Mel faced Daniel and, clearing his throat, returned to Hebrew. "Daniel, you absolutely astound us with your perspicacity. You have shown us a completely new approach to Sophia's problem, that could possibly bypass her method. However, we think it was consideration of that method which trapped us here, not of the original problem directly. For it relates to the dimensionality of time."

"Careful," Ruth warned.

"I will be."

"Time must enter into it, surely," said Daniel, "for how can motion occur if time is frozen? Motion is simply the presence of a thing here at one instant, and there at another."

"Precisely," Mel agreed. "Position as a function of time. And it is the description of this function which constitutes the solution of the problem."

"But that must vary," objected Daniel, "depending on how the body is situated originally, and on how great a knock it is given, and in what direction."

"You're absolutely right," said Ruth. "It depends on the initial conditions. There are then certain laws that relate force to motion..."

"Allow me to conjecture." Lifting his head, Daniel squinted in the bright sunlight. "Let's see, common experience would suggest that the harder one shoves on something, say a skin-boat floating in a quiet pool, the faster it—wait." He pursed his lips under the thick beard. "No." The beard trembled as his lips moved. His hands drew back, palms out, and thrust forward; once, then again more rapidly. "Ah. The faster one can bring it up to a certain speed. Is this not what truly occurs? And, of course, one needs to shove a bigger boat harder."

"Well, there goes Newton's second law. Is he going to invent calculus in the next breath?"

"Probably, if he hasn't already. Ruth, these people are smart. I always thought Bible folk were a little simple."

"Where did you get that idea? Correct again, Daniel," she said. "One must push twice as hard for a boat twice as big. Or push twice as hard to get the same boat up to speed in half the time. From this law and geometry, proceeding a little at a time, one may theoretically derive a formula, a statement, that predicts the position and movement of the body through all future time."

"But the difficulty lies in your word 'theoretically,' does it not? At times things are not so simple. Patterns are not always easy to see in events. Inspiration is required."

"Almost always," Mel agreed.

"And true inspiration, infusion by the Spirit, is from God. This we may pray for. Solomon asked for wisdom and was granted it; he wrote that we may do the same."

"He's right, Mel. I think we should pray. Again."

"Yeah? What happened last time we prayed? Nothing!"

"Are you kidding?" Her eyebrows went up. "We asked for help, and we got help! Or did you fly into Babylon by flapping your arms?"

"But that help was from people, not from God."

"Well, I'm going to try it." Ruth bowed her head over clasped hands. "Please, God, bring us home."

Daniel, who had been hearing English with patience, now planted his staff on the floor and rose to his feet. "I find," he said, "that a stroll often helps me to think. And digest. It is a beautiful day; what say you?"

10
Diagram in the Mud

When they were down walking among the crowds on the embankment in the sunshine, Mel said, "What a city! I can't get over it! Even Rio, in our time, is not so beautiful."

"Yes. King Nebuchadnezzar did a good job," Daniel agreed. "Eventually, of course, it will be gone, and never rebuilt."

"But the people seem so happy! Like children, or Polynesians."

"Before the missionaries," Mel muttered.

"I heard that. And I guess these folk are also pagans."

"Most of them," Daniel admitted. "Some have hearkened to us and become believers. As for the rest, life is easy for them, and they can choose to forget the miracles in evidence of the one true God. You see them at play, at their best. Yet they search in drink, in endless parties, in the worship of one idol or another, for that which can give meaning to their empty lives."

"But they were raised that way," protested Mel. "How can God blame them if they never heard of Him?"

"Most of them have. In fact, I am persuaded that one reason God exiled us here was to teach the Babylonians about Him. But even those who have not heard are without excuse. See you that tower?" Daniel pointed. His question was rhetorical; the tower dominated the landscape. "Even after the flood, which they still recall in their garbled Gilgamesh story, they sought to displace the Most High, to ascend to the heavens by science, to construct that diabolical astrological observatory."

"It can't be. That tower?" Mel and Ruth stared at each other.

"And God confounded their tongue, and drove them apart. Yet those who remain choose to forget these unpleasant facts. Their ruin shall be permanent. Wolves will howl here."

They walked in silence for a few moments. It seemed incredible to Mel that this teeming city, with its busy commerce, its artisans and architects, its superb climate and irrigated soil, its location at the closest approach of two navigable rivers, should one day disappear forever. Yet he knew it was true.

"You must know the truth of this," said Daniel, as if reading his thoughts. "Or can it be that Babylon is still strong in your time?"

"No," Mel admitted.

"It's been in ruins for thousands of years," Ruth said. "Now that I think of it, it's surprising that no one has managed to redevelop it in all that time. Such a good location for a city."

"Yet God saw its end, and gave the knowledge to His servants, the prophets."

"We've seen it too." Mel's eyes widened. "Ruth! God must be a time-traveler! Perhaps from our future. With technology so advanced—"

"Mel! Get hold of yourself!"

"Still, isn't it possible that Isaiah, say, was a Madison Avenue account exec who fell into a situation like ours?"

"No it isn't!" replied Ruth hotly.

"What disturbs you, my friends?" They had lapsed into English.

"My husband thinks the prophets were time-travelers, like us."

"Why do you not agree with him?"

"Well, it just seems so…it doesn't seem right. He even says it of God."

"I was only speculating; can't a guy speculate? Anyway, Daniel, isn't it worth some consideration? We ourselves tripped in time while elaborating on Sophia's idea that time is a plane, not a line."

"Mel!"

They held their breath.

"We lucked out that time," Ruth said .

"I suppose it possible that your situation is not unique. But the prophets were not so situated. For they said they spoke the word of God. Were they lying then? And otherwise never?"

"But perhaps they were deluded. Perhaps God himself…"

"Lied to them? Take care. You do not really mean that. Besides, God does not only predict future events. He travels not within the plane of time; he stands outside of time, no matter how many dimensions it should prove to have. As outside of space. The Creator of the heavens and the earth is the Sculptor of time. He configures events. He molds history as his raw material, his clay, working all things together in fine detail for the good of those who love him.

"But, Ruth, the true reason you disagree with Mel is that you are beginning to know God personally. He is standing in the fire alongside you, keeping you cool. Is it not so?"

"I think…He is." Ruth stopped short on the path. The stream of Babylonian pedestrians divided around them. "Daniel, we have been lying to you."

"You're right, Ruth," Mel said reluctantly. "Time to come clean."

"We are not wed," she confessed. "We only just met, on the airplane."

Daniel's eyes twinkled. "So the Queen suspected."

"What? When?" they chorused.

"Let me say only that she would not be surprised." He resumed walking, so they followed perforce. "She assumed from the first that you were in courtship. What did surprise her was when your letter from Pastor Nab called you man and wife. That did not fit the image she had formed of you. She is wise, and well acquainted with love, as you may have discovered."

"We were caught in the same snare together," Mel explained, "and we were afraid of what your people would think of Ruth, traveling with a man not her husband."

"Mel, we made a mistake."

"You risked being placed together," said Daniel, swinging his cane at a weed growing from a crack in the wall.

"It was an honest mistake. We had not planned on spending even one night," Mel said. "But then we were stuck with the lie."

Daniel chuckled. "It must have been difficult."

"It's been almost impossible lately," Ruth admitted.

"Ruth! I had no idea!"

"That's good."

"Fear not," Daniel reassured them. "Exiles may be excused being thrown together, and many other things, thanks be to God. Rest assured I shall not place such strong temptation in your way again."

"Thank you," said Mel. Oh, well.

"And thank you for believing in our innocence," Ruth said.

"Well, you are innocent, are you not?"

"Yes, we are," Mel said. "But we must have done something wrong, to deserve...this." He waved his arm to include Babylon at large.

"This is not necessarily a punishment," Daniel observed. "You may have simply fallen afoul of some natural law."

"Nor is it necessarily bad," conceded Ruth. "Oh, it is unnerving at times, and frightening; and so lonely, except for Mel of course. But somehow it doesn't seem so hopeless or capricious anymore. I really do feel as if God is in control. And what an adventure!"

"Wow, Ruth. You seem much better now. That's great. Wish I were. But you're right. What a tale to tell our k—" He stopped in hot-faced confusion.

"If it's a natural law," Ruth said as if nothing had happened (but she was also blushing), "then we may learn to control it. The trouble is, to do that we would need to study it."

"Experiment," added Mel.

"And you fear this," Daniel guessed.

"We fear being thrown all over time," said Mel. "We have no notion of the mechanism that does this."

"We may be traveling along some curve in the time plane," Ruth conjectured, "but there are a lot of those. And we're conscious only of ordinary, real time."

"At least, I guess it's real," said Mel. "It's what we're used to, which always seemed like linear time, on the real axis."

Daniel considered. "Stop for a moment," he suggested. "Let's go down there, where there's some nice smooth mud." They walked down the embankment, almost to the edge of the slowly rising water, to a place where no children were playing.

Squatting, Daniel drew a line in the mud with his staff. "Here you were," he said, punching a hole in the left end of the line, "and here you came." He drew a smooth arc to the right until it just intersected the line again. "You landed in Opis and then moved through space down the river system, and a few days into the future along the normal route." He drew a short dash leftward along the line, from the Opis point.

"That looks like it," agreed Mel, "only I would have put future time toward the right."

"Really? Seems backward to me. Now consider this." Daniel drew a continuation of the smooth curve below the line and back toward the left. "It is possible, isn't it, that in another jump you would continue along the same curve, thereby returning home?"

"Yes, it's possible," Ruth admitted, "but unlikely."

"Without thinking too hard about it , for I know you must be careful, is there any curve that might be canonical? That is—"

"We know," Mel said. "I vote for a circle. Ruth?"

"That would be nice. Only two intersections, then and now. Okay, I'll go with the circle."

"A circle seems simplest to me also," Daniel concurred. "Now, we shall not discuss this any more today; I feel we have been skirting the edge as it is. We shall pray, of course. Tomorrow, after we break fast, and go to ground level—"

"Wow! I never thought of that," said Mel.

"Me neither. We could have fallen, or been buried."

"—you shall begin to experiment, under controlled conditions. Is that acceptable? The only alternative I see for you is to settle down here with us—you would certainly be welcome—and raise a family."

"You know, that is tempting," Ruth said.

"Ruth, I'm surprised. Out of the question, for me. Besides, what would we do here? Teach positional notation? There isn't even any algebra yet."

"Gee, what if we introduced all that stuff a millennium early?"

"Fun to dream.... It might improve the future, too—not that it needs it."

"There is one thing," she objected.

"What?"

"Well, you'd be stuck with me."

"No I wouldn't; there were lots of cuties at that party fff—" Some of the mud she threw at him got into his mouth, through his grin.

"I assume," put in Daniel, "that you are discussing the second alternative. If you have not considered it before now, perhaps you would like some advice."

Not me, Mel thought. I know what I have to do.

"Oh, yes, Daniel. We welcome your advice." Ruth stood up, stretching her back muscles, and brushed mud off her robe.

"Well, compare the advantages and disadvantages. The advantages are: (A.) You avoid the risk of time-jumping; (B.) you could be supported for life as my guests, without lifting a finger; but, (C.) I am sure you would want to be, and could be, a valuable asset to our society; and, (D.) you like Babylon, and indeed it has many attractions, even nice innocent ones.

"The disadvantages are: (a.) disease; (b.) caprice of the king; (c.) the sheer strangeness of our ways; (d.) invasion; (e.) other, unspecified, calamities that I am sure are forestalled by your age's advanced scientific knowledge. Also, (f.) you would miss the chance to experience the Last Days—and you, Mel, already a part of the second ingathering! Not to mention (g.) your families and friends at home.

"But my main advice is to pray for God's guidance. In this matter as in all. Pray; weigh the alternatives carefully; pray again, not omitting to listen; then make your decision, and live with it. Joyfully."

"Daniel, the quickness of your mind never ceases to amaze me," Mel said. "We certainly shall take your advice." Mel's mind was made up, but it couldn't hurt to ask for God's input. "The only thing is, I don't pray very often."

"Is that an understatement, or what?" muttered Ruth.

"So could you, uh, sort of lead us in prayer? Ruth, how do you feel?"

"I don't pray very often either. I think it's just talking to God, but I've never tried to listen for an answer—would I even recognize the voice of God? So yes, Daniel, please."

"Certainly." Daniel placed his hands on their shoulders and lifted up his eyes to the heavens. "O Lord our God, Master of time and space, we praise you for your great mercy toward us, and thank you for bringing us together in this age. We ask you for wisdom and for strength to do the wise thing. In particular, we seek guidance for these young people in deciding whether to remain and make a life here and now, or risk an attempt to return to their own time.

"Please make your will clear to them, Lord, and if it is the latter alternative, please bring them safely home."

Daniel's hands fell to his sides. Mel and Ruth were no longer there.

"Merciful God in Heaven," Daniel prayed. "Your will be done. Bless them and guide them, and keep them safe. Thank you. Amen. Dear Father, amen."

11
Wolves Will Howl Here

Chilled, blinded, choking and tumbling, Mel tried to gasp in shock. His mouth filled with water. His robe, his shoes, pulled him down as he was swept along. Thrashing to the surface, he sucked air, howled "Ruth!" and was pulled under again. He had glimpsed shore in the moonlight and struggled in that direction. His flailing limbs struck something yielding. He clutched at it and held on. Feeling mud underfoot, he kicked desperately toward the river's edge. "Ruth!" His fingers clenched her robe as he stumbled and crawled up the bank.

The robe was empty.

"Ruth!" he wailed. "Ruth!"

Downstream, the moon revealed a patch of white rushing swiftly away. It submerged.

Mel staggered to his feet and lurched after it along the embankment. Briefly it appeared again, a lifeless white arm in a white blouse. "Ruth! Oh, God! No!"

Ruth's body stopped drifting, momentarily grounded on a mud bar. Mel reached her and dragged her out of the current. Rolling her onto her back, he lifted with one hand under the back of her neck. With his other hand he pinched Ruth's nose and blew four hard quick puffs into her mouth. Her chest rose and fell. Her throat wasn't blocked. Please, please!

He counted to five, gave her a breath. Counted to five, gave her a breath. Counted to five, breath. Five—

She breathed. A pulse beat dimly in her neck.

"Oh, God. Thank you. Thank you."

"Mel?" Her eyes fluttered open. "Mel!"

"Ruth. Ruth. Ruth," he said. "Oh, Ruth."

"Cold," she whispered. " So cold, cold. Hold me."

He hugged her a long minute, then pulled her up the bank to where it was dry. He ran back for her soggy robe, wrung it out, and wrapped it around her, rolling the cowl under her neck. He removed and wrung out his own robe and wrapped her in that also.

"You'll be cold."

"I'm fine." Lying next to her, he hugged her tight.

"We jumped again," she said weakly. "Why?"

"Hush. Rest now, rest. Shh. You're alive. That's enough. Rest, get warm. We're safe now."

Not far away, a wolf howled.

Ruth's head jerked up. "What's that?"

"Just an owl," he lied.

Another wolf howled, closer.

Mel looked around for something to use as a weapon. On this side of the river the bank was bare mud. Not a stick. A cloud covered the full moon. In the dark Mel thought he saw, far upriver, an eerie amber glow drifting toward them. A shadow under it could have been a skin-boat.

"Ruth, can you get up?"

Wolves chorused on three sides. Ruth rose unsteadily to her feet. Mel helped her stumble toward the mud bar. "We're going to take a little boat ride."

They waded out into the river. The amber glow drifted closer, closer. Then it went out. There was a snap, and a voice floated over the water:

"Aardvarks dark."

Along the near shore, wolves gathered under the moon.

BOOK II

Caravan to Antioch

12
The River

A wet slick on the polished tile floor reflects bare arms against pierced marble screening. Lithe bodies settle across cushions, their veiled limbs draped down the steps of a sunken pool in which smooth forms undulate. Two women, one brushing the other's hair, sit on the pool's edge, their toes trailing in the water. Slippered feet pad across the floor behind them.

Outside the ormolu door stands a burly, bare-chested guard in silk pantaloons. Wearing a plumed fez on his shaven head and a sinuous-bladed kris at his belt, he faces outward with a bored expression, his muscular arms folded.

A girl sits on a padded chair at a cherrywood dressing table, applying cream to reddened eyes. She wears bridal veils in layers that drape her to the knees but leave her navel bare over bloused silken trousers tucked into the laces of jeweled sandals. She sighs.

A woman speaks softly to the eunuch at the door, enters, and approaches the girl. "Scheherazade, it's time," she says in Arabic. "The Caliph awaits."

The girl rises reluctantly to her feet and turns to follow the woman.

With a pop! of displaced air, a young man appears bearing a laptop computer. He seizes Scheherazade around the waist. Laughing maniacally as the women scream, he presses a key and disappears with the bride.

Laughing maniacally, Chazz pulled over to the side of the road and stopped the car, its wheels at the edge of the sand. Enough daydreaming about Scheherazade; now to actually rescue her. He turned off the engine, leaving the key in the ignition, opened the door, and stepped out onto the dark road. His computer screen still displayed the Hijack Bomb Menu. He pressed the Escape key. The menu scrolled up and a DOS prompt appeared.

Standing in a tense, alert crouch, Chazz typed "harem" at the DOS prompt and vanished.

Incredible heat and bright swirling sand smote him. Wind whistled. He staggered. "Wait. This isn't the harem." He pressed a key and was gone.

Mud slid out from under his feet and he sat down involuntarily with a plop on the bank of a placid river. It was late afternoon. "Where's the car? This isn't right." The amber-backlighted LCD screen showed the cursor blinking at the DOS prompt.

Chazz picked himself up and brushed fastidiously at the seat of his pants and at his windbreaker, secured by its arms around his waist. "Must be a bug."

Propping his computer under a nearby olive tree, he called up the Trilogy source code for his Harem program. He looked at the constraints listed at the top: 7 p.m. on March 4th, A.D. 794: Scheherazade's wedding night in the palace of Caliph Haroun al-Rashid. Everything seemed O.K.

All the assertions looked good, including the standard call to the subroutine that evaluated the integral

$$\int \frac{\sum_{j=m}^{n} (j+6)P'_{mn}(t-i-j)}{P_{mn}(t)} \, dt$$

Just to check, he compared it on a split screen with the page from Sophia's lost paper, which was stored on his hard disk. There it was, symbol for symbol.

What had gone wrong? He had practiced with similar programs plenty of times before. Just short hops, though; maybe on a long jump, truncation error would accumulate. Or roundoff error.

"I might have known! Should have used 80-bit reals...*wait.*"

Maybe it was a chaotic situation.

Fear crept over him. Where was he? How could he get back?

"I'll just take short hops, that's all. I'll write a little loop."

But which way? Was he in the past, or the future? If chaos had taken over, it could have bent the curve into any shape in the time plane.

He looked around. Nothing in his immediate surroundings gave him a clue. There was this river, mud, trees, and a bedraggled plain. The horizon fuzzed out in haze or dust.

"Or smog. Let's see. If this were the future, it would be more thickly settled, wouldn't it?"

Unless there had been a war.

He suddenly realized the great risk he had taken. If his iteration were chaotic, he could have ended up anywhen. In the middle of a war, or a fire, or—

"No more of that! Got to find some people, find out when I am." He shut down the computer to let the battery recover, and started to walk downstream.

When he got out of this, he could sneak up on the harem by easy stages. Get more accuracy that way, anyway. How long was it from the time when the palace was built until Scheherazade's wedding night? Thirty years? Surely he could hop that far. He'd see exactly where the harem was, hop back before it existed, walk over into its space, then hop into its time, rescue his girl, hop away, and—

What was that? Something half-submerged at the river's edge caught his eye. He walked closer. It seemed to be some kind of primitive coracle made of leather laced around a withe frame. Some of the laces had loosened. It was freighted with mud.

"Must be the past, then. No, not necessarily. Have to be sure, or I could keep hopping farther and farther away from home.

"Wonder if I can use this boat? It would beat walking."

He set the computer in a dry spot, took off his rather muddy shoes and his socks, and rolled up his pants. He waded into the squelchy mud. "Ick."

Bending, he started to scoop the mud out of the boat with both hands. It was half-buried in the river bank, and was larger than he had at first thought: seven or eight feet across. It took him half an hour to get it free and empty enough to move. Then he was able to drag it up the bank and tip the water out of it. Water also poured through a foot-wide rent in the keel.

"It leaks. Well, sure. That's why it sank. Wonder who left it here?" He had still not seen a soul. "How can I fix that rip?" It was getting cooler as dusk approached. He absent-mindedly untied the sleeves of his windbreaker from around his waist and started to put it on.

"Wait a minute. This jacket is waterproof, isn't it? *How* waterproof?"

In the end he managed to lace his windbreaker over the hole, using its own string-ties from waist and hood. The boat still leaked slowly, but it floated.

"I can bail. Not good for the shoes, though."

He clambered aboard and launched himself into the stream, sitting in the bilges with his computer on his knees. He leaned against the gunwale, trying to find a comfortable position. The other side rose high out of the water.

"Hey!" He slumped down, stretching out his legs. The boat gave flexibly, elongating slightly, and leveled out, heading downstream with Chazz sitting in what was now the stern.

"Solid comfort." He closed his eyes.

He awoke when the water reached his hands grasping the computer. The boat was very low. He pulled off his shoe and started to bail with it. Gradually he emerged.

"Wow! If this gets wet, I'm stuck here! Maybe walking would have been a better idea after all."

The moon was almost full. Its light showed that the river had broadened and that he was in midstream. It also showed that the surrounding plain was checkered by canals into square fields of grain.

"Someone must live here. Where are they all? Home in bed, I guess." If these were farms, somewhere there must be a farmhouse, and farmers. Could he paddle down one of these irrigation canals? Maybe he'd find an electric pump. That would settle it.

Ahead to starboard the steep riverbank was cut. The water seemed to flow sluggishly into a wide, straight canal that intersected his course almost at a right angle.

"That looks promising." He paddled. The boat turned toward the canal, approached, and entered it. He drifted more slowly now. He yawned. His eyes closed and he slept again.

The boat lurched and woke him with a start. At first he thought he was back in his dorm room in Uppsala. But why was he so wet? Then it came back to him. He was lost in time.

His boat was grounded. The water in the canal had dwindled to a trickle. Ahead, the canal ended, except for a narrow stream that meandered away into the dark. The moon on the horizon showed a glint of water a mile or so ahead, where the canal apparently resumed navigability. There was no sign of life in the dark fields. No farm house. No electric pump.

"Portage time." He climbed out of the boat, tipped the water out of it, and began to carry it toward the setting moon.

Shortly after sunrise the canal debouched into another, swifter river.

"This is more like it. We can make some progress, now."

But the long day passed into night without event.

Finally, Chazz decided to try again to debug his harem program. Opening his computer, he began to hand-trace his way through the program source, a line at a time. Soon he became so engrossed he didn't notice a huge, crumbled brick ruin slip by in the dark.

A mile farther on, he concluded that there were no bugs he could find without running the program, and he certainly didn't want to try that.

Just as he thought. Right the first time. He shut the laptop with a snap.

"Aardvarks dark."

He had not heard the wolves.

13
The Skin-Boat

The first wolf stepped gingerly into the water as Mel, one arm supporting Ruth, reached with the other to grasp the rim of the skin-boat. "Help us," he asked the sailor in Hebrew. "Please h—Chazz!"

"You!"

"Take Ruth, quick! Wolves!"

The lead wolf had swum to within two yards. Chazz pulled Ruth while Mel shoved. She rolled over the wicker rail into the boat. Mel kicked at the wolf's gaping jaws, heaved on the rail and was in. The boat listed dangerously and shipped water. "Careful! She's going over!" Chazz warned. "Let's get out of here!" He reached to paddle but jerked back his hand as a wolf snapped at it. The waterline was only inches from the rail.

"We're sinking," cried Ruth. "Bail!"

Chazz threw a shoe-full of water out the stern, into the face of an approaching wolf. The wolf gargled and sank. It rose again, coughing. Others in the pack turned to it. As they thrashed, Chazz and Mel bailed and paddled toward midstream. The boat rose in the water and picked up speed, leaving the gasping, struggling wolves behind.

"My computer!" Chazz snatched it out of the bilge where it had fallen. Water ran off the case, glistening in the moonlight.

"Aardvarks wet," Mel said.

"It's no joke! That's our ticket home!"

"Just bail," advised Ruth, "or it'll be academic."

They bailed until the water was shallow in the bilge and the boat reached an uneasy stability, rushing down the river—the Euphrates, they assumed. Chazz confirmed this: "In all my practice hops, I stayed in the same place, near as I could tell."

"You know how this works?"

"It's all in Sophia's lost paper. Integrating

$$\int \frac{\sum_{j=m}^{n} (j+6)P'_{mn}(t-i-j)}{P_{mn}(t)} \, dt$$

produces a lifting into the Riemann surface of the wrapping mapping, e^{it}. This is canonically isomorphic to the earth's world line around the sun, so depending on the winding number of the lifting curve about the fixed point, your rigid body gets displaced in time by an integral number of mean solar years: all those points are on the same fibre."

"I see."

"The only thing is, Madam K. never wrote down the value of that integral: too dangerous, she said. And I couldn't figure it out. But it was easy enough to program a numerical integration using Simpson's Rule. You know that rule?"

"Evaluate an integral—" began Mel.

"—as you would have an integral evaluate you," Ruth finished.

"Hey, that's good. I must remember that. But now, if my computer's ruined, we can't do the integration! We can't jump!"

"Come on. Numerical integration was practiced long before computers. Besides—"

"—we can integrate that guy by inspection," said Ruth.

"Right, by residues," Mel agreed.

"You can? What's the answer?"

"Can't tell you."

"Wait, don't look so exasperated. He means we literally *can't* tell you, not that we won't. We can't discuss it. Just talking about it is what got us into this."

" Ruth, our results are inconclusive on that. Once it worked, once it didn't. We discussed it heavily with Daniel, remember? And nothing happened."

"Five minutes later we were in the water. Close enough. You don't think it was the prayer that did that, do you?"

"Real-time delay," said Chazz.

"What?"

"Well, I don't know what curve you get if you don't know what you're doing," Chazz explained. "I do know that when I set up curves that coincided in part with the real axis, traveling along those segments didn't feel any different from experiencing the passage of time in the ordinary way. My guess is that you got a curve that started out adhering to the real line. You were time-traveling, but you didn't notice it until your curve left the real axis. You felt it as a delay."

"We may be doing that now." Ruth shuddered. "Please, can we stop this?"

"All right, let's— "

"But no more exuberant wars."

"—change the subject. Chazz, why did you hijack our plane? Don't you know bombs can be hazardous to our health?"

"There wasn't any bomb. Anyway, I had to get to Baghdad as soon as possible—my life was passing. And Sophia's paper doesn't tell how to travel in space. Although, say! Do you suppose—"

"I refuse to discuss it."

"But why? Why Baghdad?" asked Mel.

"You'll laugh."

"No."

"No we won't."

"Everybody does. Oh, well. Ever since I first heard the music as a child, I've been in love."

"Music?"

"Then I read her stories. So clever! Chazz, I said, this is the girl for you."

"Stories? What girl?"

"Scheherazade."

A minute later, when they could catch their breath, the boat was still rocking. "Sorry, we couldn't help it," Mel told Chazz.

"Chazz, Scheherazade is a f-fictional character," Ruth gasped.

"No she isn't! That's what everybody says!"

"Well, in this case, everybody's right."

"For a change."

"No, no, no! Don't you see? There has to be a factual basis! Some groundwork of truth! There was a Caliph—"

"But not named Scheheriar."

"Oh, sure. How smart do you think it would have been, to go around telling this story on Haroun al-Rashid, using his real name? 'Say, a funny thing happened to old Haroun last night. 'FWHISSHT!" Chazz drew his finger across his throat. "I know she's there! Crying her eyes out! And I'll prove it. I'll get her! I'll bring her back! I almost did already!"

"Is that what you were—"

"Well, er, there seemed to be this, uh, slight snag. Roundoff."

"And you ended up here? In a skin-boat? Chazz, I'm disappointed," Ruth said. "A hijacker should work out every contingency."

"I dreamed about her for years—in Technicolor. I'd hear Rimsky-Korsakov's music in my sleep, and wake up. Then I'd pace.

"One night I was walking around a back corner of the Uppsala campus about three a.m.—do you know how *old* that college is?—when I saw this girl suddenly appear out of nowhere, pop!

"Of course I thought at first it was Sche, the answer to my dreams. But she was blonde, and wearing the wrong sort of clothes. She didn't see me: I was behind a shrub.

"She was carrying a manila envelope. She stepped over to the wall and casually pulled a stone out of it! A stone that looked as if the Vikings had cemented it in place! She tucked the envelope in the hole, slid the stone back—it looked so natural, I almost forgot which one it was—and disappeared.

"I retrieved the envelope as soon as I was fairly sure she wasn't coming right back. I was a junior; I already had enough mathematics to know that this really was the answer to my dreams. All I needed to do was write a quick Trilogy program, and get to Baghdad.

"That was the trouble. You can't just hitchhike into Iraq, and I was broke. Then I realized I could use the ticket the department had given me to the Sophia Centennial. It was kismet."

"Evidently not. You're here," Ruth pointed out.

"How did you expect to get out of Iraq? With a girl who didn't know what was going on, and no papers?"

"Love would find a way."

"Chazz, you're supposed to be a mathematician, a programmer, a hijacker. You should plan. What would Trilogy say if you fed it a program like that? 'INCOMPLETE ASSERTION. THAT DOES NOT COMPUTE.' Something of the sort."

"It was a stub. I was going to fill it in later. After all, I had all the time in the world."

"Blinded by love," observed Ruth. "I can almost sympathize with that."

"Yeah...almost," Mel growled. "Chazz, do you realize how serious—how downright wicked it is to hijack a plane? Someone could have had a heart attack from terror. You could have been shot. Hundreds of people were forced to be delayed, to miss appointments, who knows how important? We're missing the conference. And we're stuck here, whenever this is. Why didn't you just rob a bank?"

"Mel!"

"Well, if he was gonna do something criminal anyway? The FDIC would cover it. And we would certainly be a lot better off."

"I'm not so sure. Mel, think where we've been, what we've seen. Don't forget the miracles."

"Ruth, you seem to have been really affected—"

"Where have you been? What do you mean, miracles?"

"Just a minute, Chazz. Mel, do you remember who said this? 'Sometimes no amount of evidence will change a mind.'"

"No, who?"

"It was you, you bigot! And you've seen enough evi—"

"Hold it." Mel grinned. "You can't call a Jew a bigot. It isn't done. Ruth, I guess you've got a point. I say I have an open mind; I should act like it. You're right, those were genuine miracles. At least I can't explain them. Yet."

"Yet! What more—"

"Not to interrupt," interrupted Chazz, "but we're sinking."

"Paddle!"

"Bail!"

Leaking faster, the boat drifted sluggishly toward the right bank.

"Let's get it up on the shore," Chazz urged, "and I'll tighten the laces."

"What's that?" asked Ruth, pointing. On the shore lay a dark shadow like a felled twenty-foot palm tree without fronds.

"Looks like a log," Mel guessed.

The log slithered into the water toward them.

"Crocodile! Oh, God!" cried Chazz.

"Jesus!" Ruth prayed. "Jesus!"

The crocodile's eyes and nostrils plowed a smooth wake as it streamed toward them with powerful strokes of its tail. Their boat awash, they were practically swimming. The computer was forgotten.

"This is it," said Mel. "Ruth, I love you."

"Dear Mel. It's been so—"

The croc glided past them a yard away, heading out into midstream.

They floated, stunned, unbelieving.

"Thank God! Come on!" Mel whispered. "Out of the water!"

They swam toward shore, Chazz dragging his limp boat. Finding footing in the mud, they waded up the bank. The boat was in tatters, but still too heavy with water to drag across the mud. Chazz rescued his soggy jacket and laptop. They ran for high ground.

Something splashed in the river. They turned to look. The moonlight showed a great white-bellied tail arc out of the water. There was another splash.

"Look, it's got the wolf," observed Ruth.

"Must prefer dead meat," Chazz surmised. "Are we lucky."

"Just don't stumble on any other crocs," Mel recommended quietly.

They all looked closely at where they were placing their feet. That was how Ruth spotted the bird. Twice as big as a sandpiper, it was just visible running away into the tall grass.

"Is that a nest?" she asked.

"Can't be. Look, the croc's trail runs right past it," replied Mel.

"Well, there's something there," Chazz insisted. "I'm going to look. There may be eggs. I'm starving. Three Tootsie Rolls in two days."

"Tootsie Rolls! Do you have a wrapper?" asked Mel.

"No, I'm afraid I littered. Why?"

"Never mind." It was too late anyway. He was convinced, already. They were in the past.

"There is a nest here," Ruth said. They squatted next to it. Chazz felt gingerly through it with his fingers.

"No eggs."

"Let's get out of here," urged Mel. "That croc may be back." Leaning on his hand to rise, he broke through the sandy surface. "Hey!"

"Shh. Not so loud," Chazz advised.

"Find a hole?" asked Ruth.

"Yeah. Not a very big one. Have you still got your keys?"

"Why? Oh." She shone her penlight into the cave-in. There was a smaller hole tunneling into the sand at the bottom.

"Chazz, can you see the croc?"

"Still eating the wolf."

"Keep an eye on it. If it starts this way, we split." He carefully dug, following the tiny tunnel.

"What do you expect to find? Asterites?" Ruth asked.

"I just have a hunch—Asterites?"

"Little tiny people from the asteroids."

"I read that," said Chazz. "Buck Rogers."

"Just mind the croc, please." The tunnel was shrinking.

"Actually, I haven't seen it since you last asked. All's quiet."

"Too quiet?" asked Ruth.

"Hey-hey!" Mel exulted. "Give me that windbreaker." The tunnel had suddenly broken through into a sizable chamber. Mel began gently lifting eggs out of it and placing them in the jacket.

"Oh, oh. Here comes mama."

"Run!" Mel stood, cradling the eggs.

The crocodile was after them. It was not slithering: it was walking on webbed feet that lifted its long body clear of the sand. Then it was running.

"I didn't know they were that fast," gasped Mel. Trying to cushion the eggs, he fell behind.

Ruth glanced back. "Yipe!"

The croc was now actually galloping after them, twice as fast as before: rapidly bounding along using both hind feet together, alternately with its front claws, like a jackrabbit. It was gaining.

"Mel! Forget the eggs! Run!"

Placing the eggs gently on the sand, Mel leaped to his feet and sprinted away at an angle. He expected the croc to screech to a halt to inspect the eggs for damage.

But the crocodile, having almost caught up while he paused, veered to intercept his new path and galloped with renewed energy, snapping as it neared his heels.

"Mel!" Ruth screamed.

Mel's feet kicked sand into the croc's mouth. Arms flailing, he stumbled in a soft patch and fell. The crocodile sprang at him.

A feathered bolt skewered its jaw to the ground.

Mel lurched to his feet. The croc's tail lashed out as it pivoted, just missing his head. Another arrow plunged into its eye. It arched, spasmed, shuddered and died.

Mel looked around.

A dozen Arab horsemen surrounded them.

14
The Raid

Four horsemen, dismounted, held Ruth and Chazz firmly by the arms while their ponies pawed restlessly at the scrub. Another nocked a new arrow into his bow as two more aimed theirs at Mel. An eighth and ninth rode toward the dead crocodile to take it as a prize and retrieve the arrows, while another saw to the eggs. The last two approached Mel.

"Salaam," he said in Arabic, bowing. "Thanks for—"

A fist slammed into his head. He staggered, fell to his knees.

"Shut up. Turn around."

Dry steely fingers lashed his wrists together behind his back. Chazz and Ruth were bound similarly.

Their ropes, knotted loosely around their necks, were tied to the pommels of three ponies' saddles. The croc was rolled onto a travois pulled by a two-horse team. The band rode off toward the south, dragging their stumbling, choking captives at a jog.

Their captors were solicitous to the extent that the prisoners survived the half-mile journey to the camp, where rough hands untied them. They fell exhausted and strangling. Gradually their color returned.

"Oh, God," Ruth said hoarsely.

"Ruth," croaked Mel. "Are you all right?"

"I—"

"Shut up! No talking." The guard's Arabic was heavily accented, but his meaning was plain. The three travelers fell silent and looked around.

About forty archers, and more horses, were scattered around a half acre under a sparse grove of palms. The men sat or lay on blankets, each by his horse. Some sharpened their swords, some waxed bows, some quietly talked. In their midst stood a tent, near a small fire where several were skinning the crocodile. The archer who had slain it announced himself through the tent flap. A man with a golden cord securing his burnoose emerged. They spoke briefly, glancing at the captives.

The sheik said something to a man standing nearby, who walked toward them. "Get up. Come."

Rising stiffly, they followed him under guard to the fire. They shivered while the sheik looked them over.

"Fetch blankets," he said to a guard. "These will be useless if they die of chill." He pointed to Ruth. "Give me your robe."

These Arabs weren't like the ones at home. Had they forgotten Islam? "Ruth, take off your robes," Mel translated in a low voice. "I think he just wants to dry them off."

Ruth complied, removing both robes. The sheik handed them to a man who draped them on a rack by the fire. Warm, dry and passably clean blankets arrived, to be wrapped snugly about the captives' bodies. Still wearing their soaking modern clothes, they nevertheless began to lose their chill as the fire's warmth penetrated. The roasting crocodile meat wafted a delicious aroma.

"Let us eat," said the sheik. "Nannar will set in two hours. By then we must be at the temple." He indicated the time-travelers. "These must also be fed, then interrogated. I shall handle that myself." He motioned them down onto a blanket spread between the tent and the fire. "Be seated."

Their captors began to carve and distribute crocodile cutlets, scrambled eggs, and skins of wine. One of them brought Chazz his jacket. Taking it gratefully, he wrung it out and started threading the laces through their eyelets. Their food was served on bronze plates, steaming hot.

The sheik lifted his to the full moon. "O Nannar, mysterious consort of Ningal, we give thanks for the food, for these slaves, and for our safe and profitable night's journey."

"Slaves!" Mel hissed.

"What did you expect?" asked Chazz.

They fell to, heedless of burnt fingers. Mel wasn't sure crocodile was kosher, but gave it the benefit of the doubt. Chazz wolfed his down. In fact, part of his meat looked a little like wolf haunch. Ruth poured wine on her eggs to cool them, then scooped up the mess with a slice of croc. There was silence for a few minutes, except for the sounds of munching.

Mel caught the sheik peering at Ruth's blue eyes over his cup. Unconsciously he inched protectively closer to her on the blanket. But what can I do, he agonized. There are forty of them!

What would happen after dinner? 'Interrogation.' Would the sheik believe the truth? Maybe they could be magicians. What would these men make of Chazz's computer? Did it still work? Hardly likely. And then 'temple,' the guy said. They were going to temple services. Strange.

"You people are strange," the sheik began. "Ordinarily one first kills the crocodile, then steals her eggs."

The interrogation was relentless, the answers truthful, but the sheik didn't believe a word. He concluded that these slaves ought to fetch a good price as story-tellers for the children of wealthy Greeks. But his main interest was in Ruth, whom he planned to take for himself just as soon as the temple was relieved of its gold.

Now the three sat tied to the base of a tree, guarded by one glowering Arab, while the rest of their captors crept up on a large limestone edifice two hundred yards away. Nannar the moon-god had just set behind mountains to the west, and the night was wrapped in the darkness before dawn. The sky blazed with stars totally unfamiliar to the eyes of modern city-dwellers.

"Too bad my computer—" Chazz whispered.

"Quiet!" growled the guard, kicking him in the side.

The stillness was tense. Even the night-creatures were silent as the robbers spread to encircle the temple.

Suddenly a cry rang out from the southwest watchtower: "A raid! We're surrounded!"

"That's Hebrew!" said Ruth.

Calls and shouts echoed as the raiders rose to their feet and rushed the temple guards. Arrows whipped through the air. One of the guards fell with a feathered shaft protruding from his chest. A crack of light appeared briefly as the other guard ducked inside and slammed the bronze door. The archer in the tower returned fire. With a metallic thump, the Arabs ran a log against the door. They bashed it again; light showed around its edges as it began to buckle. A stray arrow buried itself in the ground between Ruth and Mel. They strained frantically at their bonds.

"Let us loose!" begged Mel. "We're sitting ducks here!" The guard ignored him.

With a crash, the western door of the temple gave way.

"God of Jacob, save us!" cried the watchman.

A stream of raiders poured into the temple, swords drawn. From within came screams. The Arabs encircling the temple ran to the breach at the front and jammed themselves around the buckled door, seeking entrance.

The stars were dimming overhead. Thunder rumbled in the west, behind Mel. He was taking advantage of the guard's distraction to work on his knots. So far they had not budged.

The thunder grew louder.

"Rain. That's all we need," Chazz said. "As if—"

"That's not thunder," said Ruth.

In an avalanche of rattling weapons and pounding hooves, a stampede of mounted warriors charged past their tree from behind, gouging mud, knocking the guard spinning. The horde sped toward the beleaguered temple, the vanguard swerving past it at a gallop while the rear of the column was still passing the tree.

Arrows sprouted from the backs of the Arabs at the door. As they fell screaming, the raiders inside heard and came running out, to be met by the head of the charge, which wheeled around and loosed another flight of arrows. The rest of the mounted column split off around the temple to the eastern gate, where the first rays of the sun illuminated twenty Arabs who had chosen to flee out the back door. These met a similar fate.

"Praise the Lord of hosts!" shouted the watchman.

The last few mounted archers passing the tree caught sight of the three captives tied at its base in the dawn light. Several reined to a halt and rode back to investigate.

"Help!" Mel called, in Hebrew.

"Save us!" cried Ruth. "For the love of God!"

The horsemen bent and sliced their ropes with swords. Ruth cried out in pain as the circulation returned to her hands. The cavalry leader rode up.

"A woman! What are you doing here?" he asked in Hebrew. "And you," he addressed Chazz. "Why are you wearing such strange garb? Are you a Greek?"

"What's he saying?" asked Chazz.

Mel and Ruth looked at each other and burst into exhausted laughter.

"This is where I came in," Mel said.

"It's a long story," said Ruth to the horseman, "but we'll be delighted to tell you."

"I want to look for my computer. Maybe when it dries out, it'll work."

The young captain of horse offered his hand to Ruth and helped her to her feet. "I can think of nothing that would please me more," he said, "than to listen to a long story of adventure, told by you." His gaze flashed into Ruth's, then swept to include Mel. "And your husband." Chazz had wandered over to the raiders' horses, tethered nearby, to rummage through their saddlebags.

"He's not my husband. He is my…fellow adventurer."

Mel smiled coolly at the officer. "We are exiles from a far land," he said. "Thrown together by chance. Or by the will of God."

"Exiles! Interesting. You must tell me how it feels. I am new to it, myself."

"Your pardon, sir," said an adjutant. "Your father wishes you to join him in the synagogue."

"Thank you, Tars. Please conduct these pilgrims to my wagons. See to their needs." He turned to Ruth. "Have these thieving filth injured you?"

"Not very much."

"But your wrists are raw." He took her hands in his, examined them tenderly. "And your throat! Rope burns?" He raised his hand to her cheek, gently tilted her head to the rosy light, and bent close to inspect her bruises. "Those scum! Tars, bring this girl…?"

"Ruth."

"I am Jacimus Bar-Zimri, at your service. Escort Ruth, here, to my mother's wagon, and ask her to treat her wounds."

"Ahem."

"Please excuse me?"

"My name is Mel. My companion Chazz, over there, does not speak Hebrew. Have I your permission to fetch him, that I may translate for him? He is looking for an item of equipment which these raiders took from him."

"My pleasure. Tars, take over. I must join my father. Shalom."

Tars spoke to a sergeant. "Kimu, accompany this man—Mel, is it? Melchior?—and assist him and his companion in their search, then conduct them to the captain's wagons. I leave you in charge. Come, my lady."

Mel looked at Ruth, his heart in his eyes. "See you later, Ruth."

"So long, Mel." Her own eyes downcast, she turned and followed Tars.

15
Zimri

Mel stumbled along after Kimu, thinking furiously, not paying much attention to where he was going, until he almost walked into a horse. Swerving, he saw Chazz, three ponies over, unfastening the straps of a rectangular leather bag.

"Eureka!" cried Chazz.

"So he *is* Greek," Kimu muttered. "That explains it."

"Okay, you've found it," snapped Mel. "Now let's get somewhere where we can dry off. Come on."

"What's the matter with you?"

"Nothing."

"Where's Ruth?"

"Having her 'wounds' treated."

"What wounds?"

"Rope burns."

"Oh. Mine are rather sore, also."

"Well, come on. Maybe we'll get treatment too." They followed Kimu southeastward along a canal.

"What is going on?" Mel asked him. "Who are you people? No, wait. First, what is the year?"

"A period of time twelve moons long, from Nisan until Adar."

"Ah…thank you." Mel wasn't in the mood to pursue it.

Emerging from the trees they saw the river, and along its bank a paved road, somewhat rutted and potholed. Pavement! This had to be the future, then. After a war…a big war. Parked along the road, a column of ox-drawn carts and wagons stretched for miles to the southeast. In the distance Mel could just make out a string of camels, and some tents pitched near the woods.

"Quite a caravan," Mel remarked. "What is it?"

"The exodus of Father Zimri and his relations and army from Parthia."

"All these are related? Where are they heading?"

"To an estate called Valatha, given to Zimri by Governor Saturninus."

"Whereabouts is Valatha?"

"In Antioch, by Daphne of Syria."

"I've heard of Antioch, at least."

The first two wagons were twice the size of those following; nearly thirty feet long, with iron-tired wheels, they were each pulled by four oxen. Kimu bypassed them, stopping instead at the fourteenth wagon in line, again a large one. He hailed it: "Sergeant Kimu reporting with guests!"

A fine-meshed wicker screen slid back and a stout, elderly, bald man in a white chiton looked out a window.

"What's all the ruckus? Can't a slave sleep? What time is it?"

"Dawn, O Tosthenes," the sergeant replied respectfully. "Our column surprised the Lunar Raiders robbing Beth Yehuda synagogue. All are dead, I believe. They had three captives. Captain Jacim bade me bring these two here and have their needs seen to."

"What of the third?"

"She has been taken to the wagon of Mother Bathyra."

"She! Aha! Well, come in, come in, I suppose." He pulled in his head and slid the screen shut, then reappeared opening a door in the rear of the wagon. Mel bent to peer curiously at the undercarriage, which seemed independently suspended beneath the wagon floor. Was that a gleam of iron in the slanting shadow? He straightened. Above the chassis' shoulder level the sturdy oaken framework gave way to light vertical cedar laths reaching to head height, crowned by a shingle roof.

Kimu followed Chazz and Mel up two narrow steps and through the door. It was cool and surprisingly spacious inside. Tosthenes waved his guests to seats around a table hinged with leather straps under a side window. "Please be seated," he said. "Refreshments momentarily." He passed forward through a wicker screen pivoted at top and bottom.

"Looks like a Winnebago in here," Chazz remarked.

"Chazz, have you ever been in a Winnebago?"

Chazz ignored the question. "What's going on? Any idea when we are?"

"Not yet, unless you know when Zimri was...or will be...exiled from Parthia."

"None of the above."

"What a curious tongue you speak," commented Kimu. "So clattery."

"I shall teach him Hebrew soon. How about it, Chazz? Want to learn some Hebrew?"

"Is that the predominant language now?"

"Never has been."

"Then no. I'd rather learn something a little more lingua franca."

Tosthenes returned from the front, bearing a tray of tall mugs. "Let's get outside these," he said, "then we'll see about less immediate needs."

"I'll drink to that." Mel sipped. It was cool, but not ice-cold. Of course.

"None for me, thanks," said Kimu. "I'm on duty."

"It's just grape juice. Too early in the morning for wine. Even for me."

"Well, in that case."

They drank. Tosthenes fetched dry robes and slippers, into which the travelers changed with great relief.

"And now, my friends. What brings you here? How did you get into this mess?"

"Well, Chazz, he wants to know what…or who…got us into this mess."

"Don't look at me! You and Ruth would have met in any case. You were sitting together on the plane. Blame your travel agents. If not for me, you'd probably be freezing in a yurt in prehistoric Moscow."

"With our luck we wouldn't even have a nice cozy yurt. Yeah, I guess you're right. We did it to ourselves. O Tosthenes, the proximate cause of our capture was a certain crocodile, now *karat*."

Mel had told them everything. Tosthenes was a little skeptical, but Kimu's eyes glowed. "What marvels!" he said. "And what a blessing that the two of you met at such an opportune time, on the river! God must have a special mission for you."

"Kimu says we must be on a mission for God."

"Well, open the sealed orders."

"I was hoping you had them."

"God doesn't speak to me; I'm a Lutheran."

The screened door banged open. "Ho, Tossy!" Jacimus hailed, unbuckling his jacket. "Is there something cool to drink? I see you've been entertaining our guests. At ease, Kimu."

"Hail, Jacim. No, they've been entertaining me. Wait 'til you hear their tale."

Mel groaned inwardly. He didn't feel like going through the whole thing again right away. Jacimus's next words made him feel even worse.

"Heard it already—assuming it's the same tale. I've just spent a most delightful half hour in Mother's wagon, listening to a fascinating story from the lips of their fascinating companion."

"How is Ruth?" asked Mel.

"Fascinating."

"I mean—"

"A few bruises. They should heal with no scars. A slight sniffle from being wet and cold. She's warm and dry now. Mama gave her hot chicken soup and wine. She'll be fine. No other injuries, just fatigue."

"You examined her?"

"Me? Of course not. Doctor Kaski is our resident physician. He'll be here presently; he was coming right after me, to tend to you two."

"I want to see Ruth."

"Don't blame you. But she'll be asleep by now. She was dozing off over her mulled wine when I left. Why don't you wait until Kaski treats you and you get some rest? I'm given to understand you've been up since the third hour yesterday. Or for five hundred years, in some sense."

"Chazz, we seem to be in the first century B.C."

"At last! I thought it must be the past. Great. Now if this thing only works."

"What is that object?"

"Open it for him, please."

"O.K. But I don't want to turn it on until it's dried out for a couple of days." He opened the case. Jacimus pressed a key gently, marveling at the workmanship. "Wish I had a screwdriver," Chazz said.

"Hold on a second." Mel got up, went to where his pants were hanging, and felt in a pocket. "I have one on my key ring."

"Great! But why did you bother to take your keys to Moscow?"

"Just for you." Chazz started working on a screw. As Mel replaced his pants on the hook, something fell out and rolled across the floor.

Jacimus picked it up. "The shield of David!"

"Nebuchadnezzar's widow, Queen Amytis, gave me that as a memento."

Tosthenes had returned with Jacimus's drink. "Really?" he asked. "May I see it?" Jacimus traded it for the mug.

Tosthenes examined the sigil closely, holding it in a shaft of sunlight. "A fire opal," he said. "Exquisitely carved. Set in solid gold, from the mass. Priceless." He handed it to Kimu, who was expressing a desire to see it. "Between this and that…'computer'…I find it difficult to maintain my skepticism. On the one hand we have a ring of antique workmanship, but lacking the patina of great age. On the other—" He gestured.

Chazz had the back of the case off, exposing the motherboard, hard disk, power supply, and internal modem. It seemed to be dry, and not obviously discolored. "Good, I don't think any water got in here," he said. "The keyboard's damp, though." He wiped gently at the keys and LCD screen with a corner of his robe. "Hope it didn't short out. Ask them where I can stand it up to dry where it'll be undisturbed."

"Chazz, we're in a caravan. This wagon is going to start moving soon."

"Oh, yeah."

Tosthenes continued his thought: "—here we have an object of impenetrable but indubitable futurity. Most persuasive."

"Of course it's true, Tossy. Ruth wouldn't lie to me. Anyway, just look at these people. They're obviously not our contemporaries. They don't have the attitude. They don't even move right." Mel was puzzled by this, but upon reflection he thought Jacimus might be referring to Mel's and Chazz's modern view of personal space, or perhaps to something even subtler.

Kimu handed the sigil to Mel. "To think that this was worn by...given to you by...Nebuchadnezzar's Queen herself. And that you spoke with Daniel the prophet."

"That gives me an idea," said Tosthenes. "We have a remarkable opportunity here. Wait just a moment." He went forward.

"I hope you will permit me to try to grasp the mysteries of that sleek object in the coming weeks," Jacimus requested. "Fine craftsmanship has always intrigued me."

"Certainly. Weeks?"

"I presume too much. You are going to be our guests, aren't you? We must leave this place, and we can't leave you here, helpless. In Antioch you'll find it much more civilized. Besides, Ruth has already—oh, here's the doctor now." Two figures had appeared on the steps outside the wickerwork door. "Come in, doctor." They entered. "Hi, dad. My father, this is Mel and Chazz, the other time exiles. Men, this is my father, Zimri. And this is Kaski. They seem to be in pretty good shape, Doc."

"I'll be the judge of that," the doctor chided, smiling.

"I am very pleased, and I may say heartened, to meet you," said Zimri, a lean gray wolf of a man with a burly mustache. "For centuries God has vouchsafed us no sign, no prophet. Now wonders are starting to appear again. Signs in the heavens, auspicious auguries. Something wonderful is about to happen. If you are part of this, I welcome you. Please accompany us on our exodus. We need some distraction from our heartbreak." Seeing Mel's puzzled expression, he asked, "Son, you have not told them?"

"Only the fact of our exile. I have not had a chance to elaborate."

"A common enough story," Zimri said to Mel. "Unlike yours. Political corruption, temple graft, involving some priests of Zoroaster. One of my soldiers, a member of that cult, came to me with a tale of a stolen dowry. I investigated, found more such instances. When I endeavored to expose these abuses, the priests suborned witnesses against me to our king, the Shahanshah. Though he believed me innocent, I could not prove it. He had no choice but to send me into exile. The graft continues, if less overtly."

"It doesn't get any better in the future, I'm sorry to have to tell you," Mel sympathized. "It surely must hurt to be forced to leave your home. How long have you lived here?"

"For generations. My ancestors chose not to return to Judea when Cyrus set them free."

"He did it!" exclaimed Mel.

"Sorry I took so long," Tosthenes apologized, returning with a scroll. "Oh, hello, sir. I couldn't find it right away. It had gotten buried under Seneca's 'Oratory.'"

"What had?"

"The Tenach. In particular, this book. We have a golden opportunity to verify some of the details in the Book of Daniel."

"We don't need to," protested Jacimus. "Every word is the truth."

"At it again, are you, you old skeptic?" Zimri asked.

"May I see that?" Mel reached for the scroll. "I blush to confess I've never read the Book of Daniel. But now that I've been there…"

"You should rest first," advised Zimri. "In fact, it has become rather crowded in here."

"You're right, Dad. Come on, fellows. Let's leave them in peace with the doctor. Tosthenes, Kimu, let's go. Tossy, come to my day room. I want to discuss some things." They filed out. Zimri lingered.

"You will stay?"

"Ruth is staying, right?"

"Yes."

"Then so am I."

"She was confident you would. If that makes you feel better."

"It does. Thanks for telling me that. You're a good egg, Zimri."

"Ho! A good egg! Delicious. I've never been called that. I must say I prefer it to the alternative."

"I think maybe I will learn Hebrew after all," Chazz cut in. "I'm missing all the jokes."

"We're invited to Antioch with this tribe. Are you on? It'll take several weeks."

"Not me! You go if you want. As soon as my computer dries, I'm out of here."

"You don't have to give me an answer right away. Sleep on it. At least you ought to get out of Iraq before they invent passports."

"No, I'm going back to Baghdad."

Mel sighed. "You realize you're probably stranding Ruth and me here."

"Do I hear violins?"

"Father Zimri, Chazz will accompany us for at least a few days."

"What are you telling him?"

"Fine. He may get off at our next stop, Neapolis, if he chooses. Please excuse me now. Shalom."

16
Aletha

After Mel and Chazz had been examinated and treated and their rope burns anointed with salve, Tosthenes returned. He led them to cots in one of the forward compartments of the wagon, where they sank into exhausted slumber.

When Mel awoke, the wagon was not moving, and it was dark. Letting Chazz sleep, he got up and went to the rear of the wagon to see if his clothes had dried. Finding that they had, he dressed and went outside. To his surprise, the caravan was still parked in the same location as in the morning. The oxen were ruminating, drivers chatting.

These guys were supposed to be in a hurry! Presumably they had a deadline to get out of town. What was up? Some kind of trouble?

He walked toward the big lead wagon, past smaller ones covered and uncovered, and even a few one-ox carts, reasoning that Father Zimri, and hence Mother Bathyra, would be there. And Ruth.

As he neared it, savory odors from a cook-fire just beyond reminded him he hadn't eaten all day. It must be dinnertime, he thought. He'd turn into a night person at this rate.

He mounted the steps to the back door of the lead wagon and knocked on the sturdy cedar panel. The door opened. A dark-haired young girl with warm brown eyes smiled at him. She looked around sixteen. "You must be Mel. Come in." She held the door as he entered. "You're just in time for dinner."

Candlelight dazzled him and lit a cozy domestic scene. Zimri must be rich! This wagon was furnished like Nebuchadnezzar's palace. Father and son sat at opposite ends of a short dinner table that stretched across the width of the narrow wagon. Kind of a tight squeeze, Mel thought. But I guess it'd be even tighter if they couldn't put their knees under the table. To Zimri's left sat a matron Mel didn't recognize, presumably Bathyra. On the near side of the table were two empty chairs, the one to Jacimus's left pulled out as if the girl had just risen from it. To Jacimus's right sat Ruth.

"Hello, Mel," she said.

He drank her in with his eyes, too distracted to answer. She was so...cold.

"We thought you might want to sleep through the night," said Jacimus.

"Come, join us for dinner," invited Zimri. "Sit right here." He indicated the chair at his right hand. "Some wine?"

"Thanks." Mel took a seat as the girl poured wine from a carafe on the table for him. "Thank you."

"This is Aletha, my daughter. And this is my wife Bathyra."

"I am blessed." Mel sipped. "What's wrong?" Yes, what was wrong? What had he done? "Why haven't the wagons moved?"

"It's the Sabbath, Mel," Ruth explained. "These people observe it. They don't travel on the Sabbath."

"Actually it's over now," said Jacimus. "Since sundown. But we don't travel by night, either."

"But you fight, thank God!" Mel suddenly realized he owed his freedom, if not his life, to the apparent fact that these Jews weren't as legalistic as some in his time. "And how well!"

"God did not intend the Sabbath as an opportunity for sin-worshiping thieves to loot synagogues," said Zimri. "He commanded that we keep it holy. We do."

Aletha, on Mel's right, said earnestly, "We rest, we sing praises to the Lord, we enjoy our fellowship, we study. We pray." Her cheeks dimpled. "And we eat too much." Mel noticed how the candles sparkled in her eyes.

"Talking of that, what's keeping dinner?" asked Jacimus.

"Agnes!" Zimri called. A pleasant woman appeared in the doorway behind the table, a curl of brown hair straggling down one pretty, plump cheek.

"Yes, master?"

"We have an extra guest for dinner. Water the soup."

"Water the soup indeed! The very idea! There's plenty, and it's almost ready. Two minutes."

"Thank you, Agnes."

"Welcome to you, sir. I hope you like roast duck."

"Yum!" said Mel. "So that's what smells so delicious!" Agnes blushed, smiled, curtsied and left. Mel took another sip of purple wine.

"Mel, how is Chazz doing?"

"Sleeping when I left. Maybe he will sleep all night. Ruth, we...we have to plan our next move."

"Not if it involves discussing time-travel. Mel, you ought to know this: I will not time-jump again. If I can help it."

Mel sat stunned as if Ruth had just administered him a lethal injection.

"I've thought about it," she continued, "and it's just not worth the risk. I almost died last time. I can make a life here. I'm capable. Sorry if this upsets your plans."

"I have no plans." He felt woozy. "Not now." So that was it. No, that wasn't all; there was something else. What?

"We can help you," Jacimus offered. "You'll adjust quickly. Our life is not so bad. And you have skills we can use."

"You can be of immense help to us," agreed Zimri. "Knowledge that is second nature to you, things you don't even remember you know, are undreamed-of by us."

"It isn't as easy as you think," Mel mumbled. "Technology requires a base."

"Mel, you may find this hard to believe," said Aletha, "but I am a student of mathematics. Ruth has shown me how little I know. Will you teach me? That doesn't require a lot of equipment, if I understand correctly."

He didn't teach mathematics to young girls. Not anymore.

The first course arrived: Agnes glided in carrying a steaming tureen, followed by a serving girl with a stack of bowls. She ladled out the thin soup with a flourish. Zimri blessed God and Mel tried his soup with little appetite. It burned his tongue.

What now? he wondered. What did he do now? What had gotten into her? He risked a glance across the table. Ruth was talking animatedly with Jacimus on her left. Was he the "something else"? She was getting along just fine in Hebrew...with him. Had she forgotten who taught her?

Still, she had a point, he conceded, sipping more prudently at the soup after a cooling draught of wine. She had almost died. That had been pretty dumb, risking a time-jump right on the bank of a river they had known was low. They would be more careful next time. If there was a next time.

Well, he had to get back. But how could he leave her? And he'd thought he was in trouble already! God! He'd said he'd give his life for Shoshana. But that was before he'd met Ruth.

"—dying out here?" His host was asking him something.

"I'm really sorry, sir. I was preoccupied. What did you say?"

"Nothing vital," Zimri assured him. "I was inquiring how it could happen that, though you come from so far in the future, you speak the old language so well—especially as it seems to be dying out here. Most of my brethren speak Aramaic when not forced to do otherwise, or Greek. Even our Scriptures have succumbed to the trend: the revised version is in Greek."

"Hebrew was revived almost single-handedly by a saintly Jewish scholar named Eliezer ben Yehuda," explained Mel. "Good thing for me: I wouldn't understand a word of Greek or Aramaic."

"Mel is part of the second ingathering," Ruth put in from down the table, "as prophesied by Isaiah."

So! Mel's heart leaped. She hadn't entirely forgotten him! He smiled wanly at her. She smiled back.

"How wonderful!" Aletha exclaimed to Mel. "Tell me about it!" Ruth's smile cooled a few degrees.

Mel looked at Aletha appraisingly. Was it possible? Could Ruth be jealous? Of someone so young? "Wonderful indeed," he said. "A wonderful result of a monstrously horrible deed. There was a war, and the leader of the enemy, a madman, tried to make a whole burnt offering of the sons of Israel. A holocaust. He exterminated us en masse, and one in three of all Jews died. After the war, the nations who defeated him helped the remnant migrate to Palestine. They're still returning…or will be…were when I left."

"One in three!" Bathyra spoke for the first time. "Many have tried, but not even Haman came that close to exterminating the Jewish people."

The door banged open. Tosthenes stood there breathless. "Your pardon, sirs—and ladies—I beg your pardon. Chazz is gone."

17
Chazz

"Maybe he's just strolling around the caravan," Mel suggested.

"I have searched up and down the line," objected Tosthenes. "None has seen him. His computer is missing too."

"Mel!" Ruth was half-risen from her chair. "How could you leave him? There goes our only chance of getting back without getting killed."

"He told me he wasn't going to stay with the caravan anyway," Mel protested. "He's going back to Baghdad, for Scheherazade."

"That nut! He'll never survive alone." She pushed her chair back and stood up. "We've got to find him." Jacimus rose and started toward the door.

"That'll be hard enough if he's only wandering in this time. But I agree." Mel looked toward his host. "Zimri, may we have a search party?"

"Of course. Son." Jacimus paused at this, halfway out the door. "See to your men. Describe the lost one's peculiar dress; they'll have no trouble recognizing him. Report back before you go out yourself. We need to pray."

"I'm on my way, sir." The door crashed shut behind him.

Zimri addressed Mel. "You realize that there is little hope of finding him in the dark if he wishes not to be found."

"And he has a head start. Tosthenes, when did you discover him missing?"

"Ten minutes ago. I checked with drivers of three wagons behind Jacimus's, and three before it on my way here."

"Mel," asked Aletha, "how sound asleep was he when you left him?"

"Good point. He was breathing heavily, but he could have been playing possum."

"'Playing possum'?"

"Feigning sleep. So he could have left right after I did. Say half an hour ago."

"Where is this 'Baghdad'?" asked Bathyra.

“About fifty miles up the Tigris. And six hundred years into the future.”

“If those are Roman miles, then in three days’ walking he will encounter Seleucia. He will be safe enough there from wild beasts. Not counting Greeks.”

“Very good, my dear. You’re right,” Zimri agreed. “We should concentrate our search in that direction.”

“Mel,” asked Ruth, “which way is Baghdad?”

“That way, assuming this caravan is headed toward Antioch.” He pointed forward.

“Does Chazz know we’re going to Antioch? And does he know where Antioch is?”

“‘Yes,’ and ‘I don’t know.’”

“You see my point? He could have wandered off in any direction.”

“All he had to do was find the river and head upstream. He must know we’re on the right bank.”

“It is very dangerous to walk along a dark river in these times,” Zimri observed. “Phraates Arsaces is too busy coping with rebellion to police the countryside at night.”

“Perhaps he could hail a boat heading up the river,” Mel offered. “He wouldn’t need to know the language for that.”

“A boat heading up the river? Impossible. Not to say unnatural.”

“No motorboats here, guy,” said Ruth.

“Oh.”

“But there are lions,” Aletha said. “As well as the wolves, crocodiles, and brigands you already know of.”

“Lions!”

“Just small ones.”

“What a relief.”

“Poor Chazz,” said Ruth. “Mel, we have to find him.”

The door opened and Jacimus entered. “The search is on. I have sent a runner down the train to notify the occupants of every wagon to be on the watch. If they see Chazz, they are to detain him and notify us.”

“Can we detain him legitimately?” asked Mel. “He’s a freeman.”

“Mel, he’s just a kid. He may even be under eighteen.”

“We can hold him in protective custody,” Jacimus replied, “at least long enough to impress on him the dangers of traveling alone.”

“Oh? Could you hold us also?” asked Mel.

“You are not so foolish as to wish to leave.”

“Right,” agreed Ruth.

Mel bristled. I’m leaving right now! he shouted. But only in his head.

“Besides, Chazz is a special case.” Jacimus turned to Ruth. “Was not his computer important to you?”

That's right, Mel realized. She was willing to time-jump if she could use the computer to do it. Or so it appeared. His heart leaped with hope. God, please! Bring him back!

"It's not just that," Ruth protested. "It's Chazz I'm worried about. I want to talk to him before he goes off and does something stupid."

"Hi, everybody. Am I late for dinner? Sorry."

Chazz stood in the doorway, holding his computer by the handle, a little bedraggled.

"Chazz!"

"Praise God!" cried Bathyra. Mel and Jacimus jumped to their feet. Ruth raced around the table, jostling past Jac in her haste to hug the prodigal. "Are we glad to see you!" she said. "We were afraid you'd been eaten by lions."

"Guess I should have left a note. Sorry, no paper."

"Where were you?"

Chazz stepped into the wagon. Behind him were two soldiers. "Meditating in the woods, where these guys found me. They seemed upset, so I came back with them."

"They're part of the search party," said Mel.

"Krof, pass the word to call off the search," Jacimus ordered one of the soldiers. "Then you and Zak report to me for kudos."

"Yes, sir!" They saluted and left.

"Now, Chazz," invited Ruth, "pull up a chair, have something to eat, and tell us everything. We were worried sick. Here, have some wine."

"Agnes!" Zimri called again.

18
Curriculum Planning

"Basically," Chazz began after he was seated and served, "I just wanted to meditate in solitude. I had a lot to think over. Mainly, what I should do next. And I took my computer in case the answer turned out to be 'Split.'" He bit another bite off the duck drumstick.

"Chazz, just a minute," said Ruth. "Do you mean to tell us you were seriously considering leaving us? Going off by yourself? Now, of all times, when we've just found somebody"—surely, Mel hoped, her gesture included Zimri's whole family, as well as Jacimus—"actually willing to help us?"

"Willing, maybe, but able? Besides, helping you might hinder me. We have different goals. I need to get to Baghdad. You don't care where you are, only when. But..."

"Chazz, this better be good," advised Mel, "because our hosts are eventually going to have to hear it, and if they're annoyed at you, they may decide to chuck out all three of us."

"I don't think so," Ruth murmured.

"Hey, am I giving time travel a bad name?" asked Chazz. "I was just about to say, the main thing I had to mull over was something you said."

Ruth looked at Mel. "What did you say?"

"He said if I went I'd be leaving you two stranded here," Chazz replied. "Now even though I didn't get you into this mess—"

"You certainly did!" protested Ruth. "If you hadn't hijacked the plane and catalyzed our conversation, Mel and I would have gone our separate ways in Moscow."

Probably true, Mel brooded. Like they were doing here in Parthia.

"And we'd never have achieved that synergy, discussing...that topic...that sent us here."

"Not a chance," said Chazz. "You didn't need me as a conversation piece. You two are meant for each other. I wouldn't be surprised if you're in love. It's obvious to the casual observer.

"Anyway, my Lutheran conscience was already prodding me to come back. But I must admit that wasn't the convincer."

"What was?" Mel prompted, anxious to end this painful conversation.

"Well, I could have meditated in the wagon," said Chazz. "But I wanted more facts. My excursion was partly a feasibility study. To see how traveling alone, on foot, in the dark, was."

"How was it?"

"Not the way to go," Chazz admitted. "It's scary out there. The clincher was this blood-curdling shriek right behind me: YEEEEUURROWWGHHH!"

Zimri's family, who had been sitting in polite patience waiting for the translation, leaped to their feet.

"What ails him?" Jacimus drew his sword. "Is he mad?"

"Now see what you've done," Ruth scolded.

"Chazz was telling us of an animal that he heard in the woods," explained Mel.

"An owl," Tosthenes identified, "if he imitated it correctly."

Knuckles pounded at the door. "Come in," said Zimri.

"Privates Krof and Zak reporting as ordered, sir," Krof said, entering. "Was that the alert?"

"No, it was the all-clear," said Jacimus. "At ease, men. You did a fine job, finding this lost one. You apparently rescued him from a screech owl. I commend your powers of observation. Notify Sergeant Kimu that you are to be awarded five kudos each. Dismissed."

"Thank you, sir!" They left.

"What was that animal that sounded like that?" Chazz asked. "A lion or tiger? A bear?"

"Oh, my, no," replied Ruth. "Just an owl."

"Let me get this straight," Mel interrupted. "You wandered out there to consider your options and to see if you could survive alone."

"Right."

"Leaving aside the survival thing, since you lucked out, is it fair to say that when the soldiers found you, you were on the point of deciding to accompany us to Antioch?"

"Past the point. I was heading back already; speedily, I might add. Or I thought I was. But I guess I got turned around, after the owl. The soldiers brought me at an angle to the way I had been running. An eighty-degree angle."

"But Antioch?" Ruth pressed.

"And the computer?"

"Yes, yes. If it still works. And tell them I'm sorry."

"Our companion has told us his story," Mel addressed his hosts. "He is very sorry for the inconvenience he has caused you. He took a walk in the woods to gather his thoughts on whether to accept your kind invitation to accompany the caravan to Antioch, or to strike off on his own with the computer. He realized it would not be good to abandon Ruth and me, and started back. But he lost his way. He would be wandering around out there still, or eaten, if it were not for your skillful trackers."

"Please tell him not to do it again," Jacimus said. "It is extremely dangerous out there alone. Thank God we found him in time."

"Yes, thank God," agreed Bathyra. "It is a miracle. And God knew where he was, and what we desired, even before we had time to pray."

But I did, Mel realized. I prayed. And Chazz showed up immediately afterwards. Is there really a God, then?...who answers prayer? Or was it only a coincidence?

"Chazz," Ruth admonished, "Jacimus wants it impressed upon you that you must never do a foolish stunt like that again. It is extremely dangerous out there alone. Okay?"

"Okay. Ruth, I really am sorry. And I appreciate your concern."

"Chazz, this isn't Uppsala," Mel added. "Survival won't be easy for any of us. It's a case of forced growth now. You have to think about the consequences of your actions. I don't think you really considered, for example, what a fix you'd be in if your computer got wet. You just hopped into a skin-boat."

"Lucky for us!" interjected Ruth.

"Those things don't sail themselves," Mel continued. "It's a real art, keeping them from spinning. You live too dangerously."

"And Chazz, I hate to mention this," said Ruth, "but if you had walked upstream a mile or two, you would have hit a big city—Seleucia—right near the site of Baghdad."

"But then you two would have been wolf-bait. Do you get the feeling that maybe it wasn't just luck that I boated downstream?—and on the Euphrates, at that. Originally I was on the Tigris."

"You don't know the half of it," Mel said. "The chance of our being there at that instant was even smaller." Another coincidence? Or was that an answer to prayer too? Daniel's prayer?

That settled it. He was going to have to read Daniel's book and see how many other "coincidences" turned up. He was part of the second ingathering, after all. Or would be. Or whatever the tense was. How could Isaiah have known there would be a second ingathering? Or even a first?

"What's that stuff in your hood, Chazz?" asked Ruth.

"What stuff?" Chazz tried to look down the back of his own neck, failed, and stood to remove his jacket. Caught in the hood was a lump of something slick and golden. "Yecch!" he said. It was translucent and soft to the touch, the size of a melon slice, clear and smooth except on one side, where it showed a ragged edge. "What is this?" He gingerly removed it and laid it on the table.

"That's interesting," Mel said. "What is it, beeswax? A honeycomb?" He touched the ragged edge. It was faintly sticky.

"What a sweet smell it has!" exclaimed Aletha.

"How'd it get in there?" Chazz answered his own question: "I must have broken it off a tree when I was running through the woods."

"It appears to be some kind of crystallized sap," conjectured Tosthenes.

"He says it's sap," Ruth told Chazz.

"Oh, good. That's not so bad. Actually it's kind of pretty."

"I have never seen its like," said Zimri. "Yet it reminds me of something, I can't remember what."

"Well, I'm going to keep it. I can look at it and remember what a sap I was."

Mel came to a decision. He wasn't ready to be a sap. He would not give up Ruth without a fight. Whether she wanted to time-jump or not, he'd stay with her.

First, he had to find out how she really felt. Was there a chance that he would be able to talk to her alone soon? Yeah, two chances: slim and none. They would surely be chaperoned. Besides, it wasn't going to be easy to pry her loose from Captain Jac. Still, there would be times when the captain would have to attend to his military duties.

As Mel pondered these plans, Zimri threw him a curve. "Please ask Chazz whether he would prefer to be taken to Seleucia."

"What!"

"We reach Neapolis in three days. The Tigris runs near the Euphrates there—an armed squad could escort him handily across to Seleucia. Even after remaining long enough for him to establish a base, they could easily overtake our caravan."

"You don't understand," Mel objected. "I will translate, but let me first explain. Chazz seeks a girl who never lived except in a fable. He is convinced she is real, against all evidence. Besides, there are compelling reasons for him to leave Parthia—as compelling as yours. Also, if Ruth and I are ever to return to our own time, we apparently need to use his computer to do it. This means we three must all stick together until we leave the country. Finally, Chazz has already agreed to come to Antioch."

"He may change his mind when he knows he can be escorted," replied Zimri. "However foolish or selfish his decision, it is his to make, using the best information we can give him."

"You are correct." Mel sighed. "Chazz, in a couple of days Zimri will, if you choose, provide you with an armed escort from Neapolis to Seleucia. The escort will even set you up in a room in Seleucia, where you can jump to Baghdad all you want."

"Really! That's nice of him. That changes things. I'll have to think about this."

"Please do. Think hard. And don't forget Interpol, and Iraqi jails."

"Why don't you settle down with a real girl?" urged Ruth. "Looking for Scheherazade will only break your heart."

"He'll consider your offer," Mel told Zimri. "How much notice do you need?"

"An hour or two will suffice."

"Chazz must be most baffled by our conversations," remarked Tosthenes. "With your permission, master, I will undertake to instruct him in the rudiments of Greek. In a few days I can scarcely impart much knowledge of the classics, but with diligence he can acquire a basic speaking vocabulary. Enough to enable him to find the bathhouses in Seleucia. Or avoid them."

"But you do not speak his tongue," Jacimus objected.

"Ah! That is the beauty of my plan," replied Tosthenes. "With but minor assistance from Mel or Ruth at first, I shall learn his tongue as he learns mine. It has long been one of my passions to study the kinds of men by studying their modes of expression. Imagine the opportunity to try to fathom the workings of a mind from the distant future!"

"Seems a waste of time to me," Jacimus commented. "I can already fathom Ruth's distant future mind in Hebrew. And a lovely thing it is, too."

"But have I your permission?"

"Oh, all right. So long as you do not shirk your duties."

"Thank you, master. Mel, would you help me in this? And of course present the case to Chazz?"

"Surely. Chazz was interested in learning the language most widely spoken. Does Greek fit this description?"

"*Koine*—will take him from Germania to India. The whole Alexandrine Empire—and more, as spread by Caesar—will be accessible to him."

"If that's the case, perhaps Ruth and I should learn it too. Does everyone else here speak Greek?"

"We all speak Greek, of one dialect or another," replied Aletha. "We could all instruct you. My own duties are not onerous while in caravan; perhaps I might coach you, Mel: trade Greek for mathematics lessons."

"While I coach Ruth," offered Jacimus. "I have some spare time too. And Tosthenes will be sufficiently occupied teaching Chazz."

Oh-oh! This was taking a turn Mel hadn't anticipated. An unwelcome one. Was there a gracious way out? He thought fast. Cut his losses, at least.

"A splendid idea! We shall all meet regularly for a combined course in Greek. That way, you teachers can share the work and avoid duplication, while we students will all learn the same vocabulary." And, he didn't add, they could chaperone each other. "Now excuse me while I inform Chazz."

Chazz welcomed the idea, and it was settled. The class would meet in Zimri's wagon each evening after dinner. Since Chazz might leave in a couple of days, and since he and Mel and Tosthenes were all riding with Jacimus, he would receive extra coaching during the days as well. The same applied to Ruth, who would be traveling with Aletha.

As Ruth put it, it was a familiar pattern: a main lecture and two recitation sections. In fact, the group quickly saw the possibility of establishing a sort of peripatetic school: besides Greek and English classes, there could be mathematics and riding lessons when the opportunity offered, and Bible studies, especially in the Book of Daniel, on the Sabbath.

Maybe even music lessons, Mel mused. Too bad he had lost his harmonica. Everything was under the ruins of Nebuchadnezzar's palace, including his razor. He'd just look scruffy for a while, until his beard grew out. Then he'd fit right in.

He wondered if he could make a harmonica. Maybe splint together some bamboo tubes? What about the reeds? No. If he was going to start making things, a harmonica was probably not the highest priority. What was? He'd have to see what they needed, and what they already had. He'd wait until Antioch for that. If they needed it there, they'd need it everywhere. Of course, there might be something they could use sooner, while traveling.

"Zimri, I have an idea. I've been trying to think of some way we could make some gadgets for you that wouldn't require much of a technological base. It isn't easy.

"My idea is for the three of us to meet periodically and brainstorm in English to think of inventions within our capabilities. Afterwards we could check our proposals against your needs."

"A brain storm!" Zimri exclaimed. "Most expressive! Ideas flashing like lightning, pouring forth like rain!"

"And assaulting the ears," muttered Jacimus, "like thunder."

"I can see the use of that," said Tosthenes. "Spontaneity would be essential, and possible only in your 'English,' which is most familiar to you, and embodies the required concepts."

Mel hoped Chazz wouldn't mind. If he insisted on brainstorming in Swedish, he'd be a solitary drip.

"Mel, that's an excellent idea," agreed Ruth. "And we'd better get started soon, before Chazz leaves, if he's leaving."

"What about tonight? Right after school?" Mel asked. Receiving assent, he turned to Chazz. "What we're proposing is for the three of us to have brainstorming sessions for inventions we can implement here. Sound good?"

"Okay, count me in."

"Let me consider," asked Zimri. "Where would be a good place for these brain storms?"

"It should be someplace where we would not disturb you," Mel said. "These sessions sometimes involve loud voices and late hours."

"My headquarters wagon is available," offered Jacimus. "It has a small day room, and otherwise is used only for storage."

"Mine is more comfortable, dear brother," Aletha counter-offered. "A pleasant atmosphere would seem important for the stimulus of inspiration. Not a military atmosphere."

"What's not pleasant about that?" asked Jacimus wryly. "Very well, wherever is most suitable."

"Perhaps some refreshments could be provided," Bathyra put in. "Would that help your activity, or distract?"

"Coffee!" exclaimed Mel. "There's our first invention."

"Oh, we have coffee," Aletha informed him. "From Arabia. Would you like some?"

"Coffee!" chorused Ruth and Mel. "Yes, please!" begged Ruth. "Mel, how long is it since we've tasted coffee?"

"Too long. Chazz, how about a cup of coffee?"

"Decaf?"

19
A Riding Lesson

Life in the caravan was restful. Just before dawn Mel heard the muffled voices of ox-drivers, creak of harness, lowing of cattle; he rolled over and yawned while the oxen were yoked, and was asleep again before the wagon lurched into motion. During the day it was pleasant to sit and study in his tiny room, watching the riverside amble by; it was easy to visit between the wagons, which creaked along at half walking pace; it was even enjoyable to converse with Jac over coffee in the rear of the wagon, while Tossy drilled Chazz in Greek pronunciation at the other table, occasionally asking Mel for an interpretation.

Jacimus wasn't such a bad guy after all. He fully deserved his post as commander of his father's garrison, having earned it by valor and wisdom in battle, and skill in horsemanship and tactics. He treated Ruth like cut glass, and was perfectly gentlemanly and friendly toward his rival. Mel could hardly blame him for sharing his own opinion of Ruth, and in fact quickly grew to admire the man. His troops revered him. He would make some girl a wonderful husband. Just not *my* girl, Mel thought. Please!

Life would have been even more restful if not for the tension in the air.

The main source of tension was the anxiety of everyone in the caravan to escape Parthia before the political situation soured even further. Phraates IV Arsaces could not guarantee Zimri's safe-conduct or protection once he had left his plantations near Nippur, and even though Zimri was nominally in Roman territory west of the Euphrates, the border was ill-defined. His safety was illusory, or marginal at best. Zimri had made powerful enemies, and he could only guess what plots were afoot against him.

His wagons, though not as vulnerable as those of an ordinary mercantile caravan because of his private army, were slower and more tempting, carrying all the portable wealth of a rich and powerful noble and a hundred of his relations.

Not all were trained fighting cavalry, but every soul except the young or feeble was skilled on horseback and had been drilled in defense maneuvers. For example, they had been taught to flee in a cohesive formation, rather than scattering. Each helpless member of the clan was assigned one able-bodied guardian responsible to ride him or her out of trouble in a crisis.

The time travelers had to learn to ride too, and the sooner the better. This led to another source of tension.

The second morning after the Sabbath, Mel was sitting in the booth engrossed in trying to sketch plans and calculate flight parameters for an observation balloon that could be towed behind the fifth wagon. This scheme had come out of last night's brainstorming session; it envisioned a refined version of the Opis aircraft, with a proper basket and firepot.

Mel's calculator watch was doing yeoman service, unharmed by its immersions and buffetings. But even with the wagon temporarily halted he was having difficulty sketching on rough parchment with his Uniball Micro. He didn't want to blotch, because he wasn't sure how he would erase; and the plagued compass-string kept coming loose. He tied it tighter, jammed the other end under his left thumb, and carefully swept out what was meant to be a circle but stopped as an arc when it hit the lip.

Why now, groaned Mel, just when I almost—

The lip whickered, showing huge yellow teeth.

"Yipe!" Mel jumped back.

The lip was attached to the nose of a horse, whose long neck extended into the window over the table. Reins led from the bridle out the window, where Ruth held them loosely.

"Really involved, weren't you?" she asked.

Jacimus sat on an adjacent horse. All four intruders seemed to be trying to stifle laughter.

The wagon, which had been waiting in line at a ford, lurched forward. Ruth backed her horse away from the window.

"You and Chazz come outside and saddle up," she commanded. "Time for your riding lesson. Captain Jacimus is an excellent teacher. And right now is when he's available, so now's when you ride."

"Okay." Mel rolled up the parchment and clipped the pen into his pocket protector. He spoke to her in English. "You seem to be sitting easy on that beast. Private lessons?"

"Dad bought me a pony when I was eight," explained Ruth.

"What else can you do that I don't know about?"

"Mel, let's speak Hebrew, please? Just to avoid the appearance of rudeness?"

"But then Chazz will be left out," Mel said in Hebrew.

"Well, my Greek is still just about nonexistent. Anyway, who cares about Chazz? He's going to split, you'll see. He doesn't care about us."

"Ruth, I'm shocked!" said Jacimus.

Jac shocked? How much time was he spending with her, anyway?

"I just can't be bothered. He's safe; he knows the way home; he owns the computer; he'll be out of here in two days."

"One," Jacimus corrected. "Please, Ruth, this is not like you. The boy is entitled to courtesy, however foolish his goals, however brief his visit. Don't you like others to treat you with kindness?"

"I like to be spoiled rotten," admitted Ruth. "Okay, the golden rule. But if we speak English, you'll be left out. You, our benefactor: not Dennis the Menace here. I thought my choice was wisest."

"Soon Chazz will be gone, or we shall all speak Greek," Jacimus said. "In the meantime, let's muddle through with verbatim simultaneous translation."

"Are you talking about me?" asked the subject of their conversation, looking up from his Greek.

"Yes," said Mel. "Tell you later. Let's go saddle up."

Chazz scowled but, rising, set down his vocabulary list and followed Mel outside, where Jacimus held the traces of two frisky-looking horses.

"That one's got a wild eye," Chazz said. "They can sense fear."

"Then fear not," said Ruth. "Haven't you ever gone riding?"

"Riding in a circle on a carnival pony count? I did that when I was three. Granny Helga took me."

"Chazz, I'm afraid to ask," Mel said. "Was she your mother's mother?"

"How did you know? She's the reason I've got this nickname."

"I don't want to hear it. Well, Ruth, what next? I don't see any saddles."

"Unroll that blanket and toss it over the horse's back, then jump on. It's a cinch."

Mel grinned. "I thought a cinch was what kept coming loose so you could ride upside down."

"You are a card. Here, I'll show you." She dismounted, trailing her reins on the ground. The wagon having again halted, she led Wild-Eye alongside its back door, unrolling the blanket as she did so and draping it evenly on the horse. "Use the step."

Mel obeyed and managed to mount. The horse moved docilely aside as Ruth returned with the other. "Your turn," she said to Chazz. "Open your eyes or you'll fall off the step."

"Here goes." Chazz opened one eye, raised his leg and slid onto the horse, and off the other side. "Ow!"

"Grip her with your knees, and balance. Try again."

The fall onto the soft overgrown asphalt had not injured Chazz. He re-spread the blanket and tried again.

"Good. Now sit up." Chazz was hugging the mare's neck. He carefully rose to a sitting position, knees locked tight.

"Nothing to it," he said.

"Relax," advised Ruth. "Hold the reins loosely. And open your eyes."

"Let's try walking first," Jacimus suggested. "Head down toward the creek. No, Mel, don't pull the reins; just press with the opposite knee." Ruth translated for Chazz, and soon they reached the bank of the stream the caravan was fording.

Jacimus's wagon was now eighth in line. He continued straight ahead, wading his horse into the water. "Come on." He swept his arm. "It's not deep." Ruth followed him.

"If we must," said Chazz. He and Mel splashed into the muddy creek. The cool water reached their knees in midstream. They rode the ponies up the other bank and ahead to the lead wagon, Jacimus waving to the driver as they passed.

"Now let's go a little faster," he said. "It's safe ahead for a couple of miles—been scouted." He kicked his horse into a trot. The other horses followed his lead.

"Hey!" cried Chazz, leaning forward to hug his mare's neck in a death grip. "I was just getting used to that walking gait!"

Ruth drew back alongside him. "Sit up," she called. "Watch me. Lean forward just a little, like this."

Chazz tried it. Mel, following, could see daylight blinking under Chazz's seat as he bounced.

"Don't fight the motion; go with it. Relax. There, that's better. Good." Ruth fell back. "How're you doing?"

Mel, having caught the rhythm of the trot, replied, "Surviving." But his mind was elsewhere.

Now was his chance. Jacimus was fifty feet ahead. Ruth had been all business at the brainstorming sessions, ignoring Mel's feelers. He decided on a direct approach: Ruth, will you marry me? Well, maybe not that direct. This wasn't the right occasion, trotting along a muddy ox-trail with his rival and the Kid. Not quite romantic enough. "Ruth."

"Yes?" she asked, unsmiling.

"Ruth, I want to ask you—"

"Chazz! Watch out! Your blanket is slipping!" Ruth trotted up alongside Chazz, reached over and tugged at his saddle-blanket. "You okay?"

"I think…I'm getting…the hang…of it."

"Good." She fell back beside Mel once again.

Be quick, he told himself. They were catching up to Jac. "Ruth, I love you!"

"It can't work, Mel. I won't risk a jump."

"I don't care. I just want to stay with you."

"You say that now, but—"

"Think you're ready for a canter?" asked Jacimus.

How much did he hear? mused Mel. Doesn't matter: we were talking English. The Kid could have overheard us, but I don't care. It may even have spurred his conscience.

The lesson continued with a canter, then a few seconds of full gallop. "Enough for today," said Jacimus. "Let's go back. Don't worry about being stiff and sore. You'll get used to it. Tomorrow make sure your blankets have no wrinkles, or at least wrinkles in different places."

They rode slowly back toward the caravan for a minute or two before it appeared among the trees. Jacimus's wagon had crossed the creek. Good, Mel thought: my legs just dried off.

They reined in at the wagon. After helping Chazz and Mel dismount, Jacimus rode with Ruth and the two extra ponies toward the herd behind the barracks wagons at the rear of the caravan.

"I can't believe I really did that," said Chazz. "Rode a galloping horse bareback. Pretty good, huh?"

"You'll believe it tomorrow morning, all right."

"I'm limping already. By the way, what were you and the others saying about me?" They limped into the wagon, where Tosthenes greeted them with grape juice.

"When the four of us are together, we have a dilemma: whether to talk English and leave Jac out, or talk Hebrew and leave you out. We were discussing which to do."

"Oh. Was that all?"

"Well, no," Mel admitted. "We're worried about your taking off with the computer tomorrow, if that's what you've decided."

"Is that what's bothering her. Listen, don't worry. I've thought it all out, for a change. I am going to Seleucia tomorrow, but I'll be back. I made a commitment to go to Antioch and share the computer with you guys. I haven't forgotten it."

"What's your plan, then?"

"I'll ask my escort to wait while I fetch Scheherazade. It shouldn't take long, especially since I can jump back to a few minutes after I leave."

"You have that much control?"

"I ought to, if I can avoid the chaotic region. Twenty-year hops should be safe enough, and I can loop through a few dozen of those in just a couple of minutes, subjective time."

"If the computer works."

"Of course. I'm going to try it out tonight. It'll be as dry as it's ever going to get, by then."

"Chazz, I'll tell Ruth your plan. I'm sure it'll make her feel better about you. But it still leaves me uneasy. You'll never find—"

"Don't say that! Anyway, I must try. Look at it from my point of view: this is a lifelong dream of mine. If I don't give it my best shot, what am I? I've already thrown away my career, and I'm wanted by Interpol, as you pointed out. I can't stop now."

"How about this? Give it a finite time limit. Say a week."

"Six months. I'll agree to six months, subjective. If I can't find her by then, I'll come back and rethink my life. You won't notice the difference, anyway: for you it'll be a few days at most. And going to Antioch will at least get me out of Iraq. Won't it? Where is Antioch?"

"In Turkey. That might be worse. Chazz, I still don't think you've given this plan enough thought. Fifty or so twenty-year hops mean fifty exposures to totally unknown conditions."

"Only for a few seconds."

"Want to spend those seconds in the middle of a prairie fire? Or a battle? Besides, how will you even recognize Scheherazade?"

"By her beauty. And the circumstances. And our chemistry. Look, Mel, I know I'll know her. We belong together. It's kismet."

"A Lutheran's supposed to say, 'God will lead me to her.'"

"Yeah, all right, God will lead me to her."

"How do you know? Was this His idea in the first place, or yours?"

"I just know."

"But the paradox: If you don't let her tell her tales of the Arabian nights, how will you ever have read them? You'll never have heard about her."

"Oh, you think there are alternate universes, do you? That's silly. Speaking of silly, your mustache is growing back."

"Whole beard is. Can't help it. Yours isn't; how old are you, anyway?" asked Mel.

"Seventeen. Old enough to know what I want. Don't try to talk me out of this. And don't worry. I won't abandon you."

If you live, Mel thought.

"May I intrude?"

"Certainly, Tosthenes. What is it?"

"This." He drew out a scroll. "The book of Daniel."

"Good. That'll take my mind off my sore...anyway, I've been wanting to read it. Excuse us, Chazz: a little Bible study. Or would you...?"

"Not right now. I'll go work on my Greek. *Kalimera.*"

"*Kalimera*. Tosthenes! This is Square Hebrew! I can read it much faster than Daniel's Isaiah scroll."

"Good. This is the Masoretic text, as compiled by Ezra the Scribe five centuries ago."

"Let's skip to Belshazzar's feast. That's where I came in. 'Belshazzar the king made a great feast to a thousand of his lords, and drank wine before the thousand.' But he wasn't the king," Mel objected.

"While Nabonidas was away, he was. Read on."

"'Belshazzar, while he tasted the wine, commanded to bring the golden and silver vessels which his father Nebuchadnezzar had taken out of the temple which was in Jerusalem.'—Right! That's how we got caught. Zaran never expected anybody to look in the museum. Nobody would have, either, if Belshazzar hadn't decided to desecrate the sacred vessels." He read further. "Okay...okay so far. Right. A man's hand. We all saw it, not just the king. He was really shaken: I think he wet his...ah, lost continence. I don't know what he said, but the magicians showed up."

"Were they real magicians, or fakers? My experience with so-called—"

"I never believed in magic either, Tossy, but after seeing that hand write, I was more receptive. They were real enough! It was amazing, the things they could do. But they couldn't interpret the writing.

"Whatever they did say nearly caused a riot: 'Then was king Belshazzar greatly troubled, and his countenance was changed in him, and his lords were astonied.' I'll say. They were ready to lynch the seers."

"But the Queen—"

"Right. She showed up and recommended Daniel, just as it says here. And they sent for him. Afraid I can't vouch for the details, because everyone was speaking Akkadian, but Zaran translated Daniel's interpretation for me, and it looks correct in here. And sure enough, 'In that night was Belshazzar the king of the Chaldeans slain.'"

"How?"

"Fell on a Persian's sword, I was told," replied Mel. "I was a little suspicious of that at the time. It smacked of suicide."

"Very possible."

"Let's see what happened to Daniel after we left." Mel unrolled a few more inches of the scroll and read it. "Hey!"

"What's the matter?"

"So that's why—" Mel began. "I've got to show this to Ruth. Look, there she is now!" For, indeed, Ruth and Jacimus were riding past the window at that moment. "Ruth!"

The two riders reined in. "What is it, Mel? Jac has to get back."

"This won't take a minute. Come here and look at this."

Ruth looked at Jacimus, who nodded. They dismounted and climbed into the wagon, their horses matching velocities outside.

"Listen to this, Ruth: it was Darius the Mede, not some earlier king, who 'commanded, and they brought Daniel, and cast him into the den of lions.' No wonder Daniel didn't remember the lions' den. It happened after we met him! After the fall of Babylon!"

"I knew that," said Jacimus.

"I thought he didn't remember because he was just a boy when it happened," Ruth said. "All the Sunday school pictures…"

"Some boy," said Mel. "He was ninety years old."

"Wasn't that something you thought was an error in the Bible?" she asked.

"Guess I was wrong," admitted Mel. "Bible one, Mel zero."

"I seem to remember more than one."

"Okay, okay."

"How can the word of God contain error?" asked Jacimus. "Isn't logical."

"As your tutor in logic, master," Tosthenes said, "I recommend a refresher course. Do you not remember a fallacy called 'begging the question'? What proof exists that this is the word of God? Are the letters written in fire?"

"Some of them were, as a matter of fact," muttered Mel.

"Tossy, you old atheist—" Jacimus began.

"Skeptic."

"—must we go over this yet again? The internal evidence of the prophecies and their fulfillments still does not convince?" He turned to Ruth. "Show me a man who repeats the same quibbles again and again, and I'll show you one who has some sin he does not wish to give up." He grinned. "Tossy, to which sin do you cling so lovingly?"

"All of them," admitted Tosthenes.

Mel felt a curious resonance. "What does that signify? I'm afraid I can't see the logic myself."

"It is the implications," Tosthenes explained. "Once I admit that this scripture is the word of God, King of the universe, it is only rational that I obey the commandments therein."

"But that's only rational anyway," protested Mel. "Those ten commandments are a good guide for keeping out of trouble. They're fences around holes. Fall in one of those holes, and you've got a lot of grief."

"O Mel, my favorite agnostic, that was bravely spoken. Do you remember the first of those ten?" asked Ruth.

"Uh."

"'I am the Lord thy God, which have brought thee out of the land of Egypt, out of the house of bondage,'" quoted Jacimus. "'Thou shalt have no other gods before me.'"

"Well, I have no other gods," Mel claimed. "There are none."

"Too right," agreed Tosthenes.

"But a man will often worship one of them anyway," Jacimus said, "a nothing, a vapor." The Hebrew word reminded Mel of *idol*. "Mel, we must talk more of these fascinating matters, but just now I need to inspect my troops. Coming, Ruth?"

"Right." She rose to go, plunging Mel into gloom. "See you later." She and

Jacimus left the slowly-moving wagon, mounted, and rode away.

Tosthenes observed Mel for a minute in silence broken only by the muted creak of the wagon wheels and a barely audible muttering from the direction of Chazz's cubicle:

"*Den milo tin glossa sas kala...Parakalo milate arga...epanalabate...Pou ine to banio?*"

"Brood not," said Tosthenes eventually. "It's plain she loves you."

"To you it's plain. To Chazz. To Zimri. Why not to me? Why does she spend all her time with him? Is it that he's a believer? I would believe if I could, but I just can't. I haven't got the faith. And I can't force it; that would be phony."

"Nor can I. I have seen too much of the world to believe that a loving God rules all. What justice was it when Suren was slain by the very King Orodes he protected so ably from Crassus's legions? Or how justify the unfortunate fate of the hero Pacorus? But faith is not your problem."

"No?"

"Consider: a young, handsome, able captain of horse; from a good Jewish family—meaning one in which women are at least persons: a vivid contrast to otherwise in Parthia, I assure you!—moreover, this man is clearly infatuated with the exotic, lovely woman, whose like he has never seen. Is it any wonder that she should respond?"

"That's why I'm down. I haven't got a chance in hell."

"You are mistaken," Tosthenes insisted. "Only her fears cause her to—"

"That's enough Greek for a while," said Chazz, emerging from the forward compartment. "Still studying the Bible? Learn anything?"

"Daniel was in the lions' den," Mel informed him.

"I knew that."

"How's your Greek?"

"After two days? Give me a break! I can say 'Good morning,' 'Good evening,' and 'Where is the public bath?' Hope I don't need much more than that. I can read and write it, too, since I already knew the alphabet."

"Me too, from mathematics. And the terms of science should give us a head start on the vocabulary. Did you take science?"

"Physics and chemistry. They're required for math majors at Uppsala."

"Used to be required everywhere. Now it's a wonder math is."

"But I don't find much use for the terms 'light' and 'motion' in everyday colloquial discourse," said Chazz. "I know *tele* is 'far,' but I don't know how to say 'How far is the toilet?'"

"Just follow your nose," Mel suggested.

"My *otos*," translated Chazz. "Or is it *rhinos*? So much for the terms of science."

"Yeah, I get the Greek and Latin roots mixed up. Like 'television.' That's a mixture of both. It should be 'tele-opsis' or 'tele-skopsis' or..." Mel paused.

The same thought must have struck Chazz. "Wow! Do they have glass?"

"Tosthenes, do you have glass here?" Mel used the Hebrew word, *sechuchit*, not knowing how old it was.

"Of course. All you need is sand, potash, and a bellows. Women use it for adornment. There is not much other application."

"Oh yes there is."

20
Prophecy

After Tosthenes went off to perform a feasibility study of lensmaking, and Chazz retired to his room to write the program that would allow mid-course corrections every twenty years, Mel was no longer distracted. He again sank into melancholy. Was Ruth deliberately avoiding him? If so, there was no point trying to seek her out. How could he convince her that he wanted to stay with her no matter what?

Not that he wasn't more than ready to return to 1995 himself. But not without Ruth. He'd never met anyone like her. Aletha was sweet and clever, and her attentions were flattering, but Mel wasn't tempted. He was immunized by his love for Ruth…and by something else. He'd learned that Aletha was only fourteen. Girls must mature faster here. She looked and acted ready to be betrothed, but she wasn't that much older than Shoshana. That might be okay for these folk, but he wanted no part of it. It was frightening enough that he was teaching her mathematics.

Thinking of mathematics made him wonder about the problem of control of time-travel. Would it be safe for him to study the problem by himself? Was it only their synergy that threw Ruth and him wildly across time?

Or was it wild? Was there, as Kimu thought, a purpose in their arriving at this particular time? They had encountered Chazz again; was that mere coincidence? If only Mel could remember the exact words of Daniel's final prayer. He was sure that prayer had something to do with the specifics of their jump. He didn't know how, but neither did he know how simply thinking about Sophia's work could lift him into the covering space over Earth's orbit.

Chazz seemed to have a lot of control. Why not? He had read Sophia's lost paper. Did he carry it with him? Where? He didn't seem to have anything but his jacket and that damp computer.

Maybe it was stored in the computer, on the hard disk. Maybe Chazz would let him read it. Maybe it was in Tokyo, in his luggage. Maybe the computer would work, and maybe it wouldn't.

His thoughts were chasing their tails. He was tired of thinking. Tossy had a Septuagint someplace; he'd see what further adventures Daniel had had. He could practice his Greek at the same time.

Mel couldn't find the Septuagint anywhere in the public spaces of the wagon, and he didn't want to search Tosthenes' private room. However, the Square Hebrew scroll was still lying on the table. He unrolled it and began reading. Maybe the lions just weren't hungry at the time.

Wow! They were hungry, all right. He shuddered. How many lions *were* there? Daniel had been right: those beasts were dangerous. But God, he read, "...delivereth and rescueth, and he worketh signs and wonders in heaven and in earth, who hath delivered Daniel from the power of the lions."

Mel considered this. He needed deliverance himself. A prayer couldn't hurt. God, here there be lions, too. Please help us! Meet us here with your rescue!

He resumed reading, and was soon engrossed in the puzzle of baffling visions and prophecies, barely noticing when the wagon drew to a halt.

A spill of dark hair grazed his cheek. Aletha! She was bending close to see what he was reading: "Seventy weeks are determined upon thy people and upon thy holy city, to finish the transgression, and to make an end of sins…"

"Hi, how did you get here?" Mel asked.

"Peace. Did I awaken you? You looked so solemn, poring over this scripture. Have you now understood it fully?…for it is dinner-time. This is my message.

"Besides, how can you read in such gloom?" She smiled. Indeed, her clear brown eyes were widely dilated, and her teeth flashed white in the dimness.

"It has gotten dark, hasn't it? Never noticed. But I am hungry. What's for dinner?"

"I know not. Something tasty, I'm sure. Agnes usually surprises us, but always pleasantly." As he started to rise, she placed a hand on his arm. "Wait one moment. Truly, do you comprehend what you are reading? For I have long wondered at it. It's clearly a prophecy of something, but see, here..." She unrolled the scroll almost to the end, and read: "'But thou, O Daniel, shut up the words, and seal the book, to the time of the end: many shall run to and fro, and knowledge shall be increased.' To me it is a sealed book. But perhaps not to you, since you are from 'the time of the end,' the very generation of the second ingathering. Has your knowledge been increased? What do you think it means? I am curious."

"Well, whatever the prophecy means, it has long since been fulfilled. Seventy weeks is less than a year and a half."

"No, no," she protested, laying a finger gently on his lips. "These are sevens of years, not weeks of seven days. That much is clear. The word can mean seven of anything...a heptad, the Greeks would say."

"Like a decade. That helps. I was wondering how so much could happen in so few months—the commandment to rebuild Jerusalem, the Messiah coming and being executed, and the destruction of the city and the sanctuary. And who is 'the prince that shall come?' Is he the Messiah?"

"It would seem not. He doesn't behave as would Israel's Messiah: it is his people who destroy Jerusalem. And it is he who makes it desolate, for the overspreading of abominations."

"What does that mean?"

Aletha seated herself on the bench next to Mel. "We think it means something like what was done by Antiochus the Mad in the last century. In fact, it may refer to that very deed. He sacrificed a sow upon the altar of God in the Holy Place."

"A sow!" Mel shuddered.

"Mel, I know you're not a believer, but surely you've heard of this? It provoked a revolt by the Hasmoneans. Judas Maccabeus—"

"Hanukkah! Of course! No wonder the temple had to be cleansed. We always celebrated Hanukkah, with a dredel and a Hanukkah bush, but I never was too clear about when the event happened in history. So that's what Daniel meant."

"Part of it." She slid against him to reach for the scroll with both hands, rolling it back to his original place. The sleeve of her robe fell away from her arm, which brushed briefly against his chest as she turned the parchment. Mel cringed. "Note that the seventy weeks are subdivided: seven weeks, sixty-two weeks, and one week. The abomination of desolation is committed in the middle of that last week, thus sixty-nine and one-half weeks after 'the going forth of the commandment to restore and to build Jerusalem.' Well, we happen to know exactly when that was: the first of Nisan in the twentieth year of Artaxerxes, 3556. So, as you see—"

"What year is it now? I think I'm getting your drift."

"3995. Four hundred thirty-nine years later."

"And sixty-nine weeks would be, let's see, four hundred ninety minus seven equals four hundred eighty-three. I get it—it hasn't happened yet! The time hasn't run out yet. It's close, though; only one generation more. Think you can wait?"

"It appears I must, if you can shed no more light on it." Aletha smiled.

"I'd like to discuss it again, rack my memory, consult with the others over dinner." Mel moved to rise. This was getting dangerous: Chazz was in the front, out of sight. But she was blocking his way out, so he didn't get far. "They're not Jewish, though, so it doesn't—"

"Mel, you are a Jew." Aletha did not budge.

"Yes."

"What does that mean to you? Only a tradition?"

Mel thought for a moment. "Basically," he admitted, "I guess it's that I was born and raised a Jew…that is, raised in the tacit expectation that I would remain Jewish. Even though my parents were also non-practicing, they'd be upset if I were to 'defect.' And, come to think of it, I'd lose my Israeli citizenship, too."

"But it does not mean belief. As it did to Shadrach, Meshach, and Abed-Nego."

"I'd have to say no. But I don't believe in anything supernatural, so no idols, either. My motto is, 'There's always a scientific explanation.'"

"Really! Even for all the wonders you have recently seen? Even for the prophecies and their fulfillments? And what of the creation itself? The natural world? How could all its splendor have come about without God?" She gripped his arms and looked directly into his eyes.

She was a good part of that splendor herself. "Aletha, there are reasons I won't go into to doubt even that. I don't want—"

"There's always a reason to doubt!" Her eyes flashed. "Why not a reason to believe? Look at me, Mel." Now she was pleading. "What would you lose if you truly worshiped the God of Abraham, Isaac, and Jacob?"

Bacon cheeseburgers, Mel thought. But she had a point. He certainly wouldn't lose his cultural tradition: if anything, it would be enhanced. His family wouldn't disown him. And she seemed to be hinting that he might have a great deal to gain. But all those rules! He opened his mouth to say something, anything; he wasn't sure what. But just then a cry of pain pierced the dark air.

"Chazz, you okay?" called Mel.

"Just bumped my head on a shelf. Must have dozed off."

"It's suppertime anyway."

Chazz emerged clutching a small scroll. "It's essentially done. I was only touching up the interface. Cosmetics."

They climbed down the back steps and started walking forward through the fragrant twilight. One bright star had already appeared, low in the west. Must be Venus, Mel thought. Another natural wonder. He certainly didn't want to kill Aletha's childlike faith by introducing her to the theory of evolution; that was one modern innovation that would have to await its time.

After dinner the three time-travelers retired to Aletha's wagon for their nightly "brain storm." They were joined this time by Tosthenes, but Aletha, after making them comfortable, courteously left. On the agenda was the third source of tension.

"The first order of business," Chazz said. He opened his computer. "Aardvarks bright?" He toggled it on.

The screen lit up. The words POWER ON SELF TEST. CHECKING MEMORY: 128K, 256K, 384K, 512K, 640K appeared. The disk light glowed. After a second the screen blanked out and "C>" appeared.

"It works!" yelled Chazz. "It booted from the hard disk!"

"Hooray!" Ruth cried. She clapped her hands and beamed at Mel.

"Yea!" shouted Mel. "That's some laptop!"

"Sweet baby!" Chazz cried. "Mel, let's take her out for a spin." He typed TRILOGY. "Give me a problem you know the answer to."

"Six divided by three."

The integrated Trilogy environment screen, which Mel had first seen on the plane to Moscow, appeared. Chazz pressed a few keys. "Two!" he read.

"I knew that," said Ruth.

"It's working so far," Chazz said. "How about something harder?"

"Do you have a Julian day routine in there?" asked Mel.

"Sure."

"Okay, take March 14, 445 B.C., get the Julian day, add sixty-nine-and-a-half times seven times three hundred sixty-five-and-a-quarter days, and convert it back to the Gregorian date."

"What's all this? O.K., just a second." Chazz typed. The disk light flashed. A line appeared on the screen. "October 10, A.D. 42. What happens on that day?"

"The abomination of desolation."

"The what?" asked Ruth.

"Your guess is as good as mine," Mel admitted. "It's in Daniel."

"Never heard anything about A.D. 42. Chazz?"

"Nope. Ben Hur?"

"Well, at least the computer knows six divided by three equals two. It must be okay," concluded Mel. "Maybe we're doing something wrong: software problem."

"Maybe Tosthenes knows," Ruth suggested.

"Tossy, how much of that could you follow?" asked Mel in Hebrew.

"Little. The computer works. What are those? Numbers?"

"Yes. Do you know what's significant about A.D. 42? Let me rephrase that. The seventy-weeks prophecy in Daniel: we're trying to compute the date, and we're having difficulty."

"Well, a common error is to use a year with too many days. The 'prophetic year' has three hundred sixty days in it, like the degrees of a circle. Does that help?"

"Chazz, try replacing three-hundred-sixty-five-and-a-quarter with three hundred sixty in the program," Ruth said.

"And hey. Let's try sixty-nine instead of sixty-nine and a half," suggested Mel. "The last 'week' is mentioned separately, I remember."

After a brief wait, Chazz read, "Sunday, April 6, A.D. 32. What happens then?"

"Tosthenes, what happens at the end of the sixty-nine weeks?" asked Ruth.

"Messiah the Prince shall come."

Ruth translated for Chazz.

"Wait," cried Mel. "A.D. 32—Jesus Christ!"

"Yes, that is the Greek for it: 'God's anointed salvation.' But," Tosthenes admonished, "your accent needs work."

"Mel!" exclaimed Ruth. "That must be Palm Sunday! When Jesus rode into Jerusalem on a donkey—"

"And the people greeted him with palm branches, like a king!" finished Chazz.

"But that means your Jesus is the Jewish Messiah!" Mel protested. "Who ever heard of such a thing? Christians have persecuted Jews for millennia! They're entirely opposed!"

"And after that 'shall Messiah be cut off, but not for himself,'" added Tosthenes.

"That's him, all right," Ruth said. "That's the crucifixion."

"Wait, you guys. This is too much. There must be another interpretation."

"Mel, we met Daniel. Was he devious? Or was he a plain speaker?"

"He told it as it was, and was sharp as an arrow, to boot," admitted Mel. "But it can't be. It just can't."

"The evidence is in," Ruth said. "Or do you work on the principle 'sentence first, verdict afterwards'?"

"What seems to be the problem?" asked Tosthenes. "Too much English, too fast."

"We…some of us…recognize this figure," Ruth explained. "This prophecy will be fulfilled by a man who so changes the world that the years are numbered from his birth. Wait! Wait a minute! His birth! What year is this?"

"3995," replied the slave.

"Mel, what's that in Gregorian?"

"6 B.C."

"Oh. We'll miss it. Too early. I certainly don't want to stick around six years, even for that."

"You don't? Ruth, that's won—"

"It seems to me," Chazz interrupted, "that if you're talking about Christmas, the birth of Christ wasn't in zero B.C. or A.D. It was a few years off."

"Couldn't have been zero B.C.; there was no zero B.C.," agreed Mel.

"There was no zero, period," Ruth added mistakenly. "Wait, we can settle this. Tosthenes, who is governor in Syria?"

"C. Sentius Saturninus. He it is who is giving refuge to Master Zimri and his clan, in Valatha by Daphne."

"Who's this gal Daphne?"

"Wait a minute. Tossy, does the 'C' stand for 'Cyrenius,' by any chance?"

"Gaius."

"Oh. Well, that takes care of that. Wrong period. Even a Christmas-and-Easter Christian like me knows that much from Luke Two: 'Cyrenius was governor of Syria.'"

"Daphne," Tosthenes replied to Mel's question, "is not a 'gal,' but a beautiful, exclusive suburb of Antioch, south of the Orontes River."

"How nice for Zimri!" said Ruth.

"Sentius is a good friend," Tosthenes explained. "And he appreciates military prowess. Zimri is one of the few who still apply the wisdom of Suren. In his battle against Marc Antony—"

"Now cut that out!"

"I tease you not. Antony was trying to besiege Praaspa without siege engines. Zimri served in the archery unit that chased Antony almost to Armenia, harrying him with more arrows than he expected. Why do you think our caravan includes so many camels?"

"Don't tell me just to carry arrows," Mel begged.

"Just to carry arrows."

"That makes me quiver," said Ruth. "Sorry, couldn't resist."

"You seem to be in fine feather," Mel observed. "That's the happiest you've looked in five hundred years."

"I must admit I'm relieved about the computer. And Chazz's plan. You will take care now, Chazz, won't you? Don't get lost, don't get killed, and don't forget to come back."

"Do you love me for myself alone?" Chazz asked, smiling. "Or do I detect an ulterior motive?"

"Well, I admit it," replied Ruth. "But even if you have to throw the computer to the wolves, we want you back safe and sound."

"I'll be fine. I modified the program to give me a preliminary glimpse of the situation before committing."

"How does that work?" asked Mel.

"I jump twenty years ahead for a quarter-second and automatically jump back. Only if it looks safe do I then jump and wait to stabilize. Otherwise, I try again at nineteen years, eleven months. And so forth."

"Sounds pretty safe," Mel conceded.

"Just don't blink at the wrong time," warned Ruth.

21
Baldy

The next morning, Chazz sat heading a mounted column of sixteen light cavalry archers ready to escort him to Seleucia, twenty miles east on the Tigris. His computer was secured in a well-padded saddlebag strapped around his pony's neck. Half a mile to the east, the Euphrates glinted in the dawn light. Birds rioted. Ahead, the temple towers of Neapolis gleamed on the horizon.

Mel stood near Chazz. "Keep your powder dry, this time," he advised.

"Right, don't worry, I will."

Riding up to Chazz's other side, Ruth leaned close and hugged him. "Follow your dream. Don't worry about us."

Jacimus, Zimri, and Aletha made their farewells. Zimri, standing with his wife next to Mel, had already asked God to protect Chazz in his journey. The caravan was in the last stages of breaking camp to move on into Neapolis, where they would rest an extra day to await the squad's return.

Bathyra moved toward Chazz. "My son—" she began.

A cry pierced the air. From far down the baggage-train a figure on horseback raced a cloud of dust toward them.

Jacimus wheeled his horse around and galloped to meet the rider. As he drew close, he appeared to recognize the newcomer, hailing him and turning to accompany him as he rode back to where Zimri waited.

Mel had never seen him before. But Zimri recognized him. "Ho, Baldy!" he shouted. "Welcome, friend! What is your news? Trouble?" Baldy's horse was drenched with sweat and blowing lather. Not an archer's pony, this beast was one of the biggest horses Mel had ever seen. For all its power, the fine Nesæan charger was barely equal to its burden: a burly giant in chain mail shirt and hose, wearing a conical helmet with iron-mesh veil. The horse, staggering as if ready to drop, was also draped in mail.

The giant dismounted, removed his helmet, and wiped his hand across a shiny, perfectly bald scalp, calloused by the iron.

"See to the horse, Arik," ordered Jacimus. "Try to save him."

"Zamaris, old friend," the bald one said, striding toward Zimri with a metallic rustling sound. "At last I've caught up with you. I may yet be in time."

"What is the matter?"

"Your enemy is upon you. His scouts cannot be more than three hours behind me. Mithradates has returned."

"The usurper!" exclaimed Jacimus.

"Aye, and he has leagued himself and his army with the priests of Zoroaster. As we speak, they pursue you."

"How many?" Zimri asked. "On which bank of the river?"

"Two thousand light archery, a hundred clibanarii, I know not how many infantry, making speed up the left bank. Flee, my friend! They mean to exterminate your clan."

"How are they supplied?"

"For only a brief sortie. They travel fast and light."

"Do they know you rode to warn me?"

"I think not. I slipped away at night."

"Then perhaps we can escape." Zimri turned to his son. "Start the caravan. Head straight west, into the desert. Now."

Jacimus saluted and rode over to the lead driver.

Zimri turned to Mel. "Inform your friend that we can no longer spare his escort. We now flee for our lives. I'm sorry, but he must change his plans."

Jacimus, returning from where the lead driver was goading his oxen into a tight turn, overheard. He called to his adjutant, who led the escort. "Tars! The Seleucia trip is canceled. Battle stations, at once."

"Yes, sir!" The adjutant barked an order to his squad. They performed an amazing right-flanking maneuver on their horses and galloped rearward in two ranks, to join their army.

"Hey!" Chazz yelled. "What's going on?"

"Sorry, buddy," said Mel. "Emergency. Your excursion is canceled. We'll be lucky to get away with our lives."

"No!" Chazz shouted. "So close! I can't stand it!" He clutched his mount's neck, kneed him fiercely, and spurred away eastward at a gallop.

"Chazz!" yelled Ruth, starting after him.

"Ruth! Come back!" Jacimus reared back on his horse and wheeled around to follow her.

"Aletha!" cried Mel. She rode over. He reached for her hand, grasped it, and tugged her sprawling off her pony. "Sorry!" Mel leaped aboard her horse and joined the pursuit.

"West!" Zimri called after them. "I said west!"

Mel quickly overtook Jacimus, who had caught up to Ruth and was reaching for her reins. Jac clutched them and skidded both mounts to a halt.

"Let me go! Get away!" Ruth screamed, beating fiercely at his hand with her riding-crop.

Mel thundered past, not waiting to see how it came out. He crested a rise. There was Chazz, down by the Euphrates, casting back and forth looking for a place to ford the river.

"This time he wants to make sure his computer stays dry," Mel muttered grimly. "Good, that slows him down." He pounded down the hill toward Chazz, drew alongside, grabbed his arm, and pulled.

Both riders fell to the ground. Unfortunately, Mel landed underneath. "Aaaphhh!" he grunted, the wind knocked out of him.

Chazz leaped to his feet, ran to his horse, and drew the computer out of its bag. He opened the case. "Aardvarks bright!"

Mel struggled to his feet. Chazz was going to disappear! Escape into the future! Summoning a reserve of strength, he ran.

Chazz, cradling the computer, typed a frantic command. Still ten feet away, Mel watched in anguish as Chazz laughed maniacally and pressed 'Enter.'

22
Flight

As Mel returned over the rise, he saw that Jacimus had managed to move Ruth from her pony to his own, and was clasping her firmly about the waist. Aletha had found another mount and was galloping toward them. Seeing Mel, she halted. Both girls wore dark scowls. Jac had the beginnings of a black eye.

"I have some good news and some bad news," Mel called.

The good news became evident, and the girls' countenances brightened considerably, as Chazz rode over the crest of the rise behind Mel.

"Hallelujah!" said Jacimus, grinning, and wincing. "You got him!"

"What's the bad news?" asked Ruth as they rode up.

"The battery is dead."

"No!" Ruth protested.

"It's a NiCad," Chazz explained. "Nickel-Cadmium with potassium hydroxide electrolyte. Wonderful batteries. They last and last, and even recharge slightly when idle. Their discharge curve is nearly flat, until the end. When they go, they go."

"Chazz fired up the computer," said Mel. "He was going to slip away."

"I typed the command name, glanced up, and pressed 'Enter.' Nothing happened. When I looked at the screen, it was dark. That's that. I guess it's up to you guys now."

"Aardvark's dead," Ruth murmured softly. A tear rolled down her cheek. With a sob she relaxed back into Jacimus's arms.

"Sorry again. I won't cause any more trouble," said Chazz.

"We're wasting time," warned Jacimus. "Come." But he didn't relax his hold on Ruth.

I should have hand copied Sophia's paper, Mel reproached himself. Or at least read the crucial part, instead of being satisfied to see that it was there.

"Hurry," urged Jacimus. As they approached the camp they saw that the wagons were traversing a wide arc, traveling at twice normal speed toward an empty western horizon. Jacimus's wagon was already some distance away.

How was this going to work? Mel wondered. He couldn't picture wagon wheels making any speed through sand dunes. Maybe there was a track.

They reached the line of march. "Mel, take Chazz to my wagon and both of you stay in it, out of harm's way," Jacimus ordered.

Out of your way, you mean, thought Mel.

"Just let the horses go. They'll come back. Ruth, you ride very well; will you serve as courier?"

"I'll do all I can."

He swung down. "Here." He lifted Ruth onto her pony and remounted his own.

"Wait a minute!" Mel protested. "I want to help too. I'm...I was in the IDF, the Israel Defense Force. I studied tactics."

"All right. But Chazz sits in my wagon for the duration."

"Chazz," said Mel, "ride to our wagon and stay there. Your mission is to safeguard the computer."

"Oh, sure. If this ever fell into enemy hands, it'd be devastating. You just want me out of the way."

"Too right. And you won't cause any trouble, remember?"

"I remember." Chazz rode forward.

"Come, then. Quickly," said Jacimus to Mel and Ruth. They followed him to the headquarters wagon, between the troop carriers and the horse herd.

Zimri was already there with Tars and an orderly. He looked up from a map when they entered. "What is this? We have urgent matters to attend to that preclude socializing."

"No frivolity intended, sir. Ruth is an excellent horsewoman and has volunteered to ride courier for us. Mel has a military background, including the study of tactics."

"We do need every soldier we can get," Zimri granted. "Ruth can release Kimu for archery duty. And the tactics of the future may be of some use. Have you studied desert warfare?"

"The battle of El Alamein. Rommel's panzers."

"Panzers?"

"I'm not sure that battle's directly applicable," admitted Mel.

"All right. Your mind is good, Tosthenes tells me. You can sit in. If you catch us in a mistake, say so."

"Thank you, sir."

"Orders, father?"

"You have a difficult task. Take all the cavalry and ride into Neapolis from the east. Better cross the river here, then cross back below the city. Ride in with great pomp and ceremony. Make sure they know it's the army of Zamaris the Jewish Wolf. Be arrogant."

"Sounds easy so far."

"Remember, Mithradates thinks we know nothing of his approach; behave accordingly. Act as if you had ample time. Hire two nights' lodging for the officers. Then comes the difficult part."

"Yes?"

"Sneak out the back door as inconspicuously as possible. Leave a skeleton guard around the area of your lodging to keep anyone from seeing that there's no one there. Trickle out the western gate and rejoin us...here." Zimri jabbed a point on the map. "Just past this defile in the hills, and to the left."

"I see. Mithradates will naturally assume we stopped in Neapolis."

"I want nothing to show we didn't. Detail some civilians to follow the wagon train, brushing out our tracks and their own."

"He'll think we rode up the left bank anyway."

"Correct, and your trail will confirm it. Now go. You should be back before the ninth hour."

"Yes, sir." Jacimus went.

"I hesitate to mention this," Mel offered, "but I was taught never to divide my forces in the face of the enemy."

Zimri smiled. "So was Mithradates."

By noon the western horizon had resolved into a ripple of low hills marking the boundary of the Euphrates flood plain. Zimri apparently knew the countryside well, for the caravan was headed straight for a low pass in the hills. So far the oxen had made no difficulty pulling the wagons over the hard-packed alluvial pan. In fact, the unrutted way was somewhat easier going than the regular ill-paved trade route. Still, the accelerated pace could not be maintained for long, and there was trackless steppe ahead: the Syrian Desert, a stony hamada of lava outcrops and gravel beds. The only route through this waste, far to the north, led to the oasis at Palmyra, over a week away.

None would expect Zimri to try to escape by this route, not even Mel. When he learned the geographic situation, he waited patiently for an opportunity, then asked: "What's the plan?"

"We're outnumbered five or ten to one. By Parthians, not just Romans. So we'd lose a face-to-face battle. Besides, they have heavy cavalry. They would truly exterminate us."

Mel swallowed.

"Nor could we hide two hundred wagons in open country, not for long," Zimri continued. "Among yon hills, there is a chance."

"Can we reach them in time?" Mel asked.

"It has been five hours since Balthasar arrived," said Zimri. "We must assume our ruse succeeded, or Mithradates would have caught us ere now. He was only three hours behind Baldy."

Baldy, eh? Mel smiled to himself. It appeared nicknames had been in use practically as long as names had. "Who is Baldy, anyway?"

"A neighbor of mine in Nippur," Zimri replied. "A semi-retired clibanarius, and a good friend. As you see. He loved that horse."

"So Mithradates is parked at Neapolis?"

"Yes, and he is in the position of Antony before Praaspa."

"No siege-engines," guessed Mel.

"You have heard of that campaign? Correct, else he would make short work of that city's defenses. As it is, to construct an earthen ramp fit to bear cavalry over the wall, he must employ his mailed clibanarii. And many of those will fall to the arrows of the Neapolis militia."

"There's something I don't understand," Ruth mused. "Neapolis will admit the army of Zamaris the Jewish Wolf, but repel Mithradates?"

"They know that usurper of old," explained the Wolf. "Every man's hand will be against him. When word reaches Arsaces' Arabarch that he has returned, he'll be put to rout in short order. Again. He doubtless found it opportune that the priests of Zoroaster would ally with him in return for his help in wreaking their vengeance against me."

"So while he shovels mud..."

"We hide," Zimri said. "Night will bring a new game."

Small units of Jacimus's detachment began to straggle in around two in the afternoon. At three, Jacimus himself returned.

"Remarkable, Dad, how well-concealed this camp is. The cousins did a good job covering your tracks: I almost rode right by. And whose idea was it to pull the wagons into a circle?"

"Mel suggested that. It does seem more defensible, doesn't it? But let's pray it doesn't come to that. What news of Mithradates?"

"His scouts appeared about the fourth hour, right on schedule," Jacimus said. "They demanded the Wolf be turned over to them. The militia replied with a flight of arrows. Soon after, the main force showed up, and began digging. The clibanarii didn't look too pleased—arrows falling like hailstones seeking chinks in their armor while they, after a two days' ride, and covered in mail, scrape dirt in the midday sun."

"Didn't they surround the city?" asked Mel. "How did you get out?"

"We'd already left," Jacimus explained. "On our arrival, we were warmly greeted by the Neapolitans. While we were riding in through the eastern gate in all pomp, diverting the attention of the populace, those first in were already sneaking out the western gate. A few remained to alert the militia that the enemy was coming, spread the rumors, and guard our empty district. If Neapolis harbors any sympathizers of Mithradates, they will be deceived.

"We backed off a mile to the northwest and hid in a canal, watching to see what happened."

"Did the telescope help?" asked Mel.

"Wonderfully well. That's how I spotted the scouting party. Have you any more little devices like that up your sleeve? Something that destroys siege engines from a safe distance would be appreciated." Jacimus smiled.

"Sorry, but I don't know the recipe for gunpowder," Mel confessed. "We'll see what we can come up with, though."

"Maybe we do have a chance to survive," said Ruth.

"Survive? Yes, a chance, unless we grow overconfident," Zimri cautioned. "And we must be sure that Mithradates learns of my absence before he can breach the wall."

"And of the reinforcements. I spread the Syrian rumor. It may well even be true. I also sent out two couriers with the news of Mithradates' return, to find the Arabarch. If he can be found, and is able, he will indeed come. In any case I made sure that Mithradates' soldiers heard he was on his way."

"What is the Syrian rumor?" asked Ruth.

"Why, that Saturninus has sent the Sixteenth Legion from Syria to escort his good friend the Wolf to Antioch," Zimri replied. "And that this army is expected in Neapolis at any moment."

"The rumor had some effect," remarked Jacimus. "Shortly after the knights started digging, a small scouting party departed the enemy camp heading north."

"Then Mithradates must know by now that the rumor is false," Mel pointed out. "At least that the Syrians' arrival is not imminent."

"I don't think so. Those scouts didn't return."

"Good work, my son!" Zimri beamed. "Now we must do some estimating. How long did the ride from Neapolis take you?"

"Almost an hour. Of course, I went slowly, at first."

"And the progress of the ramp?"

"Slow. I'd guess six to ten hours before it's finished."

"Six hours is barely enough time." Zimri frowned. "We don't want them charging into the city before you can return to lure them away. Let's hope they're slower than you think. Perhaps they'll tire."

"Excuse me," said Mel. "How high is the city wall?"

"Twenty cubits."

"How wide is the ramp, and how far back did they start it?"

"It's narrow: they're in a hurry. Say five cubits on top. Barely room for two heavy cavalry units abreast, or four infantry. And they started a hundred cubits away. Well within bowshot."

"Okay, hold on a minute, please." Mel mumbled: "Thirty by one-fifty, that's forty-five hundred, by eight—no, better make it seven, that's thirty-one and a half thousand; divide by two, fifteen thousand seven hundred fifty." He turned to Jacimus. "A hundred armored laborers?"

"Yes."

"Thank you." Mel didn't like what he saw: if each worker had to move only one hundred fifty-seven cubic feet, they'd be done in no time. Zimri and Jacimus had returned to a discussion of probable timings of events to come. Mel sketched a ramp on a scrap of parchment. "Ruth," he asked quietly, "can you please look at this? I don't trust my calculations."

"Is that your model?" she asked. "That looks more like a wedge. It's too steep at the sides. The dirt will collapse."

"Of course. What was I thinking of? Here, if I add sides, like this, tapering back…a thirty-sixty-ninety right triangle…take the average, it'll be fifteen feet high, about twenty-six feet wide, a hundred fifty feet long. Two of them: an extra fifty-eight thousand five hundred cubic feet. That's not right."

"Yes it is. Look, you drew your wedge way out of proportion," Ruth pointed out. "It should look tall and skinny. Most of the mud will be in the side supports."

"So that's," Mel summed, "seventy-four thousand two hundred fifty cubic feet. With lots of assumptions."

"Seems conservative to me."

"Good. And three sixty into that is over two hundred cubic feet a minute, to finish in six hours. Can they move dirt that fast?"

"We need more information. Size of shovels, mean distance to carry dirt, fatigue. Still, I'd say no," Ruth guessed. "Figure a shovel is half a cubic foot: that's one every fifteen seconds for every digger."

"I think they could do it, meaning that Jac's estimate was pretty good in the first place," admitted Mel. "I was hoping for a narrower range."

"He's done this before."

"Still—" Mel addressed Jacimus. "Excuse me, but if I could have more information on the ramp-building operation?"

"Let's see," Jacimus obliged. "Their shovels are like ours. Tars, please fetch a shovel to show Mel. They haven't many: ten or twelve."

"Then how…"

"Not having carts, or enough shovels, they move earth by bucket brigades extending up the ramp, sheltered by a human tortuga of mailed knights holding shields aloft. They're also protected by light archery, but the bowmen on the walls have the advantage of height and cover, of course."

"Well, there go most of our assumptions," said Ruth.

"Let's see your sketch," Jacimus requested. "That's about right. Their ramp is not so wide: steeper on the sides. But it's essentially as you show it."

Tars entered with a spade. It appeared to hold about half a cubic foot of mud.

"I guessed right on that, at least," said Ruth.

"What are they using for buckets?"

"Shields. When I left they had twenty men in each of four columns dumping a load every second."

"Okay. There'd be spillage," said Mel, "but let's say two cubic feet a second."

"And gaps when an arrow removes a man from the line," Jacimus pointed out.

"Well, seventy-two hundred into seventy-four thousand two hundred fifty is over ten hours. At earliest."

"Parallel processing beats pipelining every time," said Ruth. "Good thing they don't have enough shovels."

"Don't forget," Zimri put in, "that as they approach the wall, the ramp itself will afford some protection. They will shorten their lines and use more of them...perhaps even dig with their shields."

"And that's where the bulk of the dirt's needed," added Jacimus. "Still, perhaps my low estimate was too conservative."

"Let's hope so. We need them stalled until the eleventh hour, assuming it will take them two hours to reach their western camp."

"Their western camp?" Mel asked.

"I intend to lure them west, to a spot north of us, at a time when it is too dark to search us out. There they must encamp."

"The main thing is to divert them before they can enter the city," Jacimus said. "They would kill everyone in it."

Mel saw Ruth shudder. He felt cold himself. This was risky business. They weren't playing games.

"To provide a margin of safety, you had better leave immediately," recommended Zimri. "Take fresh horses and save their strength for the return trip. God go with you."

"Thank you, sir." Jacimus strode out the door.

"What can we do?" Mel wanted to know.

"Nothing, until they return. Or, rather, there is one thing."

"What?" asked Ruth.

"Pray for a miracle."

23
Gideon

At dusk the detachment returned.

"Praise the Lord!" cried Zimri. "You lost them!"

"We finally lost them in a maze of hills," Jacimus agreed, dismounting, "but for a while it was risk and run." A crew of children ran up to take the horses.

"Have they given up the chase?"

"Probably, by now. We last saw them two miles north of here, heading away."

"Rest now. Eat. The equipment is ready. We have at least an hour to wait for full dark. Then we shall take out their guardposts. Come, tell me of the siege."

Mel and Ruth followed them into Zimri's wagon, where the women were setting out dinner. Jacimus sank gratefully into his place at the table. Zimri thanked God. After waiting for a few minutes to let Jac unwind, he asked, "What happened?"

"Our estimates were way off," Jacimus said. "The ramp was already finished when we got to where we could see it, from the canal north of the city. While we rode into range, the clibanarii were mounting for their charge. We stood on the north bank of the canal and lobbed a few arrows into the enemy troops, to get their attention, yelling 'Greetings from the Wolf!'

"But the clibanarii didn't notice us. They charged. We saw we could lose the city while waiting for them to see us, if even one of them got inside and opened the gate.

"So a few of us crossed the canal and launched an attack through their infantry at the side of the ramp that was protected from the wall. But we knew we were too late." He paused for a deep draught of juice.

"Too late!" cried Aletha.

"That poor city!" said Ruth. "After they tried to help us!"

"Fret not," said Jacimus. "It soon became obvious the Neapolitans had some tricks to play. As the first knight reached the wall, his horse went out from under him. Then the whole top of the ramp collapsed. The defenders had sluiced a jet of water onto it from their reservoir! What a mess! Mud, horses, men, all in a kind of stew. And the ramp was useless, for the moment.

"Then they saw us. We got back across the canal with no losses, thanks to the surprise, chased by cries of 'Ormazd! They're out here!' and 'They're getting away!'

"Rather than start digging all over again, and probably fearful of Saturninus or the Arabarch, Mithradates sent his whole army after us." Jacimus wiped his brow as if sweating even at the memory.

"Soon we were strung out across the plain: our light cavalry, their light cavalry, their heavy cavalry, and I suppose their infantry, too. I didn't wait around to see. We had only five or ten minutes' lead.

"Thanks be to God, we maintained that lead, and got into the hills before they did. We had time to split and leave tracks in five different directions, all trending northward, then cross some rocks and work our way south again." He sighed and, pushing his chair back, stretched his legs out under the table. "I never would have believed it possible. Was someone praying?"

An hour before moonrise Mel found himself crawling, with all the other able-bodied men in Zimri's clan, through pitch darkness toward the enemy lines.

An advance party had already located and silently eliminated the guards posted around the camp.

"How do you know where they are?" Mel remembered inquiring.

"I ask myself where I would station them, given the lay of the land," Zimri had replied. "Then the tricky part is to make sure of including all the exceptions."

Mel hoped they had all been included. Well, Zimri was an old campaigner, and a survivor; he wasn't called the Jewish Wolf for nothing. And so far no alarm had been raised.

On the other side of this very hill, down in a wide meadow, the enemy rested after their forced march. Mel imagined he could hear snores.

And on the other side of the meadow, two hundred paces away, was another hill similar to this one; and on the other side of that, he hoped, Ruth was crawling as he was, face also blackened with soot, the lone woman in the assault. She was included because she had the only other wristwatch and had refused to give it up. It was synchronized with Mel's. When he held his near the lip of the pitcher he carried, the light from the lamp within showed that it was 8:51.

He reached the top of the hill. On both sides others, spaced about a yard apart, were also assembling along the crest in a great circle surrounding the camp of the enemy below, where all but a few apparently slept exhausted in the dim red glow of dying campfires.

Mel drew a fist-sized rock out of his pocket and set it on the ground where he could quickly find it by feel in the blackness. He raised his trumpet to his lips, and waited.

Peep—peep—peep—peep! his watch signaled. Nine o'clock. He took a deep breath and blew a resounding blast on the shofar. From across the valley he heard an echoing wail: Ruth was right on time. A fraction of a second later the whole circle reverberated with trumpet calls. Soldiers stirred in the camp below. Mel grabbed his rock. He smashed the pitcher, uncovering his lamp. Similar bright sparks appeared around the circle of hills. Grasping the parchment megaphone clipped to his belt, he roared, "The sword of the Lord, and of the Wolf!" Alternately yelling and blowing their trumpets, Zimri's men rose to their feet as one, lifting their lamps high. The clamor was tremendous.

The confused, half-asleep soldiers in the camp below cried out in alarm and milled about, swords drawn. Colliding with one another in the dark, they panicked and swung wildly. Howls of pain added to the tumult.

Now Zimri's five hundred archers, spaced around the meadow, loosed a volley of arrows at maximum distance toward the far sides of the camp. "The Wolf is among us!" rose the cry from below, as many of the feathered bolts found their marks in the dark. The enemy bowmen began shooting in desperation at random targets in the middle of their own seething mob.

While his archers fired flight after deceptive flight of arrows into the horde, Zimri's clan continued shouting and blowing their trumpets. The sound was lost by now in the screaming melee that was rapidly making a shambles of Mithradates' army.

Finally, the ring of lights parted at a point in the northwest quadrant and the arms of the arc retracted toward the southeast. At the same time, the sparks on that southeast side began a measured advance down the hillsides toward the meadow.

Seeing this, the surviving enemy soldiers broke and ran in terror toward the northwest. Some, retaining an atom of self-possession, were able to mount horses and ride out. Others were mauled under hooves or crushed in the stampede. Mithradates' headquarters pavilion burst into flame. The fire quickly spread to the priests' tents. The center of the meadow became a trampled mass of broken bodies, burning canvas, screaming horses, and fleeing troops. These last streamed into the desert as if pursued by demons.

Zimri whirled his lamp in a circle and flung it high into the air. It fell and smashed, spraying burning oil. At this signal his archers withdrew over the hills toward their mounts, tethered just south of the meadow. In a few minutes, they formed ranks and, equipped with the spare quivers lashed to their horses sides, thundered off toward the northwest in close pursuit of the decimated army.

Mel thrust his trumpet through his belt. Holding his lamp high, he began to circle to the right around the ring of hills, looking for the spark that was Ruth.

24
Lead-Acid

After escorting a shaken Ruth back to Aletha's wagon, Mel returned to Jac's. He found Chazz already there.

"There he is," Chazz greeted him. "Another survivor. Did you see Ruth? Is she okay?"

"Yes, but she's going to have nightmares. She says next time she'll stay home with the rest of the women."

"I hope there is no next time. That battle will haunt me for long enough."

"Me too. Even if our side took no losses, which I believe is the case."

"That in itself is amazing," marveled Chazz. "We must have been outnumbered five to one, yet we slaughtered them. Where did Zimri get that tactic, anyway?"

"He said something about Gideon vs. Midian. Something in the Scriptures."

"That figures. What advantage would a Jewish Parthian have over a Gentile Parthian? Answer: whatever tactics he could glean from the Hebrew scriptures. They'd be a big surprise to a follower of Zoroaster."

"Right, whereas standard Parthian tactics wouldn't. Still, it was risky," Mel said. "We really lucked out. Mithradates' troops must have thought the whole Syrian army was attacking."

"Any tactic is risky at five-to-one odds. Myself, I think it was an authentic miracle."

"Maybe it was. We did pray for one. But look, you said before the battle you had some kind of an idea. Want to discuss it now?"

"Why not. We're not going to get any sleep tonight anyway. Tossy isn't even back yet, let alone Jac."

"Shall we include Ruth?"

"Sure; it concerns her. Let's go see if she's up."

In fact, Ruth and Aletha were both still awake when Chazz and Mel arrived at their wagon. When they entered in response to Aletha's "Come in," Mel was surprised to find Ruth sitting on the sofa, sobbing in the younger girl's arms.

He'd seen sabras, native Israelis, react similarly. "Tough desert cactus" or not, women weren't meant to go into battle. Even "liberated" women.

"Ruth." He put his arm around her shoulders. "Come on, honey. It's okay." He held her wordlessly for a moment, while her sobs subsided. "What's the matter? You weren't feeling this bad before."

"I guess I was numb. It just hit me."

"It's bothering me too," Mel confessed. "I try not to think about it. They would have done worse to us."

"I know, but—"

"Look, we came over because Chazz has an idea about the computer."

"He does?" Ruth looked up with a glimmer of hope.

"I don't want to get your hopes up prematurely," said Chazz, "but I've been thinking about this all day in the wagon, and I need your help. There are still parts I don't know how to do."

"Should I leave?" Aletha asked.

"No, please stay," begged Ruth. "You've been such a comfort."

"You may be able to help," Mel added. "Chazz, what's your idea?" He motioned for the young man to sit down.

"Well, the computer seemed to be working fine. All it needs is a battery charge."

"Sure, just plug it in the wall," suggested Mel. "Why don't we use it to go up to the twentieth century and find an outlet?"

"Wait!" Ruth cried. "Chazz, how sensitive is it? Does it need one-ten AC?"

"Holy smoke. Chazz, have you actually thought of a way to charge the battery? AC in B.C.?"

"At least DC. Maybe. It depends on what we can find around here. But no, it isn't too particular. House current would work, but I can also use DC if I bypass the adapter. Just a few volts, trickle charging it for half a day or so, and it'd be good as new."

"Just a few volts of electricity?!" exclaimed Ruth. "That's all that's standing between us and home? Surely we can generate that."

"You'd think so, wouldn't you? But how?"

"A hand-cranked generator?" Mel offered. "Or horse-powered?"

"There's no shortage of willing hands, or hooves, here," agreed Ruth. "But you've thought about this, and you see some snag, right? What could go wrong? I don't know much physics, but I certainly do know Maxwell's equations, and I know all you have to do is move a wire past a magnet and you get an electric current."

"Right there are two possible snags: a permanent magnet, and lots of good wire. I don't know if we can find or make either one of those."

"Wait," said Mel. "I seem to recall you don't need a permanent magnet."

"Yes, there's some way to wind it so you get an electromagnet that provides the field. We could probably find that by experiment if not theory. It's the wire we'll have trouble with. I don't think they can draw wire to any great length, here."

"And insulation," Mel pointed out. "It's got to be insulated wire."

"Things we take for granted," agreed Ruth. "And brushes! Don't forget brushes. Hard graphite blocks, machined smooth."

"And tough little springs to hold them against the armature," Chazz added. "Not to mention bearings."

"Spring steel! Ugh! Well, Chazz, let's have it," prompted Mel. "You've obviously thought of an easier way."

"I hope it's easier. A battery. Lead-acid. They have plenty of lead. All we need is sulfuric acid."

"Of course! Sure!"

"Is that all!" Ruth cried in relief. "They must have that here. Sulfuric acid is common."

"And has been for a long time," agreed Chazz. "'Oil of vitriol,' the alchemists called it. The only thing is, I don't know *how* long."

"Let's ask Aletha," Ruth suggested. "Can you describe it?"

"Sure. It's a heavy, oily liquid. Reacts violently in water. Dissolves metals, except gold. Smells bad; in fact, it burns your eyes and nose, as you might expect."

Aletha had never heard of such a substance. "But let me inquire among our metal-workers," she volunteered. "Or perhaps Tosthenes would know."

"Tossy! Of course!" agreed Mel. "After the short work he made of that telescope, he'll have us a car battery in no time."

"How did he make a telescope so fast?" Ruth inquired. "I've been meaning to ask."

Good, thought Mel, she was distracted from thinking about the battle. For the moment. "He found a jeweler who had a few lumps of glass . . . cullet saved for the next batch" he said. "He cast the lenses in the bottom of a smooth glazed pot. They came out flat on one side, of course. Polishing took a long time, but the tricky part was mounting them coaxially in those two tubes. Then it just took Jac a little practice to get used to seeing the world upside-down."

"Well, that ties it," declared Ruth. "We've changed the future. Good-bye Galileo."

"It doesn't work that way," Chazz insisted. "Anyway, if you think early optics will have an impact, what about early electricity?"

"Yeah, that'll really be shocking," said Mel.

"What's the matter?" Aletha asked. "Why did everyone groan?"

It was not that Jacimus was particularly noisy when he came in, exhausted, at four a.m. No, what woke Mel and Chazz were the shouts greeting the entire complement of one hundred archers who returned at the same time.

"We purged the land of them," Jac said, unstringing his bow. "An army of stragglers." Gore dripped from his sword as he wiped it with an oiled cloth. "Like target practice." He poked a clean cloth through his leather scabbard with an iron rod, and tugged it, no longer clean, out the small hole in the tip. "The heart was gone out of them." He stood his empty quiver in the corner rack next to his bow. "Lots of business for the fletchers."

"You killed all your enemies?" Mel asked, yawning. "That's good. Now I guess you'll turn around and go home."

"Can't. Still in exile. Remember the 'Law of the Medes and Persians'? Well, Phraates has the same conceit. Likes to pretend he's in the line of the Achæmenids. Won't change his mind.

"And I think my father wants to try living somewhere a little more civilized now. Parthians are good fighters, but their empire is declining."

"Did the Arabarch ever show up?"

"Never did find him. Probably putting down a rebellion somewhere else. See, that's what I mean. Dad's going to try to help matters a little, though: one last contribution to stability. Put the fear of God into these rebels, if Phraates takes advantage of it."

"How?"

"Mithradates is dead. We came across his body. Dad thought it would be edifying to leave it for Phraates as a present."

The next day they returned to Neapolis. After the jubilant city hosted them at a victory feast, Balthasar went about his business, purchasing materials in the town. Mel and Ruth accompanied him to see the sights, while Chazz was closeted with Tosthenes, exploring sulfuric possibilities in a halting but improving pidgin of Greek and English.

Baldy spoke good Hebrew. Though he had no professional dealings with Jews, he had been socially acquainted with Zimri, or "Zamaris" as he called him, for many years. "Ever since he took this old Babylonian bachelor under his wing. I had been lonely, I confess. My profession, though necessary, made me rather an outcast. Zamaris is about my only real friend."

"You certainly repaid his friendship," said Ruth. "Sorry about your horse."

"Hammurabi died a hero's death. What a great-hearted steed! It won't be easy finding a replacement for him. In fact, it will really be impossible. After so many years of care and training, he could almost anticipate my commands. He saved my life in many a battle. Perhaps I ought to retire from the reserve militia, and devote full time to business. The Romans will have their own war tricks, anyway, and I'm a little too set in my ways to learn them."

"You're coming to Antioch, then?" Mel asked.

"Yes. Zamaris offered me a place in his household, nominally as his bodyguard, but I think I'd prefer to set up my own establishment. There's always a call for my services. More and more, lately, it seems."

"What do you do?" asked Ruth.

"I'm an embalmer. I'm shopping for the things I need to gift-wrap Mithradates."

Ruth bravely did not wince, and it proved fascinating, though grisly, following Baldy into the charnel district, in a remote corner of the city, to see what materials were required for the preparation of a body for burial. But she politely declined to observe the actual process.

The local practitioners seemed to be unusually busy, probably because of yesterday's battle at the city wall, so they had no objection to Baldy's freelancing.

"We can take these with us," Baldy said, loading the pannier on their donkey with several jars of various pungent aromatic ointments and salves, two large containers of liquid, and a shroud. "At the next stop, though, we'll have to arrange delivery."

They approached a brickyard, where dust hung in the air and clay muddied the ground. Baldy led Mel and Ruth to a stack of large ceramic objects in a corner. With a practiced eye he selected one of the right size, marking it with an "X" in mud.

"What's this?" asked Ruth. "Looks like Paul Bunyan's kazoo." The object was cylindrical, six feet long and flat on the bottom, with a large round opening framed by a wide cylindrical flange molded to the top of one end. It resembled a slipper for a very slender-footed giant.

"It's a coffin."

"Why the shape?" Mel asked. "Why not just a box?"

"That's the way they've always made them," explained Baldy. "To use the wrong shape coffin would be disrespectful to the dead."

On the way back, Baldy led them down the colonnaded main street under the aqueduct through the bustling agora. As the donkey clip-clopped over the stone pavement, past stalls and counters displaying silks from China and linens from Elam, jewelry and pottery, aromatic frying lamb and chicken, a blast of heat struck them, radiating from a fiery glow inside a dark stall that resounded with the clang of hammer on metal.

A woman behind a table in front of the stall caught their glance. She smiled at Ruth. "*Bizou? Mia hara bizou gia tin oraia kyria*!"

"Oh, Mel, I want to stop. I think it's a jewelry store."

"It's up to Baldy."

"Certainly, but not too long. Mithradates won't keep."

"*Kathiste*," the woman invited, indicating a stool at the counter. Ruth sat and began examining the pieces spread before her.

"I'd like to look inside. Want to come?" Mel asked the giant.

"No, thanks. I'll stay out here where it's cool."

It was certainly hot in the shop. Mel approached the goldsmith, who was rolling a cubit-long rod of gold under one horny, blackened hand, while beating on it with an iron hammer held in the other hand. He paused and looked up. "*Te thelete*?"

"Do you speak Hebrew?"

"Eh?"

"*Skopein*," said Mel, smiling and pointing first at his eyes, then at the interior of the shop.

The jeweler shrugged, nodded, and resumed his pounding.

Mel stepped over to the furnace, not too near, bent, and peered inside. On a grille rested a ceramic tray with a gold brick melting at the edges like a pound of butter sitting in the sun. The tray had long, narrow grooves baked into its top surface. Aha! he thought. That's where he gets the golden rods.

In fact, behind the smith was another such tray, all but one of its grooves filled with gold. Mel saw the air shimmering above the tray, and he knew better than to touch even cool gold belonging to a stranger. He glanced again at the smith as he passed him on the way out. He'd seen enough, and it was hot. His eyes fastened on the rod of gold under the hammer.

It was now four feet long, much thinner, and its end whipped around flexibly as it rolled, like—

He spun on his heel, and collided with Ruth. "Mel!" she cried. "Come see what I've found!"

On the counter lay a necklace of milky glass beads strung on gold wire.

25
H_2SO_4

"Nobody ever heard of sulfuric acid." Chazz sighed.

The trio was once again brainstorming in Aletha's wagon as Tosthenes looked on. Zimri had gladly funded ten cubits of fine gold wire, and Chazz had spliced lead-in wires to the terminals of his computer's nine-volt battery pack. Now the problem was to do something useful with the other ends of those leads.

"I sort of remember getting some juice out of a lemon in high school general science," offered Mel. "I mean, not for lemonade, but we just stuck a copper wire and a nail into the lemon, and it produced enough electricity to make a galvanometer wiggle."

"Right; it seems to me all you need is two dissimilar metals in an electrolyte," Ruth agreed. "Do we really need sulfuric acid?"

"Making a compass point west is one thing," explained Chazz. "What we need here is sustained power. At least nine volts, and several ampere-hours. Lead-acid is the simplest way I can think of to get that. Oh, sure, you could use salt water. That's how Alessandro Volta did it. He got about enough power to make a frog's leg twitch."

"Don't you just have to link up more cells?" Ruth asked.

"Right, about a hundred bowls of salt water, a hundred pieces of silver, ditto zinc, ditto gold wire; two hundred connections; what do you think the chances are of that kind of setup working? Or even if it works, what'll be the efficiency? We'll do it that way if we have to, but let's try a little harder for sulfuric acid," urged Chazz. "After all, sulfur is everywhere. Life needs it."

"Especially ours, right now," Ruth agreed.

"You're the resident chemist, Chazz," said Mel. "If we can't buy sulfuric acid, can we make it from this omnipresent sulfur? Where exactly is it?"

"In eggs, for example. You've smelled rotten eggs: that's hydrogen sulfide. But I hope we can get off easier than letting a thousand of Zimri's eggs rot. That's pushing even his hospitality. Besides, I don't exactly see us processing the gas. Bulky equipment, to hold that many eggs; besides, it'd take too long waiting for them to spoil."

"Anyway, that's still not sulfuric acid," Ruth pointed out. "There must be more steps to the process."

"Right," agreed Chazz.

"What'll we do, then?" Mel asked. "I assume we can't use twentieth-century methods, whatever they are. Can we?"

"Not being in Texas or Louisiana, we can't use the Frasch process, to extract sulfur from beds of the pure element. Even if we had the equipment, I wouldn't know where to dig."

"Too bad we don't have a little palladium," said Mel. "Could use cold fusion."

"Yes, and warm superconductors while we're at it," Ruth added.

Tosthenes, having previously discussed some of this with Chazz, had understood part of the conversation. "I know this smell. Rotten egg from no egg," he said in English.

"Tossy," said Mel, "you can't imagine how it makes me feel, hearing English spoken again."

"That's really excellent, Tosthenes," Ruth agreed. "I had no idea you'd learned so much English already."

Tosthenes beamed. "Talking to Chazz all day is a big help. He speaks good Greek, too."

"Where was this 'no egg'?" asked Chazz. "Uh...*pou ine ohi avga*?"

"*Ladi*. I do not know the English word." Tosthenes switched to Hebrew. "Oil. While sojourning in a region where oil bubbles up from the ground, I have smelled the rotten-egg odor. It's hard to miss."

"Oil," Mel translated for Chazz. "*Ladi* is oil. He smelled it near tar pits. Or springs."

"Hot sulfur springs! Of course! Ask him if there are any on our route."

Tosthenes said no, he knew of none in this part of Parthia. His experience had been while traveling in Media Atropatene, the mountainous northeastern region.

"Too bad."

"Wait a minute, Chazz," Ruth said. "This Frasch process. Is that the only way to get sulfur? From a pure source? What about ores?"

"Smog," said Mel. "Too bad the air's so clean. Smog has sulfur dioxide in it."

"Actually that's a source that's becoming more important lately: stack scrubbers. But there are minerals that contain sulfates. I think gypsum is one. Ask Tossy if he knows about gypsum."

"Can't," Mel admitted. "I don't know the Hebrew word for it."

"Mel! I'm shocked!" Ruth grinned.

"We know of *gypsos*," said Tosthenes, "if that's the right substance. A grayish powdery mineral? *Geves* in Hebrew. We make plaster from it."

"Hooray! Another cognate!" Mel said. "Tossy, we're glad you sat in."

"Then what?" asked Ruth. "What do you do to gypsum?"

"Extract the sulfur."

"I knew that."

"Well, I don't know how," Chazz confessed. "We'll just have to get some, and try various processes."

"I'm sure glad it's not gunpowder we're after," muttered Mel.

By the time the caravan arrived at Dura, nine days later, Chazz's frustration was intense. Was it to be rotten eggs after all? Or a hundred voltaic cells?

He had tried heating the gypsum and got hot gypsum.

He had tried dissolving it in water: wet gypsum.

He had tried heating the wet gypsum and succeeded in boiling off the water.

"If I only had some reagents," he complained to Tosthenes, who was assisting him. "Some acid. Then I could make acid."

"Oh, our life would be so placid," sang Ruth, "if we only had some—"

She and Mel were doing fine in their parts of the project. She had insulated a length of wire by coating it with bitumen and wrapping it in linen. Winding this into a coil, she had a working galvanometer which could make a compass point west. For the compass, she had first magnetized a sliver of soft iron using her coil and a lemon, then floated the iron sliver on a wood shaving in a bowl of water.

"Notice that this always points north," she showed Jacimus, "no matter how I turn it."

"Most intriguing. What else can it do?"

"Uh, that's all it does."

"Diverting. Pity there's no application. We already know which way is north: up the river."

Mel, for his part, had assembled a battery of lead plates in a ceramic tank, with a rope of gold wires "soldered" between alternate pairs: the wires were twisted together, then heated until they fused, and their ends melted into the lead. The connections were good, according to the lemonometer. All that was needed was sulfuric acid in water.

The critical path now went straight through Chazz.

26
Playing in the Tub

That the next day was the Sabbath was "no accident," said Zimri, returning from Synagogue with the women, Baldy, and Jacimus to the latter's wagon, to invite Chazz, Mel and Tosthenes into town. "Civilization has its uses."

Dura Europus was a large, bustling city on a bluff overlooking the river, with colonnaded sidewalks, interior plumbing, and monumental architecture.

"Something like Washington, D.C.," Mel observed to Ruth.

Chazz, lost in thought, must have overheard the end of Mel's sentence. "DC! How many volts?"

"Let it simmer for a while, Chazz," advised Ruth. To Mel she said, "Yes, it's so modern-looking, isn't it? Makes me feel rather scruffy."

"We shall take care of that," Zimri promised. "Ah, here we are."

They had rounded a corner and now stood gawking on the edge of a wide public square. Horse, wagon, chariot and pedestrian traffic was moving smoothly in four directions on paved, well-marked lanes around the square. At its center stood a large statuary group surrounding a marble fountain.

"The Six Genies." Zimri pointed. "And over there is where we're going." They started threading cautiously through the traffic.

Across the square loomed a vast stone structure, with fluted Corinthian columns attached to the front of buttresses that supported an elaborate frieze portraying some spectacle with a cast of thousands.

They climbed the steps into the shade of the portico, where men and women sat at tables sipping Arabian coffee or fruit punches.

"Here's where we part," Zimri said. "Dura has one of the few public baths with separate facilities for men and women. That's because of the large Jewish population. In through there, ladies; we'll meet you outside here in three hours, then go to lunch."

"A bath! Hooray!" cried Ruth.

"Come, my dear," Bathyra invited. She and Aletha led Ruth in through a tall archway surmounted by a bas-relief of a demurely-robed female figure.

The men followed Zimri down the portico. Three hours, thought Mel. He'd be wrinkled as a prune.

"This will remove the grime of the road, all right," Jacimus said.

"And the fatigue," added Zimri. "We all needed a day of pure rest. Especially the troops."

"Those wagons do jounce," Chazz agreed.

They entered through another archway. A young man at a long table across the room rose to his feet and rang a bell.

"Good morning, gentlemen. Six? The standard course?"

"The deluxe course," Zimri corrected him.

"Certainly, sir. Right through there."

In the next room, attendants with baskets whisked their clothes away to be laundered, while others led them through yet another archway to steaming shower stalls.

Soap! exulted Mel.

They showered, plunged into a cold pool, then lay relaxing on warm marble slabs in the steam room while masseurs pummeled them expertly.

Mel declined, with Jacimus, having his beard plucked like Baldy's and Zimri's; for Chazz the decision was moot. Mel's and Jac's beards were trimmed, Tosthenes' was brushed out, and all but he and Baldy were given stylish haircuts.

Anointed with salves and unguents, they finally sat draped in towels on benches in a sauna, sipping cool cups of mint tea.

"This heat sure feels good," Chazz sighed.

"Almost makes you forget your saddle sores, doesn't it?" asked Jacimus. "You're doing very well, by the way. Improved a lot."

"I still miss the post with half my arrows."

"That'll come with time. We'll have you shooting over the crupper like a true Parthian before we get to Antioch."

"That's amazing, the way you guys do that," Mel said. "It must really be a surprise to someone chasing you."

"Yes, usually the last surprise they ever see."

"Thus speaks an expert," said Baldy. "Tail-archer Jac."

"You're no amateur yourself, Leviathan. How about that time you skewered three rebels at once on your lance?"

"They were lined up."

"That was the other time Mithradates tried some evil, was it not?" Tosthenes asked.

"Yes," replied Zimri. "It's good to have him finally out of the way. Perhaps there will be peace now for a while. Well, it's no longer my affair."

Mel ladled a pint of water onto the hot rocks. "Is Antioch so modern?" he asked through the hissing cloud. "This seems as good as it gets."

"Yes," agreed Chazz. "This sauna is as posh as any in Sweden."

"Antioch makes Dura look sick," Jacimus contended. "It's huge. Got baths this size just for private homes. Whole street roofed over for ten miles through the center of town."

"In a sense, however, Antioch is the sick town," remarked Zimri. "Overcivilized. Decadent to a fault."

"So I've heard," Baldy said. "Even the women are shameless."

"Speaking of women," interrupted Zimri, "I wonder how the ladies are doing."

"They're having fun, I bet," Mel guessed, "if their side is anything like ours."

"Yes," agreed Jacimus. "Ruth always likes a long soaky bath."

Mel glowered. "Speaking of that—"

"Hey, come on, guys," protested Chazz. "I'm trying not to think about the girls at the moment. It's hard enough being seventeen without—"

"It's getting too hot in here," Baldy interrupted. "I'm for a cold plunge, then a long soaky bath myself. Anyone care to join me?"

"Yes, let's go," agreed Zimri. "I'm done on both sides."

"Aahhhh," he sighed, leaning back until he was immersed to the chin in the warm foaming tub.

"My sentiments exactly," endorsed Baldy.

"These guys really know how to live, don't they?" Mel asked Chazz.

"At times, yes. Times like this, anyway."

"Come on! We have lots of good times," proclaimed Jacimus. "Riding, shooting, battle."

"Feasts, wine…" Baldy adduced.

"Agnes's cooking…" put in Zimri.

"And good conversations," Tosthenes pointed out, "like this one."

"Not to mention the joys of conjugal love," added Zimri.

"Right! Let's not mention them," Baldy protested. "Some of us have not the advantages enjoyed by…some of us. Hey!" he added, as Zimri splashed him. "Why, you old goat!" he spluttered, reaching to duck Zimri.

Jacimus intervened. "Now, boys," he began, reasonably enough; but at the same time he stealthily placed a firm hand on his father's grizzled head and one on Baldy's dome, and pushed them both under.

They came up sputtering, allied now against Jac. "Two against wub!" he protested as he sank.

"You guys are having too much fun," cried Chazz. "Come on, Mel!" They launched themselves into the dripping fray.

Tosthenes, muttering "Horseplay, is it? They shall have horseplay, eh? Well, I know a trick or two, when it comes to horseplay," began to circle around the combatants in a sinister flanking maneuver.

Five of them soon discovered that they needed to gang up on the sixth, but the discovery availed them little; after a valiant struggle, Jac and Mel found themselves locked by the neck under Baldy's left arm, while Zimri, Tossy and Chazz thrashed near extinction under his right.

"Say uncle!" Baldy insisted.

"Never!" Zimri refused, and was consequently dunked, along with the rest.

"Say uncle!"

This time there was a mixed chorus of "No!" and "Uncle!" and "Help!"

"Say uncle!"

This time "uncle" carried unanimously. Baldy let them go.

"You win, you old cataphractus," Jacimus conceded. "This time."

"Wait till next year," warned Mel.

They rested, glad to be breathing air. Finally Jacimus said, "I'm ready to dry off. How about it, dad?"

"Yes, I believe I've had enough water for a year." They climbed out of the bath, rinsed briefly under showers, and, toweled down vigorously by attendants and rubbed with more lotions and potions, retired to a lounge where they reclined in flannel robes on long low couches surrounding a low table laden with appetizers. Baldy overhung the end of his couch by two feet.

"Don't spoil your appetites," advised Zimri, as Jacimus was reaching for his third marinated squab. "We're going to a nice inn for lunch."

"I'm hungry now," Jac protested. "We can always stop off at a vomitorium on the way."

"Jacimus!"

"Just teasing, dad. Just wanted to raise a laugh out of you."

"Ha! You managed to raise my gorge, instead. The food God gives us is not to be wasted."

"One of the hallmarks of decadence," agreed Tosthenes. "Too bad that the benefits of civilization are used to provide a surfeit of food for the few, rather than adequate nutrition for all. Imperial concerns don't extend to the masses, beyond keeping them tractable. Had democracy survived…"

"Democracy!" Mel said. "Sure, that's right; it started with the Greeks, didn't it?"

"Started and ended, I regret to say." Tosthenes flicked a nearly invisible speck of lint off the gold-embroidered hem of his robe. "It failed to survive the war."

"When we cross into the Roman Empire in a few weeks," warned Jacimus, "you'd better watch your seditious tongue. I don't want a slave of mine thrown into the arena. It'd sully my record."

"Thanks."

"What is our schedule, anyway?" Mel asked. "When do we arrive at Antioch?"

"In about twenty days," replied Zimri. "Including Sabbaths."

Chazz rolled over onto his other elbow. "We flew all the way from London in ten hours," he lamented.

"Excise that nonsense!"

"It's true," confirmed Mel. "When Daniel said 'Many shall run to and fro,' he wasn't kidding."

"Daniel who?" Baldy asked.

"Daniel the prophet," answered Zimri. "You know. I've told you about him. Remember? The handwriting on the wall, the lions' den?"

"Oh, that Daniel. I remember now. It's just that I never met a prophet myself, so I tend to forget." The giant peeled a grape, carefully.

But I have met one, Mel thought. So why do I forget?

"There have been no prophets for centuries," said Zimri. "Since the time of Daniel. No miracles at all, in fact, except the day's supply of oil that lasted eight days."

"Hanukkah," Mel said.

"Correct. God's people hunger and thirst for some further word of guidance and love from Him. They have sought long and carefully, and have not found. That's why it's so exciting to see these new signs and wonders in our present time."

"What signs and wonders, exactly?" asked Chazz, rising to sit propped on both elbows. "What's been happening lately?"

"He means us, Chazz. Strange visitors from another time, who—"

"Actually, I think not," Zimri cut in. "Strange and wonderful, yes. Prophetic? A sign from God? It seems doubtful, now."

"Besides, we started seeing it before we met you," added Jacimus. "Not long before, admittedly."

"Seeing what?" Mel asked.

"The star." Jacimus waved vaguely toward the high domed ceiling.

"A bright new star in the west," explained Tosthenes. "Even I have seen it; haven't you?"

"Now that you mention it," Mel agreed, "I have seen something. I thought it was Venus, the 'evening star.' I don't know much astronomy, but are you sure it isn't a planet? Or a conjunction of planets?"

"Come on." Jacimus grinned. "Trust we know something."

"Any child can keep track of the four planets," Baldy attested. "This is something new."

"Maybe a nova, or supernova rather," suggested Mel.

"No," Tosthenes objected. "We know of those, but this is different. Were there truly supernatural events, this would be one of them. It's enough to make even me doubt my doubt."

"What is so strange about it?" asked Chazz.

"You called it the evening star," Zimri said. "But we also see it in the morning. And at midnight. Always in the west."

"A synchronous satellite!" Mel tingled from head to toe. "My God!"

"'Synchronous attendant?'" asked Chazz, but then the Greek apparently became clear to him. "Oh. No, wait a minute!" he clamored. "What we have here is obviously—"

"Good God in Heaven!" continued Mel, still chilled.

"Precisely," Zimri said. "Or at least the Forerunner."

"Listen, it's obviously an unidentified flying object," declared Chazz. "Maybe it'll pick us up. Take us to a telephone."

"Chazz, do you seriously believe in UFO's?"

"Don't you? If they don't exist, then where is everybody? With life evolving on a billion planets in this galaxy alone—"

"Slow down," Jacimus said. "This is fascinating. Science! Mysteries! I love it! But you used a word just then that I didn't understand. What is 'evolving'?" He popped a morsel of chicken into his mouth.

Here it comes, Mel thought. He couldn't avoid it any longer. He raised one finger while taking a healthy swig from his cup, then wiped his lips with the edge of his towel and began. "Evolution is the way plants and animals change into different, higher ones," he explained. "Life began in a very tiny form in the sea, in a sort of soup where the chemistry was just right. Then it grew and developed over millions of years into all the plants, animals, and us."

"From goo to you by way of the zoo," muttered Chazz in English.

"That's why Chazz said that life must have evolved on lots of other worlds: since there are so many of them, there must be many on which the chemistry was also just right."

"Whoa." Jacimus raised a hand. "One world at a time, please."

"This is truly amazing," Tosthenes said. "Have you, yourself, seen it?"

"Seen what?"

"Why, seen God change an animal into a different one," said Zimri.

"No, no. You don't understand. God doesn't do this. It just happens."

"How?" Zimri asked.

"Well, let's see. Suppose one giraffe has a slightly longer—"

"One what?"

"Uh. Strike that. Suppose one wolf is cleverer than the rest."

"That's you, dad." Jacimus grinned.

"Hush. Let the man speak. This is interesting."

"Suppose game becomes scarce. Then this clever wolf is more likely to catch some and not starve. So he will survive to pass on his ge— his cleverness to his cubs. The dumb wolves die out. So the pack improves. That's called 'survival of the fittest.'"

"I see," said Tosthenes. "Those who turn out to have survived thereby prove their fitness to survive. A perfect circle."

"Selective breeding, that's what you've got here," Baldy said. "Men have always done that. That's where a mighty steed like Hammurabi comes from," he raised his cup aloft. "God rest his equine soul. Select the best ones—the 'fittest,' as you would say. Only here it means fittest for the man's purpose—and breed them together. Improve the race."

"Right," Mel agreed. "You've got it."

"But even an ignorant rancher like me knows you can only push selective breeding so far," argued Zimri. "You can't breed a rabbit into a horse, no matter how nice you make it for the horsy rabbits."

"And that's by intentional design," Jacimus added. "How could it ever happen your way, with nobody doing the selecting?"

"It's called natural selection," Mel began.

"Sounds like blind chance to me," opined Tosthenes, rolling away to reach a tart across the table.

"Well, yes, but acting over millions of years—"

"What millions? We've got three thousand nine hundred ninety-five years of recorded history, going all the way back to Adam. That's it," Jacimus declared.

"And nothing happens by chance," said Zimri.

"Even if it did," Baldy added, "seems to me a mina of design is worth a talent of chance."

"You guys are ganging up on me," grumbled Mel. "Chazz, you got me into this, with your dumb UFO's. How come I don't hear any helpful words from you already?"

"You're holding up our side wonderfully well," Chazz said. "I couldn't improve on it."

"What time is it?" asked Zimri. "We'd better get dressed. We'll be late for the ladies."

"Why is it that just when you're having an interesting conversation about life, the universe, and everything," Tosthenes asked, "you have to drop it and go somewhere else?"

"Sure as taxes," Zimri agreed.

"Don't you hate it when that happens?" asked Jacimus.

"What? Taxes?"

The laundry was ready: their clothes were warm, dry and clean. As Mel and Jacimus were climbing into their tunics and baggy leggings, they found themselves slightly apart from the rest.

"What's this about Ruth liking long soaky baths?" Mel asked in a low voice. "How would you know?"

"She told me. Mel, some friendly advice: Give up. Ruth's not right for you. She's a believer, Mel. That gives her more in common with me than any amount of twentieth-century comfort does with you. Rides well, too. Here's an idea for you, just a suggestion: Why don't you go off with Chazz, help him look for Scheherazade, keep him out of trouble? Maybe Sche has a sister."

Mel finally found his voice. "What a colossal nerve. It's you who's not right for Ruth, not me. I love her! She's coming with me, back where she belongs."

"Where she 'belongs' is debatable. Anyway, that'll be up to her, won't it?"

Zimri approached. "Ready?" he asked. "Let's go, we're late."

The ladies had apparently not been waiting long. At least, they were chatting amiably as the men approached, and did not seem annoyed at their tardiness.

Mel was disconcerted to see that Ruth and Aletha appeared to be on the best of terms. As if they weren't rivals for my affection, he thought. Maybe Jac is right. No! Let it never be!

He approached her determinedly. "Ruth," he said.

"Hi, Mel?" She fell into step beside him, following the others.

"Remember we were kidding about Landsat's having us in its lens two weeks ago? Ruth, there's a satellite up there in synchronous orbit right now! I've seen it! Must be time travelers. We have to get their attention somehow. I think we need to build a radio."

"Do you mean the star?"

"Yes. You know about it?"

"All the girls in there were talking of nothing else... Well, almost nothing else." Her cheeks grew slightly more rosy. "I haven't seen it, myself, but I'm going to look for it as soon as it gets dark."

"I figure if we can find a galena crystal—"

"That's for a receiver. We'd need a transmitter. Electricity again. But, Mel, it can't be a synchronous satellite. It's nearly straight west of here. Where is synchronous orbit?"

"Over the equator. Oh."

"Right. We're too far north. It would be more south of us than west."

"Then what is it? Wait: it could be maintaining its position by rockets. Not be in a free orbit at all."

"I don't think so. I think it's something...special."

"A sign from God? Ruth, are you a believer?"

"Yes," she acknowledged. "I know God's been with me, since Babylon anyway, if not before. When you saved me from drowning, He was there, or I'd be dead now. Couldn't you feel His presence?"

Mel remembered that desperate moonlit night. He remembered his panic at finding Ruth's robe empty, and seeing a flash of white rushing downstream, faster than he could run. "God! No!" he had cried. And she had stopped, grounded on a bar. Coincidence?

"I confess I prayed," he said. "And you're alive."

"I have a confession too," Ruth admitted. "Sometimes I still get scared. Even though I know He's in control. And then I act like a fool."

"No you don't."

"Mel, even if it is a satellite up there, what difference does it make? We certainly can't build the word 'HELP' in letters like the Great Wall of China. You're right, we'd need a radio. And for that we need electricity. And as soon as we get electricity, or a few hours later…"

"We go home?"

"Well, we can try." She slowed him down with a hand on his arm, so that they fell farther behind the others. "Frankly, I'm not convinced Chazz has as much control as he thinks he has."

"I agree. But it's our best hope. Anyway, the battery isn't turning out to be as simple as we thought. Do we really need sulfuric acid?"

"Your guess is as good as mine. I took biology, not chemistry. Chazz is the closest thing we've got to an expert."

"It's all up to him now. We should help him all we can. Our own projects are done."

"Right. Let's catch up before we scandalize everybody."

"Okay. Nice talking to you. We ought to do this more often. Oh, one more thing: do you like long soaky baths?"

"No thanks, not right now; just had one. I'm a raisin."

That night they all went outside to look at the star. Mel wasn't sure, but he thought it was a little south of where he remembered seeing it.

"That's Venus over there," Baldy said, pointing. "The evening star. And Mars; Jupiter; Saturn; all pretty close together—there does happen to be a conjunction. But watch."

In half an hour Venus set, but the star was still the same altitude above the western horizon.

"It's so bright," said Ruth. "How could I have missed it?"

"You have to be looking up," Bathyra said.

"It's too light at night back home," said Chazz. "We got out of the habit of looking at the sky."

27
Alumen

Soon after leaving the high citadel of Dura Europus, the caravan reached the ford where the Royal Syria-Babylon Road crossed to the left bank of the Euphrates.

"Partly because of the terrain," Jacimus explained to Mel, "but mostly to avoid the Roman Empire: the border runs along the river from here north."

As usual, there was a long wait at the river crossing. Zimri was using it to their advantage. They were being fitted for new riding habits of soft kidskin while they waited. Because Zimri wanted to make a maximum military impression when his army rode into Antioch, everyone who could ride acceptably was to be mounted and armed, and in uniform.

"It's going to take a lot to impress the Romans," he had said. "I don't want us looking like a ragtag band of brigands."

The time-travelers were at a dead end regarding the sulfuric acid project. Worse yet, the caravan's supply of salt was low, so the Voltaic alternative would have to wait until they arrived at the next town, Circesium. Chazz seemed reluctant to start that chancy project in any case; perhaps that was why he had neglected to look into the salt supply before they left Dura.

Chazz had also found that the locals had a hard time distinguishing zinc from tin, and that the cost of a hundred silver electrodes would be enough to buy six of the caravan's wagons, complete with oxen and furnishings.

So now, squatted by the tanner's fire, he was occupying the time at the ford by experimenting with something else.

The others, standing around him, watched with interest (but from upwind) as he heated a bucket of asphalt.

In a small ovoid pottery jar he placed a copper sheet rolled into a cylinder, clipping a gold wire to it with a small wood-and-thong clamp. On the ground nearby was an iron rod with another gold wire attached to it, and beyond that, a jar of brine.

When the asphalt became warm enough to pour, Chazz braced the pottery jar between rocks and gingerly picked up the bucket with fleece hot-pads.

"Ugh," he grunted as he poured an inch of the hot resin into the copper cylinder. "Stinks."

He set down the bucket and inserted the iron rod carefully into the center of the copper cylinder, standing it up in the soft bitumen plug.

"Now where's that salt water?" He looked around, spotted it just out of his grasp, and twisted to reach it. Leaning too far in his precarious position, he lost his balance and fell into the fire. "Ow!" Flailing to remove himself from it, he knocked over a tall amphora. A handful of white powder spilled into the flames.

A cloud of thick white smoke hissed up.

"Hey!" cried the tanner. "Wasting good alumen! Pick that up, quick…and don't breathe the smoke."

"Too late," Ruth wheezed through tears. Even upwind, choking wisps of the stench had reached them.

"What (kha!) is that?" coughed Chazz. "Holy smoke!"

Jacimus righted the amphora, then held his nose while trying to brush the powder out of the fire with a stick.

"Give up," Aletha advised him. "Get back."

"Get away! Get away!" They all ran away except Chazz, who moved to a foolhardy position downwind of the fire and sniffed the smoke!

"AAaaggh! I thought so!" He staggered away and joined the others.

"Did someone die without bathing?" gasped Jacimus.

"That *is* quite acrid," Mel agreed, retching.

"You're going to have to get used to it," said Chazz. "What did you call that stuff?"

"Alumen," the tanner replied. "That's the Latin name. It tans leather very well."

"Mother makes pickles with it," added Aletha. "I must give you her recipe," she offered Ruth.

"Alum!" Ruth exclaimed.

"Whatever," said Chazz. "The smoke is sulfur trioxide. We're back in business."

The following Sabbath found them encamped on the riverbank above Nicephorium.

With the help of Zimri's smith-armorer, Chazz and Mel had constructed a bulky, angular hood to trap the thick white smoke from heated alum and force it, past a somewhat leaky tar seal, through a ceramic tub of water. Each evening the device was fired up (downwind of the caravan) and tended through the night by a bleary-eyed Chazz, and each morning it was dismantled and packed before the trek resumed, its precious product carefully poured off into pottery jars which were then sealed with wax and wrapped in layers of fleece.

Chazz had tried to sleep days, with spotty results. Only excited anticipation kept him from becoming grouchy.

Ruth, meanwhile, had been trying to make a hydrometer, with little success. The small clay jars sank too fast in water.

Finally, the afternoon before, as the caravan was arriving in Nicephorium, she, Mel and Jacimus had ridden ahead to walk through the bazaar before the Sabbath fell.

On the prowl for new technology, they headed straight for the jewelry shop, and there struck paydirt. Jacimus had never seen such skill.

The jeweler was blowing glass.

On the spot, Jacimus made him a generous offer to join his fortunes with Zimri's: to accompany them to Antioch and there work as the family's lensmaker. While they were negotiating, Ruth purchased six slim glass perfume bottles of varying colors and sizes, complete with stoppers because, as she told Mel later, "they reminded me of test-tubes."

Now they knew for certain they had something potent in those sealed, padded jars. A sand-weighted vial that sank slowly in water floated in Chazz's solution.

It was time for the acid test

By the time Ruth and the others returned from Synagogue, Chazz and Mel had set up the battery and computer in the middle of a cleared patch of ground, next to their three jars of what they hoped was a good strong electrolyte. The group stood in a circle at a respectful distance to watch.

Ruth stepped over to Mel and Chazz, who were scraping the wax out of the jars. "Mel," she said quietly.

They paused. "Yes?" Mel asked.

"Something's not quite right. I have this feeling. It came over me while we were praying for the success of this experiment this morning."

"Can you be a little more vague about that?" Mel smiled.

"Not exactly. It's something about lead, acid, lead. Which way is the current going to flow?"

"Does a car start?" Chazz riposted. "It'll flow. Trust me. Just get your galvanometer ready. And watch out: it'll probably melt."

The coil, wrapped around the compass-bowl, was already connected to one of the battery's leads. Ruth knelt where she could connect the other.

"We'll have all day to charge up," said Chazz as he and Mel cautiously poured the fluid into the battery tank. "That should do it. Then, tonight, we can do a few trial jumps. Say an hour into the future. Watch out, don't breathe those fumes."

The liquid level reached nearly to the top of the plates.

"Ready?" Ruth asked.

"Okay; now be careful, and use the fleece pads. That gold's going to get hot."

Ruth gingerly brought the bare ends of the wires together, watching the compass needle. They touched.

The needle did not flicker.

"Nothing," she reported.

"What? Let's see that. You're right. Must be a loose connection. Mel, help me check. Careful."

All the connections were firm.

"Well," Mel remarked, "at least it didn't melt."

"*Fee farn*!" cursed Chazz. "Look, let's take that coil out of the circuit. We should get a fat spark." He tore the twisted gold wires apart, then pressed the battery leads together. Nothing happened.

"All right, let's get the juice back into the jars, while we figure out what went wrong," Chazz said irritably. "Somebody please melt this wax."

Baldy bent to gather the pieces of sealing-wax. The rest made sympathetic sounds of condolence. All except Jacimus, who stood somewhat apart, with an expression not quite as gloomy as the others'.

On the one hand, Mel thought as his horse clopped onto the pontoon bridge, Chazz was right: cars did—would—start, using lead-acid batteries: lead and sulfuric acid alone.

On the other hand, their lead-acid battery didn't work. It wouldn't start a grounded mosquito. Something was obviously wrong. There was some missing ingredient. Ruth had furnished a clue: their battery was too symmetric. What would make current more likely to flow in one direction than the other?

It was the third day after the Sabbath, and the caravan was finally crossing into the Roman Empire. This time there was no waiting at a ford: they had set out from Apamea that morning, only half an hour ago, and already most of the wagons, and half the army, were moving unhurriedly up the slope of the right bank of the Euphrates toward the conical acropolis which, with its colonnaded Temple of Zeus, dominated the eastern approach to Zeugma.

Chazz had spent the rest of the Sabbath mumbling about sulfate ions, electrode chemistry, hydrogen gas, and valence. Once he asked Mel if he happened to remember the periodic table.

"The whole thing?"

"You can skip the lanthanides and actinides."

"Right."

Ruth was more help. She actually remembered the atomic number of lead. "Eighty-two," she supplied. "Just happened to stick with me. It's such a leaden number. I know all the flavors of quarks, too: up, down, top, bottom, strange, and charmed. Is that any help?"

"We mathematicians are a useless lot, aren't we?" Chazz asked.

"Art for art's sake," Mel said. "If you play Beethoven sonatas in a henhouse, you can increase egg production."

"So that's why Beethoven wrote them," mused Ruth.

Finally Chazz threw down his pen. "Well," he sighed, "I'm fairly sure you get lead sulfate."

"At both terminals?" Mel asked.

"Ya. At one you get lead sulfate and electrons; at the other you take in electrons and make lead sulfate out of them."

"Neat. Exactly how is this accomplished? By wishing real hard?"

"It'll come to me. Let's go see if supper's ready."

"Dissimilar metals," Ruth had suggested later, at the brain storm. "Stick some gold in there."

"Sulfuric acid has no effect on gold," Chazz pointed out. "Or do we have to set up nitric and hydrochloric acid projects too?"

"Well, how about iron? or copper?" she persisted.

"It's just that we're close. I know it. Nobody calls it a lead-iron or copper-lead battery."

"Look, Chazz," Mel said. "You've thought about this a lot. Now let it rest."

"Stop thinking, start praying," advised Ruth.

"Did you know Poincaré could actually watch his unconscious mind at work?" Mel quoted: "'Ideas rose in crowds; I felt them collide until pairs interlocked, so to speak, making a stable combination.' Of course, that was after too much black coffee."

"I know; that's what I meant—let your unconscious mind work, Chazz. You've got all the hooks stirred up and flying around loose. Let them organize themselves onto the appropriate eyes."

"Okay. Let's assume we'll get past this last hurdle," agreed Chazz. "Let's work out the steps to take when we have a fully charged computer again."

"You mentioned a test," Mel recalled. "A short hop."

"Yes, an hour or so at first, just to be safe. I want to calibrate the boundaries of chaos."

"Let's table this discussion," warned Ruth, "or I'm leaving."

"One way or another," Mel remarked.

The bridge swayed in the swift current of midstream. Made of interlocked rafts, it was remarkably stable for a pontoon bridge. Mel's pony negotiated the tilting planks with no difficulty. The dovetailed beams were secured with thick iron staples, supplementing the rope lashing at the stress points.

The crossing into Seleucia-on-the-Euphrates, nicknamed "Bridge" ("Zeugma" in Greek), was a dress rehearsal for the entrance into Antioch. All available personnel were mustered as cavalry and told to look as confident and ferocious as possible. Zimri and Jacimus led the frontal body of archers; then came the wagons; then Mel, Ruth and Chazz, riding abreast at the head of the remaining cavalry. The camel train brought up the rear, bristling with arrows.

At least we have an excuse not to be marching in step, Mel thought: we're crossing a bridge. Otherwise these guys would hardly be impressed.

They were crossing under the suspicious gaze of the city's garrison. The entire Sixteenth Legion of the Roman Empire was drawn up in shining ranks on the heights ahead, watching them closely.

Out of the corner of his eye, Mel tried to monitor their reaction. The Parthians' longtime foes, the Romans had only recently become allies. Some of these, Mel mused, may remember Antony's campaign. He couldn't tell: from this distance, their faces might have been frozen.

Bet they'd enjoy some action, Mel thought. Probably bored silly with nothing to do but pull guard duty and maintain this bridge. Needs a lot of maintenance, too—look at that staple; it's rusted almost through.

He saw Chazz's eyes follow his glance, then widen and fill with a wild light.

BOOK III

Faufi

28
The Secret Diary

The young girl awoke in confusion. A figure stood by her bed. What's happening? she thought. Who is this?

Suddenly her eyes widened in horror as she recognized the visitor to her dim bedroom. "Mummy!" she shrieked. "But—"

The gaunt figure clamped a gentle hand firmly over the girl's mouth. "Hush," she admonished. "Oh, my darling, you look so fine! It is so good to see you this way...so grown up! Don't make a sound. I'll explain everything." She released the girl.

"But...Mummy, is it really you? But you're dead!"

"Shhh. I'm not dead; do I look dead?" The woman smiled. "Never fear, when I'm dead, I'll let you know! Be patient, my own. All will be explained. Have you been keeping up with your lessons?"

"Mummy! It *is* you!" The girl sat up, scrambled to her knees in the soft bed, and hugged her mother fiercely. "Oh, Mummy! Mama! They told me you were never coming back. I knew that meant dead."

"Dearest." The woman sobbed. "Dearest Faufi. How lovely you are! What a fine young woman!"

"Mummy! Mama! Don't ever go away again. Promise! How I have missed you! Where have you been? Why did you go away?"

"Patience, patience." The woman smoothed Faufi's hair with gentle strokes. "Patience is a virtue, remember? I promise to explain everything. But it will take time. And, my girl, you will have to be trained. You will have to study hard."

"I do, Mama. Listen: 'I met a traveler from an antique land / Who said—'"

"Not now, dear. But we shall have time together, I promise you. Time for all the things we want to do together. 'Time to grow, time to know...'"

"'...and time for tanning leather!' Oh, Mama!"

"Bags of time, Faufi. Time for all your training. But now..."

Faufi's expression darkened. She sank back to a sitting position. "Now you must go. Is that it, Mama?"

"No! Of course not! May it never be! All I was going to say was, now we must arrange for all that time. We must set up appointments so that we can be together."

"I knew it." Faufi pouted. "I want to be with you always."

"Now, dear, you know better. You know that can't be. You're a busy young lady! Do you want me to sit through all your lessons with you? I have learned those lessons already; they would bore me. Or perhaps you are ready to skip your lessons? What do you think this is, Heaven?"

"Yes, Mama."

"Well it isn't. Although, at this moment...Oh! Faufi!" She hugged her tight.

"Don't cry, Mama. Mama, please don't cry."

"I'm so happy, darling. What a miracle! What a gift from God!"

Faufi stroked her mother's hair until her tears dried.

"Now, Faufi. Let me see your appointment book."

The girl jumped out of bed and ran to her writing desk. Opening it, she withdrew a slim leather-bound calendar for 1893. She brought it back to where her mother sat on the bed. "Here, Mama."

"It is very early in the morning. Show me your first appointment for today."

Faufi turned the leaves to Monday, June 12. "Eight o'clock, see, Mama? Breakfast with Aunt Ellen."

"There you are! We have an hour to spend together until you must prepare for your first appointment."

"But Aunt Ellen will be wild to see you, Mama; won't you join us for breakfast? She will be pleased to poach an extra egg—"

"No."

"But why?"

"Always you are asking why. And always I have answered you, have I not?"

"Yes. At least, mostly."

"Always, Fufu, when you could understand the answer, and when I knew it myself. What are the second most important three words a mathematician can say?"

"I don't know."

"You remember! And what are the *most* important three words a mathematician can say?"

"I love you. Oh, Mama, I love you so!" Faufi threw her arms around her mother.

"And I love you, Fufu. You love me, then trust me. Aunt Ellen could not understand why I am here. She would be upset, very upset. So she must never know. We must never let anyone know. It shall be our secret. Won't that be fun?"

Faufi pulled away. A terrible fear filled her.

"Mama, I am going mad. You are not really here."

"Oh, no, Faufi! Never think that! Never think that! You can see me, touch me." She squeezed the girl's cheek. "It is only that I can trust no one else with this secret. No one but you. Wait, wait. I can prove it. You know about proof. You are studying Euclid, aren't you?"

"I'm talking to myself. Or maybe I'm only dreaming! Yes, that's it! It's only a dream! When I wake up I'll be sane! What a relief! What did you ask, Mama?"

"Euclid," the woman prompted.

"Oh, yes. No, Mama, I have finished the thirteen books of the Elements and am now studying the differential calculus!"

"Faufi, you are fourteen already! Why are you not studying the integral calculus?"

"I shall master it tomorrow, Mama. Oh, this dream is fun! Now you shall prove you're real, and I shall be convinced, and go back to sleep, and when I wake up, I shan't remember the details of the proof. Oh, if only it were true! If only I could never wake up!" Faufi began to weep bitterly.

"Compose yourself, daughter! Pay attention, I see I must prove it to you. Well, time is short now; it's almost six, so I shall tell you only two things.

"First, you must never tell anyone you are seeing me—don't cry, hear me out—until you marry, Faufi. This is my first time with you—don't ask me yet what that means (All will be explained! Have patience!), but I know in my heart you will meet a fine young man someday, and love and trust him, and marry him. You may share our secret with him.

"Second, we must arrange our next appointment. Are you free this afternoon?"

Faufi consulted her appointment book.

"Between tea-time and Rhetoric I have two hours to play, Mama." She got up to dip a pen in the inkwell.

"That will be fine. But don't write it in there. Here, this is for you." She took out of her purse a black diary with lock and key. "You must write our appointments only in this book. You must keep it locked, and you must never let anyone read it. Hang the key around your neck and wear it always." She smiled. "You are at the age when a girl may be expected to begin to keep a private diary: for her fondest wishes, her attempts at poetry, her gossip, and other secrets.

"Write for June twelfth: appointment with Mama, five-thirty to seven-thirty."

Faufi did, then looked up. "Where, Mama?"

"In the old gazebo in the secret garden. No one will interrupt us there." Faufi wrote. "Now lock that up. Here's the key. Hang it around your neck. Put the diary where you'll be sure to see it as soon as you wake up.

"That will be your proof.

"Now let me tuck you in and sing you a lullaby. And I'll be waiting for you in the gazebo at half past five. There." She kissed her, and began to sing softly:

"Like a furry bear cub cuddled in her den,

"Dreaming sunny honey dreams till springtime comes again..."

Faufi fell asleep smiling.

The woman carefully stood up, removed a small intricate brass mechanism from her purse, adjusted a setting, wound a spring, and pushed a lever.

There was a soft click, and Sophia Vasilievna Kovalevskaya vanished from the room.

The light brightened. The birds sang louder. At seven-thirty the bedroom door opened, and Anna, the upstairs maid, came in and drew open the curtains. Morning sunlight flooded across the smooth cheeks and golden curls of the sleeping girl. She stirred.

"Wake up, sleepy bones!" said Anna cheerfully. "Time to get up! Come on, time to get ready for breakfast!"

"Ohhhh!" Faufi yawned and stretched luxuriously. She sat up in bed. "Good morning, Anna."

"Good morning, Mistress." Anna bustled about the room, pouring water from a pitcher on her cart into a bowl on the nightstand, flicking an invisible speck of dust from the dresser, and opening the window to the early June breeze.

"Oh, Anna, I had the most marvelous dream!"

"Tell me all about it! I love dreams!" Anna poured a glass of water from the pitcher and brought it to Faufi's bedside table. "What's this?"

"A glass of water. Riddles, so early?"

"No, this." Anna held up a black book with a brass lock. "Where did you get this?"

"Oh!" Faufi's hand flew to her throat. A silken cord hung there, holding a small brass key just out of sight under the collar of her nightgown.

Then it was real!

A thrill stole all over her, and became a profound glow of warmth and pleasure. She basked in it. Mama was back! Really, really back! There was the diary, and Anna could see it too! She wasn't going mad. Surely she could not be imagining Anna. Her imagination wasn't *that* good.

Anna waited. "Well?" She examined the diary more closely. She sniffed. "This has a nice scent. Are you using scent now? No? You'd better not be! Don't worry, I shan't tell Madame Ellen. But where'd this come from?"

"Anna, can't a girl have any secrets at all?" Faufi pouted prettily while thinking furiously.

"Not from her maid and best friend and confidante. Oh, please! Tell me. I love secrets even more than dreams."

"But if I tell you, then it won't be a secret anymore." What could she say? How could she explain it? Let's see, where had she been yesterday? To church, of course. And then Mr. Williams had taken the girls boating on the lake in the afternoon. He had sent Faufi to fetch ices from the kiosk in the esplanade.

"Oh, poor Anna! Don't look so sad. I bought it yesterday in the market by the lake. There, now you know, but please don't tell, or everyone will be wanting to read what I write in it, and will be pestering me endlessly. Do you keep a diary? You do? What is it like? What kinds of things does one write in it? Is it exciting? I thought it would be, but now I can think of nothing to put down."

"You will. You'll see how much fun it can be, having secrets. Don't worry, I shan't pry, and I shan't tell anyone you have a diary. And you must learn not to leave it out in plain sight, where any—Goodness! It's nearly eight! Here." She tossed Faufi her dressing gown. Faufi hopped out of bed and put it on, tucking the diary in one of its deep pockets. "Now scamper downstairs before your egg grows cold!"

All the long day Faufi could hardly contain her excitement. She could not concentrate on anything. At breakfast she ate half her eggshell. In Logic she left a middle undistributed and earned an extra sorites for homework as a penalty. In Differential Calculus (which, to be fair, she was only beginning) she momentarily forgot the Quotient Formula. And in English Literature she lost the thread of Mr. Shelley's sonnet. It was quite embarrassing.

But what a secret! In a moment of privacy she had unlocked the diary and read the entry for June 12. There it was: "Appointment with Mama, five-thirty to seven-thirty, old gazebo." The ink was a little smeared against the facing page. She locked it and, pondering where to hide it, tucked it away in her book-bag for the present.

If only Anna wouldn't tell! Faufi was afraid the secret was already compromised. Dear Anna could keep a secret exactly until she encountered the best opportunity to reveal it.

What could she do? Perhaps Mama would know.

There was no thought of not telling Mama that Anna had seen the diary.

After what seemed months and years, tea time arrived. Faufi fairly vibrated with impatience. But she steeled herself and got through it with no one's seeming to notice anything untoward in her behavior.

At last she was free to play. She packed two biscuits in a napkin, fetched Lang's Red Fairy Book from the library, and walked down the back lawn toward the secret garden.

Mama was waiting in the kiosk under the great Cape chestnut. Faufi cried with joy. All day long she had suppressed fears of disappointment.

"There, there, dear," Sophia said. "Of course I'm here. I know how difficult it must have been, to keep hoping all day. But here we are, together once again. Thank you for your faithfulness."

"Oh, Mama, there's something I must tell you." She told her about Anna. "What can we do?"

"That was quick thinking, Faufi. There is a stall on the esplanade that sells diaries, isn't there?" Faufi nodded. "Then the first thing we must do is make your story true. After that we can consider how to disarm Anna's curiosity."

"Make it true, Mama? But how? I didn't buy the diary there; you gave it to me. I only bought ices for the girls."

"Well, I'm sure we shall find it there, too. But I'm glad Anna saw it, Faufi; do you know why?"

"I think so. I realized at the time that if the diary were real enough for Anna to see and touch, then I was not mad."

"Good, darling. Yes, there is your proof. It's all real. You must hang onto that through what you're about to see: it's all real, and you have convincing proof of that."

"Yes, Mama."

"Then come with me." Sophia got up and extended her hand to her daughter. Hand in hand they walked out the bottom of the secret garden and through the city to the lake. It was not crowded, but there were several townspeople out for a before-dinner stroll in the fine late sunshine. The market stalls were open but not doing much business.

Sophia led her daughter behind the stationer's stall. "Give me the diary, please. Wait here a moment." She walked around to the front, returning a moment later. "Now I shall take you to yesterday," she explained. "You will find your diary in with the lace-trimmed lavender envelopes. Purchase it and that will be that. You have some money, haven't you?" Faufi nodded. "Good. Three kronor is what the others are marked. Don't buy the wrong one!"

"I shan't, Mama. But how does one go to yesterday?"

"Like this...it's simple, really: First you decide when you would like to go to. Then you draw a curve that loops back or forward to that moment from this. Add up the residues at the poles of a special formula that lie within the loop formed by this curve and two or three others I'll tell you about later. I've had so much practice I can now do it in my head."

"Residues? Poles? I don't understand."

"That is why you need training, dear. You must be well versed in the Integral Calculus, the Theory of Elliptic Functions, and Contour Integration. A little Analysis Situs wouldn't hurt, either."

"But that will take months!"

"It will and it won't. Patience. The last step is to multiply by two pi i; that gives the integral. But the most important step must be done before that, and that is to spin the Kovalevskian Gyroscope." She took out the small brass device.

"Did you invent that, Mama?"

"No, dear." She smiled. "A Dr. Delone built the first one based upon principles in my prize paper. He called it that, and I have kept the name. I had these small copies made by a skilled mechanic." She showed Faufi another identical device in her purse. "This one is for you, when you have learned to handle it."

"How does it work?"

"It adds psychomanipulative stability to prevent chaotic tumbling of the median axis of the rigid body about the fixed point."

"No, I meant—"

"Oh. See this key here? This winds it up." She twisted the key; the ratchet clicked as the coil spring tightened. "This lever here must be set to either the 'P' or 'F' position, for 'Past' or 'Future.' That shifts the gears to reverse the axis of rotation. And this is the release switch." She pressed it. The little gyroscope began to spin, and they went to Sunday afternoon.

29
Yesterday

Faufi and her mama spent a glorious afternoon together on the opposite end of the lake from where the previous Faufi was spending it with Mr. Williams and the girls. They soaked up the sunshine, talked of old times, and basked in each other's love.

Sophia introduced Faufi to the outline of what she wished her to do. It was to preserve the secret of time travel, in two senses: to make sure that the technique was not lost, and to keep it secret.

"For suppose Napoleon had had it, Faufi. We would all now be his subjects in a world-wide empire, and we should be speaking French at this moment."

"Thank God he didn't, Mama."

"But he still might, don't you see? Someone might go back to his time and teach him. Then it would take a miracle to keep the world from tearing itself in two. For he would be able to win all his battles, even Waterloo.

"You must guard the secret as well as you can, and pass it on to your children. I've written a paper that explains the theoretical basis of time travel. I almost sent a copy of it to Dr. Hermite, but realized my error in time. I'll show you where to hide it; I have a good place in mind.

"Even that paper does not describe the use of the Gyroscope. Some secrets are better never written down.

"And we must pray no one rediscovers the big secret; or, at least, that the discoverer will be a man of good will and good sense. For I know of no earthly way to prevent rediscovery."

In the twilight they walked back to the garden and entered the dark gazebo. Sophia spun the device; the sun popped out: it was six-thirty Monday afternoon.

"I must go back now, and you must prepare for your Rhetoric lesson. We'll meet here again after tea tomorrow: write that down, and hide your diary so that Anna will forget about it."

"Yes, Mama."

"I love you, Faufi."

"I love you, Mama. Good-bye."

"Good-bye." Sophia disappeared. Faufi went to Rhetoric, tired, drawn, and somewhat sobered by the new responsibility she had been given. But she resolved to discharge it to the best of her ability. And hoped she would not make any mistakes.

Two years later and three years older, she had made only one. She had let someone see her hide her mother's paper in the wall of the old college.

When Faufi returned after a month to retrieve the paper and found it missing, she almost panicked. She almost visited her mother in the past, to ask her advice.

Sophia had warned her never to do that. "I shouldn't recognize you, I shouldn't believe you, and I shouldn't be of any assistance to you. You see," she had explained, "the me of then knew nothing of any of this. And the me of now has only a finite number of seconds of life left, practically all of which are already being spent with you."

Her mother had looked more gaunt than ever when she said this. The extra years and the secrecy were taking their toll.

"You are young, my Faufi. The young have excess energy. And this task, and its secrecy, are vitally necessary; equally necessary. Still I feel guilty."

"Oh, no, Mother!" Faufi protested. "Never think that you are wasting my youth. You are enhancing it. God has given us time together that we might never have had."

But the time finally ran out. Sophia eventually told Faufi that her visits, ever more stringently rationed, were at an end.

"Dearly beloved, we shall meet again in Heaven. You must carry the burden alone now. I shall always love you. Farewell."

The pain of that parting was still with Faufi. Tears could still spring to her eyes unexpectedly. She had thrown herself into her studies and advanced quite rapidly, thanks to her extra maturity and coaching, and to her endeavors to dull the pain by working herself to exhaustion each evening.

And now, this.

Pull yourself together, Faufi thought. Mama taught you well. What would she do? Not panic, surely. "Patience," she would say.

Anna! Remember Anna? What a crisis that was, and how calmly Mama dealt with it! "I'm glad Anna saw it," she said. She would doubtless find good even in this calamity too.

She would simply find that thief and...

And what? Confront him? Ask him to return the paper? What if he'd already read it? It had been a month.

Faufi unlocked her diary. She had long since learned to log all her time jumps carefully, like scientific experiments (which of course they were, but not for publication), so she had no difficulty in returning to the exact instant.

She watched a young man watching her hide the paper.

She saw herself vanish, saw him remove the paper, and followed him to his room in the dormitory.

Fortunately for her purpose, in 1995 no one blinked to see a boy and girl enter the same dorm. How shocked she had been, at first, by the future! More shocking still, perhaps, was the readiness with which she accepted the relaxation in the rules. Some of them.

It could not be doubted that the Victorian era, as she had come to think of it, had some rules that were simply unnecessary. As a native of that period, she had sometimes chafed at them. Why shouldn't a woman become a mathematician?

But from her unique point of view, she could see that the precious innocence and law-abiding peacefulness of that century stemmed in large part from the very rules which hedged young people away from impropriety.

If the young were angels, they could be trusted. The Victorians knew that they were not, and wisely curtailed their "occasions of sin" or, at least, tried not to place temptation too blatantly in their path.

One hundred years later it was just the opposite.

And some of the young, it developed, proved worthy of trust. Some did not.

As Faufi stood in the hall waiting for the crack of light under the boy's door to go out, she hoped he was one of the former.

She would wait an hour after his light went out, to give him time to fall asleep, then go in—a locked door was no barrier—and retrieve the paper.

The light stayed on.

A few minutes' work with the gyroscope told her that it would stay on all night. He was too interested in reading the paper to sleep. Well, he would have to sleep sometime.

As for herself, Faufi could hardly keep her eyes open. But she could remedy that. There was always time to catch a few hours of sleep, or an extra half-day to study for an examination or to finish writing a paper.

Mama had admonished her not to use the technique frivolously, lest she be caught at it. Faufi obeyed. But getting good grades was certainly not frivolous. And there were many demands on her time. And she was always very careful not to abuse the ability. She didn't want to age too fast.

Returning to the same minute after a refreshing eight hours' nap in a nearby room which her scouting had assured her would remain vacant, she considered that it had not been frivolity that had endangered the secret. She had only been doing her duty. The secret paper on the articulation of time was always to be kept behind the loose stone when not in use.

Well, I was a bit careless, she confessed to herself. I was tired. I should have checked the bushes—What's that?

Soft strains of classical music were emanating from the boy's room: "Scheherazade," by Nikolai Rimsky-Korsakov.

Good. She had heard worse, much worse, in this century. Perhaps the boy was a moral being.

Perhaps he never slept.

I'll change the parametrization, Faufi thought.I can fast forward until he leaves or falls asleep. No. That would be another mistake, worse than the first. Suppose someone comes through the hall and sees this statue of a girl, frozen in plain sight? But if I hide, I can't watch. Or...there's the keyhole of the room across the corridor... No. Anyone could zip up and open the door in a flash, long beforeI could react, and see me crouching there like a ceramic frog. Fast-forward is too dangerous except in very special circumstances. I'll just have to wait.

What's that clicking? Is he typing? Worse and worse; he must be copying the paper. Why doesn't he make a photocopy? Well, what *is* he doing?

Why don't I just knock, introduce myself, snatch the paper and go?

But if he's already read it?

What a squirm I'm in!

30
Through the Keyhole

Finally overcoming her reluctance, Faufi bent and placed her eye to the keyhole. The young man was typing something into a small computer on his desk. Her mother's paper was nowhere to be seen.

He paused, waiting for the computer to catch up, typed again, waited again, and said "Ah." The screen went blank. He typed one word and then, with the cursor blinking at the end of the word, reached over and disconnected the power cord from the wall and then from the computer. The cursor was still blinking. He must have switched over to battery power.

He pressed a key and vanished.

Faufi let out a muffled shriek and banged her head on the doorknob. Surely this boy was a mere undergraduate! How could he have mastered the inversion of hyperelliptic functions? Yet he had obviously time-jumped. He was already able to put her mother's paper into application.

Perhaps he had found another way to perform the integration of the fourth first integra…Of course! He had used the computer, not knowing how dangerous that was. Well, he wouldn't get far that way. And without a gyroscope—

"Yea! It worked! The clock jumped!" came a cry from inside the room. She looked through the keyhole again.

The boy was back. As she watched, he clicked shut the computer, murmuring something about…could it be aardvarks?…scooped a jacket off the back of his chair and an envelope off the desk, thrust an arm through a jacket sleeve and gripped the computer's handle, jammed the envelope through the other sleeve and into a pocket, threw some books and a blanket into a suitcase, and strode toward the door.

In her haste to hide she almost fell. Scrambling, she barely made it to the corner of the corridor before he was out the door, slamming it and leaving the light on. She had missed his exit in her scouting! She struggled into her overcoat and followed him out into the chilly night.

She had no difficulty keeping up with him on the train to Stockholm. When he took the airport shuttle, she managed to board behind him without being noticed. But when he caught the early morning flight to London with only minutes to spare, she conceded that she had been outmaneuvered.

She had no ticket. She wasn't carrying enough modern money to buy one. She had no passport. Nobody needed one where she came from. Even if she had, it would have been long out of date.

As she watched her quarry escape through the boarding gate, she wished, not for the first time, that her mother's technique extended to traveling through space as well as time.

Well, in a manner of speaking, it did. At least it could be used effectively to speed up the process. She opened her diary and made a careful note of the time and flight number. Then she took the shuttle back into the city. At least she was in Stockholm. Home.

She returned to 1895 and caught a carriage to her usual terminus, the lakeside esplanade two blocks from Aunt Ellen's house, where she lived when not away at school. At this moment she *was* away at school, so she had to be careful not to be seen in town by anyone who knew her schedule. That was simply a matter of the proper timing.

She walked around the horses and vanished.

It was now midnight and proper Stockholm was sleeping. She hurried home to her room and extracted certain gold ornaments her mother had left her. She got away without waking anyone.

I never expected to need money this badly, Faufi thought at ten the next morning, as she walked through a shop door over which hung three gold balls. From the pawnshop she walked ten blocks to the best part of the business district, and opened a savings account.

Ten years later, she withdrew the money with accrued interest, closed the account, returned to 1895, and opened another account. She repeated this procedure until she felt hungry enough to break for lunch.

After treating herself to a modest lunch in a restaurant she knew Aunt Ellen disliked, she walked back to the pawnshop and redeemed her heirlooms minutes after pawning them, saying she had changed her mind. She returned them to her bedroom shortly after the previous Faufi had removed them, not bumping into her or anyone else.

Returning downtown, she placed her now-sizable fortune in a checking account and ordered a packet of checks engraved with her name, for delivery to her aunt's home. She haunted the front hall of that home at each mail delivery, every day for two weeks, until she saw the checks drop through the slot. She took them and disappeared just before Anna came downstairs to fetch the mail. There was little danger of being seen, since she was reparametrized; in fact, she was able to read the address on each piece of mail while it was falling through the air.

Finally she returned downtown and, writing a check for half her fortune, opened a numbered savings account in a bank she knew would still be thriving a century later. Then she boarded the first of several southbound trains, first class sleepers all the way, terminating in King's Cross Station, London.

Exhausted by the travel, but not as weary as if she hadn't gone fast-forward lying in her locked cabins, she booked a room at Claridge's and rested for the remainder of the evening.

Almost there, she thought as she dropped off to sleep after a light supper. I've almost got him.

The next morning she jumped to 1995 and walked to the nearest Bank of England branch. She opened an account with funds wired from her numbered Stockholm account, which was now astronomical.

She was served quickly and politely. Even the B of E had not seen many young millionairesses lately. Old money, too.

Olof Palme's taxes had gotten most of it, of course. Faufi didn't begrudge it to him. Easy come, easy go.

She rode the underground to Heathrow and was waiting for the young man's flight from Stockholm when it landed. Who needs passports, she thought smugly.

But he did not disembark.

31
Passport

The international section of Heathrow was separated from the domestic by passport control, which Faufi could not penetrate. Since Chazz was only passing through London on his way to Moscow, he did not emerge but, after jumping unnoticed five minutes into the past—just for practice and to beat the crowd—simply walked over to gate seven, from which Flight 17 was to depart. It was already boarding. He entered, found his seat, and resumed programming his computer, forty minutes after Melvin Schwartz's keys beeped.

When Faufi finally gave up waiting, and realized that the young man could have departed to any of six hundred destinations world-wide, she did not despair. She got mad.

She needed a passport. This was only a problem. She'd solved much harder problems in her life, just in mathematics. She had all the time and money she needed, so this should be easy. But first there was something to take care of.

She returned to Uppsala by cruising in fast forward on a Scandinavian Liner in 1913, entered the young man's dorm room, and finally found the secret paper. It was stacked next to the computer printer on the desk, with the last page still rolled around the platen.

Printer! Why? Then, to her chagrin, she saw that there was an optical scanner attached to the dot matrix printhead. He had copied the paper, after all. Into his computer.

She retrieved the paper, concealed it behind the stone again, and set about to obtain a passport valid in 1995, when she would be one hundred seventeen.

She knew very well that passports could be bought. But she wanted to do this as nearly legally as possible, falsifying only her birth date, since that was certainly a necessity if she were to keep the Secret. Nevertheless, even that disturbed her.

Did the end of keeping the Secret justify any means at all? If so, she would be no better than Napoleon, or even Stalin.

No, of course it didn't. Only necessary means were justified. And only means intimately and inextricably bound up with the end, at that. Like falsifying her birthdate. Bother all this paperwork anyway!

Having reached a moral standoff, Faufi put it out of her mind and set to work.

After doing many things she would have formerly been surprised at, not least of which was altering two digits on her birth record in the few seconds of a bureaucrat's inattention, Faufi obtained her Swedish passport, with her own name and lovely picture on it. She was now officially eighteen in 1995, and wealthy to boot.

Now let's see him get away!

At Heathrow she needed an overseas ticket to gain entry to the international-flights concourse. Seeing no advantage in any one particular destination over another, she was ready to purchase a ticket at random when she remembered having played the game "Going to Jerusalem" as a child.

Why not, she thought.

Ticket in hand, she proceeded to Gate 92, where the early-bird flight from Stockholm was expected. Arriving two minutes before it was scheduled to land, she stationed herself where she could see everyone who disembarked. That should have included every passenger, as the flight did not continue past London.

But no young man. Or, at least, not the right one.

Faufi had lost the trail. She couldn't understand how.

Well, she was inexperienced. She ought to do it right the next time: she would hire a private investigator and let him suffer the confusion, while she took a rest in 1895 studying algebraic topology under Dr. Poincare.

Right now it was back to Claridge's for some lunch. She absolutely could not continue.

She bought a lurid London faxoid, *Now,* outside the inn's entrance to read over lunch. It had a chess column. Faufi liked that. She also liked to read the science and technology news. She was especially interested in seeing how the gaps in the fossil record had closed up since Mr. Darwin's time, but so far had come across no mention of this. She never read the headlines; politics was too depressing, ever since October, 1917, when her mother's homeland had been destroyed.

Having arrived at Claridge's at the peak of the lunchtime crowd, Faufi perforce shared a table with a young man dining on plaice and chips. He did not seem to be too displeased.

She did not expect him to attempt to strike up a conversation—the British were so insular—so when she unfolded her newspaper and began to turn to the chess column, he surprised her by speaking. "I see those ruddy skyjackers have struck again."

"Mmmm?" mumbled Faufi around a bite of tuna sandwich.

He gestured at the outside page of her newspaper. "Have a look."

The front page revealed the usual secrets of the latest government sex scandal. From the back page, a picture of her young quarry stared up at her. The headline blared, "Swedish Math Whiz Hijacks 747 to Bagdad."

Spilling her tea, Faufi leaped to her feet, fatigue and tuna forgotten. "So nice to talk to you," she said absently. If she caught the tube right away, she'd just make her flight to Jerusalem, and from there it was only a short distance to Baghdad. How opportune that she hadn't bought a ticket to Timbuctu!

The young man looked after her departing form forlornly.

"Was it something I said?" He sighed. "All that and a Swedish accent too."

She found out before long, of course, that there were no scheduled flights at all from Israel to Iraq. But by then she was in Lod Airport, in Tel Aviv.

Lord, why is this happening? she wondered. Even if Saddam Airport was closed down because of the bomb threat, she could have gone there the day before the hijacking. Why hadn't He let her think of that?

Well? She listened. No direct answer was forthcoming. However, she did get the comforting feeling that God was in control. And she knew she could regain the time.

Meanwhile, why not relax for a little while? Perhaps then she would stop making mistakes at such a great rate. And she had always wanted to see the Holy City.

Faufi stood on the Temple Mount admiring the Dome of the Rock. It certainly was beautiful. No wonder the Jews had left it standing in 1967. She had to admire them for that decision, since it blocked any plans they may have had to rebuild the Temple.

She walked across the vast flat area, away from the Western Wall, circling the mosque just outside the courtyard that was forbidden to infidels.

What else was there to visit up here? She consulted her tourbook. Perhaps there would be something of interest in the Dome of Solomon, near the old site of the Fortress of Antonia. The Fortress, she read, had been destroyed by the Romans in A.D. 70.

She walked past the Dome of the Chain toward Solomon's Dome in the northwest corner of the flat, got perhaps a third of the way there, and stopped.

Why had she stopped?

What was here? What had made her pause here?

There was nothing nearby, not even a tourist. She might have been in a parking lot for all there was of interest.

Silly! she thought. Come on, let's go! But she didn't want to. Not just yet. Although the sun was blistering hot, a shiver passed through her. What was going on?

Her hand strayed into her purse where it encountered the gyroscope. *Be ready*, came an unbidden thought.

Slowly, not knowing why, she drew the device out of her purse, and wound the spring. She touched the lever to push it to the position marked 'F.'

Is this you, Lord? Well, I'm ready. Thy will be done.

Suddenly she was in Hell.

Smoke stung her eyes. Blistering heat, ruddy light, smote her from a wall of flame nearby. The clamor was deafening, the shreiks of the damned agonizing.

I wasn't ready for this, she thought. Dear Lord, get me out of here!

BOOK IV

The Roman Empire

32
Antioch

C. Junius Aulus was sitting at a table on the patio of Daphne's Inn in Antioch with a lady friend, sipping Falernian wine, when a commotion down the Mall caught his attention.

"What is it, Gaius?"

"I don't know. Parade of some sort? Down there."

A mounted column appeared around the corner from Eastern Drive. Queer small ponies, Gaius mused. And the riders were more so. Leather tunics and leggings; swords and bows. He wondered who they were. They seemed peaceful enough, so far. Jupiter! How many were there?

For the column kept coming, seeming to flow endlessly around the corner. The sounds of hooves on the cobbles and swords striking spurs, accompanied by a babble of voices from the excited citizenry, reached him and increased as the riders drew closer.

The first rank of horses, six abreast, kept perfect time as they approached. Their riders wore a soft tawny uniform topped with a tall domed headpiece, and each, he saw as more detail became evident, bore a full quiver of arrows slung behind the left shoulder. The obvious leader, a lean, grizzled man with a broad, gray mustache, rode in the middle. A younger, bearded man, who looked related, rode on his right. Nearest to Aulus rode another shaggy one, but the other three were mere beardless youths.

He started. At the same instant the lady, named Juliana, spoke: "Gaius, look! Women!"

"Yes, I see. And what women! They ride like men!" He took a drink. "And the men like legionaries. What is this? I must find out what's going on."

"I'm surprised you don't already know," said Juliana. "Haven't you repeatedly assured me you know everything?"

He grinned. "You've found me out."

"But this indeed would seem to be in your purview. It's clearly a military mission."

"Hush. They approach." The first rank was ten paces away. Aulus didn't really expect to overhear them talking; they appeared too disciplined for that, too stone-faced. It was one of those faces he was interested in.

The black-haired woman, between the two bearded men—she of the most striking, exotic beauty—her eyes were blue! And regally alert. They darted, piercing, around the crowd, assessing it. Assessing him! They locked on his eyes. He looked away. She could be a queen, he thought. Another Musa.

His gaze, wandering, focused on a bright reflection from a ring worn by the nearest rider as the front rank drew abreast.

A Star of David! These people were Jews!

"My dear, I'm sorry, but I'll have to take my leave," he said, rising. "Please excuse me. Another time."

"I was afraid of this," glowered Juliana. "I saw that woman look you over."

"What woman? It's only that—look. You're right, this is an army. So where are Saturninus's legions? Nowhere in sight! These must be friends of his. In town by prearrangement."

"And you knew nothing of this?"

"Sentius doesn't confide in Herod's agent. We have a, shall we say, cordial relationship. As in cordial dislike. I must ferret out facts myself. And this is one example."

"All right, go."

"Juliana! This will only take a few days."

"Take as long as you like. There's plenty to keep a girl occupied in Antioch." She rose to her feet also, turned, and stalked away.

Throwing a coin on the table, Aulus gathered up the trailing folds of his toga and set out at a brisk pace to follow the head of the column, which was still passing.

It took him two hours to locate someone in the caravan who was willing to speak to him and whom he could understand. They all seemed blissfully ignorant of Latin, speaking Aramaic or some even more barbarous tongue. Finally he found a Graecophone ox driver who was nothing loath to converse with someone other than his oxen.

"'Tis my master Zamaris, with his family and army, come from Babylon to settle in Valatha at the governor's invitation," this worthy informed him.

"And they— you—are Jews?" Aulus inquired.

"Aye, good fighting Parthian Jews, most of us," replied the driver, "though some of the troops be still heathen worshipers of Astarte or Marduk or suchlike. But we're workin' on 'em. Now tell me more of Antioch. Is't true what they say of the ladies?"

"All you've doubtless heard is true," Aulus assured him. "And worse." He loped away on aching feet. "*Kalimera.*"

"Hey! Come back! I want to know—" The driver's voice faded behind him. Aulus had heard enough. He had to get word to Herod immediately.

As soon as they were well within the gates of the estate, the six column leaders burst out laughing.

"Ha! Did you see their faces?" asked Jacimus.

"Quite a performance," Zimri said. "It's not easy, looking grim and competent for ten miles."

"It was fun, though," said Mel.

"They looked as if they'd never seen a woman before," Ruth remarked.

"They haven't: not like us," said Aletha.

"Think they were suitably impressed?" Chazz asked.

"I do believe so." Zimri chuckled. "Come on, let's get out of these hot uniforms." He broke into a gallop. The entire column raced after him, cheering, toward the main buildings visible above the trees on the hill.

"Our new home! At last!" cried Aletha, pounding along beside Chazz.

Mel heard Chazz answer something about "charging up." He didn't think he was talking about charging up the hill.

33
Sacrifice

That afternoon Zimri stood in the center of a clearing on a hill overlooking the verdant estate. Mel could glimpse white marble among the trees below: a column here, a cupola there; occasionally, as the breeze swayed the leafy branches, a facade or an entire building. The breeze fanned the flame of a torch in Bathyra's hand; sparks whipped away across the stones piled before her.

Between Bathyra and Zimri, Jacimus stood holding the tether of a seventh-year bullock. Balthasar and several husky cousins surrounded the bullock. The time travelers stood behind Zimri with Aletha, Tosthenes, and Kaski the physician. Zimri's entire army was drawn up in ranks, on foot, in dress tans. The rest of his relatives encircled him in respectful silence among the freshly-cut low stumps that dotted the clearing.

The rock pile, occupying the highest point, was neatly laid with square corners. Like an outdoor barbecue, thought Mel. He had hefted some of those uncut stones himself, after helping chop down the phallic trees. The peeled logs were now arranged on the pile over kindling. At Zimri's nod, Bathyra applied her torch to them, then stepped back. Smoke began to drift across the clearing.

Zimri raised his hands and face to the sky, and prayed: "Blessed art thou, O Lord our God, king of the universe, who delivers us out of the hands of our enemies. We praise you for your holiness, mercy, and might. We thank you for bringing us safely to this place, and for the redemption of this idolatrous grove. We offer this sacrifice to you for the sanctification of this your altar, which I name *El palat*: 'the Lord delivereth.' Most holy God, loving Father, may this sacrifice be acceptable to you. May it be a sweet savor to you for our thanksgiving. We praise you and bless you forever. Amen."

Jacimus handed the tether to his father and grasped the horns of the bullock. Zimri untied the rope and drew his sword. The bull lowed as Jacimus twisted its horns and pulled them toward the fire, stretching the animal's neck. Zimri slit its throat. Blood spurted over the altar. The bull buckled in death.

While the strong men heaved the body onto the altar, Ruth swayed and collapsed.

Flames licked up around the offering as Mel dropped to his knees by Ruth's side and cradled her head. The others were there only a beat later.

"Back," commanded the physician in a low voice. "Stand back. Let me see." He knelt by Ruth, placed a hand on her forehead, then felt her throat. "She'll be all right. She's fainted, that's all. Mel, Jac: move her into the shade."

In five minutes Ruth was sitting propped up against a tree, awake but dizzy.

"Ruth, are you feeling all right now? What happened?" Jacimus asked.

Mel looked at him in puzzlement. Didn't he know?

"That was *awful.*" Ruth's voice was weak but vehement.

"What—" Jacimus began, but Zimri interrupted him.

"Yes. It was. Blood sacrifice is awful. That is no accident. Its purpose is to show us the gravity of sin. Sin is awful, too. Sin is death."

"Didn't you know what was coming?" asked Jacimus.

"But *seeing* it—all the blood..."

"It's my fault," Mel said. "I should have realized."

"I was feeling a little sick myself," put in Chazz.

"Brother," Aletha asked, "don't you remember my first time at a sacrifice? I screamed. I had nightmares for days."

"I remember your first time," said Bathyra to Jacimus. "You were bothered also. As you should have been."

"Our trouble is," Aletha confessed, "we've grown used to these sacrifices. As Father said, they are meant to be horrible, to show us the way sin looks in the sight of God. I thank you, Ruth, for your reaction—for showing us the horror through fresh eyes."

"What sin?" asked Ruth. "Whose?"

"The unspeakable practices that were committed in this grove," Zimri replied. "God cannot tolerate sin. Were we to dwell here without having purified this place, he could not look on our home without loathing. The only cure for sin is blood sacrifice. We're glad there is a cure for our sins. Other than our own blood."

"Enough," ordered Kaski. "The lady needs rest and quiet now. Let's get her back to the house."

34
Eden

That evening another Sabbath began. The bare minimum of furnishings had been unpacked: enough to let the travelers spend the night comfortably in their new quarters. For Chazz, Mel and Ruth, this minimum included the electrical gear.

After dinner, Chazz and Mel again poured the electrolyte into the battery tank, which rested on a table in a cross-ventilated corner. Six of its twelve lead plates were now coated with a thick layer of rust.

"Okay, try it," Chazz requested.

Ruth made the connection. A fat white spark leaped across to the coil. The compass needle whipped around to the west, quivering tightly. Smoke began to rise from the insulation covering the gold wire.

"Hooray!" Chazz shouted.

"Ouch!" cried Ruth. "That's hot!" She yanked the wires apart, to the accompaniment of another spark. "It didn't quite melt," she observed.

"That's OK; plenty of amps for our purposes," said Chazz. "Let's hook up the computer battery."

"You sure this won't fry it?" Mel asked.

"No, I'm not."

"Then we should—"began Ruth.

"Look, this battery's just a boat anchor as it stands," Chazz urged. "We can't hurt it. We've got to try something."

"He's right, Ruth. This is our best chance."

"All right. What are we waiting for? Go for it."

"Let's see," mumbled Chazz, "the lead peroxide is reduced to lead sulfate, so it needs electrons to feed the protons, so it's the positive terminal." He connected the computer battery's positive lead to that terminal. "Let's see that galvanometer." He hooked it up in series, all but the last connection. "Watch the needle. It should move the same way as before." He twisted the last pair of wires together through fleece mitts. The needle swung west.

"It did," Ruth said.

"Then it's charging. All we do now is wait."

"We've waited a month already,"said Mel. "What's another few hours?"

That night Mel had another dream. It began pleasantly enough. He was back in the British Airways jet flying toward Moscow. He was seated between Chazz and Ruth as before, but instead of a folio of mathematics, there was a Bible on his tray table. He opened it to the first page and read, "In the beginning God created the Big Bang..."

Chazz rang for the steward and tried to hijack the plane, but this time the pilot came back from the cabin wearing a grim expression. It was Jacimus. "My hero!" cried Ruth, flinging herself into his arms. He drew a sword from inside his flight jacket and slit Chazz's throat. Chazz hit a key as he died, and the plane exploded, flinging Mel into space.

Mel hung suspended comfortably in black space with a bird's-eye view of the solar system. He could see the earth, which was a cube of six colors, clicking around the sun in its orbit, while rotating, in jerks like a flashcube, on its axis. Each time it passed a certain point, sunlight reflected off its blue face into Mel's eyes. He knew that it was rotating exactly 360 times in each revolution about the sun.

Suddenly there was a missed beat in the regular clicking as a blurry red object streaked past the planet. Mel's viewpoint drew back and became four-dimensional as the earth entered a slightly enlarged orbit. He could see its whole history as a series of cubes arranged in a helix, like a spring coiled around the bright wire of the sun's track through time. The places where the light flashed off earth's blue face were strung out in a line of square beads, running up one side of the helix. Above the red blur, there was a kink in the helix as in a broken Slinky, and the blue beads were, from that point up, interspersed by beads of different colors: red, yellow, green, blue, red, yellow, green, blue, red. The original blue faces formed a string that was no longer a straight line running up one side of the helix but instead looped gradually around it, returning to its original position (he knew) every sixty-eight and four sevenths years.

As he was wondering what this meant, the scene changed. Instead of floating in space, he was hovering on feathery wings among the branches of a large fruit tree in the middle of a beautiful garden. Ruth was with him, clothed in light, and they were suffused with joy, immersed in love.

There was a sudden blur of red, a feeling of tension, and she was offering him a taste of a fruit she had plucked and bitten. He had the most anguished sense of loss and despair he had ever felt. "Ruth, you shouldn't have done that," he cried.

"I...know," she answered. "Care to join me?"

You're in trouble now, he pictured himself saying. Ruth! How can I not join you? Yet he knew he must not.

Loving her too much, he reached for the fruit, bit, chewed and swallowed.

His wings disappeared and he fell, crashing through rough-barked branches to land painfully in mud and thorns, dirty, scratched and naked.

"No-o-o-o..." he wailed, and awoke sweating and knowing exactly what he had lost, and what he had to do.

35
Yes

"The program is set to take me an hour into the future, then pause and, when I press Enter, take me back an hour into the past," explained Chazz.

He, Mel, Ruth, Aletha, Zimri, Jacimus and Tosthenes stood near the altar. Chazz held the laptop computer. It was about ten a.m. Ruth wore a long Grecian gown and sandals. The white linen, blowing softly across her athletic figure, set off her tanned arms to perfection. Stunning! thought Mel.

"I'll just stay there long enough to say hello to us, then come back," Chazz continued. "To you I'll only be gone a minute; an hour later, there'll be two of me here for a minute." A light breeze overturned a feather of ash on the altar behind him.

"Amazing," Zimri marveled.

"I'll have to see this," declared Tosthenes.

"That disrupts my mind, just trying to think about it," Jacimus complained.

"Are you sure it's quite safe?" asked Aletha in a concerned tone. A gray sparrow landed on the ground near a blackened scrap of meat, pecked at it, and flew off.

Chazz smiled. "I'll be fine," he reassured her. "Don't worry."

"I don't understand how you can travel only an hour," said Ruth, "if points on the fibre are an integral number of mean solar years apart."

Jacimus looked at her, eyes wide.

"I think I may know something about that," began Mel. "I had a dream—"

"Do you want to go into all that now?" Chazz interrupted. "Let's get this test over with, then I'll explain it. Controlled differential fibrillation is the key…"

"Okay, okay," conceded Ruth. "It can wait."

"Everybody ready? Here goes." Chazz typed a command. "See you shortly." He pressed Enter and vanished.

The only sound was that of a fly as it buzzed through the immobile group, heading for the altar.

"Holy God of Jacob," Jacimus finally whispered.

"So it's all really true," said Tosthenes.

"He certainly makes it look easy," Ruth admitted.

"Routine," agreed Mel. "Piece of cake. Just press a button." Mel gazed at the horizon, where he could barely see a bend of the Orontes sparkling in the sun. A wisp of smoke rose in the foreground, momentarily obscuring it. "Ruth, we've got to look at that paper of Sophie's. I'll copy it off the hard disk by hand if necessary."

"Let me ask something," Zimri said. "Chazz vanished from our sight because he traveled into the future?"

"Right."

"Without passing through the intervening instants? For if he did, we should still be seeing him, though perhaps frozen."

"Very perceptive of you," noted Ruth. "You are correct. He looped outside the intervening interval. More than that I don't dare say just now."

Aletha frowned. "I also have a question."

"Yes?" Mel prompted.

"Chazz said he would stay in the future only long enough to say hello—"

"Well, long enough to verify the time by our watches," said Mel. "It should be about eleven when he gets there; it's a little after ten now."

"That should not take long," Aletha persisted.

"No, less than a minute," agreed Ruth.

"Then where is he?"

"She's right," Mel said. His gaze fell on a burned bone fragment lying on the uncut stones. He looked away. Suddenly the bright morning held chill. "He should be back by now."

"Don't panic," said Ruth. "He's probably chatting with himself."

"Let's give him a few more minutes," Jacimus urged.

"Until what?" asked Mel. "What can we do?"

"It's not just a question of sending out a search party this time," observed Tosthenes.

"No, but, as then, there is something we can do," Zimri pointed out.

"Of course." Mel reached out to the others, who gathered in a circle, holding hands. "Dear loving father in heaven, we need your help desperately once more. Please keep Chazz safe. Protect him and bring him back to us, soon."

"Amen," said the rest.

"And, Lord, thank you again for our new brother," Zimri added.

"Amen!" agreed Ruth heartily.

At ten-thirty Chazz was still absent, but there was a flurry of activity down the hill. After a few moments, Kimu could be seen running toward them.

"I wonder what it is?" Zimri started to walk toward him. "I'd better go see."

"The satrap," Kimu called as he neared the group. "Governor Saturninus has come to pay a call."

"Ah! Come, son. We must attend him." Zimri turned to the others. "You will please excuse us. I'm confident Chazz will be all right. He was probably detained by something trivial but compelling. In any case we must not slight our Syrian benefactor. Aletha? Tosthenes?"

"I'd like to wait here, please," Aletha begged. "You don't need me for protocol. I'll meet Sentius later."

"Chazz should show up in half an hour," said Mel. "At least one copy of him."

"Very well. Let me know as soon as he does. I'll see you later." Zimri walked down the hill with Kimu, Jacimus and Tosthenes.

"He will return." Aletha sat down on a tree stump and clasped her arms around her knees. "I know he will."

"I'm afraid for him," said Ruth in a low voice. "Even if he decided to go get Scheherazade, and spent years trying, he should have been able to return before now. I think he's dead."

"No!" cried Aletha.

"Let's not be hasty," Mel said. Ruth seated herself on the soft leather computer case where it lay on the sunny grass. Mel took a seat on a nearby stump. "He may just not have that much control."

"But he said he'd done plenty of short jumps before," argued Ruth. "He seemed to know all about the theory."

"Quit using past tense," Mel protested. "Can you picture Chazz knowing more than he thinks he does?"

"No, but I can't picture him being Mr. Prudent, either."

"I have a feeling—in fact, I'm sure—Chazz is not dead." Aletha, stretching out her legs, studied the toe of her boot. "That he's doing, or trying to do, exactly what he said he'd do."

"Then you think he must have goofed," Mel said. "You trust him. So do I."

"Trust him to goof, sure," Ruth agreed. "Actually, he has been acting more responsible lately. And pretty trustworthy—for a skyjacker. But suppose he 'prudently' decided to fetch a couple of spare batteries from 1995?"

"Ruth, we've talked it all out with him. He's a little thoughtless, maybe, but he's not dumb. I think he's just unable to return to the right minute. He missed the mark."

"Well, it's nearly eleven now." Ruth leaned back, resting her hands on the grass behind her. "We'll soon find out if he even managed to go to the right minute."

"He's not here," Mel observed at five minutes after eleven.

"Thank you, Dick Tracy. Now what?"

"Actually I'm relieved," replied Mel. "If he couldn't even go accurately, it's no wonder he couldn't return accurately. But since he was trying to jump only an hour, it's hard to believe he could be off by more than a few weeks."

"Mel, you know chaos," Ruth objected. "Chaos has a short memory. It acts like a discontinuity. Unpredictable."

"You're saying he could be anywhen."

"I'm afraid so."

Aletha looked up from her contemplation of the ground beside her stump. "I thought integration was supposed to be a smoothing process." She tried a smile.

"What else have you been teaching her?" Ruth asked in English.

"English."

"Oops."

"What did you say?" asked Aletha tactfully.

"Just a joke," Mel said. "It doesn't translate. But she's right, Ruth. It is a smoothing process. And consider: when Chazz tried for the seventh century A.D., he got 6 B.C."

"That was on the return," countered Ruth. "God only knows when he went to on the initial jump."

"Yes, He does. Remember, He brought you together once, at the river," Aletha reminded them. "He can do so again."

"Moreover," continued Mel, "even with that long a jump, the miss was in the same ball park as the intended interval. At least on the return. Surely if he only aimed for an hour, he—"

"Yes, all right," Ruth conceded. "Anyway, it's our only hope."

"It's good that you didn't try this experiment while we were still on the road." Aletha waved her hand at the date palms and jacaranda trees blooming down the hillside. "Now we're in our permanent home. No matter when Chazz shows up, he will find his friends."

"At least if he shows up in the future," Mel amended.

"We know he didn't go into the past here," reasoned Ruth. "We would have heard of it. He surely would have left a message for us."

"That's right! So, as long as he doesn't wander too far off and get lost—"

"I think he knows better than that," Aletha put in.

"Then he'll show up here eventually. We have to stop worrying, just keep him in prayer."

"What time is it now?" Aletha asked.

"Eleven-thirty," replied Mel. "I don't think there's much point in standing around any longer. There's nothing more we can do here." He rose to his feet and stretched, hands on the small of his back. "I think I'm going down to meet the Governor of Syria. Coming, ladies?"

"Yes, I think you're right," Ruth said. "Chazz can find us when he shows up. It could be hours. Or weeks." She stood and dusted off her hands. "Aletha?"

"I'll wait here a while longer. You go on ahead."

As they walked down through the trees Ruth said, "It looks like Aletha has more than a passing interest in our young friend."

"Yes, it does. Do you think he'll reciprocate?"

"Or even catch on? He's obsessed with a fantasy."

"I think Aletha would be perfect for him. She's pretty, bright—"

"And even a bit unreal. Just what he should like."

"Unreal?" Mel looked at her. "What makes you say that?"

"It's only that she's a girl from the past. To us she's been dust for millennia. Of course, she's alive now, vibrantly alive."

"She certainly is. But I see what you mean." He recalled the charred femur smoking in the ashes. "It hurts to think about it. Still, it's no more tragic than the normal condition of mankind."

"Death is not normal! It's hateful. Usual, maybe, but not normal." Her hands balled into fists. "Life is normal."

"I know. I misspoke."

"I misspoke too. Aletha is certainly real. She's the realest thing in Chazz's life, if he would only see it."

"And think of the problems it would solve!" exclaimed Mel. "From a purely practical point of view, I mean. If Chazz settled down here, Interpol would never find him."

"Unless they learned time travel. Oh, Mel! Can you imagine what a modern state would be like, with that power?"

"No wonder Sophia tried to hide it."

"Even if history can't be significantly changed, as Chazz seems to believe."

"Yes. 'It doesn't work that way,' he would say. Well, how does it work?"

"I've been giving that some thought."

"Ruth! You dared?"

"I'm still here, aren't I? I don't think we can jump without being together. Synergy, as you put it. Since we're together now, all I will say is this, and you'll have to work out the details on your own: Can strict materialistic causality coexist with free will? Or do there have to be a certain number of mid-course corrections? There, that's enough. The rest is left as an exercise for the student."

"'I can't think about that now,'" Mel quoted. "'I'll think about it tomorrow. After all….'"

"'…tomorrow is another day,'" finished Ruth. "Didn't you just love that movie?"

"Best movie ever made," Mel agreed. He paused briefly. "Ruth, will you marry me?"

36
Taxes

"Mel! Put me down!"

"But I'm so happy!" He kissed her.

"Mmm. But not out here, in broad daylight."

"There's nobody around. Let's get married right away."

"Don't forget where we are. Bathyra told me if we were publicly betrothed, we'd have to be separated."

"Separated!"

"To prepare. Then, one night, a messenger arrives to announce the bridegroom's imminent return. The bride fills her lamp and goes out with her bridesmaids to wait."

"In the middle of the night?" he asked, incredulous.

Ruth treated him to a sly grin. "It's the custom."

"Let's elope."

"Not an option here. You want to really be married, don't you?"

"Yes. Yes! Oh, Ruth, I can hardly believe it!"

"Believe it. Mel, I do love you. There was a time when I thought I would never be able to leave this place. That I was trapped here." She turned her head away from him. "I was frantic with fear. I couldn't inflict that fear on you—trap you here with me."

"With you it wouldn't be a trap. Anywhere. It would be…will be!…a pleasure dome. A home. You're not afraid now?"

"My fear was a sin. I should have trusted in God's love…and yours. I finally realized I couldn't face being separated from you. Bathyra was a great help. She is so wise! And what a good woman."

"I'll have to thank her for giving my honey such good counsel." He swung her hand as they walked down the white gravel path.

"Mel, it's going to be so hard to leave these people, all these wonderful friends."

"We're not out of the woods yet."

"I think we will be. Please, Mel, can we wait until we give it our best shot? I'd rather be married back home with my family. It'll probably be quicker in the long run."

"You have a persuasive argument there." Stopping, he kissed her again.

They continued down the hill. As they approached the terrace of the big house, loud voices reached Mel's ears: Zimri's, and another he didn't recognize.

". . . must know I'm disappointed," Zimri was saying.

"What could I do? I tell you, the order came directly from Caesar."

They went up the steps, through the cloister, past a delicate life-sized marble Artemis aiming her bow across the archway, and into the house.

"You are my friend and benefactor, Gaius." Zimri's voice, a little quieter, came from the lounge ahead. "Thus I feel I can speak honestly. Here, let me pour you some more wine."

Mel and Ruth reached the doorway of the grand lounge. A Roman centurion guarded it on the right; an exquisite winged Apollo, naturally colored, on the left. Inside there was quite a crowd: another centurion guarded the far archway, with two more at the side entrances; eight guards stood in back-to-back pairs in the corners, pila grounded at rest; four Romans Mel didn't recognize—Sentius's retainers, he thought—sat on the large sofa to his right that curved around a low oval table holding wine glasses and carafes; and at a symmetrical grouping on his left Zimri sat facing away, conversing with an elderly Roman in a toga, evidently the governor of Syria. Farther down sat Jacimus; Tosthenes stood behind the sofa at Zimri's back, and a Roman holding a pouch of scrolls waited behind the governor. Keira, Agnes's serving maid, bent near the table opposite, offering a tray of sweet cakes to one of the retainers. He smiled at her and selected one; she placed the tray on the table.

As Mel and Ruth approached their host, the governor was saying, "Thank you, Zimri. As if times weren't difficult enough—" Seeing them, he broke off.

Zimri looked around. "Oh, good. Please join us. Is Chazz back? Sit here. Keira, two more cups."

"Thank you," said Mel. "No, but he will return eventually, we're sure."

"I am sure also. Gaius, these are Mel and Ruth: two friends of mine from a place so distant even Caesar never heard of it. Their story is amazing."

"Incredible, perhaps? No offense meant, of course."

"You wouldn't believe it. None taken. Mel and Ruth, this unimaginative old soul is our illustrious governor, C. Sentius Saturninus. He was just telling me how he has reneged on his promise."

"I would not put it quite that way. Glad to meet you."

"We are honored, sir," Mel said.

"Are you sure we're not in the way?" asked Ruth. "We could—"

"No, no, no," Zimri protested. "Sit. Stay. Old friends and new, together. One can never have too many."

"Agreed," said Saturninus. "Welcome." Jacimus slid down the couch, making a place for Ruth next to the governor and, after the briefest hesitation, for Mel to sit next to her.

They would have to tell Jacimus right away, Mel thought as he sank gratefully to the cushions. It wouldn't be fair to let him keep hoping.

"After all, it's only a small matter," Zimri resumed, "uprooting our entire clan, coming all this way for nothing." He sipped some wine to conceal his grin.

"Nothing!" Saturninus waved his hand to indicate the luxurious room, the palatial buildings, the broad estate.

"Still. Wasn't there some way you could have petitioned Caesar to grant an exception?"

"What seems to be the problem?" asked Mel.

"This person before you," Zimri indicated Gaius, "promised me tax relief. Now he says he cannot give it."

"You see," Saturninus turned to address the newcomers, "it has just recently come to pass that there went out a decree from Caesar Augustus, that all the world should be taxed."

Mel saw gooseflesh rise on Ruth's bare arms. Her jaw dropped. Before she could speak, Zimri said: "It's only that all my life I have been persecuted by these taxes." He pronounced the word as though it were "typhus." "I had thought to see the load lifted at last."

"You can well afford it," said Gaius.

"It's a question of what's right. The Lord God himself requires only a tithe. What gives Caesar the arrogance—"

The Roman attendants tried to stifle a gasp. One of the retainers across the room half-rose, sloshing his wine on the walnut table. Pulling a rag from her pocket, Keira hurried toward the puddle.

"—to demand more than God?"

"Dad!" Jacimus whispered.

"I didn't hear what you said, Zamaris. Neither did anyone else. Please," begged Saturninus, "don't repeat it." He glared meaningfully around the room. There was a tense silence.

"I heard only something about Caesar's being God," Tosthenes offered.

"Yes." The Romans nodded. "Quite right." "That was it."

"This certainly is excellent wine," remarked Saturninus. "I believe I'll have another cup." Keira stepped around the table with a carafe and poured.

"I also." Zimri held out his cup. "It is a local vintage. Good, isn't it? We purchased it on our way into town yesterday."

The company relaxed.

"As if times weren't difficult enough," Saturninus resumed, "divine Caesar has ordained a census, to prepare for this taxation. Frankly, and with all due respect, it is a bureaucratic nightmare! My friend, you have never seen such traffic! Such confusion!"

"Why, what's going on?" inquired Jacimus.

"Let me guess," Ruth interjected. "All must go to be taxed: everyone into his own city. Right?"

Saturninus caught his breath. "How could you know that?"

"Yes, how?" asked Zimri. "I'm tolerably well-informed, and I hadn't heard of this census." He glared at Saturninus. "Nor the tax, needless to say."

"But it can't be," Ruth mumbled. "You're not Cyrenius. Or do you have a nickname?"

"Cyrenius? Never heard of him," replied Saturninus. "I am certainly not he."

"*Babakas*! Daddy!" Aletha stood in the doorway, one hand on Apollo's tan shoulder. "Excuse me," she said. "Chazz is back! And he says..." She paused.

"Come in, come in," invited Zimri. Aletha moved into the room with Chazz behind her. "Gaius, this is my daughter Aletha. And Chazz, another foreigner from that distant place. Youngsters, the governor."

"Delighted," said Sentius.

"I've been looking forward to this, sir," Aletha greeted him.

"Pleased to meet you," said Chazz. They stepped to the rounded end of the table, before Zimri and his guest.

"Now, son," Zimri prompted, "tell us of your adventures. Where have you been?" Aletha frowned momentarily.

"Where have I been?" asked Chazz. "Where were you? Couldn't you wait just a couple of minutes? At least Aletha had the courtesy—"

"Chazz, look at my watch," directed Ruth, leaning past the governor to offer her wrist.

"It's fast. Says noon."

"It is noon. You've been gone two hours. Check Mel's watch.'"

"Anyway. That's not important."

"Not important!" Ruth hissed.

"No. Wait till you hear my news. You—"

"Chazz, we're *so* glad to have you back," Aletha interrupted. She hugged Chazz around the waist, stood on tiptoe and kissed him on the mouth.

"Daughter!" exploded Zimri.

"Hey!" Chazz said, when he could.

"Just a sisterly peck, Daddy," reassured Aletha

"You'd better not try it on *me*," Jacimus muttered.

"No harm done."

"Gaius, I must apologize for my daughter."

"Looked perfectly innocent to me. Remember, this is Antioch."

"I know. That's what I'm afraid of: it may be contagious."

"Don't worry about *that*, Daddy."

Chazz still appeared to want to say something. Ruth looked him in the eye. "Chazz, we were just discussing some affairs of state; we can hear all about your adventures later, understand?"

Zimri also caught on. "Yes, later. I am interested, but another time. We have important company."

"Don't delay on my account," protested Saturninus. "At any rate, I fear I must take my leave now. A luncheon engagement with the ambassador. I have said what I came to say. Sorry to be the bearer of such bad news, but I thought you ought to know as soon as possible. And the good news is that you are welcome here, and that I'm delighted to see that you've arrived safe and sound."

"Well, I thank you for your visit, and it certainly was a pleasure seeing you again. Sorry you can't stay for lunch. You know Agnes's cooking."

"Agnes! Is she still with you? Perhaps I could give the ambassador some excuse." Saturninus turned and addressed his secretary behind the couch. "Claudius, are you quite sure that appointment was for today?"

"Here it is, excellency," said Claudius, unrolling a little scroll. "'Caesar's ambassador, lunch, eighth hour, Saturday.'"

"Well, duty calls." Sentius sighed. "One thing after another. It's enough to make me wish for a six-day work week."

Zimri smiled. "Yes, isn't it?"

"Well!" Zimri said when the Romans had left, "you certainly picked a dramatic way to silence Chazz. The cure was almost worse than the disease."

"Yes. I mean no! I mean, what was that all about? Not," Chazz assured Aletha, "that I minded in the least."

"Sorry I embarrassed you, Daddy," she apologized. "It was all I could think to do on the spur of the moment, when I realized it might not be a good idea for the governor to hear the news."

"I thought that was it," Ruth said. "What is the news?"

"I'll let Chazz tell it," said Aletha.

"First I'd like to know what the bad news was, that the governor brought."

"Chazz—" Mel began.

"Patience," said Zimri. "It is a matter of taxes," he told Chazz. "When Saturninus invited us here, one of his inducements was immunity from taxes. Now he says it cannot be."

"Can't you go elsewhere?" asked Mel.

"We could have originally. There were offers from several rulers and satraps who would have liked an elite troop of Parthian archers to help defend their territories. I fear those options are now closed."

"Interesting," Chazz mused. "Now I'll tell you what happened to me. I went into the future as planned, but not just an hour."

"We know," said Mel. "We waited."

"Chaos must have taken over sooner than I expected."

"So much for your series of twenty-year jumps," Ruth said. "What about all your experiments back in Sweden? I thought you—"

"Well, it worked fine at five minute intervals. I assumed—"

"What! Five minutes?" cried Ruth.

"You went from five minutes to fourteen centuries?" Mel asked. "Just like that?"

"It seemed to be working," defended Chazz. "How was I to know?"

"All right, all right," Mel said. "How far did you jump this time?"

"I wasn't sure, at first. Later I figured it couldn't be more than two or three days. Flies were still buzzing around the scraps on the altar; the stumps looked freshly cut; things in general looked about the same."

"Why didn't you just check with us?" asked Ruth.

"You were gone."

"Gone!" Mel exclaimed.

"We were? Hooray! That means we did manage to find a way to jump—"

"Hold it, hold it. I mean you were *all* gone. The whole clan. I looked all over. The estate was deserted. Wagons, camels and all."

"Looks like one of those options opened again," remarked Mel.

"See, Daddy? That was the news I didn't want Sentius to hear. It might have seemed as if we didn't appreciate his hospitality."

"Quick thinking, daughter. You did well. I'm sorry I yelled at you."

"Well, it did look a little unseemly," Jacimus reproved.

"It was necessary," said Aletha. "Fun, too," she added mischievously.

"So that's why you were so sure you wouldn't catch Antioch-itis," Tosthenes said.

"Correct. We won't be around long enough."

"Unfortunately, I don't share that vision," said Zimri. "I have no intention of leaving. We have nowhere to go."

"It isn't a 'vision.'" Chazz insisted. "It's the future."

"Maybe it's just *a* future," suggested Mel. "A possibility."

"It doesn't work that way," Chazz and Ruth said in unison.

"This will be a good test, then, won't it?" asked Mel.

37
On the Articulation of Time

After lunch, Chazz proposed, "Well, let's try five minutes."

"Can if you want," said Mel. "I don't see much point. If you can only jump five minutes reliably, the whole project falls apart. It just isn't feasible any more."

"An hour was supposed to be the low end," Ruth added. "Working up toward twenty years. Even that was going to take a hundred jumps."

"I know what I saw," argued Chazz. "Sophia had no trouble. She seemed to have complete control. And there's nothing in her paper about any limitations."

"She must have left something out, for extra security," Ruth guessed.

"Anyway, I'd like to copy the paper before something else goes wrong," requested Mel, "if you don't mind."

"Sure. Here. Just turn it on and type 'TYPE SOPHIA.LST.' Control-S will pause the scrolling."

"I'd better leave the room while you do that," Ruth cautioned. "We'll read the paper independently and see what we come up with."

"Wish we could discuss it."

"At least I haven't had that problem," said Chazz. "I jump only when I want to. Possibly each of you could discuss it with me."

"One step at a time," advised Ruth. "I'm going to my room and lie down, maybe do a little reading of Scripture. It is the Sabbath."

"Me too. I've had a longer day than you guys," Chazz pointed out. "Just bring the computer to my room when you're finished with it."

"Okay. See you." Mel opened the laptop as they left. He had already collected a dozen sheets of fine papyrus. "Hope my pen doesn't run out of ink," he muttered, turning on the power. He waited while it booted, then typed as instructed. Sophia's lost paper began to scroll up the screen. He paused it, and settled down to copying:

On the Articulation of Time
by
Sophia V. Kovalevskaya

ABSTRACT. A method is presented which applies the concept of time as a complex variable to the construction of particular liftings in a certain Riemannian manifold.
KEY WORDS. Differential fibrillation, Fixed point, Lifting, Psychomanipulation, Riemannian manifold, Rigid body, Telechronic translation, Universal covering space.
INTRODUCTION. In the investigation of the motions of a rigid body about a fixed point [1], [6], it is found crucial to the discovery of the fourth first integral to treat the time, t, as a complex variable. This leads to a consideration of paths in the t-plane…

The Sabbath was nearly over, and the room was quite dim, when Mel finished copying. He clicked off the power; the amber symbols vanished. He snapped the case closed, gathered the white sheets into a sheaf, and sat thinking in the gloomy lounge.

So much was now clear! Why hadn't he done this long ago? He saw now how to specify a particular path in the time plane. It was the inverse of a certain map, that carried the fixed point into now, composed with one of its liftings into the helix.

It still wasn't clear what that fixed point was. He couldn't believe what the symbolism seemed to imply: that it was the center of rotation of the entire spacetime universe, the point about which all things hinged.

But it was clear how to use the kink in the helix, where the fibres' singular intersection had pulled away from the sun's world-line, to swing from one to another and, sliding back down the projection map, arrive only minutes away from where one started.

This was "controlled differential fibrillation." Mel's unconscious mind had put it almost entirely together from what Chazz had said in the ruins of Babylon, plus Tosthenes' remark about the three hundred sixty-day "prophetic year." Like Henri Poincaré's, Mel's undermind had recombined his hidden thoughts while he slept, then displayed them in a dream.

But that was the less significant part of the dream, Mel realized. The main part, which he was sure was a true vision, was the realization of what it meant to be enfolded in God's love…and then to be separated from it by sin. Everything else was secondary.

He marveled that it had only been this morning when he had gone to talk to Zimri about his problem.

Why hadn't he done *that* long ago?

Sometimes no amount of evidence will change a mind, he remembered saying. Sometimes it took a kick in the slats, a fall in the thorns.

Thank you, Lord. And it was so simple.

Never mind the hundreds of rules, Zimri had told him. The important thing was to love God with your whole being, as it said in the Sh'ma, and then to love your neighbor as yourself.

Where had Mel heard that before? Simply resolve to do the will of God—"Him only shalt thou serve," Zimri had quoted—and everything else would be made clear. Well, that seemed to be working.

And more is promised, Mel thought. Someday, according to Isaiah, there will come an Anointed One who will be wounded for our transgressions, and have laid on him the iniquity of us all. "By his knowledge shall my righteous servant justify many; for he shall bear their iniquities."

The ultimate blood sacrifice!

Mel had always been told that that servant was Israel. That wasn't how Zimri saw it. But the important thing was the love of God, and obedience to him. The rest he would learn in due time.

Wow! Look how dark it is, Mel noticed. I'd better return Chazz's computer. I know why he's having trouble with long jumps, and I think I can safely tell him.

"But I don't know what to do about it," he said in Chazz's suite. "It's the old unstable IVP. An initial value problem."

"Are you sure?" Chazz sat forward on the scrollbacked velvet couch. "I would have thought it was a boundary value problem. After all, you know what time you want to end up at, as well as what time you're leaving from."

"Yeah but see, you only know one dimension of the time. That's the concept underlying this whole technique." Mel turned to trace an evanescent diagram on the silken wall-hanging with his finger. "Your end boundary is a line, not a point. Sure, you end up on that line, but where? Finding the other coordinate is the initial value problem. And it's evidently unstable: a slight change in the initial conditions leads to wild variations in the final answer, if you try to go too far."

"Chaos! And 'too far' is less than an hour."

"Apparently." Mel pulled back the chair at the low table across from Chazz, sat, and crossed his legs.

"And a 'slight change' is down in the roundoff, where my computer can't divide two by three without approximating it."

"So it would seem. But there may be some hope. Sophia could do it. Maybe we can find out how."

"That's right, and she didn't have a computer. Or when did Babbage—"

"You can put that out of your mind. His Analytical Engine was never built."

"Hey!" Chazz snapped his fingers. "You guys can do that integration by hand. That avoids roundoff."

"We're not even going to discuss that," Mel objected, "until we know a lot more. But I admit there do seem to be possibilities up that avenue." He rose and turned toward the curtained outer portal. "I'm on my way to take this paper to Ruth. Want to walk over?"

"Sure." They stepped outside. The dark, starry night was fragrant with jasmine and jacaranda.

"Will you look at that!" said Chazz, pointing up past the blossom-laden branches of a nearby orange tree. "Look how bright it is!"

The star, which they had not been keeping track of, was thirty degrees above the southern horizon.

"It's in the south now. See, there's the big dipper."

"When did it move?" Chazz asked.

"I think I've seen it move a little before. Southward. Wait!" cried Mel. "It's us...we've been traveling north! It's standing still!"

"Stars don't do that, as a rule."

"You're right," Mel acknowledged. "It's behaving like a light at the top of a very tall tower. Fixed over one spot on the ground."

"Like a beacon of some sort. For what? To warn off low-flying angels?"

38
Gaius Junius Aulus

Mel awoke the next morning still warmed by the secret glances of love Ruth had cast at him in Chazz's presence the night before. He wanted to tell the whole world of their betrothal. So far only Bathyra and Zimri knew, and Jacimus, of necessity.

They advised waiting. To go public would impel Ruth and Mel into inexorable forms of custom and propriety that would severely curtail their freedom for a month. And so many possibilities were opening up just now that they felt they needed to postpone the onset of that month. A little longer, anyway.

Today they were to start unpacking in earnest. The time travelers hadn't arrived in Parthia with much luggage, but they had since accumulated a surprising pile of personal belongings that had come as gifts from their gracious hosts: clothing, utensils, tack, weapons, electrical equipment, and bedding. All had to be stored away in their apartments, after thorough cleaning from the weeks on the road.

In regards to cleaning, Mel had a related exploration in mind. He intended to try to find the bathhouse he'd heard was here. All he wanted was a shower, but he was curious to see if the facility were truly built on the scale of the one in Dura Europus.

The sun was well up, the day already warm, when he emerged from his terrace in the guest palace and strolled down the marble steps onto the dewy lawn. A peacock preened a few yards away, then strutted off around a white corner. Other birds sang in morning concert as Mel followed a tree-lined path of smooth white pebbles around the curve of a rise.

Once in sight of the main gatehouse, he noticed a two-horse chariot, attended by a charioteer in Roman military dress, parked on the public road outside.

Visitors again! he thought. Zimri's a popular guy. Let's go check this out.

Turning toward the big house, he saw Jacimus with a tall Roman wearing the toga. Evidently the visitor had just arrived. Jacimus was only now escorting him up the portico steps.

Mel followed them inside, pausing just past the marble huntress but close enough behind Jacimus to hear him concluding his introductions: "…and a friend of the family, Ruth."

"And another friend, Mel," Zimri added, seeing him. Aletha and Balthasar were present, as was Agnes's serving maid, Keira. The family and Ruth were seated in a cozy group of lounges near a writing table. "Mel, this is Legate C. Junius Aulus, who has appeared at our door with what he claims is an irresistible offer. I am intrigued. Would you care for some refreshment before we begin, sir, or…sir? Aulus?"

The legate's back was turned, but Mel knew what had caught his attention. And she was staring back at him in cool amusement, one arm draped along the scrolled back of her couch.

"A cup of coffee after your hard ride, Legate Aulus?" asked Ruth. She turned toward Zimri. "I have seen our visitor before. Two days ago, in the crowd watching our parade."

"Ahh…yes," Aulus admitted, finally tearing his gaze away. "Coffee. Yes. Please, I was intrigued, myself. I made some inquiries. Parthian Jews! And evidently in the process of relocating—" He broke off.

"How did you know about my hard ride?" he asked in amazement.

"You seemed uncommonly interested in us," explained Ruth. "Too interested to postpone paying us a call for two days. Unless you had an urgent errand. But then you would hurry on that errand." She smiled. "Just a lucky guess."

Mel glowed with pride. He exchanged glances with Zimri. There she goes again! Knows all, sees all!

And she'd known about this good-looking guy for two days. Known he'd call because he was fascinated with her, just as Jac was. And still she accepted me! Thank you, Lord!

"A stunning mind," Aulus said. "Tell me, have you heard of a woman named Musa?"

Ruth looked blank, but the Parthians bristled.

"That scheming harlot!" snarled Jacimus. "You're not comparing—"

"My profoundest apologies," Aulus begged. "I spoke from ignorance. We have heard no news of her for years, and then only how clever and enterprising she was. And captivating."

"Do not mention her again," warned Zimri. "Especially in the same breath with Ruth. You have not started off on the best of footings, my good man."

"I think it might be well," Baldy growled, rising from his divan, "if our visitor stated his business and departed."

"Yes. Make your offer, sir."

"Uh—" Aulus looked stricken.

Was he worried about his career? thought Mel. Ruth certainly wasn't offended. Although perhaps she would be when she knew more. Who was this Musa, anyway? He didn't dare ask, not just yet. But he could afford to feel sorry for Aulus now that his love was secure. "Hey, cut him some slack. The poor guy obviously meant it as a compliment. Let's relax and start over. Besides, I'd like some coffee too."

"Yes, please," Aulus appealed. "I certainly didn't intend—"

"Oh, all right," granted Zimri. "I suppose we shouldn't have trodden on you so heavily. Please bring us all some coffee, Keira. But you touched a sensitive topic, young man. That woman is responsible for much that is going wrong in Parthia today."

"Again, I humbly apologize; I'll be more careful."

"Please proceed," prompted Aletha. "I'm curious."

"Gladly. My job is to be the representative in Antioch of the interests of the king of Judea. He is concerned, naturally, for the defense of his borders. Brigands in the Trachonitis have been raiding across them of late, harrying the settlements of Batanea. Saturninus will or can do nothing about this. His concern apparently extends no farther south than Damascus.

"My master needs someone to take charge in Batanea. Someone in whose interest it will be to assure law and order, and beat back these raiders."

Like the Lunar Raiders, Mel thought. He saw where this conversation was going.

So did Zimri, for he said, "We just got here."

"We've been traveling for weeks," added Jacimus.

"Hear me out, please. When I saw the migration of a clan of the best fighters in the world I was already interested. But then to learn that you were Jews! It was too much. It was perfect.

"I had hoped to bring this offer before you were settled in. I left as early as possible Friday morning, for Jerusalem. But no matter that I changed horses and commandeered charioteers at every courier relay station, not stopping to sleep, I could not reach the palace before Saturday morning.

"The king saw me immediately and agreed that this opportunity had to be seized. He wasted no time drawing up a letter of inducement." Aulus brought forth a parchment scroll sealed with the royal stamp. "I rushed it back here just as urgently. But I fear you have already unpacked."

"As a mat—" Mel began, until he caught Ruth's covert glare.

Keira returned bearing a tray steaming with cups of coffee, which she distributed.

Zimri took the scroll and broke the seal. He skimmed the contents, sipping gingerly at his coffee.

"Do you know what's in this?" he asked Aulus.

"In substance. It is an offer of land in Batanea, with permission—encouragement, rather—to build cities, settle, populate the countryside. And to be ruler: wield the police power. In return, it is assumed that you will keep the peace in that province, in your own interest as well as the king's."

"Legalese aside, that is essentially correct. Not interested." Zimri rolled up the scroll and stuffed it into a pocket of his tunic.

"But—"

"Now that our business is out of the way, you must be our guest," offered Zimri. "Relax. Rest after your travels. I know how it feels: that's all we want to do right now. Keira!"

"Yes, sir?" she responded.

"Please escort this citizen to the guest suite. Be sure to show him where the baths are, on the way. Ask Agnes to prepare refreshment for one, to be delivered to his rooms." He turned to Aulus. "We are civilized here. You cannot be allowed to leave before you have had a chance to rest, to partake of our humble hospitality."

"No need to insist. I am as grateful as I am exhausted. But will you not—"

"Now, now. No more talk of that. You won't change my mind. Our business is done; it's time to recuperate, get to know each other, have some fun. When you are refreshed, I'd like to show you around the estate." Zimri rose and walked to the door with Aulus and the girl.

"You are most kind," said Aulus.

"We are commanded by God to treat strangers thus. We know the mind of a stranger, having been strangers ourselves in Egypt."

"And my driver?"

"He will be seen to. And your horses. Jacimus?"

"Without delay, sir."

"As you know, Antioch has many amenities. And Valatha is the most beautiful estate in Daphne. We anticipate many happy years here." Zimri paused at the door. "Enjoy your rest. When you are ready, return here and we'll go for a walking tour."

As Jacimus returned from arranging the care of the legate's charioteer and horses, Aletha spoke. "Daddy, you're just awful!"

"Whatever do you mean, my darling daughter?"

Ruth laughed, leaning her head on the curled back of the couch.

"Yes, what?" asked Mel, confused. "I think it's a good idea, staying here where it's civilized."

"But my father doesn't."

"Am I so transparent?"

"Well, I noticed you didn't return his scroll," Jacimus remarked. Zimri glanced at him, grinning, and withdrew the scroll from his tunic.

"And you didn't let him get away," added Ruth.

Mel was stunned. "But you said he wouldn't change your mind!"

"He won't. Come here and look at this, all of you." Zimri spread the scroll on the table as they gathered around to read it. "Look here."

Mel made sure to stand next to Ruth. "'Seven hundred stadia,'" he read, "'to Zamaris of Babylon, his clan and army, and all their descendants in perpetuity…' How long is a stadion?"

"About nine to the mile," replied Zimri. "It's a sizable province. We get it all, including populous cities like Gerasa, but read on. You have yet to reach the good part."

Mel continued: "'…and the right and duty to establish justice, insure domestic tranquility, provide for strategic defense, and levy taxes, assessments, and fees, as he and they shall deem right and proper, in perpetuity, without the necessity of paying any such taxes, assessments, nor fees, neither to Caesar Augustus nor to any succeeding Caesar, nor to the King of Judea nor any of his successors, nor to any other king, satrap, ruler or lord, in perpetuity.'" He glanced at Zimri. "Wow! You said it!"

"Don't unpack," Zimri advised. "Truly an offer we can't refuse."

"Just what you wanted," agreed Ruth. She glanced sidewise at Mel, eyes twinkling. Imperceptibly her hand, resting on the table, moved a fraction of an inch to make contact with his.

Mel glowed. "Whereabouts is Batanea?" he asked.

"South of the Trachonitis."

"Oh."

"It's only a few days from here," explained Zimri. "The oxen and mounts are already fed and rested; we could be cleared out by tomorrow—" He paused.

"Just as Chazz saw," Mel noted uneasily.

"Well. That is somewhat frightening," said Zimri. "Can he do that again?"

"We don't know," Ruth admitted. "That's the problem. It's unreliable."

"Even so. Many would kill for this power."

"You're right, sir. We'll have to keep it a secret," said Jacimus. "So we are going, then? Why didn't you say so to Aulus?"

"Tradesman's instinct. Also, he will spend the next couple of hours trying to think up further inducements and concessions to persuade us. It will be interesting to see what those are."

"Assuming he has plenipotentiary power, and can commit his king," Ruth qualified.

"Yes, I do assume that. I think it likely, within limits, because of the delay in communications between here and Jerusalem."

An idea occurred to Mel. "What you need is a heliograph. A system of towers, with mirrors and telescopes."

"Why not a telegraph?" suggested Ruth. "We have electricity now."

"Yeah, yeah! I can work out a Morse code for the Hebrew alphabet."

"Mel code."

"But there is a more compelling reason for circumspection," Zimri resumed. "It isn't so much that we can't trust Herod—"

"'Trust Herod,'" muttered Ruth. "Oxymoron of the year."

"— since we have his seal and mark on this contract," Zimri continued. "It is this: How is he able to offer us tax-free status when Saturninus could not?"

"That's a good point," agreed Ruth. "Think it's a lie?"

"I intend to find out," Zimri declared. "I shall 'feel out,' as you would say, our guest on the general subject of taxes, specifically Caesar's recent decree, and see if he has any information not available to Saturninus."

"Without divulging why you're interested," said Jacimus. "Good idea."

"Conditions may be different in Judea," Baldy pointed out. "Aulus has just returned from there. He will have the latest news."

"We're going in any case. A whole province! Cities! The reins of government!" Zimri reveled. "I can't pass up this chance."

"We could build a Utopia," agreed Mel.

"And with this document, I have at the least an excuse to omit paying taxes. The onus will shift to Herod."

"Zimri, I don't want to change the subject," said Ruth, "but who is this woman Musa?"

Jacimus scowled, but Zimri, though apparently reluctant, answered. "An Italian slave of surpassing beauty and evil, given to the Shahanshah as a concubine—planted, if I'm any judge—by Caesar. Clever, persuasive, and absolutely unscrupulous. She holds Parthia in thrall, having bewitched Phraates Arsaces to the extent of promising the succession to her by-blow—even sending his legitimate sons to Augustus as hostages!"

"She'll stop at nothing," added Jacimus. "She means no good for Phraates, or for Parthia. We're well out of it."

39
The Trachonitis

Three days later the caravan reached the still-smoking ruins of a small village. Burnt thatch roofs and broken stucco walls marked the site of no more than a dozen dwellings grouped around a common once-green pasture, now blackened. Stock pens were smashed and empty. The simple pole-and-bucket irrigation pump was reduced to a few sticks of charcoal. Flies swarmed around bloated, purple bodies. The stench was overpowering.

"Those murdering dogs," muttered Zimri through clenched teeth.

"Get Chazz out of here," Mel told a pale Ruth. "Take him back to the wagon. Stay with him." Chazz was hunched over on his horse and looking a sickly green.

"Right. Come on, Chazz." Ruth gathered his reins with hers and, half-supporting him with a hand on his shoulder, led him away.

"It's gotten worse," noted Aulus. "They've never been this bold before. So close to the border."

Mel shook his head. "It is a shock, finding such an atrocity only a day's ride from Damascus and civilization."

They had left Antioch the second morning after the Sabbath, Zimri having satisfied himself that the offer of tax-free status was as sound as could be expected in these troubled times.

"I dare say Aulus is congratulating himself right now," Zimri had told Mel then, "for talking me into accepting the offer, thus saving his career."

Aulus's "further inducements and concessions" were offers of palace jobs to Zimri's son, other relatives, or any ten he chose: as administrators, bodyguards, clerks, servants, tutors.

As to the tax, Zimri had finally, after getting to know the legate, disclosed the details of the king's offer. Aulus had been sanguine.

"He told me," Zimri had reported, "that Sentius doesn't know the least of the furor that's going on in Judea. Half the population is on the move! Since it's taking so long, they're forced to seek permanent residences. Well, of course, no one is coordinating this: how could anyone? So there are incredible waiting lists, overcrowding of housing, congestion. He says it must be seen to be believed. It could take decades before the dust settles enough for them to get around to actually collecting the tax. And by then our 'august' emperor could be dead and gone. I'm sure he realizes what a mistake he's made, but how could he admit it? He's stuck with it.

"Aulus says Herod is quite willing to let it be on his own head. Apparently he needs a police force urgently," Zimri had concluded.

Now, surveying the smoking charnel before him, Mel could see why. The countryside was an ideal hiding place for bandits. All day yesterday the wagons had struggled through a cracked and crumpled maze of lava ridges and gullies: the Trachonitis. As nearly as Mel could reckon, it seemed to be an area east of the Golan Heights. I'm behind enemy lines, he thought. Better not try jumping home from here.

"I wonder," mused Aulus.

"What?" Jacimus inquired.

"Caesar did not take well Herod's invasion of Arabia. Is it possible the bandits know this? That would go far to explain their boldness."

The border with Batanea lay just a mile south of this village. Normally, that would be enough to afford it some protection by the militia of Bostra. But unluckily for these hapless folk, the abnormal had occurred.

"Herod invaded Arabia?" asked Zimri. "I would have thought he had enough to occupy him elsewhere."

"Arabia gave sanctuary to the bandits when Herod first drove them out of Trachonitis," Aulus explained. "He could not allow that. To pursue them, and to punish Arabia, he invaded...not too successfully, I fear. At the same time, he resettled three thousand of his fellow Idumaeans here, to fill the vacuum."

"The fool!" growled Jacimus. "Observe the result."

Zimri agreed. "He should never have let unprotected civilians settle here."

"Of course not, but his military was occupied elsewhere. Now the bandits are back, and worse than ever. But notice that they have not come near this caravan. I am confident that you can set things to rights."

"I shall," Zimri vowed. "I will bring law and order to this land, with the help of God, so that even travelers on their way to the feasts at Jerusalem may sojourn safely here. To begin with, I shall build a fort at the border by this unfortunate village."

"A fitting memorial," affirmed Aulus.

"Now we must turn to unhappy but pressing matters. Son, take a detail and go ask Balthasar to assist you in digging a mass grave and arranging a burial service. Then we must purify any who touch the dead. Have our physician Kaski help you plan to minimize the contamination, according to the Law."

But Kaski doesn't know anything about germs or infection, Mel thought. Good grief! Why haven't I told him?

It hadn't come up, he excused himself. Nobody had become sick and they'd taken no casualties, except one horse, and the germ theory couldn't have helped Baldy's brave old Hammurabi. Well, now was the time to tell Kaski, if ever. Ignorance—

He suddenly realized that, although Kaski didn't know about germs, the Law did. God knew. That helped explain why this tribe was so healthy. It also gave a reason, if any were needed, for some of those "rules": the ritual washings in the Law.

Mel had once been told that there were not ten but 613 commandments in the Tenach. He saw now that he was probably already obeying many of them out of reverence for modern biological science alone. The germ theory decreed many of the same commandments. Another large subset was for the Levites, the priests, to instruct them in the rituals of atonement for the sins of the people. If Ruth were right, he wouldn't be needing those, either.

"That's the Star of Bethlehem," she had said in reference to the brilliant light in the sky the night he brought her the copy of Madame Kovalevskaya's paper. "You know that star you put on the top of a Hanukkah bush?"

She was convinced, and had nearly convinced Mel, that somewhere, right now, lying in a crib, was the newborn Messiah of Israel, and his name was Jeshua ben-Joseph, translated 'Jesus' by the Greeks.

"In Bethlehem, beneath the Star." She had shown it to him in the Scriptures: "'But thou, Bethlehem Ephratah, though thou be little among the thousands of Judah, yet out of thee shall he come forth unto me that is to be ruler in Israel: whose goings forth have been from of old, from everlasting.' That's your Messiah, Mel: the Lamb of God, the Scapegoat, the seventh-year Bullock."

"Ruth, isn't it enough that I've finally become a real Jew? Now you expect me to become a Christian, and give up all I've only just found?"

"Give up what? You're only gaining, not giving up. Mel, Jesus is *your* Messiah: the Jews' Messiah. He's the one the Hebrew prophets foretold. But you'll see. 'Cause you wanna hear something *really* crazy?"

"I'm not sure. Can I take it?"

"Be a man," she teased. "Sit down if you want. Here it is: I believe we're being led to him right now."

"What do you mean?"

"Led…we're being led; we have been since Daniel prayed, if not before. Mel! I never told you! How could I have forgotten? I reconstructed when it was that the Star first appeared. Mel, it was the same day—the same hour, I think—that we arrived in this time, in the river."

"That's it! Now I remember! Ruth, I've been trying for weeks to remember exactly what it was Daniel prayed, that landed us here. It was for God to—"

"—to bring us home," she finished. "Home to Himself. And everything since then has been leading or driving us in that direction, toward Bethlehem."

After burying the dead, they continued on into Batanea. The lava gullies had given way to gently rolling semiarid ranchland when, not far from the border, Zimri called a halt on a hilltop. A valley lay before them, broad and grassy, bisected by a swift tree-lined stream. A soft breeze played with Ruth's dark hair and the mane of Mel's pony. The only sound was birdsong.

Balthasar and Bathyra walked up from the lead wagon to join the mounted party. After a pause, Zimri turned to his wife and asked, "What do you think, my dear?"

"For a city, you mean? I love it. It's so peaceful."

"Yes. I had a feeling you would. This valley… it's no Valatha, I know."

"It will be. Better."

"There is a peace about it that speaks to my spirit. Since you agree, I feel God has brought us here, and here we shall build our home. Aulus!"

"Yes, sir?"

"I will build my first city here, in this valley. You may so inform your master."

"An excellent location, if I may say so. Close enough to the border to defend it in depth. Yet fertile and quiet. What name shall I tell Herod, for his rolls? Have you thought of one?"

Zimri smiled and glanced sidelong at his wife. "Tell him the city is named Bathyra."

Color rose to Bathyra's cheeks. "Oh!" She glowed. "Thank you, dear."

"And now," Zimri continued, "I propose we waste no time paying Herod our respects. Son, I leave to you the details of establishing camp here, with a view to a permanent settlement. I shall return in a week, no longer. Meantime, besides maintaining the defense of the caravan while they unpack, see what you can do about protecting those Idumaean villages north of here."

"Yes, Father. I propose sending a courier around to them with the news of our presence. He will also provide them some instruction in the rudiments of civil defense."

"Excellent. You might suggest that they consolidate into larger villages, for one thing. At least until we are in a position to eradicate the bandits for good. Again, I leave the details to you. Be sure our guests are well-protected and comfortable until I return."

Ruth started. "Wait! Uh…excuse me. I mean, I thought we were going along. To Jerusalem."

"I don't recommend it," said Jacimus. "Bandits are still a danger, and you won't have an army to protect you, or a wagon to ride in. Wait until we're settled here. Pentecost is coming soon; then we'll all go up. That'll give you a chance to see the city."

"Pentecost? That's a Christian holiday!"

"What is 'Christian'?"

Mel smiled. "These Gentiles. Ruth, Pentecost is a Jewish festival: the Feast of Weeks. Shavuot. Seven weeks after Passover."

"But! Anyway, we *must* go. I—"

"No, my son is right. We'll travel fast and light: just Baldy and Aulus and I. Half a day's brisk ride."

"Sorry," objected Balthasar, "but if that's the case then I can't go either."

"What! But you have an appointment to discuss a situation at the court," Zimri expostulated. "Or don't you want to be Herod's bodyguard?"

"It's not that," explained Baldy. "It's these tiny ponies of yours. I can travel fast or light, but not both."

"Bless God! I forgot. We still haven't found a replacement for your horse. Well, we'll take one of the smaller wagons. Hitch a couple of ponies to it; it won't slow us down that much. We can leave early tomorrow."

"A wagon?" prompted Ruth.

"You really are determined to do this, aren't you?" Zimri smiled. "Oh, all right...no harm in it. Since we're taking a wagon anyway. Though I fail to see the urgency. I assume," he added, turning to Mel and Chazz, "that you two want to come too?" They both nodded. "Somehow I thought as much."

"Daddy?"

"Absolutely not. I must draw the line somewhere. You stay here and keep your brother out of trouble."

"That's not what I meant. Didn't your contract provide for up to nine more positions?"

"Yes, according to Aulus here."

"That much discretionary authority I have," Aulus confirmed.

"I get your drift," said Mel. "What sort of positions do you think we'd be suited for? Court mathematicians?"

"Court jesters?" asked Chazz sotto voce.

"I won't work for Herod," Ruth declared. "In fact, I'm a little surprised that you will, Father Zimri."

"Why, what has he done?" asked Aletha.

"The man is a monster," Ruth bit off.

"I've seen worse," said Zimri. "Herod has certainly not stinted in schemings and murderings to maintain his throne. Perhaps even more than most kings. But royal families all share that trait, even the Arsacid. Assassination is an occupational hazard. And Herod's not called 'Great' for nothing. His economic reforms, his public works...the Temple itself..."

"Still..."

"Look at it this way," Zimri argued. "The particular job Herod's hired me for needs doing, does it not? You saw that settlement."

"Yes, it certainly does."

"Herod can do God's work, perhaps in spite of himself. And I and my clan are particularly well suited to this job, are we not?"

"I can't imagine anyone I'd rather have protecting me. Sorry, Mel, but your army's too small." She grinned.

"Well, then," Zimri concluded.

"Besides," added Jacimus, "Herod may be evil, but Father's good, right? So he's extracting evil's money and resources, and applying them to the good. What's your objection?"

"Those Herod has slaughtered for political reasons have not been exactly innocent themselves—" Zimri broke off. "Is anything the matter?"

"Something plucked at my memory," said Ruth. "I can't put my finger on it, though."

"Then it's settled. We will set out for Jerusalem at first light tomorrow. Son, we'll need a wagon and seven horses, and ask Agnes to pack a lunch."

40
City on a Hill

"Looks different," Mel commented.

They were approaching Jerusalem from the Damascus road.

It was with a growing sense of foreboding that Mel had been contemplating the impending meeting with Herod. But he had to admit Mount Zion looked a lot better crowned with the king's magnificent Temple than with the Dome of the Rock. And the lush greenery of its environs suggested a park, or at least an expensive suburb. What ever happened to all those trees?

"A lot smaller, of course," he continued. "Just what we call the 'Old City' where we're from. But, Ruth! isn't it beautiful?"

"Yes. I had no idea."

"So that's Jerusalem," said Chazz. "About what I expected."

Zimri looked askance at him. "He who has not seen the Temple of Herod has never in his life seen a beautiful building."

Aulus pointed. "That's Herod's upper palace; see those three towers, just to the right of the Fortress of Antonia?"

"It looks as if some kind of visitation is going on," Baldy observed. "There are many camels."

"There's always much traffic near the Palace-Temple area," remarked Aulus. "You should see it on a feast day. Three million Jews, from all over the world, thronged into a small area. One can hardly move."

"That many!" Ruth marveled. "How do they fit? Will we be staying at the Palace?"

"I'm assuming we won't," replied Zimri. "I'll arrange lodging at an inn. Unless the census has made that impossible."

"There may be room," Aulus said. "It's crowded, but not as bad as it was at first, when everyone was anxious to be prompt in obeying the Imperial edict. Now they've realized it's not going to be over soon, and new inns have been built."

"Windfall profits for the innkeepers," commented Mel.

"Yes," Zimri agreed. "Even an ill wind blows down some ripe apples."

"I've never heard that put so well," said Chazz.

That evening Mel, Chazz and Ruth sat on Mel's balcony to catch a cool breeze that blew out of the west. Zimri and Baldy had gone out with Aulus to walk around the town. Zimri had found rather luxurious accommodations for the six of them in a large new inn just north of the First Wall. From Mel's south-facing balcony the three had a fine view of the palace, lit within and without by torches, and of the Temple Mount off to the left. The sky was clear and moonless. The last vestiges of a spectacular sunset had just faded. For a long time no one spoke: they only sipped their wine and gazed out at the view.

Finally Ruth said, "What a breathtaking display."

"God does good work," agreed Chazz.

"Here's to God." Mel raised his cup in a toast. They clinked glasses and drank.

"Mel, remember our first night in Rabbi Nab's house?"

"Rabbi who?" he teased. She swatted him and he smiled. "I'm not likely to ever forget that. We were so scared."

"I was scared, too," said Chazz, "when I found out I was a victim of chaos."

"Why bring those times up now? I haven't thought about them in a month."

"Neither have I," Ruth agreed. "We've been well taken care of for that month. And we're still under Zimri's protection, and God's. But you know what?"

"I can guess. You're scared again," said Chazz. "I know I am."

"Right," Ruth admitted. "I keep telling myself that it's silly to be afraid, because God is in control. But I am."

"But why? What is it about this past couple of days?" asked Mel. "Here we are in the City of Peace, yet we have no peace. 'Why is this night different from all other nights?'"

Silently they turned to look out toward the Palace.

"It's Herod. I dread meeting him," Ruth confessed. "Mel, I just know something terrible is going to happen."

"And yet you had to come. Don't forget, we expect something wonderful to happen too."

"Sort of like Ph.D. prelims," observed Chazz. "I dread taking those, but I know I need—" He paused. "Sorry, I forgot. That life is gone."

"Chazz, what are we going to do about you?" Ruth asked. "Even if we get back to 1995, that's only the beginning for you."

Mel tried to reassure him. "Look, you're still just a kid. Excuse the expression: I know you're an expert at the Parthian shot. But, I mean, what can the law do to you? And Ruth and I will support you all we can. We'll testify that you meant no harm, had no bomb, and are completely penitent."

"I hijacked a plane," Chazz pointed out unnecessarily. "A whole big plane full of people. There are those who don't take that lightly."

"Look, we're talking ourselves into a hole already," said Mel. "Let's leave off worrying about that. There's nothing we can do about it yet anyway."

"'Sufficient unto the day is the evil thereof,'" Chazz quoted.

"Who said that?" asked Mel.

"The Person we're going to meet," Ruth told him, "if all goes well."

"I take it you don't mean Herod."

"No. Just the opposite. Now *there's* a good change of subject. Imagine! Meeting the Babe, Messiah the Prince, face to face! Under the Star—"

She broke off. They followed her gaze skyward.

"Where is it?" asked Chazz.

"It's gone!" Ruth cried.

"*That's* why this night is different." Mel's skin crawled. "No Star."

A silence fell on them.

"Oh, God, what if I was wrong?" Ruth buried her face in her hands and began to sob. "What if we're too late?"

"What could have happened to it?" asked Chazz. "It's been so steady all these weeks."

"When did we last see it? Wasn't it there just last night, in Bathyra?"

"Yes, I d-distinctly remember that," Ruth confirmed. "It was so high."

"Maybe it's washed out by the bright lights of the city."

"What bright lights?" asked Mel. "Look, there's the Milky Way. The Star was a lot brighter than that."

"What if he's not here?"

"We know he's in Bethlehem," Mel reminded her. "We can go there and ask around. It's only a few miles."

"I know; that's why I wanted to come. It certainly wasn't to meet Herod."

"Unfortunately, Aulus has already set up the appointment," said Mel. "We can't duck out. Parthians keep their word. Fourth hour, sharp, tomorrow in the palace atrium."

"Still, I wish—" But what she wished Mel had to guess, because the return of their three companions interrupted her.

Zimri sank into a balcony seat with a grateful sigh. "I suppose you've noticed the Star is gone."

"We were just discussing that," Mel acknowledged.

"Ho! You and all Jerusalem," said Baldy.

"You know those camels we saw near the palace? Look." Aulus pointed. "They're still there."

"It turns out," said Zimri, "that the Star never has been visible from here.

But that camel caravan has been following it for weeks. They expect it to lead them to a newborn King."

Ruth sighed in relief. "So do we, as you know," she said.

"Yes. Well, it led them here, then it was gone. They've been asking everyone where the newborn King is. The whole city is abuzz."

"I learned," said Aulus, "that they have an audience at the palace scheduled for the fifth hour tomorrow. They think Herod, or his wise men, will know."

"Herod's not going to like their finding another King," Mel observed. "*We* could tell them where to go. Save them a lot of trouble."

"No, that turns out not to be the case," countered Aulus. "My sources indicate that Herod was quite pleased, and will be delighted to help them all he can."

"My source indicates otherwise," Ruth muttered.

41
Herod

Scrubbed and pressed, the party waited nervously in the king's antechamber. Idumaean soldiers dressed in the uniform of the elite palace guard stood posted around the marble room at parade rest. It was ten minutes past the fourth hour. Herod was late. The six were seated on a long couch against one wall. No refreshments had been offered them.

"Perhaps an oversight," excused Zimri.

"No, it's policy, arising from Herod's nervous stomach," Aulus said. "Oversights are not tolerated in this court."

Zimri's plan was to leave directly from the Palace. They had already checked out of the inn; their wagon and mounts were waiting outside, lost in the throng of camels and richly-decorated coaches of the caravan from Anatolia.

"I wish he'd show up," muttered Chazz. "I want to get this over with."

"Do you think we should have waited outside?" Mel asked Aulus.

"Herod is used to visits from admirers. He always endeavors to stay popular with the people. You'll see: he can be quite charming. I'll just introduce you as fans from Babylon, friends of Zimri's, and a few polite words later it will all be over. Set your minds at rest. Of course, he'll probably want a private chat with Zimri—shh! Rise!"

The door to the inner chamber was opening. They rose to their feet and stood waiting respectfully as Herod's major-domo strode toward them.

"His majesty will see you now. Please come this way." He led them through the inner door into the dazzling sunlight of the atrium.

The party filed guardedly over tiles cooled by the dappled shade of trees surrounding a pool fed by a marble central fountain shaped in the form of a dolphin. Sparrows chirped in the acacias, and hummingbirds hovered over yucca blossoms. Cacti and acanthus bloomed in stone planters beside the walk.

It's so...*nice*, thought Mel. He had never known Herod was a nature lover.

As his eyes adjusted, he made out a recess in the far cloister toward which they walked: an alcove in which seven chairs were set around a circular table. In one—Was that a man? He gaped. Nobody had warned him.

Seated in the most remote chair was an incredibly old, sick, feeble-looking creature. The skin of his face was drawn tight against his skull. Black eyes gleamed out of cavernous sockets. No crown adorned his brow. Instead, the king wore a gold skullcap which matched his golden robe of state, onto which something had recently dribbled. His right hand held a cloth with which he dabbed at his runny nose. With his left hand, he waved the party forward.

"Welcome," Herod wheezed. "You may be seated."

Six more guards stood at attention like statues around the alcove.

The major-domo approached the king, bent, and spoke something into his ear. "Later," croaked the king in a half-whisper.

Aulus motioned Zimri and Baldy to seats at the king's right. He himself sat on Herod's left. After seating Ruth, Mel took the chair next to Aulus, while Chazz moved to the vacant place on Ruth's left, next to Baldy.

Herod began without preamble, addressing Zimri hoarsely in cultivated Greek. "You must stop them. Stop them at any cost. Our border must be safe."

"I shall, Your Majesty. My army is—"

"Yes, yes. So Aulus has informed Us. Only let Us impress upon you the extreme urgency of your mission, *extreme* urgency. Exterminate them! Completely. Defend Our border!"

The king's skeletal left hand reached across to catch Zimri's wrist like a claw. Trembling, he coughed and spat on the floor, then wiped his mouth on the rag.

"You shall be a prince! Anything! Anything at all! Only serve Us well. Defend Us well. Remember."

Zimri nodded.

Charming, Mel thought. Ruth's right; the man is a monster.

"Please excuse Our temporary indisposition," whispered Herod, as though reading Mel's mind. "We are not Ourself today." He leered across the table. "Aulus, We observe you have brought Us a beauteous lady among Our guests. Our curiosity is aroused. We are extremely interested in making their acquaintance. Please introduce Us."

"Your Highness, this large person is Balthasar, an old friend and neighbor of Zimri's. He desires employment as your bodyguard. Eminently suited to it, I'm sure you'll agree. The others, also friends of Zimri's, are travelers from a far-distant land."

"Exactly where?" Herod interrupted.

Oh-oh, worried Mel. He's going to give our cover story a good workout.

"Why, I don't know, your highness," Aulus confessed. "It never came up. As it was evidently too far to concern us in a military sense, I dismissed it."

Herod glared at him.

Mel spoke quickly. They had prepared for this. "We will be glad to tell you, your majesty. We come from a place too obscure to interest mighty Caesar, a few hours' travel west of Raetia." By 747. "It is called America."

"We did not know there were any Jews in Germania," wheezed Herod. "You are obviously Jewish. As to these others, are they then Jutes? They appear too civilized."

"We have learned much of your ways, majesty, since joining our lot to Zimri's," Ruth explained. "We have adopted the local garb, as you see, and the local customs. We no longer paint our bodies with woad."

Might be fun, though, thought Mel.

"And your names?"

"This is Ruth, your highness," Aulus said. "And Caspar, and Melchior."

Ruth blanched and swayed, as though woozy. She and Chazz stared at each other, then over at Balthasar.

"What are you doing here?" Herod asked. "So far from home?"

He won't let up, thought Mel. "Sire, it is an interesting tale." And I hope I can remember it correctly. "I was raised among the small colony of mathematicians and astronomers who inhabit Babylon. When almost grown, my questing mind was struck by the similarities between my Zoroastrian faith and the Judaism of some of my friends. I came to believe in the one true God of Abraham, Isaac, and Jacob." That much was true, at least! And he had been raised among mathematicians, in a sense.

But his intent was to deceive, as in any cover story. All spies had the same dilemma. And Herod would certainly consider them spies. Had Joshua and Caleb had a plausible excuse ready for being in Canaan?

"A party of us traveled to the farthest north reaches of the Empire to test a prediction of an eclipse. In Noricum, a blinding blizzard separated me from the rest." Many minds had collaborated on this story. And there had been much debate over what to say. Tosthenes' governing philosophy had been the weirder the better: the more bizarre the details, the more likely they were to be believed. Mel silently thanked God for Tosthenes' encyclopedic geographic knowledge, to fortify this lie. Mel himself hated lying—though he'd sometimes done it, he admitted—and *his* rule was, "As much truth as possible."

"I stumbled through drifted snow for what seemed like hours. Finally there came a hill I was simply too exhausted to climb. I lay down in my furs and slept. I remember the blissful warmth that stole over me."

Herod's eyes were hooded, but did not waver. He was interested, all right. Mel wondered how much he knew about snow. Probably only hearsay, but a lot of that: his spies were everywhere.

"We have heard of that deceptive warmth," hissed Herod. "You are fortunate to have lived to tell this tale."

"Indeed, sire. I owe my life to these friends." And that's no lie! "I returned to consciousness in their igloo—"

"We do not recognize that word."

"A word of the far north. One builds a hut by cutting blocks of snow and stacking them into a hemisphere. This is called an igloo. Inside, out of the wind, one's body heat can make it quite warm, especially with the aid of a small fire."

"A house of snow, warm? Beware lest We conclude that your tale lacks credibility."

Wouldn't that beat all! mused Mel. To be thought lying in the truest part of the story. "I could hardly believe it myself, your highness. Nevertheless, here I sit, alive. It seems that just on the other side of the hill where I had fallen dwelt Ruth and Caspar's tribe of Jutes in their igloo village. One of their sled dogs had wandered off in the blizzard. Trying to track him, my friends stumbled upon me." Lies, all lies, but only unimportant details. Right. He was aware of irony. Authenticating details.

"Dogs that pull sleds? Ingenious." Herod leaned forward. "And what became of the poor thing?"

"She wandered back after the storm, safe and sound," Ruth reassured him.

Herod relaxed visibly. "And the eclipse? Did it occur as predicted?"

"I never found out, your highness. I was unconscious at the scheduled time, and I never found any trace of the rest of my scientific party. The storm kept the villagers indoors, no one saw whether it grew dark for a few minutes—at the height of the storm, it would have been already dim, and the eclipse was predicted for shortly before sunset...We could usually predict eclipses; what we could not predict was the weather. In Babylon, as you are aware, it is quite different."

"Yes. You call to Our mind Alexander's tale of the Babylonian water that burns. We suppose that if water can burn, snow can warm."

"The world contains many wonders, does it not?" asked Ruth.

"Continue with your tale," Herod prompted. "There you were, recuperating in an...igloo."

Why hadn't they just waited outside? wondered Mel. But he knew the answer. Once Aulus made the appointment for all six of them, six had to show up. Well, he was over the hump. The rest was true. Mostly.

"A bond grew between my rescuers and me. We became fast friends. After they learned Greek, I told them of the true God, and they believed. When I could again travel, they accompanied me back to Mesopotamia, to study. For formerly ignorant savages, you will find them both remarkably well-versed in mathematics.

"We joined Zimri's caravan as a convenient way to travel up to Jerusalem for the feast of Pentecost. When we found he was to have an audience with you, we could not miss the chance to meet you, O great king." Any questions? Mel asked silently. He fervently hoped not.

"We find this tale fascinating, and We would question you further, but the press of business forbids," wheezed Herod. "There waits even now a delegation of kings seeking guidance from Us. In fact, Aulus, We have already made arrangements for you to accompany them when they depart, and report to Us where they find the babe they seek.

"Meantime We wish to speak privately to Zimri, as ruler to ruler." He rose to his feet unassisted. "Connubius, escort Zimri to Our private audience chamber. We shall follow in a moment."

Zimri also stood and, taking leave of his friends, followed the major-domo out the far door. It closed solidly behind him.

Herod made an inconspicuous gesture with his left hand. The six Idumaean guards drew their short swords and stepped forward to surround the table: three behind Baldy, and one each behind Ruth, Chazz and Mel.

"What—" Mel scrambled to his feet, but froze when he felt the point of a sword prick his back. Chazz knocked over his chair. A guard held each of Baldy's arms fast, while the third's sword pressed against the back of his neck. Ruth opened her mouth to shriek; a rough hand stopped it.

"Sire?" protested Aulus.

"Silence!" Herod rasped. "You have been careless, Legate, extremely careless. These spies could have assassinated Us. You must exercise increased zeal in the future, if you wish Us to retain you in Our good graces. Search them. Thoroughly."

Mel and Ruth were unencumbered. Baldy carried a pouch which disclosed a jar of ointment. But Chazz—

"What's this?" asked Aulus. He held up an object in each hand. One was a soft purse that moved fluidly. The other was a leather rectangle on a sling.

"Open them," Herod ordered.

Aulus loosened the string of the purse. It proved to be silk-lined and to contain a crystal-white powder. Exposed to air, the powder gave off a sweet, musky odor.

"*Libanum*?" asked Herod. "Where did you obtain so much of this expensive incense?"

"It fell off a tree," Chazz said. "It looked like sap then, but it disintegrated to powder on the journey. I thought I could sell it at the Temple."

"So you say. Don't try to fool King Herod. Again. What is in the other case?"

Aulus undid the straps, removed a padded object, and unwrapped it. It was the laptop computer.

Herod sucked in his breath with a noisy hiss.

Aulus caressed the polycarbonate shell with a finger. "Miraculous, such workmanship! Never have I seen stone so smooth and light. Or is it metal?"

"Well?" demanded Herod. "What is this?"

"An astronomical instrument, your majesty," Chazz stammered. "It can be used to predict eclipses."

"Show Us how it works."

"Do you have an astronomy simulation program on line?" asked Ruth under her breath.

Snapping open the case, Chazz whispered, "No, but I have—"

"Silence, or We shall have your tongues cut out."

Chazz switched on the power. The guards gasped as the light-emitting diodes flashed and the hard disk hummed. When the screen displayed the DOS prompt in glowing amber, even Herod grew pale.

Chazz typed a command. The disk whirred.

Suddenly the screen filled with zooming asteroids under the title, "ASTROBLIGHT! Copyright 1989 by Pirasoft, Inc." The speaker crashed, crackled, and beeped. The guards, startled out of their wits, lowered their swords.

Baldy saw his chance. Lunging to his feet, he easily wrested the sword out of his guard's grip. He clutched Herod around the throat and pressed the sword against his breast. Herod choked and struggled feebly.

"Back!" cried Baldy as the guards advanced. They hesitated. "Drop your swords. Release my friends. Quickly, or your king dies."

"Aulus," Herod croaked. "Save Us!"

"Do as he says," ordered Aulus. The swords clattered to the tiled floor. "Stand back."

Chazz replaced the computer. Bending to gather up the fallen swords, Mel asked Aulus, "Is there a back door? A quick way out?" Baldy pricked Herod's skin for emphasis.

"Answer him, you fool!" snapped Herod.

"Yes, behind the throne in the king's private chamber." Aulus indicated the door through which the major-domo had led Zimri.

It swung open. The major-domo stood in the doorway. He sprang back with a yell, slamming the door just as Mel reached it.

"Locked! Now what?" On the other side of the door, Connubius's shouts receded, as did the sound of his hurried steps on the hard tile floor.

"O king," Baldy menaced, "you will see that we escape before more guards appear, or you will be first to die."

"Aulus," gasped Herod, "you got Us into this. Now get Us out."

"Lie down on your bellies," Aulus told the guards. They obeyed. "Mel, run that pilum through their helmet straps."

Mel set down the swords and hefted a seven-foot bronze spear standing in a corner. "This?" Aulus nodded. Mel pushed the shaft through the gap between each guard's neck and helmet strap. This bound the guards together with helmets locked tight. They gasped in the effort to breathe.

"Stay there," Aulus told them unnecessarily. "Balthasar, move your sword to the king's back. Sire, you must now dissemble. Pretend you and I are peaceably ushering our visitors to the exit. Your life depends on it."

"Dissemble! We?"

"Come," urged Aulus. They walked around the pool to the front. Mel tossed the swords in the water, where they sank out of sight.

Aulus opened the front door a crack and peered out into the gloom. "All clear so far." They stepped through into the antechamber. The guards still stood at parade rest along the walls.

"Not so much as a wink," Baldy whispered. The folds of his tunic concealed his sword, tilted up against Herod's spine.

"Chat," muttered Aulus.

"How wonderful, O sweet king," Ruth gushed, "to be able to tell my children that I was once granted the honor of an audience with your majesty."

"And your grandchildren," added Mel. They were halfway to the outer door. "Don't forget your grandchildren."

Herod grunted. Baldy pressed more firmly. "We shall never forget this meeting, and your gracious hospitality, your highness. (Say something nice!)"

"Nor shall We." Herod looked daggers at Aulus. "Truly a memorable occasion, for which We have Our most astute legate to thank."

A trickle of sweat ran down behind Aulus's ear from under his helmet. "Regrettably, this pleasant occasion is about to come to an end, as all things must." He reached the door and grasped the handle. Stepping to one side, he opened the door and bowed to let Herod and Baldy precede him.

Mel could see their wagon, waiting at the bottom of the stairs outside, with a clear street in front of it. The driver from the inn sat holding the reins, ready to go. Just a few more steps, Mel thought.

Herod stepped out the door, followed closely by Baldy, who stooped to get through it. But instead of straightening up, Baldy crumpled to the ground.

Almost before Herod could turn and croak, "Kill them not!" the guards were lunging toward the three travelers.

Aulus gripped Ruth firmly by the arms from behind. Two guards grabbed Mel and Chazz. Under Herod's urging, the burly soldier who had clubbed Baldy down backed into the antechamber dragging the giant's prone form by the heels.

Herod followed him inside and closed the door. "The driver saw nothing. You! Take this coin and pay him off. Dismiss him. Bid him return whence he came. Say his passengers have found other, more comfortable conveyance." He glared at the captives. "They will not be needing his."

The soldier hurried out the door.

"You rat!" Ruth spat at Aulus. "How could you!" She twisted in his grasp and kicked at his shins. Aulus grunted and held her tightly, using only one leg to bear his weight. Fortunately for him, Ruth's riding-boots were of soft leather and lacked spike heels.

"Be quiet, or I'll let one of the others hold you!" he hissed in her ear.

"Well, Legate, We have survived again, despite your best efforts. We must consider what will be an appropriate chastisement for your carelessness. In the meantime, consider yourself on final probation. You know We do not tolerate such sloppiness twice. Bringing German spies into Our very atrium!"

My God, Mel thought. Trapped because he *believed* our story! Never underestimate the paranoia of a Herod.

The king shuffled over to the long couch against the wall and collapsed wheezing onto it. "Listen carefully now," he said. "Here is what you must do. Deviate from these instructions by a hair's breadth and your fate will make theirs seem tender. Do you understand?"

Aulus saluted. "Yes, indeed, your majesty."

"You will convey these spies to the dungeon below. Treat them with the utmost care. We want no harm to come to them until We have had a chance to interrogate them to the full. Then there will be time for harm. Oh, yes, grievous bodily harm. Ample, slow time. While We watch."

"Sire."

"Yes?" At Herod's tone, the two nearest guards posted along the wall stiffened and advanced toward Aulus, gladii drawn.

"Your pardon, sire. The woman and boy too? Are they to be put to the question?"

"Yes, of course." Herod rubbed his hands together with a dry, rasping sound. "Especially the boy. He will first be given time and—shall We say—incentive...to instruct Us thoroughly on the true nature, purpose and use of that astronomical instrument. We see power in it. We will have that power."

"Your Majesty!" Aulus clicked his heels. "As you wish."

"That is better. You may yet survive. We have not liked what We perceive in the trend of your thoughts. Be very, very careful not to press Us." Herod rose slowly from the couch, bearing heavily on the arm of a guard. "Legate!"

"Yes, sire!"

"Are you quite sure you understand these simple instructions?"

"Yes, sire!"

"There will be no deviation?" Herod tapped his sandaled foot emphatically on the tiles. "No sloppiness?"

"None, sire!"

"Then do as you are ordered. We must see to Zimri. He cannot be allowed to suspect anything. We still need him, and the services of his army in Batanea. Our borders must be made safe! Safe! Now go!"

Herod strode away, ignoring Aulus's salute, and passed through the door into the inner palace.

"Corporal! You heard the king. Fetch a litter for the giant, and escort me and these spies to the dungeon. Now!"

42
Disguises

The cell was not dank. Rather, it was stifling hot and dry. The only illumination came through a small barred grille set in the iron door: its source, a sconce flickering on the wall down the corridor. The prisoners lay stunned where they had been thrown.

Scanning the stone walls for some chink as his eyes adjusted to the dimness, Mel watched a huge black spider scuttle across a faint patch of light on the dark surface. Words were carved there: "CARNVS XVII AN." Poor Carnus!

"On the whole, I'd rather be in Philadelphia," he said in English.

"'A few polite words,'" Ruth quoted. "That rat! He seemed pretty decent at first, for one of Herod's minions." She sat up and rubbed her arms. "Ow! He didn't have to be so rough, either."

"Is this the end, then?" asked Chazz.

A low groan answered him.

"Baldy!" Ruth moved to his side and cradled his head. "Are you—" she began in Greek.

"Ow! Don't touch that part. The part with the lump."

Mel wished he could see Baldy's pupils. If he had a concussion or subdural bleeding…But none of them seemed to have a very good prognosis. Unless—

"Ruth, don't give up hope. We may get out of here yet."

"Why do you say that?"

"Zimri. He's bound to find out we're locked up here. And he has something Herod wants."

"I don't think so," she said.

"What? How come?"

She gently placed Balthasar's head on the soft bag of frankincense, and stood. "If Zimri ever learns what Herod's done to us, how can he serve him after that? The whole deal will be off. No. Herod won't let him find out. And think how easy it'll be."

"Easy?" said Mel.

"Herod has a secret weapon he doesn't even know about," she explained, "but he's sure to stumble on it. All he has to do is plead ignorance: we left the audience chamber and he never saw us again."

"Why would Zimri believe we just disappeared into thin air?" asked Chazz.

"Because he saw you do exactly that."

"I get it," Mel said. "He'll think we discovered some way to jump home."

"And he'll know it's futile to look for us," added Ruth.

"But what about Baldy?" Chazz asked.

"That's easy," supplied the giant. "I work for Herod now, remember? Herod can tell him I was needed for an urgent mission in Spain or India."

"Great," Chazz said. "You've managed to convince me we're going to be tortured to death."

"Cheer up," said Mel. He could now see sinister dark stains on the floor. "Things could be worse."

"How?"

"We still have the computer."

"That's right!" Chazz exclaimed. "We can while away these tense hours playing Astroblight."

"I mean we can jump. Or at least you can. Maybe all four of us. Even if it's chaotic, it can't be worse—or no!" cried Mel. "You say five minutes worked?"

"Both times. I mean every time, every time," Chazz said as they pummeled him. "Just kidding."

"And we don't have to go two thousand years. Just until we find the cell door open. Program that loop, boy!"

"I don't think it'll be necessary," countered Ruth. "I *know* we're going to get out of here. You should too, Chazz, if you'd think about it."

"Oh, yeah."

"Why? What's this?" Mel asked.

"It's because of your Hebrew name." Ruth explained the tradition.

"That's eerie!" Mel shivered. "But...we're not kings."

"Well, it's tradition; it isn't gospel," admitted Ruth. "It can get garbled."

"Still," Chazz pointed out, "maybe the means of our escape is time jumping."

"That's true," agreed Ruth. "So you'd better—"

"Hisst!" The sound came from the barred opening.

Mel bounced to his feet and peered out. "Aulus! What—"

A key grated in the lock. "Quiet. No time." Aulus swung the iron door open. "Put these on." He passed out white robes. They draped them over their Parthian riding habits. Baldy's hung only to his knees. "No good way to conceal you, big fellow," Aulus said. "We must rely on speed. Come."

He closed the cell door and locked it, then led them back up the corridor the way they had been dragged. They encountered no one.

At the top of the stairs, once more on ground level, Aulus paused to peer through a doorway. He waved them on. They slipped through the door, across a court, and into a sumptuously curtained room with a throne at one end.

"Herod's private audience chamber," said Aulus. "He's out front seeing the kings off."

"Where's Zimri?" Baldy asked.

"Long gone. Herod told him an ox-and-bird story about not knowing what happened to you. Strangely, Zimri seemed to believe it. I didn't have time to talk to him in private; I had to let you loose." He led them past the throne. "Quickly! Behind this arras." Drawing back a hanging curtain, he inserted his fingers in a decorative slot, and slid aside a door concealed in the wall.

"Aulus, I misjudged you," Ruth apologized as the party ducked through the door. It was now pitch dark.

"I can find better things to do with my life than torture women. Watch these steps. Count nineteen of them, then straight ahead. Follow me, hands on shoulders."

They filed blindly down the stairs and through a long, cobwebby tunnel, then up more stairs. They began to hear faint voices. Aulus halted.

"Out into the open again," he said. "Wait till I check."

"Where are we now?" asked Mel as Aulus cracked open a door. Light glared through. The voices rose to a babble.

"The Holy Place. They're preparing for the feast. Now. Nobody's looking; come on."

They emerged quickly and quietly into the outer sanctum of Herod's Temple. Several Levites were polishing the sacred furniture: the table of showbread, the Menorah, the brazen altar.

Their robes, Mel thought, they're just like ours. Clever.

Aulus led them with confident, businesslike strides toward an archway on the other side of the brazen altar. The priests paid them no heed as they hurried down the sanctuary steps, past a huge bronze bowl and out a door to the right.

Once they were through the door, the noise increased. They found themselves facing the source of the noise across a low railing of stone latticework a few yards away. It looked like the trading floor of the stock exchange. Was this supposed to be holy ground?

Almost an acre of outer court was mobbed with yelling, gesticulating merchants and their customers and wares. The wares resembled a petting zoo. Cages of birds cooed and chirped; pens of lambs and goats baaed and bleated; bullocks and heifers hitched to posts lowed and mooed.

The menagerie provided a noisy, smelly accompaniment to the continual yells of negotiating merchants and the persistent obbligato of clinking money.

Weary pilgrims, singly or in family groups, were purchasing sacrificial animals, asking directions, and changing out-of-town cash into the local coinage, leaving a small fee with the brokers.

Aulus led the party swiftly down a flight of fourteen steps toward an opening in the low railing. As they passed through it, Mel's attention was caught by a sign inscribed in Greek.

> No foreigner is to enter within the balustrade and enclosure around the Temple area. Whoever is caught will have himself to blame for his death which will follow.

Mel shivered and quickened his step to catch up to the others. He decided not to mention the sign.

They followed Aulus swiftly through the dusty, busy throng toward the western gate. "Once we're outside, head for the camel train," he directed. "We must be under cover before the king finds you missing, and under way before he thinks where to look."

They emerged onto the walkway atop the wall leading to the palace. "Leave the robes here," said Aulus. They dropped them in a corner and proceeded along the wall to where some camel drivers were prodding their beasts to their feet.

Running down a stair, Aulus strode up to the first in line, flinging the train of his toga over his shoulder. "I am C. Junius Aulus, legate of his majesty King Herod, authorized to accompany this expedition to its destination. These are my retinue. Which is our conveyance?"

"Legate, at last! We've been expecting you. We are about to depart. Your accommodations are right over here, sir. I trust they will be adequate."

"I trust. Driver!"

"Sir?"

"You would have departed without me?"

"Ah…I'm afraid so, sir. The masters, the kings, are rather anxious to get on. And you are a little late. We were going to allow you five minutes more. My humble apolo—"

"Good."

"Sir?"

"Good, I say. You have waited long enough. I did not appear. You left without me. Do you understand?"

"I'm afraid not, sir. Are you going or aren't you?"

Aulus spoke quietly to Mel, "Mel, the rest of you…get aboard! Quickly!" Then he turned back to the driver. "Let me explain, driver. Here, perhaps this fifty-denarius coin will help you concentrate. Now: you must surely obey your kings and go when they say go. Correct?"

"Correct." The man took the coin reflexively and stared at it in puzzlement.

"Put it in your pocket; that's better. I, too, must obey my king, Herod. He wishes no one to know of my presence on this caravan. No one! This is a secret mission. Do you understand?"

"A secret mission."

"Correct. If anyone should ask you whether I or any of my retinue are aboard, what will you say?"

"Will you be aboard?"

"Yes, but you say no. That is the nature of a secret mission."

"Yes but no."

"Should any come impersonating an envoy of Herod, and ask for me, you have not seen me."

"I have not seen you."

"Good. Even if Herod himself should ask you?"

"Uh..."

"It will be a test, man, a test! A test of the mission security! You must deny seeing me. Were Herod to find you a security risk, do you know what would become of you?"

"Something bad?"

"Yes. So just say 'No,' whoever asks."

"Just say no."

"I realize this is difficult." Aulus mounted the step to the enclosed carriage. "Here is another fifty denarii as difficult-duty pay."

"Thank you. Rely on me. I have not seen you."

"Good. Proceed. Let's depart." Brushing under the valence, Aulus ducked through the door Mel was holding ajar and sank into the cushioned seat.

Cries of "Ready to go!" echoed down the line of camels, and their carriage lurched into motion. Aulus was flung against Ruth. Instead of giving way, Ruth threw her arms around him and kissed him. His eyebrows rose and his face turned a warm red.

"Gaius, you were wonderful!" Ruth released him.

"Yes," agreed Mel in admiration. "What a con artist."

"Worth it. Worth it," Aulus gasped.

"Hope it works," said Chazz.

"Right; we're not quite there yet." Mel turned and inspected the seat cushions. "Is there anyplace to hide in this carriage?"

"Looking for dimes?" Chazz asked.

"Just trying to see if—Ah!" The padded top of the seat slid away from the wall. "Baldy, please get up a minute."

Baldy stood crouched over, holding on to a strap, while Mel pulled the seat off its frame. A sharp aroma rose from a small jar lodged in one corner of the bare wooden space, which was otherwise empty. It was big enough to conceal Ruth or Chazz, even with the computer, but not both. And not comfortably.

"Well, let's hope they don't search." Mel replaced the seat.

"Let's try and think of something else," advised Aulus, "just in case they do."

Finally Ruth asked, "Mel, have you or Chazz read Poe's story of the purloined letter?" She grinned. "I know a 'new' way to hide."

"Halt!"

The young Idumaean centurion swung his horse in front of the lead carriage. Its oxen lumbered to a standstill.

An elderly, crowned head peered out one of the carriage windows. "Why have you stopped us?" asked the king.

"Your pardon, sire. We fear some escaped criminals have hidden themselves in your caravan. We must request your permission to search it."

"Permission granted. We would cooperate with all duly constituted authority." The crowned head withdrew and another, even more elderly, took its place.

"But do please be quick," the elder king requested, "as we are quite anxious to complete our journey."

"This won't take long." The centurion turned in the saddle to face his squad. "All right, men. You have the descriptions. Search quickly but thoroughly." He himself rode over to the kings' window and peered in. Satisfied, he rode back along the line, past carriages and wagons, slaves and drivers, horses and camels, checking to see that his squad examined each possible place of concealment. Finally he came to the carriage whose driver was sworn to secrecy. "You! Driver!" he hailed. "Are you not the one I arranged with this morning to carry the legate Aulus?"

"Yes, I believe so. You look familiar."

"Well, where is he?"

"He showed up too late. I mean, he did not show up in time. We could not wait. We left without him. Sorry!"

"Are you quite sure?"

"Oh, yes. He is not here. And this," the driver pointed, "is the very wagon he is not in!"

"Mind if I have a look?"

"You will not find him."

"Move aside." The centurion swung off his horse and onto the running board of the suspect carriage. Calling "Stand by!" to two of his men who were closest, he opened the door.

The carriage was empty.

"Juno!" he swore. "I was sure I had him."

"I told you so."

"So you did. Men, finish up! Check the others and let's go. Evidently our quarry missed the caravan."

But they searched the rest of the caravan anyway. Finally the centurion rode to the front, where he apologized to the kings and released the caravan. He and his squad departed. The caravan resumed its journey out of town.

A bearded, hawk-nosed potentate in a turban, riding a camel near the front of the line, shook the golden cords leading from his saddle to the necks of the two half-naked Nubian slaves walking in front of him. "They're gone," he said in a stage whisper. "Ease on back to the carriage. I'm going to let the foxes out of their boxes."

He loosed the ends of the golden cords, letting them trail in the dust, and sidled his camel out of the line on the side opposite that of the cooperative driver. Dropping back until he rode next to the empty carriage, he managed to swing down out of the camel-saddle to the running board. As the camel returned to its place in line, he eased the door open and, ducking to clear his turban, stepped inside.

He bent down and spoke to the seats. "They're gone." He heard movement under the seat cushions, and slid them away from the walls.

"Help me out," groaned Ruth. "I'll be stiff forever." She managed to lift one arm out of the box. Mel removed his turban, bent, and lifted her to a sitting position. Chazz was clambering awkwardly out of his own seat across the cabin. Mel helped Ruth out and replaced her cushion, and they sat down.

Chazz sat facing them. "Oh! Oh! Oh! Am I sore! Muscles I didn't know I had are sore!"

The carriage door Mel had come through opened again, and Aulus and Baldy slipped in.

"Don't complain." Aulus tossed the coiled golden cord on the seat. "At least you got to ride." He reached for Mel's robe. "May I? I feel naked without my toga."

Baldy reached under Chazz's seat for his tunic. "And at least you didn't have to be stained brown." He rolled down the cuffs of his leggings. "Too bad about that valence." He tossed his own golden leash in the box and replaced the seat.

"It does look a little ragged without its edging," Ruth agreed with a glance up at the denuded valence.

"And you're lucky we found that harness polish," observed Chazz. "Without it, that guy would have recognized Aulus for sure."

43
The Fixed Point

Night fell as they reached the outskirts of Bethlehem. Suddenly they heard an outcry from up the line.

"What's happening?" asked Aulus. "Another search?"

"Sounds too happy for that," Ruth objected. "Let's see." She cautiously leaned out the window and tilted her head.

She drew back inside, looking more beautiful and joyful than Mel had ever seen her. And that was saying a lot.

"Take a look," she urged.

Encouraged by her smile, they opened the door of the rumbling carriage and stepped outside.

At first Mel could see nothing untoward in the luminous night. The city lay just ahead, bathed in moonlight…

No. There was no moon. It was the star.

"It's back!" he exclaimed.

It was directly overhead. They could now see a faint beam shining down from it onto a certain spot in the city.

"Let's walk forward and meet the kings," suggested Ruth, "and celebrate the star's reappearance with them."

The wagons of the caravan could not negotiate the streets of the town. Leaving them outside, the party, leading a single pack animal, picked its way carefully along a narrow, dusty lane between close-set houses whose walls seemed to glow. Elsewhere the star shone with the brightness of a full moon, but here Mel could faintly distinguish green highlights in ivy clinging to pale stucco, a golden glint of Hebrew letters written on a doorpost, purple stripes on the awning of a souk. And the colors beckoned more brightly as the group progressed in a subdued silence punctuated by the muffled echoes of the camel's hoofsteps.

Ruth reached for Mel's hand and clasped it. "It's so bright," she whispered.

"It's," Mel began, then fell silent.

"What?"

Mel knew he had to admit this. "It's holy ground." Ruth greeted his words with silence. Thanks, he thought; he didn't feel like talking.

They reached a crossing, more like a three-way branch of bending alleyways. The Kings stopped, peering. Mel and Ruth stepped apart as the camel caught up to them and nosed its ungainly way between them before clomping to a halt. It snorted softly. What a beautiful camel, Mel thought. And it *was* beautiful: beautifully appropriate and right, somehow. Everything was happening as if long-rehearsed and eagerly awaited, like a command performance. Everything was falling into place. But not *déjà vu*, *enfin vu*: at long last seen. The certainty that all his life had been preparing him for this feeling of a rough patch of wall against his hand, the scuff of *this* step of his booted foot in *this* rut in the dust just *here*. So this is where it led. The slippery slope. Why had he resisted so long?

The Kings had evidently decided which way was brightest. They were moving again, into the middle lane. As the camel dropped back, Mel took Ruth's hand again. She turned to him with a smile that seemed to light its own halo. Why me? thought Mel. God, why have You chosen me to bless with these wonders? I never gave You two thoughts in a row. Never cracked open Your book since my Bar Mitzvah. Surrounded by colleagues and fellow students just like me, not knowing and not caring to know. But calling ourselves Jews just the same. And absorbing the traditions by osmosis. The taboos we broke with hardly a twinge. The focus on persecution. The view of Christianity as the religion of the oppressors, the inquisitors—at best, a religion for *them*. The Gentiles' way to God. They have the New Testament, we have the Talmud. God through Jesus Christ versus God through the study of Scripture. Then I met Zimri.

Mel became aware of his surroundings as the party paused again. They had entered a crossroad that widened into a little plaza with shuttered shops, a cafe—all dark and silent now—and a wide arched portal before which sawdust speckled the ground. Next to this, their destination: a polished, sturdy oak door gleaming in the face of a small stucco dwelling. The light, brightest here, seemed to glow from within as well as above.

Zimri didn't have the Talmud to confuse him, Mel thought. He had the Isaiah scroll, and he took it literally: the Messiah would suffer and die. Just as the Dead Sea scrolls said! No wonder they were spiked for forty years; they corroborated Ruth's story—the gospel story. An outside source.

But that meant...He was struck by it. I know Rabbinical Judaism didn't arise as early as the first century, he thought. But the scrolls confirm that *Jewish Christianity did*! He recalled a snatch of the translation released just a few years ago. "And they put to death the leader of the community, the branch of David."

Jews who believed in Jesus Christ wrote these things! I'm not the first!

King Orondes unstrapped a heavy-looking sack from the camel's saddle, then advanced to the illuminated door as King Atuman took his position beside him, leaning on a staff. Caspar, Melchior and brown Balthasar stood just behind them with their gifts. Ruth and Aulus hung back a little, Ruth's hand on Mel's arm. Aulus looped the camel's lead around an iron railing.

When the King knocked gently, the star winked out. The alley was plunged in darkness as if the shadow of a great wing had passed over it. Ruth gasped, and her fingers dug into Mel's arm.

Suddenly he knew what had happened. "Its job is done." His skin prickled. "*It was only waiting for us*."

The door opened on its pivots. A full-bearded young man stood there. He looked about Mel's age. "Yes?" he said.

"Where is he that is born King of the Jews?" Orondes asked. "For we have seen his star in Anatolia, and are come to worship him."

"He is here," Joseph replied. Turning, he led them around a screen into the living area. Baldy stooped deeply under the low ceiling. As they filed in, they filled the room.

And when they were come into the house, they saw the young child with Mary his mother, and fell down, and worshipped him; and when they had opened their treasures, they presented unto him gifts.

Dropping to one knee when his turn came, Melchior slid Queen Amytis' ring off his finger and placed it on the stack of gold coins and chains. It was the most precious thing he had.

Caspar draped his purse of frankincense on the heap of costly powders.

Balthasar removed the jar of myrrh from his pouch and set it on the lovingly handcrafted table next to a crystal box of spikenard. "It's not much," he said quietly, "but somehow it seems appropriate."

Appropriate! How? That was the stuff he packed corpses in—Oh. Mel shuddered.

Little Jesus smiled and gurgled in his mother Mary's arms. Barely two months old, he seemed to be enjoying the attention: his keen blue eyes peered curiously at the exotic visitors and the heap of bright gifts on the table. His chubby arms waved in pleasure.

As Mel rose from the firm sweet-smelling sawdust, he caught the eye of the woman seated on cushions behind the table.

Aletha! This girl had the same warm brown eyes, the same welcoming smile. And she wasn't much older, fifteen or so.

Yet there was something else. Something that made him lower his eyes and turn his head away as if to make sure he wouldn't bump into anything when he stood up.

A glint of steel. Her eyes blazed triumph.

Brazen! he would have thought only a few weeks ago.He knew perfectly well what the Talmud said about this woman and her child. But that interpretation fell apart under the beams from the star that had singled out this very house—and in light of all he had recently seen. No, this was the woman given as a sign for King Ahaz: *Behold, a virgin shall conceive, and bear a son....*

Mel tried to imagine Aletha pregnant. Out of wedlock.

He pictured Zimri's reaction and winced. But of course she would never do such a thing...But what if she were given the choice by an angel? What would she say?

He realized, dimly, a small part of the courage this girl had shown. The penalty for what everyone would believe she had done was to be stoned to death. He knew his own faith would never be equal to such a deed. He could not risk stoning for a virtuous act, let alone one with such shame, such disgrace attached to it.

Blessed shall she be above women.... The thought from his childhood flashed unbidden through his mind, a line remembered from Hebrew *shool.* He couldn't remember the context, except that it was somehow connected with an act of great courage. Rising clumsily to his feet under the low ceiling, Mel risked another glance at Mary's face. Yes, that was it. Courage. So great that it abashed him. He who had slapped a king knew he couldn't compare, could hardly face this woman. That wasn't courage, that was just plain stupid impulse. But what she did: that took great, considered courage. And it was courage rewarded, a daring obedience vindicated, somehow by *him.* Or his presence here.

The memory verse's context suddenly came to him with a chill that turned his knees to water. He staggered, recalling the rest of Deborah's song: *Blessed above women shall Jael the wife of Heber the Kenite be, blessed shall she be above women in the tent.* He remembered what Jael's act of great courage had been. One that involved great personal danger, and shame too: a breach of the traditional hospitality—wait a minute! What was Sisera doing in the women's tent anyway?

Mary smiled and thanked them. "He that is mighty has done to me great things; and holy is his name."

"Through the tender mercy of our God," added Joseph, "the dayspring from on high has visited us."

His bride glanced up at him. Zeal flashed in her eyes. "And his mercy is on them that fear him from generation to generation." Her gaze fell on Ruth, kneeling at the table. She held the babe out to her. "Would you like to hold him?"

"I..."

Mel was glad the offer hadn't been made to him. Then he noticed Ruth's hesitancy. Surely she couldn't be feeling the same inadequacy, the same guilt? Come on, Ruth, he urged silently. You can do it. You, the Christian, the innocent. You have nothing to fear.

Ruth rose to her feet. "Yes." She lifted the baby Jesus in her arms. His tiny hand clutched at her dark curls. He cooed. She gazed down at his face, enrapt.

"My Lord and my God," she murmured. "Look, Mel. Isn't he beautiful?"

Mel had barely recovered enough to face anyone, never mind the Holy One of Israel. "Yes. He's beautiful."

"You're not even looking."

Mel gulped and took a peek. He was not struck dead, and he saw he'd been right: the baby *was* beautiful. For a baby, at least. Mel was rather color-blind in that area, having no younger siblings. This one looked like an ordinary, healthy baby boy. Jesus had no halo, no piercing gaze of infinite knowledge, although his eyes were a bit unusual for a Semite.

Ruth says he's God, Mel thought. Nobody's gonna believe that—

He suddenly saw what that meant, what this babe was facing. What they'd do to him when he grew up and spoke out, made his claims.

They're gonna crucify him! With the best excuse in the world. Blasphemy. But if he is God, or—how did Isaiah put it? The mighty God, The everlasting Father—He's given all that up. It doesn't show. He's just a man. And in this context, that means...Vulnerable.

My God! How could he do that? Why? For...

For me?

Chazz looked over Ruth's shoulder. "This is it!" he whispered. "The fixed point at the center of the universe!"

"Of course!" she said. "So that's why we would automatically time jump to the moment of his birth, by default."

"Right," Mel agreed. "If there's anything central to all of space-time, this is it." Jesus, he saw, was indeed the Fixed Point around Whom the universe revolved, and toward Whom all their adventures had been leading them. Shiloh has come, and He has met us here, in our need. God's eternal Project, His Plan of redemption.

The fixed point yawned.

"He's sleepy," said his mother. "Let me put him to bed now. Then we can visit. I'll see if I have any refreshments fit for kings."

44
Epiphany

When Jesus was asleep, Mary served tea and honey cakes on the low table, then took her seat next to the kings on the couch. Aulus and the time travelers sat on cushions on the opposite side of the table. Baldy sprawled at full length on one elbow on the sawdust-covered stone floor. The entry screen had been opened to expose the company to the warmth radiating from the cook stove.

Joseph settled at the end of the table, under a lamp fixed to the wall, and turned to the elder king, nearest him. "You have journeyed far," he prompted with a smile.

"I am Atuman, King-emeritus of Anatolia," the king introduced himself, "and this is my son Orondes, the current regent. We fancy ourselves astronomers and scholars. The fact is, we are mere dabblers."

"Amateurs," agreed Orondes. "We do love searching out the mysteries of ancient knowledge. Thanks to a peaceful and prosperous kingdom, we have the means to continually augment our collection of books, and the time to devote to their study."

"When the star appeared," his father continued, "we knew it signified something of import. But what? Usually such an omen is associated with a calamity, a royal death, a war." He sipped from his cup.

"Also," he went on, "commonly the nova or comet or whatever it is flares briefly in the heavens and is gone in a few days. This was different. We searched our library diligently. Finally we found a reference in your Torah to a star coming out of Jacob. It was associated with a Sceptre's rising, one that should have dominion.

"We saw a chance to give our worship to one who would be a King blessed by the God we love. So we organized this expedition, hoping we would not be too late."

"These things always take longer than one expects," added Orondes. "But God smiled upon us. We have found him in time." He leaned forward, looking earnestly past his father at Joseph. "We have read again your sacred writings on our journey. Please tell us: is this the great light seen by the people who dwell in darkness?"

"Son, need you ask?" said Atuman. "Can you not feel it? Peace itself, its Prince, is here. As the shadow of a great rock in a weary land."

Mel agreed. He looked down the table at Joseph, sitting cross-legged and calm under the oil lamp, its flame a bright, still tear. The peace which had enveloped him after his dream-inspired talk with Zimri, the loving presence that had embraced him when he had resolved in his heart to obey the will of God as far as he could understand it. That peace had its source here. That presence dwelt here. This baby was truly the Messiah of Israel, and was also, mysteriously, the Holy One of Israel: God himself, the everlasting Father. The culmination of what it meant to be a Jew.

"He shall be exalted and extolled, and be very high," quoted Joseph. "So shall he sprinkle many nations…for that which had not been told them shall they see; and that which they had not heard shall they consider."

Chazz, seated between Ruth and Aulus, paused in the act of taking another sweet-cake from the table before him. "What does that mean, 'sprinkle many nations'?" he asked.

"It means you and me, Chazz," answered Ruth. "We're not Jews, yet we've been adopted into his family anyway. Just out of the love and faith he gives us."

Aulus looked around Chazz at her. "Are the Romans also sprinkled?" he asked. "I am a Roman citizen. A product of the finest, most modern civilization the world has ever seen. A resident of Antioch, the most cosmopolitan and beautiful city of that world. A high-ranking member of the elite, entitled to wear the toga, favored by the gods, as I believed."

He turned his face toward Mary, across the table. "Yet somehow that's irrelevant now. All of it. Meaningless. Even minor, like a hangnail, to be excised or ignored. The gods…Juno I have never met. Mercury I have never seen. *This* is the God. The only God. The love here…it cannot be fathomed. My career, my life even, were well lost, to have found this."

The young mother smiled at him. "Yes, even Romans are included. The angel brought the shepherds 'good tidings of great joy, which shall be to all people.' I particularly remember that, because we had supposed beforetime that the Messiah would be for the Jews alone.

"When the archangel announced to me that I would bear him, he said, 'the Lord God shall give unto him the throne of his father David: and he shall reign over the house of Jacob for ever. . .' Nothing about Gentiles. I kept all these things, and pondered them in my heart; we puzzled over them for days, didn't we, Joseph?"

"Yes. And after we had moved here, and were more settled, we searched the scriptures diligently for the answer. Then we began to find hints, like the passage from Isaiah, that salvation…Jeshua…is for the Gentiles also."

"And you," Mary told them all, "are the confirmation of that scripture. For you are the first Gentiles to visit us. Husband, what was that other prophecy we read? Oh, yes: 'And the Gentiles shall come to thy light, and kings to the brightness of thy rising.' And here you are."

Mel was chilled with awe. Did it really say that in there?

"Yes," continued Joseph: "'…the forces of the Gentiles shall come unto thee. The multitude of camels shall cover thee…they shall bring gold and incense; and they shall show forth the praises of the Lord.'"

"Praise the Lord," Mel whispered.

"There are some parts of these prophecies that are still unclear," mused Joseph. "We don't recognize the events they speak of. They must refer to the future: prophecies not yet fulfilled."

The time travelers glanced at each other. Maybe *we* would recognize these events, Mel thought.

"But we are confident," continued Joseph, "from seeing the parts that have been fulfilled, that the rest will be also. God is so gracious! He knows our faith is weak and needs strengthening from time to time. So he grants us prophetic fulfillments in the near term, to sustain our hope and faith for the distant future."

"It is real, then. I had never thought it possible," Balthasar marveled. "An old idolatrous dog like me… The God of Abraham has been gracious to me beyond hope… But what is to become of this babe?"

"The myrrh you brought," replied Mary, "reminded me of one of the most puzzling parts of all, and one I hope does not apply to my son! Isaiah says the Messiah must suffer: 'He is despised and rejected of men; a man of sorrows, and acquainted with grief…' and this is the same man who shall be 'very high,' and 'sprinkle many nations'! How can this be?"

"As nearly as I can discern," Joseph offered, "the passage seems to indicate that it is precisely by being tortured, by being beaten beyond recognition as human, that this man will sprinkle many nations.

"That tells me that the sprinkling will be with his blood."

"God forbid," prayed Mary, "that this should happen to my son!"

"'Yet it pleased the Lord to bruise him,'" Joseph quoted.

"What?!" said Mel and Ruth together.

"A difficult passage indeed," King Atuman agreed. "*I* cannot fathom it, at any rate. And it is followed by another even more difficult—self-contradictory, in fact: 'he shall divide the spoil with the strong; because he hath poured out his soul unto death.' How can anyone take a spoil after he is dead?"

"That's easy," replied Chazz. "He'll come back to life again, after three days."

"Where does it say that?" Orondes asked.

"It's in all four gos—" Chazz stopped short. "Ruth? A little help here?"

"You're asking the wrong lady," admitted Ruth. "But it's true!" she assured the others. "We know it's true! Jesus will be crucified and then rise from the dead—"

Seeing the ashen expression on his mother's face, she stopped. Her own face clouded. Burying it in her hands, she broke into heart-rending sobs. "It's so easy," she choked out, "when it's just *history!*"

Chazz too looked stricken. There was a pause.

"Well, who can know the future?" asked Joseph. "Only God, and those to whom he reveals it. It may be that some other interpretation is true. Or it may be that Messiah himself has to suffer. We his parents, of course, hope that he need not. But someone must; Isaiah makes that clear. Someone must bear the punishment for our sins."

Mary reached across the table to lay her hand on Ruth's shaking shoulder. "It is not your fault. It is a mystery—though a sorrowful one. God will give me the strength to bear it at the proper time. And if what you say is true, there is a joyful mystery at the end of it all."

"Oh, yes," sobbed Ruth. "He will return to life. He will live forever. So shall we all. There's a happy ending." She wiped her eyes. "At least for his followers."

"So this is what it all means, in reality," Chazz reflected. "To know him personally. To know that you know that you are his. When I longed to find the Scheherazade of my dreams, I *knew* that such longing, so acute that it was itself a thing to be desired, could not exist in the world without there also existing some object that would satisfy that longing." A tear welled out of his eye. He brushed it away and continued.

"But I see now that my longing for a figment betrayed my unconscious despair—my hidden belief that its object couldn't truly exist at all. I was wrong. Here is that object."

"The object of my heart's desire," agreed Ruth. "Of everyone's. But to us it's been given to find him. We've been chosen. The Lord is good."

Later, as they shared a stoup of wine before retiring, Mel asked Joseph, "'It *pleased* the Lord to bruise him'?"

"I am far from plumbing the depths of God, but I think it gives some indication of his love for us, his strayed sheep: God loves us so much that he is glad there is a way to save us, even if it means sacrificing his anointed one."

Tears stung Mel's eyes, surprising him. "So much love…for us?"

"That is my interpretation, yes. That he loves us enough to die for us even while we are still sinning. Men would call it almost a demented love—totally undeserved, its object totally unworthy. In any case, we know from experience that if the Holy Spirit gave it to Isaiah to write down, it will be found to be true."

"Everything? Every verse in the Bible? What about the contradictions?"
I don't *care* about them, Mel realized, sipping his wine. It was the central message, which had survived the corruption of centuries, that was important. Not all those pickers' nits.

"There are no contradictions," Joseph asserted. "None. For example, did you know there is a curse upon me and my entire line?"

"No!" Mel was shocked.

"Messiah was to be of the house and lineage of David. I am of the house and lineage of David, through his son Solomon. Unfortunately, or providentially, as it turns out, one of my ancestors was King Jeconiah, or Jehoiachin. Do you know of Jeconiah?"

The name was familiar. Who—

Ruth placed her hand on Mel's arm. "We had lunch with him in Daniel's apartment," she reminded him in English. "Remember? The blind king's nephew?"

Oh yes! Mel remembered that old fellow quite well now. "Yes," he said to Joseph. "I see what you mean. His uncle fulfilled two apparently contradictory prophecies. But what's this about a curse?"

"Jeconiah was accursed of God, he and his descendants to all generations. That includes me," said Joseph. "That would include Jeshua, also, except—"

"— he is not your child, by blood," Ruth supplied.

"You know?" asked Joseph, surprised. "Correct. My bride is the virgin spoken of by Isaiah."

Chazz chimed in from Ruth's other side. "'Behold, a virgin shall conceive, and bear a son.'"

"And I," Mary added, "am of the lineage of David also, in the line through his son Nathan. No curse attaches to that line. Do you see?"

"Do you see how the Lord fits it all together perfectly?" concluded Joseph. "There is no room for any contradictions."

A lot of my friends in 1995, Mel thought, are going to be very surprised.

45
Death Squads

That night, sleeping in the camel caravan, Mel did not dream. Others did.

Aulus shook him awake just before dawn. "Sorry to do this, but get up right away and come to the front. King Atuman has an announcement."

The kings were packed and dressed for travel when Mel got there, still rubbing his eyes and yawning.

"Dear friends," said King Atuman, "how I have longed for this rendezvous. How I wish that we could remain here forever, at the feet of this child, learning more of his love, coming to know him better and better. But we cannot.

"God has warned me in a dream that we must depart into our own country by another way. We must leave immediately, and remove all trace of our having been here. For Herod will seek the young child to destroy him."

"It is best that we leave now," King Orondes added, "as quietly as possible, before the neighbors awaken. I would that we might see this family once again, and bid them farewell; but we must not tarry. I have already sent a rider west to Ascalon to charter a boat. Herod's writ does not run there: it is a free port."

"We shall convey your farewell, and your warning, when the family awakens," said Aulus. "We cannot accompany you, for we must return to a different land, eastward. The five of us are less conspicuous than a camel caravan, so we hope to slip by Jerusalem without being apprehended."

"God go with you," the king blessed them.

"And with you also," replied Mel.

"We'll meet again," Ruth declared. "That's certain."

Joseph also had dreamed.

"Just before I awoke," he told Mel, "the angel of the Lord appeared to me in a dream, saying, 'Arise, and take the young child and his mother, and flee into Egypt, and be thou there until I bring thee word.'"

"Yes. We were going to warn you. It won't be long before Herod realizes nobody is going to tell him where to find you. He'll try to hunt you down. He'll probably institute a house-to-house search."

"We'll help you pack," Ruth offered.

"Thank you," said Mary. "We don't have much. We traveled light when we came up from Galilee, and haven't had time to accumulate many possessions."

"We sold our beast to set up shop in this house," Joseph added. "Now we must purchase another."

"With all that gold," Aulus noted, "you should be able to travel to Egypt in some comfort."

"'I will sing unto the Lord, because he hath dealt bountifully with me,'" quoted Joseph. "'I will call upon the Lord, who is worthy to be praised: so shall I be saved from mine enemies.' His providence is wonderful."

"Wonderful indeed," Ruth agreed. "To think that he has brought us here, and met us here. In the bosom of his family."

"*You* are as family," said Mary. "Our brothers and sister in the Lord. 'Behold how good and how pleasant it is for brethren to dwell together in unity!' We have rejoiced to know you. One day we'll be able to know you even better, to share all we have, all we are, in his presence again.

"But now we must part. Come, I'll show you what things to pack."

Within two hours the holy family had packed, loaded their few belongings into a donkey cart Aulus and Joseph had purchased in the town, and departed to the south along the Gaza Road.

"Now what?" asked Baldy.

"Now we sneak back to Batanea," Aulus said. "We won't be safe until we're under Zimri's protection again."

"Wait till he hears what Herod did to us," predicted Chazz. "He'll reconsider paying taxes."

"It certainly will strain relations, at the very least," Baldy agreed. "And there goes my job as Herod's bodyguard." They laughed.

The five got as far as the outskirts of Bethlehem before Aulus muttered, "Hold it. Trouble."

They ducked into an alley and peered around the corner. Down the quiet street a mounted party of helmeted figures rode toward them.

"Idumaeans," said Aulus.

They watched cautiously as the troop halted before a house, dismounted, and entered, leaving several soldiers to guard the horses.

"They *are* searching house-to-house," Mel whispered.

But he was wrong.

"What's that?" asked Baldy. "A scream?"

The soldiers emerged from the house. One held a short sword. A woman followed him, beating on his armor, clawing at his face. The soldier shoved her roughly to the ground and swung onto his horse. The troop rode on to the next door. Townspeople began to step out into the road in fear and curiosity.

"Back!" shouted the leader of the soldiers. "Back into your houses, all of you, or you will be killed." The people scurried indoors.

"Something evil is happening," Baldy guessed. "What can we do?"

"Can we take them?" asked Mel.

"No," Aulus replied. "They are sixteen, a full squad, armed and armored. Let's get out of here."

They ran quietly up the alley. At its end, Aulus and Mel looked out. Another squad was just leaving a house on the parallel street, a block away. Aulus pulled Mel back. "If they see us—"

"Are they looking for us, or for Jesus?"

"I don't know. But we are wanted men," Aulus reminded him. "They must have our description."

"What'll we do?" asked Ruth. "We're surrounded."

"Or soon will be," Aulus agreed. "They're being rather thorough."

Suddenly there was a new scream, from just around the corner: "Murderers! Oh, my angels!"

"Rachel, Rachel," came a man's voice. But Rachel would not be comforted; she continued to scream.

"Oh, no," Ruth cried. "No! How could I have forgotten *that*?"

"What is it?" asked Mel.

"No time now," Aulus hissed. "Quickly! In there!" They took cover behind the first house on the alley, sheltered between its wall and a stable.

"We can't let them do this," whispered Ruth urgently. "They're—"

"Quiet," Aulus cut her off. "I don't think they saw us, but they'll hear you."

Through a curtained rear window, Mel saw the family cowering in the one room: the mother, a little girl about ten, and a boy who was no more than a toddler. Where was the man of the house?

Suddenly the front door burst open and two soldiers entered. The woman stepped protectively in front of the young ones. "What do you want of us? What does this mean?"

Three more soldiers crowded into the room. Baldy joined Mel at the window. Ruth crouched on the ground, face in hands. Chazz put an arm around her shaking shoulders. Aulus watched the alley.

Two soldiers seized the woman and dragged her away from her children.

"You can't do this!" she shrieked. "King Herod will catch you. He'll have you punished."

"Silence, woman," the sergeant growled. "Know this: We are acting under the orders of King Herod." He spat on the floor. "You think we'd do this of ourselves?" He spoke to one of his troop, indicating the toddler with a glance. "That one."

Mel barely had time to realize what was about to happen when the soldier drew his bloody gladius and ran it into the child's breast.

With a roar, Balthasar vaulted through the window, taking the curtains and half the frame with him. He smote the executioner's head with one huge fist, snatching the man's short sword as he fell. Berserk, Baldy whirled the sword through the necks of the sergeant and his corporal, decapitating them instantly. The soldiers holding the now hysterical woman yelled and released her. The little girl ran to her arms, crying.

Baldy stepped forward and ran one of the soldiers through before he could move. The other turned to the front door and collided with several who were coming through it in response to his yells. Baldy skewered two of them with the gladius. As they fell, he leaped over them after the rest, who turned and ran toward their horses.

"Come on," Aulus shouted. "It's all up now. He needs help."

Chazz, Mel and Ruth followed Aulus as he ran around the side of the house to the front, flinging off his toga and drawing an ornamental dagger from his belt. Mel picked up a rock from the dusty street.

Rounding the corner, he saw Baldy surrounded by yelling Idumaean auxiliaries, none of whom seemed eager to be first to approach within reach of the giant's short sword. Yet the circle was pressing closer.

The soldiers' horses had skittered across the street and reared, neighing in terror, on the verge of stampeding. Chazz and Ruth hung back, uncertain what to do. Chazz, clutching the computer tightly with one hand, scooped up Aulus's toga with the other.

Unnoticed, Aulus ran up behind the nearest auxilius and drove his poniard between the laces of the man's armor, into his back. The man fell. The two nearest him turned and saw Aulus and Mel. "More of them!" one shouted. Mel hurled the rock, catching him in the face with enough force to drive his helmet's cheek-plate into the bone. He screamed and dropped his sword. Aulus bent to retrieve it as Baldy took advantage of the other's distraction to leap through the hole in the circle, bowling his man over.

"The horses!" Baldy yelled.

While he menaced the eight remaining troopers with his whirling sword, his friends ran to the milling horses and scrambled on. Backing toward the largest mount, Baldy twisted a seven-foot pilum from its loop; suddenly his radius of action was doubled, catching the nearest Idumaeans by surprise. Three fell from blows to the head. The remaining five turned and bolted. Baldy bestrode the big horse.

The squad down the alley, roused by the noise, raced toward them.

"Come on!" shouted Aulus. "Ride for your lives!"

They spurred their mounts to a gallop toward the east. Baldy whacked the riderless horses and roared as he rode past them, stampeding them westwards to collide with the fresh troops just rounding the corner of the alley. Mel saw two knocked down, but three others galloped past the melee and began to catch up.

Baldy's mount reeled under its burden. The pursuing riders were gaining fast. Aulus dropped back alongside Mel.

"Get out of here! I'll cover your exit."

"No! You'll be killed!"

"Aulus, you can't!" cried Ruth.

"We can handle it," Chazz insisted. "Here! Hold this, and get out of the way!" He leaned over and passed Aulus the laptop computer. Aulus grabbed it reflexively.

What does that kid think he's doing? Mel wondered, watching Chazz yank a bow from its socket and whack Aulus's horse on the rump with it. The horse bolted ahead.

Light suddenly dawned as Mel saw Chazz raise the bow vertically, high in the air, holding its string fast in its groove, and start to lift his right leg. *He's stringing it!* Mel followed suit, performing the tricky but well-practiced Parthian maneuver, ending with the bow flexed under his right leg and over his left knee, which freed his left hand to fix the lower loop into its cut.

As he swept the strung bow down and off his right leg, Mel noticed that Ruth, also grasping Chazz's plan, had strung her own bow. The Idumaeans were only five lengths behind and coming up fast, shielding their eyes against the dust.

Mel plucked an arrow from the saddle-quiver and nocked it onto his bowstring, seeing the others do likewise out of the corner of his eye. Gripping the horse between his knees and allowing it to slacken its speed the merest trifle, he extended the bow in front of him and paused an instant until Ruth and Chazz acknowledged with the same signal.

At Chazz's far side, Ruth had sped up a trifle. Now riding in echelon, the three simultaneously swung their left arms to the side while drawing their bows. In a smooth continuation of the movement, they pivoted left at the waist, aiming rearward. Time seemed to stretch out for Mel as he fell into the familiar maneuver. He had leisure to choose his target and absolute confidence in his well-rehearsed skill. Compensating flexibly for the violent motion of his mount, he set the iron point of his arrow on the center of the soldier's armored chest, pausing imperceptibly to synchronize with the others.

Just as his grip relaxed it struck him: this was not a volunteer, not practice, not a padded arrow streaking on its way.

He was killing a man.

So were they all.

Time leapt forward: their arrows flew in unison over the horses' cruppers directly into the breastplates of the pursuing troops, at point-blank range. A perfect Parthian shot.

The three Idumaeans exploded from their saddles and flew through the air, dead before the surprise could fully register on their faces. Before Mel saw them hit the dirt, he and his companions wheeled around a corner into another alley.

"Nice shooting!" yelled Aulus.

As they pounded out the far end of the alley, the five saw a third company of Idumaeans making their methodical way westward on the main street. These, several blocks away to the west, were not looking toward the fugitives, whose horses' hoofbeats were muffled by wailing and sobbing as they strove to widen the gap.

"They're sweeping the whole district," Aulus called.

"Oh God, it's horrible!" cried Ruth. "Why didn't I remember sooner?"

An angry mob was starting to gather in the street as they galloped by the last house at the east end of town. A stone whipped past Mel's ear.

They're blaming us!

Then they were out of range, leaving the howling crowd in their dust. They thundered southeastward for ten minutes, under the umbrella pines lining the Herodium Road.

Finally Baldy called a halt. His animal was the first to tire. He quickly dismounted and began to walk his horse, his long strides easily keeping up with the rest as they rode at a walk. No more pursuit was evident.

Chazz handed Aulus his toga, trading for the computer. Aulus donned it gratefully. "That was amazing," he said. "Where did you learn to do that?"

"That's the way Parthians do it," replied Chazz.

"You have learned fast," Baldy approved. "But now we need water. Soon. Otherwise the horses will be useless."

The road stretched featureless ahead of them for miles, rising gradually to a fold of purple hills dominated by a castle on a round crag.

"Think they can make it that far?" Mel indicated the castle. "There doesn't seem to be water any closer."

Baldy had removed his tunic and was wiping down his lathered horse as he walked. "I hope so. This one's in a bad way."

No wonder, thought Mel. Even without armor, Baldy was pretty hard on horses. That one was big, but he was no clibanarius.

"We'll know in an hour," Aulus said. "We should be up there by then. We'll have to be cautious whom we ask for water, though."

"Why?" asked Ruth. "They won't know anything about us there, will they?"

It's not as if they could broadcast an APB, Mel thought.

"They might," replied Aulus. "That's Herodium: Herod's summer palace. He may even be there, God forbid. We're walking into the lion's den."

46
Crossroads

The breeze was noticeably cooler as the five friends rode slowly through the open gate of the high village under Herod's castle. Two bored Idumaean gatekeepers ignored them.

The weary horses stepped up their pace a bit as they carried the five down the main street through the afternoon shade.

"There must be a stable up ahead," Aulus guessed. "They scent food and water."

They found the livery stable two blocks farther on, between an inn and a smithy. It fronted a square at the intersection of another main road running north and south. A well stood under trees in the center of the square.

Aulus handed Baldy his toga. "Wait by the well with Ruth, while I arrange feed and a rubdown for the horses. You might draw some water for them. Try to be inconspicuous. Mel, lend me your tunic? My toga is *not* inconspicuous."

"Sure." Mel took it off and handed it to the legate, who walked over to the stable and entered. He emerged shortly with a boy who gathered the reins of the still-thirsty horses and led them into the shadows of the stable's interior. Aulus walked over and joined them, sitting on the grass by the well.

Baldy drew up a fresh bucket of chill water and gave it to Ruth, who drank from a cupped hand, wiped her face with the remaining moisture, and passed the bucket to Chazz. They all drank in turn.

"How long before they'll be coming after us?" Chazz asked. "I'm hungry."

"An hour; no less, I hope," said Aulus. "The horses must rest at least that long. We'll risk a meal in the inn."

"Nobody seems to have heard of us here yet," Mel observed.

"No, but they'll remember us. Let's hope we're gone long before then." Aulus got up and dusted himself off. The others followed him into the inn.

They were just leaving the inn after a quiet lunch of lamb brisket and rice pilaf. A cloud of sadness still hung over them from the recent tragic events in Bethlehem. "Still, I wish we could have warned them," lamented Ruth.

"The whole town? Where could they have gone that was safe?" Mel asked.

"If I had remembered sooner," she began.

"We've been over all this," said Mel. "You can't blame yourself."

"At least the holy family got out in time," Chazz pointed out.

"Probably," said Aulus. "They were—what's that?"

"Somebody shouting," Baldy pronounced. "At the western gate."

"This is it." Aulus hurried toward the stable. "Let's get the horses, quickly."

They were mounting when a rider on a dusty steed dashed through the square from the west. Close on his heels ran an angry mob. Some carried hoes, hay forks, or winnowing shovels. They passed through the square toward the east.

"They're not after us," observed Mel. "They're heading toward the castle."

"What's he yelling?" Chazz asked. "Doesn't sound like Greek." He still clutched the computer, now wrapped in the toga.

"It's Aramaic." Baldy translated: "'Down with Herod, murderer of babies!'"

As the five rode away toward the north, Mel saw the blacksmith run out of his smithy after the mob, crowbar in one hand and a firebrand in the other.

"There goes the summer palace," he said.

"Too bad," sighed Baldy. "Herod's not there."

"Isn't this going to get them in trouble?" Chazz asked.

"It will no doubt soon call down Herod's wrath on them," replied Aulus. "More slaughter. We must be well into Batanea before then, lest we be caught up in it."

"Maybe this will take Herod's mind off us," Ruth suggested.

"Yes," agreed Mel. "If it becomes a widespread revolt, he'll be too busy defending Jerusalem to worry about us."

"Where does this road lead, by the way?" Chazz inquired.

"Jerusalem."

Reaching the base of the Mount of Olives at dusk, they halted at a crossroads. Jerusalem loomed ahead and to their left. Bethany lay straight ahead, Jericho and the Jordan river-crossing at Bethabara to the right.

"Here is where we part," Baldy announced.

"What!" cried Mel, stunned.

"You must cross the river now, but I have unfinished business in Jerusalem."

"You can't go into the city," said Aulus.

"I will take care. It will be dark soon. Please, beloved friends, don't make this harder than need be. There is a thing I must do, or never live with the failure to do it."

"You'll be killed," said Mel. "Don't even think of it."

"Don't be foolish," Ruth urged. "Come with us. We need you."

Balthasar sat patiently through their protests. Then he pulled on the reins. His horse reared and whirled westward. "Don't try to follow me," he called back. "Farewell. We'll meet again someday."

They watched his departing silhouette in indecision for a few moments.

"Come on," said Mel. "Let's go after him. We've got to stop him."

Aulus placed a restraining hand on his arm. "Should we not respect his wishes? Besides, the four of us together could not stop him."

"Then let's go with him, watch over him..." Mel hesitated, realizing how absurd that sounded. Any danger that would daunt Balthasar would surely overwhelm the rest of them.

They continued to watch until the tiny figure of the giant was lost against the shadow of Mount Zion.

"We'd better be going too," Aulus urged. They turned back toward the darkening east.

Torches borne by a company of mounted soldiers were advancing toward them from the eastern road.

As they hesitated between routes, the soldiers saw them.

"Halt!" came the faint cry as the troops began to charge. "Halt in the name of Caesar Augustus!"

"Romans!" hissed Aulus. "Ride!"

They spurred their weary horses into a gallop up the rising road toward Jerusalem. Behind them, the armored cavalry of the VIIth Maniple of the XIXth Auxiliary, Judea, strung out into a line in pursuit.

In five minutes the pavement under the pounding hooves of their lathered mounts changed to cobblestone streets. In two more they were through the just-closing eastern gate of the Old City. The heavy armor of their pursuers had prolonged the stern chase—until now.

Chazz being the lightest, his horse was in the lead. Fatigue, and a loose cobblestone, doomed him. With a crack of bone and a scream of agony, the horse lurched sideways as it pitched forward in a twisting half-somersault, cracking its head on the stone corner of an alley. Chazz and the computer flew in separate arcs. Chazz landed on top of his silent horse with a grunt.

The computer slid out of its padding toga in midair and smashed to chips against a stone wall.

Aulus hauled desperately on the reins to stop his own mount from trampling Chazz. Ruth and Mel had more time to react. Ruth leaped from her horse as it sank to its knees, and ran to Chazz's side. He was moaning. Mel was there an instant later.

"He's alive," he said in relief.

Aulus ran to them and snatched up his telltale toga. *"Hai!"* he cried, slapping Ruth's mount on the rump. It bolted away, followed by Mel's. Aulus's own horse was already gone. "They're right behind us. Help me here, Mel." The two men sat bracing their backs against a wall and shoved at the body of Chazz's horse. Slowly, then faster as it hit a patch of slime, the animal slid into the alley. "Quick!" Aulus leaped to Chazz's head. "Lift his feet."

They dragged Chazz into a narrow arched passage and held their breath.

Seconds later the Roman maniple thundered by, overlooking the dead horse in the gloomy side alley. In a minute they were gone.

Chazz was dazed. "Can you walk?" Aulus asked him.

"I—I think so."

"What now?" asked Ruth. "We're down to three horses, if we can find them."

"Leave them," Aulus ordered. "We must hide."

Already, cries and shouts of command echoed from the Temple mount. The soldiers were retracing their path.

Aulus led them, Mel half-supporting Chazz, through a maze of twisty alleys, all alike, until they emerged at the edge of a brightly lighted quad. They had encountered no one on their meanderings. Mel thought it strange, and said so.

"Curfew, because of the revolt," guessed Aulus. "That must be why they challenged us. We were out after curfew."

"What's that building?" Ruth pointed across the quad.

"Don't recognize it in the dark, eh? Herod's palace. They'll never think of looking for us there. Come on."

With misgivings, Mel raced silently after Aulus across the quad with Ruth and Chazz. Chazz had recovered enough that he didn't need Mel's support. "My computer!" he exclaimed in a stricken voice.

"It doesn't matter now," Ruth consoled him. "It accomplished its purpose."

"Where to?" Mel asked Aulus. They were crouching in the shadow of a vast ornamental marble stair. Mel recognized it as the one down whose length he had looked, from inside the door at the top, to see his wagon awaiting him among the camels.

"Freight entrance. I have the key." At the base of the steps, in the corner where they met the wall, was a huge iron door. Aulus inserted a large notched bar of iron into a slot near its edge, and twisted. A murderous shriek of abused metal rent the air, followed by a clank and a thud from the internal mechanism.

"Needs oil," Aulus complained. "The maintenance staff has been lax."

"Let's not tell Herod," advised Mel.

The hinges were oiled, however: the great door swung open silently and they slipped inside. Aulus clicked it shut after them. They were in total darkness.

"Ruth," Mel whispered, "by any chance, do you still have your—"

"Have what?" came a raspy, sneering voice.

Sudden light dazzled their eyes. They were surrounded by guards. Herod stood there, dangling the shattered computer by its handle.

47
The Temple

"So you are back," he hissed. "We knew you would return. Having failed to assassinate Us once, you meant to try again. Filthy spies!"

"They're not—"

"Silence, traitor. We see now that it was not 'sloppiness' but malign purpose that moved you. A special fate awaits you.

"As for you," he croaked to the time travelers, "your infernal device cannot save you now. And We shall not be distracted by a caravan of lying kings this time.

"Bring them to Our private audience chamber. Immediately."

As the guards hustled them in businesslike grips through the ground level of the palace toward the back stairs, Mel called out in English, "Ruth! The integral of

$$\int \frac{\sum_{j=m}^{n} (j+6)P'_{mn}(t-i-j)}{P_{mn}(t)} \, dt$$

along a path composed of the inverse of—"

A blow from a large hairy fist stunned him. "Shut up, spy," growled the guard. "You'll get me in trouble."

In the audience chamber Connubius, the major-domo, tended a fire in a brazier that had been set up next to the throne. Certain metal instruments lay in the fire, wooden handles extending over the side. The sight of them brought bile to the back of Mel's throat.

"This one first," Herod rasped. Ruth stumbled as her guards thrust her forward.

"Ruth! No!" cried Mel.

"Too much clamor," his guard said. "We'll put a stop to this." He picked a set of tongs out of the fire. "Hold his mouth open." The other guard clenched Mel's jaw by the beard with one hand and yanked back on his hair with the other. The smoking tongs drew closer. Ruth screamed. Mel's lips began to parch.

"Enough!" commanded Herod. "Do not rip his tongue out yet, lest he be unable to divulge his secrets."

"Yes, sire." The guard replaced the tongs in the fire.

"I'll tell you anything you want to know," Mel said. "Only let Ruth go free."

Herod cackled. "Yes, you shall tell Us everything. All the sooner, after We first soften you up with the screams of your fellow spy. Is she your woman? Better yet."

He took a thick cloth glove from a tray table next to the throne and began to pull it onto his left hand, finger by finger. The implements in the fire were starting to glow dull red.

King Herod saw this. "Hot enough." Examining the metal tools, he selected one that looked like a potato-masher. He gingerly picked it up in his gloved hand. "Strip her," he ordered. The guard reached to tear Ruth's jacket open.

Through a haze of helpless fury and anguish Mel saw the arras behind the throne billow. Some curiously detached portion of his brain wondered where the breeze was coming from.

Balthasar emerged from behind the throne and pressed Herod's face down into the fire. With his other hand he crushed the throat of the guard who had grasped Ruth's jacket. Herod stopped kicking. Baldy dropped him on the potato-masher. The golden robe began to smolder.

Stooping swiftly, Aulus picked up the dead guard's short sword and tossed it to Mel. The rest of Herod's guards were just starting to respond to the new situation when Aulus slit the throat of the one nearest him with his poniard. Mel stabbed another. Baldy cracked two heads together. Ruth hooked her foot behind the pedestal of the brazier and pulled the fiery tools down against her other guard as she twisted away from him. She grabbed up his fallen sword and swung wildly, leaving a red gash down his face. His tunic ablaze, he fell back and stumbled into the arras. It ignited like a torch.

A guard menaced Baldy from behind with his sword. Snatching up the smashed computer, Chazz flailed out with it. The heavy power supply swung out at the end of its cable and caught the guard in the temple. He dropped, senseless.

The major-domo was running for help toward the atrium door when Aulus's poniard thudded into his kidney. He went down and skidded into the wall.

The five looked around. No enemies remained standing.

In the sudden relative silence the crackling of the burning arras caught their attention. "Quick!" urged Baldy. "Back down the tunnel!"

Mel cut away the fiery cloth in front of the hidden door, thrust his hand into the ornamental slot, and heaved. "Ouch! Hot!" The panel slid aside. The five raced through. Mel turned to close the portal behind them and saw the far door slam off its hinges as reinforcements, summoned by the noise of battle, burst into the chamber.

"Aulus," he whispered, sliding the panel firmly closed, "is there a way to lock this from inside?"

"There should be a bar...yes." Aulus's groping fingers found an iron bar behind the panel and hinged it into place with a click. "Now. Watch out for these steps."

A pale yellow ray of light beamed from Ruth's hand.

"You do have it!" whispered Mel. "Now we can make time."

They hurried down the steps and through the long tunnel, guided by Ruth's penlight, then ran up the steps under the Temple. They paused at the door.

Aulus opened it a crack. A delicious odor of roasting meat wafted through, accompanying the shaft of light from the sanctuary.

"The sacrifices have begun," Aulus observed. "Curfew does not apply to the Temple. The priests carry on no matter what happens."

"Priests!" exclaimed Mel. "We're not wearing the priests' robes this time. Except Baldy."

"That could be a problem," Aulus admitted. "Only the Levites are allowed in here."

Mel remembered the sign in Greek. He shuddered.

"For that matter, Baldy, where'd you get that robe?" asked Ruth. "And one that almost fits, too."

"There's a room full of them under the gallery," Baldy explained. "And another of musical instruments, with a passageway—"

Far back down Herod's secret tunnel, they heard a crash.

"They're coming!" cried Ruth. "Is there any other way out of here?"

"I was just coming to that. The passageway from the music room led to the sanctuary porch. Across the porch I saw a door. That's it right there." Baldy pointed to a door on their left.

Mel opened that door a crack. Sure enough, it gave onto the porch. But the porch was thronged with priests. He quickly closed it. Now they could hear shouts behind them, and booted feet pounding up the tunnel.

"They're almost here," Chazz warned.

"There must be some other exit, or somewhere to hide," said Ruth, swinging her penlight around. "Herod wouldn't—"

A third door glowed palely to the right.

"This has to be it," Aulus whispered. "Quickly."

They were through the door in seconds, closing it softly after them. Mel looked for some way to secure it. Nothing.

Too late anyway, he thought. Here they are. Lord, let them not see this door!

Feet and outcry rushed past outside the dark chamber where Mel and the others huddled. "What is the meaning of this?" they heard the priests shout as the soldiers emerged into the sanctuary.

"Stop them!" the soldiers answered. "They have murdered King Herod!"

"Ladders!" cried an authoritative voice. "Fetch the ladders and crowbars!"

"Ladders?" Ruth whispered.

They looked around. By the penlight they saw they were in a bare stone chamber inside the temple wall. Opposite the entry door, another door led to a short hallway and another chamber. Just at the limit of illumination Mel thought he saw yet another doorway. But next to the nearest door was a spiral staircase. They ran to it and shone the beam up and down, but saw only steps.

"Up's a dead end," said Aulus. "This sanctuary is an island."

From downstairs there came a faint breath of air, and a sound as of gurgling water.

"Down it is, then." Aulus led them down the twisting steps, Ruth close behind, shining her light at his feet. The others followed as well as they could. They came to a landing. A dark corridor led off to the right.

"Which way does that go?" Chazz asked. "I'm all turned around."

"Be nice if it took us under the porch, wouldn't it?" commented Mel. They moved down the corridor. Torchlight glimmered ahead. They emerged under a stairway.

"I know where we are," Baldy whispered. "These steps lead up to the porch. And across there: that's where I came from—the music room."

They raced down the passage to the music room. At its far side, past the racks of flutes and timbrels, was a door.

"That door comes out in the Court of the Women, beside the circular steps."

Baldy slowly eased it open a crack. He softly and silently closed it again, pressed his back against it, and took off his conical white silk hat. "It's full of soldiers out there." He wiped his glistening pate. "Not only the palace militia after us: Roman auxiliaries, too."

"Did they see you?" asked Aulus.

"I think not. It's dark out there. But they will soon find this door."

"What are Romans doing in here?" Ruth asked. "It's taboo."

"A mystery to me." They ran up the steps to the Chamber of Vestments.

"At last," breathed Mel. "Grab four of those, hats too. We'll put them on upstairs." The hue and cry of the mob was just outside their door. That's not all for us, is it? he wondered. Sounds like fighting.

The stairs continued up to the gallery above the Nicanor Gate. Torches in the priests' court below cast the shadow of the balustrade over the fugitives. They started to don the robes.

Ruth happened to glance across to the brightly illuminated facade of the temple as she tucked her long black hair up under the silk cap.

"So that's it," she whispered.

The others turned to look. Two young priests on ladders were prying and hammering at a great golden eagle mounted on the marble above the Temple gate. Roman and Idumaean soldiers were struggling with priests defending the ladders' feet. As Mel watched, the eagle came crashing down behind the altar, in a patter of marble chips. A great cheer rose from the throats of the onlooking priests and Levites.

"They're desecrating the Temple, and cheering?" Mel was incredulous.

"Herod's eagle was desecrating it," explained Aulus. "He couldn't resist putting it up there, to please the Romans: it's our standard. I advised against it, but he thought he could ride out the furor. And furor there was."

"Now it's down," Mel said. "Maybe that'll distract the troops long enough for us to get out of here. Everybody! Into a huddle!"

"Now or never, I guess," agreed Ruth. The five formed a circle, arms on shoulders. "Hug tight! The integral of

$$\int \frac{\sum_{j=m}^{n} (j+6)P'_{mn}(t-i-j)}{P_{mn}(t)} \, dt$$

along a path from here to the fixed point and lifted two thousand sheets of the manifold..."

"....is the sum of the residues inside the path in the time plane," Mel continued, "which form a finite arithmetic series..."

"...whose sum is 1,991,000..." added Ruth.

"...so the integral is that times two pi i, or 3,982,000 pi i!" Mel concluded, holding his breath and squeezing his eyes shut.

"Hey!" cried Chazz.

Mel opened his eyes. Nothing had changed.

The eagle was still down. The soldiers had toppled one of the ladders and were beating the young priest.

"It didn't work!" exclaimed Mel.

"We're stuck here after all!" Ruth wailed.

"Real time delay!" yelled Chazz. "Chaos crumpled your path! And a good thing too! You forgot the river!"

Mel and Ruth looked at each other in horror. "He's right!" Ruth cried. "Ground level! We've got to get downstairs!"

They looked over the balcony. It was a long way down.

"Come on!" yelled Mel, starting down the stairs. "We could go any minute! We'll be smashed on the Dome of the Rock!"

"Chazz, how do you know the difference?" Ruth panted. "How can we tell whether we're time jumping along the real line, or just living as usual?"

"Can't, unless there's a change of parametrization—"

"Oof!" Ruth, Chazz and Aulus piled up on the steps, colliding with Mel, who had skidded to a stop.

Roman auxiliaries were advancing up the stairway.

The five ran back up to the gallery.

"Where to?" Mel shouted.

"That way!" Ruth pointed north—

48
Chaos

—and stumbled into Mel. A flute played peaceful music. The sun shone brightly into the Temple. The two of them were alone on the gallery. Down in the Court of the Priests, a man in a blue surcoat with a fancy vest was singing, "O Lord, thou hast brought up my soul from the grave…" to an orderly congregation that included many not in priestly white. The people waved sheaves of barley before the altar. Through the open curtain of the sanctuary, Mel thought he could see a ragged edge of torn drapery within.

"Where are they?" asked Ruth, panic rising in her voice. "Where's Chazz?" Heads turned in the crowd below. A beadle started toward them.

"We left them behind!"

"We've got to go back!" she cried.

"Can't. We're not in—" The floor dropped out from under him.

"—control!" Everything turned black. But instead of smashing onto the Dome of the Rock, he fell to the gallery floor, clinging to Ruth while the earth rolled and buckled beneath them.

The earthquake subsided. He struggled to rise, and was helping Ruth to her feet when he heard a ripping sound, like adhesive tape being stripped from a giant wound. He turned. And stared.

"Why is it so dark?" asked Ruth. "Where are the torches? What's that?"

"Don't you recognize it?" Mel asked in reply. "From Nebuchadnezzar's attic museum?"

Across the Court of the Priests, through the open curtain of the sanctuary, the light from the Menorah showed the great curtain concealing the Holy of Holies—torn in two from top to bottom.

Inside, resting on the bare floor, was a curious object like a baby's bathtub, with two dragons mounted on its massive gold lid.

"The Ark of the Covenant," gasped Ruth. "Cyrus must have returned it."

"But what ripped the curtain?"

Light flooded the day as though the sun had been switched on. A bell struck nine.

"Oh, God, Mel! Jesus!"

"What is it?"

"Darkness at noon! They've just crucified Jesus!"

Mel's heart sank. He knew she was right. All that love—that helpless baby, that innocent Presence—slaughtered like a Passover lamb.

"Ruth, listen. 'It pleased the Lord to bruise him.' Remember that."

"If only we'd never sinned!" she sobbed. "Never incurred the death penalty!"

"Pull yourself together. We did, and he paid the price. Now let's get down to ground level, fast, or we'll die too. We've been lucky so far." He urged her northward along the gallery, in the direction they had started to take—thirty-three years ago. They reached the corner before the next jump.

The sunlight's angle changed suddenly and the noise level increased. The priest in the blue surcoat was shouting something from the top of the sanctuary steps. It barely carried over the babble of conversation in the Court of the Priests.

"What's he saying?"

"Shhh." Mel watched the high priest grasp his blue lapels firmly, one in each hand. As more of the crowd noticed what he was doing, quiet spread.

He repeated his announcement: "The sceptre has departed from Judah, but Shiloh is not come! *The Torah is wrong!*"

He ripped his robe apart from collar to fringe in one swift spasm. Anguished cries rose from some of the audience nearest him.

"Ruth, did you see what I just saw? The Bible is wrong? How can that be?"

"Easy, Mel. Calm down." She pointed down over the balcony. "There's the answer."

Almost directly beneath them, at the north end of the long narrow Court of the Israelites, an adolescent boy perched on one of the polished ashlars, surrounded by bearded men and by Levites sitting on the steps that led up to the priests' court. His clear voice drifted up to them: ". . .our Father in heaven only wishes his people to trust him. He loves us. He will never leave us or forsake us. Which one of you who is a father will not run after his small daughter as she runs along the beach, happy at her joy in freedom, yet ever ready to catch her should she stumble? Willing to die gladly, rather than have her come to any harm from the wild waves? So is our Father in heaven."

Foreshortened though they were by the angle, Mel could see that the elders were deeply moved. One or two wiped their eyes. Others murmured assent to each other. Some of the men lifted their hands toward the sanctuary and praised the Lord.

"The Torah is right. There's no mistaking that Presence." Mel's panic was gone. "Ruth, let's go down to him."

"If we can."

They made their way along the north gallery to a structure like a small marble house of four rooms, built above a gate in the north wall. They entered, seeking an unguarded stairway. Seeing one by a window, they hurried toward it and again Mel felt that disorientation, that discontinuity in his surroundings that signaled a time jump.

Loud voices raised in dispute caught their attention outside the window. Down in the crowded Court of the Gentiles, a man was overturning tables, opening cages of doves, untying tethered lambs. The merchants and money changers shouted at him and called for the Temple guards. Ignoring them, he resolutely went about his work until he had gathered several of the tethers in his hand.

Mel and Ruth watched, fascinated, as he tied the cords into a knot at one end.

Gripping this knot, he whipped the scourge—crack!—down onto one of the tables.

"Take these things away," he commanded. "It is written: 'My house shall be called by all nations the house of prayer;' but you have made it a den of thieves."

They scattered. The whole court was clearing out. Just one man!—but what authority! The blind and the lame came to him in the temple; and he healed them.

"Look." Ruth pointed. "Some of them are still carrying their palm branches."

"And here come the priests. They're carrying chips on their shoulders. They don't like this one bit."

"What can they do? Look at the size of that crowd, shouting hosanna."

"Messiah the Prince has come."

"'He came unto his own, and his own received him not.' I was wondering if you realized who that was."

"I know him now, Ruth. I'll never lose him. Or vice-versa."

"Look! The high priest is heading out there. What's he going to do?"

Mel leaned his head out the window—

—and suddenly yanked it back as a flaming torch flew in, missing him by inches. He coughed: the air was thick with smoke. The court was full of armored soldiers, milling horses, screaming zealots.

The torch sailed over the parapet and landed, scattering sparks among closely-packed defenders in the priests' court below. A bowl of anointing oil went up with a whumpf! Mel saw another firebrand ignite the Temple curtain. The heavy silk blossomed into flame. The entire Temple was an inferno.

"Mel!"

Mel turned back to the window just in time to see a helmeted Roman face pop up, then an arm holding a sword.

He ducked the legionary's swing and slammed his booted foot against the arm, trapping it against the window frame. Hopping closer on his other foot, he reached out, grabbed the top of the ladder, and shoved. He fell backward into the room as the Roman's sword arm disappeared out the window and the man toppled to the courtyard with a yell.

"Mel! Are you hurt?"

"Downstairs, quick!" he managed to choke out. "There's not going to be a Temple here much longer!"

But the stairs were a chimney of flame. Singed and choking, they ran out of the small compartment, west along the gallery. In the next chamber was a large central basin of water.

"Get wet!" cried Ruth. They plunged into the basin and out again, soaked robes dripping on the hot tiles.

"Look," Mel shouted over the screams and fire's roar. A spiral staircase descended into dark depths.

Ruth led the way down, stepping warily as they left the light above for cooler air.

"Turn on your light," said Mel. "I'll hang on to you."

"Sorry, I already did. It finally went. Do you think we're at ground lev—"

Ruth's hand snatched out of his. He heard a splash. "Ruth!"

"Ulg. Watch out for that last step. I'm treading water."

Mel felt his way down. His foot sank into cool depths. "Grab my leg. I'll help you out. This cistern must be below aqueduct level. Good enough: they follow contour lines."

Ruth clambered up, to stand close to Mel on the dark stair. She was shaking.

"Cold?"

"Mostly scared. Again. So we can just wait here, can we? Until the next jump?"

"I think so."

"Mel, we've been looping through manifestations of the fixed point. It must be a strong attractor."

"You mean strange attractor."

"Whatever. You're the chaos expert. But now where are we? Where's Jesus?"

He's here. "He's never left us."

"You're right."

"But we seem to have left the fixed point. Good; maybe the next jump will be the big one."

"I hope so. Mel, that means we just made it! To ground level."

"Some coincidence."

"So he is still in control. Of course."

They shivered in silence.

"Mel."

"What?"

"How do we know we're still traveling? How do we know that our synergy hasn't just run out of steam?"

"We can wait a while, and if nothing happens, try again."

"No way to tell the difference."

"Chazz said not."

"Poor Chazz! Will we ever see him again?" moaned Ruth.

"You know we will. All of them."

"I mean in this life."

"I hope so. Ruth, I just thought of something."

"What?"

"After we get home," if we do, "we can learn more about this stuff and exactly how it's chaotic, and practice with short jumps—"

"— and come back and rescue Chazz! Great! Wait a minute."

"Something wrong with my idea?"

"No, no. That's not what he said."

Mel was puzzled. "That's not what who said?"

"Chazz. He said there was no way to tell the difference, unless—"

"That's right, unless there was a change of parametrization."

"What does that mean?"

"Don't you remember reading—"

A threshold was passed.

He could see!

The dim red light came from above. He glanced up.

Two yards overhead, a huge, flaming timber plunged down the stairwell.

He recoiled in horror.

The burning beam hung there. Its heat blistered his face. It was falling, but so slowly!

The bulge of flame enveloping it was not the normal color. It was a little too red.

"Dive!" shouted Mel. He and Ruth launched themselves off the steps into the cool water of the stone cistern. Surfacing ten feet away, they stroked toward a wall where waves lapped against the vaulted ceiling of a low opening running under the Court of the Priests.

"In there!"

"Can we breathe?" asked Ruth.

"Swim on your back—"

The light brightened, blued. With a roar and a hiss, the huge beam plunged into the water where they had been standing. As it surged back up, extinguished, a wave flooded over them and flung them into the pitch-black tunnel.

Mel swallowed water, held his breath, and pumped with desperate strokes of his limbs. Where was Ruth? Which way was the air?

He rolled onto his back, reached. Touching the stone ceiling, he risked a breath. Air!

"Rooglph!" A wave caught his cry. Was this ceiling level? Or was she trapped, drowning again?

"Mel!"

A surge of joy sent him lunging toward Ruth's voice. "Thank God!" The waves subsided. He caught her hand. They floated on their backs, paddling down the tunnel, barely able to breathe. But they were together!

"Where do you suppose this comes out?" asked Ruth.

"It can't go on forever like this; we'll be off the Temple Mount."

They paddled on, using their unlinked hands.

"Mel, what saved us? What kept that beam from crushing us? It was just hanging there, in midair."

"That must be what Chazz meant. Our time path got a change of parametrization. Two or three of our minutes coincided with just a second of the real line."

"Then it changed back," she guessed.

"Yes. Either that, or we're not 'traveling' anymore. Our synergy ran out of psychomanipulative oomph."

"That's more likely, isn't it? Rather than postulating two changes of parametrization so close together, just by chaos."

Chaos isn't in charge, he thought. "Nothing happens by chance."

"I can't believe you said that! Right, the change came just in time to save us. Well, we'll have to try again."

"Ruth! I never thought I'd hear you say *that*."

"This time we'll take our time, be more careful, get to a stable ground level."

"The Temple Mount level stayed the same for centuries after Herod planed it off," said Mel. "Ouch!"

"What happened?"

"I think the ceiling's coming lower. My nose scraped against it." He reached up to feel it. "Ow! It's hot!"

Ruddy light and a loud clamor came from down the tunnel. Wisps of smoke floated along the low ceiling. Steam rose from the water. They paddled faster toward the light.

"Let's get out of here."

"Whoa," Mel whispered. "Slow down. Let's see what's out there first."

As the ceiling began to curve upward, they silently rolled over and, treading water gently, looked out just above water level.

Mel saw a small chamber hewn out of the rock, filled with water up to a ledge that ran along the far wall. A ladder rose from the ledge to an open trap door. The noise and flickering light came through that opening.

"A way out, at last," whispered Ruth.

"I'd feel better if we could get up there. Closer to ground level. Wonder where we are?"

"Still in the thick of it. Mel, what happened to Herod's temple?"

"Titus burned it to the ground in A.D. 70."

"Did anyone get out alive?"

"Not after the fire started. Some of the Zealots hid for a while in tunnels under—"

"They'll be coming down here!"

"Swim!"

They swam across the chamber and dragged themselves up onto the ledge. Through the open trapdoor Mel saw men fighting amid flames. The flickering light glinted off a segment of curved surface, like the underside of an enormous polished bowl.

"We're under the laver," he said. "This must be where they draw the water."

"Can we begin integrating down here, climb the ladder, and finish up there?"

"Sounds like a plan. You start."

"This time," Ruth began, grasping the ladder and placing her foot on the bottom rung, "we want the path to span 1925 sheets of the Riemann—"

A rock fell from the opening onto her head. She dropped senseless to the ledge at the foot of the ladder.

"Ruth!" Mel sank to her side. "Oh, God! Ruth!" He scooped her limp form up in his arms. Realizing he couldn't climb the ladder that way, he shifted to a fireman's carry. The rough iron rungs were already warm under his hand.

"Lift the path 1925 sheets, the residues add up to 1988525, so the integral is—" He reached the top. "3,977,050 pi i!"

Nothing happened.

"I can't do it alone!"

He lay Ruth down on the hot marble floor, kneeling by her side to avoid the smoke. The air seared his lungs. He could hear water boiling in the laver above him. The altar to his right was a wall of flame. The fighting had moved away toward the blazing stockyard area.

Suddenly two figures stumbled out of the smoke, trading sword blows: a Roman and a Zealot priest. As Mel watched in horror, the priest, leaping aside to avoid a thrust, stumbled against the altar. His linen robe burst into flames. He screamed and fell in a burning heap.

The Roman noticed Mel, still wearing his priestly vestments. With a yell, the Roman raised his gladius and advanced on him.

"Jesus, save us!" Mel cried. "Save us!"

49
Back to the Future

Chazz stumbled to a stop.

Ruth had pointed north and had disappeared, along with Mel.

"Wait!" he shouted. "Wait for me! Come back!" What now? He looked wildly around the gallery. Aulus and Baldy had also paused in flight, looking for their vanished friends.

A Roman helmet appeared in the stairwell. In seconds the auxiliary would reach the top, turn, and see them. Quick as thought, Aulus tore off his priestly robe and flung it into the shadows. It seemed to hang up on something, a lumpy obstacle that crumpled to the floor under it. There was a clink, and a bright object danced out from under the folds, spinning like a top. Colliding with the wall, it skittered off and spun like a brass ballerina toward the railing of the stairwell.

Chazz saw it poise between the railing supports; then its whirling, shrouded toe stepped into the void, its wheel-guard glanced off the stone edge, and it was gone. He heard a *tonk!* from below, followed by a surprised "Quid?" from an ascending guard; then Aulus, now clad in the toga, seized his arm and hissed, "You're my captives!" in his ear, simultaneously gesturing to Balthasar with his poniard.

Chazz assumed the meek, stooped stance of a prisoner. Even Baldy managed to look innocuous. It had worked before. Could they be so lucky twice?

As the auxiliary sergeant approached from the stairwell, the robe Aulus had discarded moved in the shadows. What was under there?

To Faufi's left was a waterfall of fire, a flaming body at its base. Ahead, two damned souls crouched under a steaming cauldron. One looked female. She was unconscious.

"Look out!" cried the other…in English!

Faufi spun around and saw, through the smoke, a demon in armor advancing on her with a sword dripping blood. Panicked, she turned back to the couple on the floor.

"Get us out of here, for Christ's sake!" the man implored.

She must have time-jumped; there was no other explanation. But it had been involuntary; she had no idea when she was. What could she do?

The man was looking at her in desperate hope.

An angel? No. With those clothes she had to be another time-traveler. Sophia! Mel spoke quickly. "Nineteen-twenty-five sheets, sum of the residues 1,988,525, the integral is—"

"Wait!" The blonde pressed a button on a funny-looking brass gadget she held. Mel gripped Ruth's limp arm tightly as the young woman stepped close and finished, "3,977,050 pi i!"

The fires went out. The noise ceased. Bright dusty daylight surrounded them.

Mel knelt in the middle of the Temple Mount. Ruth, lying beside him, was beginning to stir. The only sound was the diminishing whir of the gadget spinning in the girl's hand. To the east, high on the Mount of Olives, sun glinted off the huge windows of the restaurant in the Intercontinental Hotel overlooking the amphitheater. The Dome of the Rock rose in the middle distance, fifty yards to the south.

"Thank you," breathed Mel fervently. "Madame Kovalevskaya, I presume?"

"Thank the Lord, rather. How did you know my name? But it's Miss."

"It's a long story, but I'll be delighted to tell you."

"Owww," Ruth groaned, tenderly feeling her head.

"Ruth!" Mel hugged her.

"Careful," she said. "Pain hurts." She pulled the tall conical priest's cap off her head, releasing her mass of dark hair, and wrung it out. "What's that smell?"

"Smog," replied Mel. "You get used to it after a while."

"So…we're back, then? We're finally, finally safe?" Ruth looked around the quiet mount. "Where's Chazz?"

"He didn't make it." Mel was unconcerned. "Don't you remember? We tried to bring them all, but they got left behind—"

"Chazz!" Ruth cried. "That's right, he's still there! We have to get him! Now!"

"Quiet!" hissed Faufi. "The Waqf guards—"

"Ruth," Mel whispered urgently, "calm down! We have time, remember? In the palm of our hand. This is the gal who wrote the book on it."

"Oh. But will she—"

"You're both soaking wet," the girl observed. "Let me invite you to my hotel."

"First, will you please help us rescue a friend?" begged Ruth. "And may we call you Sophia?"

"If you wish, but I usually go by 'Faufi' because Sophia was my mother's name too. Who is this friend?"

"Chazz, we call him, but his name is really Caspar Lundquist," Mel replied.

"Praise the Lord!" exulted Faufi. "God, you were in control all along! King of all the ages!"

Mel and Ruth looked at each other. Ruth smiled, still a little anxiously. "A sister," she said.

"Let's go get dried off," Mel suggested.

"A moment, please." Faufi...*blinked.* Not her eyes. For just one instant Mel saw *through* her, saw the Dome of the Rock where Faufi's head and shoulders had been. Then, before his eyes could change focus, she was back. "Come on," she said, reaching to join hands with them.

Suddenly Mel's surroundings altered in a way that had become familiar. The Dome was still there behind Faufi, but there was a different taste to the air and the light.

"How can we remember this spot again?" mused Faufi. "Help me out. Let's see, each of you choose two lined-up pairs of features in the distance, at right angles."

"Where are we?" asked Ruth. "I mean, when?"

"In 1926, same fibre, same time of year. A fairly quiet modern period. Let's go. Can you walk...Ruth?"

"Sure, thanks." They started walking toward the street leading up the Mount of Olives.

As they trudged across the Kidron Valley, Faufi explained her momentary absence. "The guards were starting to get suspicious. I went to find a time when we'd have free access to that spot, since we know where it connects to in the past."

"What do you have in mind?" asked Mel, carrying their priestly robes over one arm. The twenties, he thought. Flappers. Our Parthian riding outfits, tunic and leggings, aren't too far out of place here. Tourists can wear anything. At least nobody's run away screaming yet. He nevertheless unlaced the front of his tunic so it more nearly resembled a sport jacket.

"Training first," Faufi answered, "then rescue."

They walked up the hill to a nondescript thorn bush just off the road, and behind it joined hands again. Night fell, instantly. Mel found himself standing on the asphalt of a dark parking lot behind an enormous modern hotel.

"Wait here, in this corner," Faufi said. She pushed through the revolving glass door into the lobby and was gone.

The dripping couple wordlessly embraced.

"Home at last, 1995," Mel said. "Oh, Ruth." He kissed her tenderly. "Feeling better?"

"A lot." She explored her scalp. "But I'll have a lump; that rock hit hard. Or whatever it was. Thank God for those priest hats."

"And that they stayed on through it all."

"Amen." Ruth leaned her head against Mel's chest. Then she looked up. "'Faufi'?"

"I think it's Sophia's daughter. Here she comes now."

Faufi emerged from the lobby. "I've taken another suite. Come, I'll bring you in through the side entrance, by the pool. No one will mind if you drip there."

As they climbed the steps of the pool terrace Ruth stumbled. Mel, holding her arm, caught her. "All right?"

"Just exhausted. That last mile, up the hill, did it."

"You poor dear." Faufi held the door for her. "The elevator is right here."

"Air conditioning!" Ruth sighed as she entered the hall.

"I remember that," said Mel.

Faufi stepped to the elevator and touched the up arrow. The car was waiting; with a ding! the door slid open. Inside, Faufi pressed twenty. As the car rose, she handed Mel a key tagged "2011."

At the twentieth floor she led them in tired silence to Room 2011, then said, "Here's your room, Mel. We're right next door, 2013, if you want anything."

"I want thirty hours' sleep and a bath. In either order."

"Second that," said Ruth. "'Night, Mel."

He hugged her. "Good night. You, too, Faufi. We can never thank you enough."

"It's not me you have to thank, I told you." She smiled. "Good night." Mel turned and went into 2011. The door clicked behind him. The women walked to the next suite.

"Where do you know Chazz from?" asked Ruth as Faufi inserted the key in her door.

"From watching him steal my mother's paper." She let Ruth in, then followed and closed the door. "The shower's right through there."

"Thanks," Ruth said with feeling. "And do you have some aspirin?"

"Look in the medicine cabinet."

Removing her jacket, Ruth ducked under the strap of her red patent-leather handbag and hung it on the doorknob, then exited into the bathroom. Faufi heard the medicine cabinet door open, then water running, as she lay down on the bed to rest and think.

I need a bath too, she thought. I can still smell smoke on my clothes. Clothes! Ruth can borrow mine. Perhaps the hotel shop will have some that fit Mel.

Her eyes drifted shut, then flew open. She rolled to a sitting position on the bed. Mustn't sleep yet, not 'til I decide. Rising, she walked slowly to the desk and pulled out the chair.

The secret was out. She sat, picked up a pencil, and began doodling on the notepad. Maybe not. Maybe she'd have help. It had been tiring, going on alone. She must enlist them.

What if she couldn't? What then? She'd burn that bridge when she came to it, she decided. Either way, this phase was ended.

The bathroom door opened. Ruth appeared, swathed in a huge white towel, turbanned in a smaller one. Her skin glowed.

"So, how's your week been going?" asked Faufi.

Ruth laughed without restraint. "It's good to laugh again," she said when she could talk. She sank on the bed.

"How did you ever get into that mess? What were you doing?"

"Oh, Faufi! Jesus!"

"That's my Lord you're taking—"

"It's not in vain!" Ruth sat up. "We met him…in his home. I…I held him in my arms!"

"Jesus Christ?—as a babe?"

"Yesterday. The love, the peace…oh, God, was it only yesterday? And yet—" she faltered.

"Ruth!" *Is she ill?* "What's the matter?" Faufi moved quickly to Ruth's side.

"I killed a man." Ruth broke into racking sobs.

What do I say to that? Faufi cradled Ruth's damp, towel-wrapped head wordlessly against her ruffled bosom. A terrorist, and now a murderess? What pit was she falling into? Beginning with a forged passport….She lifted her head to the pale ceiling and squeezed her eyes shut. Mama! Your task is hard!

"You think I'm awful," said Ruth.

"Well…"

"It was self-defense."

"That's different. And Mel? is he a m—Did he also—"

"Yes. Chazz too." Ruth's clouded blue eyes sought her own. "We had to, to get away from the death squads."

"I…see." *No I don't! Not quite yet. But I trust this sister. Somehow.*

"They were slaughtering all the children," Ruth whispered, "to get the Christ."

"Oh!" Faufi's hand flew to her mouth. "You were caught up in *that?*"

"We barely made it out alive."

"Let's talk of something else."

"Gladly," said Ruth. "You're really Sophia Kovalevskaya's daughter? But of course, you must be."

"Yes."

"I'm an avid fan of hers. Do...did you ever see your father?"

"Papa Vlad? Not often, and never for long." But how joyous the occasions! How happy he could make Mama and me! Faufi paused, fighting tears. "He had to stay in Russia. But there were no chances there for a woman who loved mathematics as my mother did."

"I could see that love. We read her paper. None too soon."

"And that copy? What became of it? It's very secret, you know—or was."

"There were two, I'm afraid. One was on Chazz's hard disk." She smiled. "That crashed. The other was a hard copy; I last saw it—Wait!" Ruth reached to the doorknob. "It's right here, in my purse!" She ripped open the velcro seal and, withdrawing the folded sheets, handed them to Faufi. "It's pretty dry now, considering."

"Thank you. Then I won't have to retrieve the original. We can use this."

"What for?"

"Your training. I must enlist you as allies if I can, in keeping the secret of time travel. As persons of good will, which I believe you are, you must surely see the importance of this."

"Certainly. Gladly. I know I can speak for Mel, and I think even Chazz. We kept the secret from Herod, at great cost."

"Herod!" Faufi shuddered. "*Good.* So, then. You must be trained. Not only for the rescue."

"What are your plans for that?" asked Ruth.

"Let's sleep first, then plan when Mel can join us," Faufi replied. If I'm exhausted, how must she feel?

"Fine...I have to tell you, though, we left Chazz sixty feet in the air."

"No more than he deserves." Faufi smiled to show she was teasing. "Actually he's rather cute."

"He's lost some of his raw edges," Ruth said, "in the two months since you saw him."

"Yesterday."

"He's matured, mellowed." Ruth took a breath. The bedspring creaked as she twisted around to sit facing Faufi directly. Her look was serious, almost pleading. "I find I like him a lot. Does that shock you?"

She wants to protect him from the police. Well, we'll see. "Not...exactly."

Mel was ravenous when he joined the women the next morning dressed in a shirt and jeans delivered to his room by room service. Over breakfast at a window table, they discussed theory. Eastern sunlight blazed off the golden dome on the Temple Mount.

"Like the risers of a spiral staircase—the fibre is actually a plane, not a line, of course. The wrapping mapping sends $t+i\tau$ to the circle of radius $e^{-\tau}$, so as you go farther up the plane the image point gets closer to the sun! There's no danger, though, as long as your path doesn't terminate there."

"But earth's orbit is an ellipse," Mel objected, "not a circle."

"More's the pity," said Faufi, "otherwise we wouldn't have to use elliptic integrals."

"What exactly caused this 'Transgression'?" asked Ruth. "Men from Mars?"

"Either a close approach, a flyby, or a severe resonance effect, involving some large body. Mars? I don't think so, but..."

But it was red, thought Mel; at least in my dream.

In Faufi's absence Mel discussed his understanding of the theory with Ruth, very carefully. "What's required," he said, "seems to be a certain amount of mathematical maturity. It's a talent that can be developed, like playing the flute—there's nothing mystical or 'psychic' involved. How can a psychological theory be involved when no two psychologists agree?"

"Like economics," Ruth agreed. "As my sister Helen says, any two economists have at least three theories."

"You have a sister?" he asked.

"A twin, but—"

Ruth was interrupted by the sudden appearance of Faufi, pop!, who offered a small brown paper bag. Mel took it. It was heavy, and something clinked inside.

"Those are for you," Faufi said. "I also got a few more, as spares." Mel scooped out the contents.

Two Kovalevskian Gyroscopes gleamed on the tablecloth, rotors turning idly.

"They're dual powered, spring and battery; they can spin for an hour," said Faufi. "I had to go to Tel Aviv to find a machine shop that could make them."

"Yeah," said Mel, "sometimes I think the only industry in Jerusalem is tourism." He reached to pick up one of the devices and hefted it speculatively.

"It turns out that if you stay in real time, you don't need the gyroscope," Faufi explained. "Stability is inherent, from rational closure of the reals."

"What about reparametrization?" asked Mel.

"Mel, how long since your prelims?" teased Ruth. "Contour integration is independent of the parameter, remember?"

"Yes," said Faufi, "so the final path-lifting in 5-space isn't subject to parametric influence. Chaos can still arise, but it's unrelated."

"I knew that," Mel muttered.

Their training began with simple, controlled single-fibre time jumps from one year to the next or the previous, always in the same season. Control was provided by Delone's gyroscope. Just as important—"More so!" commented Ruth—was avoidance of time jumping when not desired. The involuntary kind, though rare, was disconcerting and dangerous. If the talent for wandering in the imaginary dimension of the time plane was like a gift for music, "time-stumbling," as Faufi called it, was whistling at a funeral. With ordinary care and attention, it could be avoided. Ignorance was the main contributing factor.

"But that's how my mother discovered it," said Faufi. "She time-stumbled. As luck, or Providence, would have it, she ended up in the time of the Transgression, and saw the possibilities. We'll save that aspect for later."

The next lesson, reparametrization, was more fun, as well as safer. One stuck to real time, so there was no chaos to worry about. Of course, it was not possible to avoid a speeding bullet; even Faufi wasn't that fast at stretching her curve. And to take on an imaginary component, to time jump, required all the objects transported to be parametrized identically. The problem of transportage—of what one could bring along when one jumped—was still on the fringes of research; this necessary condition was one of the few results known.

But reparametrization was what made scouting feasible, and that was their final lesson, for now. To scout a time period, one stretched one's curve by a large factor, usually thirty-six hundred for convenience, before jumping into the target interval.

"You can look around for half a minute," Faufi pointed out, "and that's still less than a hundredth of a second for the locals. There's no way they can see you."

Mel set his cup on the coffee table, in the space he had cleared for it among their scattered notes. They met in Faufi's spacious, luxurious living room. He'd had a lot of fun with mathematics, he thought, but never this much. And it was *applied* mathematics, at that! "A lot can happen in a hundredth of a second."

"Of course, it's not perfectly safe," Faufi admitted. "Don't jump into a nuclear explosion. Or even a very hot fire. But it's safer than crossing the street, and a lot better than jumping blind."

"You know, it's a pity," remarked Ruth.

"What is?" they asked.

"That this has to be a secret, particularly from my freshmen. What a motivation for learning mathematics!"

50
Contact With the Enemy

As ready as ever, Mel thought. He and the girls had gone over the plan until they couldn't find any more bugs in it. Now, as they walked down from the thorn bush in the dawn silence of a 1926 spring morning, he couldn't help reviewing it once again in his mind.

It seemed simple enough. Simple and direct as a kiss. They would go to the Temple Mount in 1926, jump into the Temple itself in A.D. 67, when it was quiet; walk upstairs to the balcony; Faufi would find the right spot by scouting, then take them to that fibre.

Mel and Ruth knew about CDF, controlled differential fibrillation, from reading Sophia's paper, as well as from Chazz, but neither of them had ever actually tried it. It involved looping around the essential singularity where the fibres intersected, in a small five-dimensional neighborhood of 701 B.C. where that intersection had torn away from the sun's world-line. In this neighborhood, called the Transgression, any fibre was accessible from any other; it was merely a matter of adding a fractional year to the integral, possible only when the lifting path looped through the Transgression. Faufi had omitted it from their training as an unnecessary complication. After the rescue, she had said. First things first.

They would rescue the guys, and go home. Cut and dried. He stumbled in a dark-concealed pothole, caught himself, and wondered where Aulus and Balthasar would want to be dropped off. Or rather, when. The past week's training made him feel supremely confident, so he had no fear of what could happen in the next hour; his main concern was for the two first-century rescuees. He stepped up onto the first of the stone steps of the footbridge over the Kidron Brook, gurgling below. They were almost to Solomon's Stables, ready to follow the trail that wound around and up to the Temple Mount—no Temple on it now, of course, only the Dome, and a few bored British tommies keeping things quiet. Which they usually were nowadays, and would be for years; that was the point of choosing this period as a staging area.

Ruth said something he didn't catch. "Hmm?"

"I said it's strange, but I feel more conspicuous in this twenties getup than I did in the Parthian tunic."

"You look great!" he said as they reached the level of the Mount plateau.

"Not so loud, please," warned Faufi. "It's all right to talk, but we don't want to call undue attention to ourselves."

"At least they're not as trigger happy as the Waqf."

"No, but they have to be alert for over-eager Zionists. Ever since the Balfour declaration, some Jews have been impatient to rebuild the Temple." Faufi had learned a lot about the local politics in the past few days.

"Well, we know the Dome isn't in its way," said Mel.

"But they don't, so the guards—"

"Halt!"

"Oh-oh," Faufi muttered. "You're about to learn another side of time travel." She smiled innocently at the advancing corporal. "Is something wrong, sir?"

The soldier, who wore the name "SMITHERS" on a patch sewn over his breast, ignored her. "State your name and your business here," he ordered Mel.

"I live here," said Mel. "These are friends of mine, they're tourists. My name's Mel; this is Ruth and this is Faufi."

"Tourists, ey?" Now Smithers could turn his attention on the girls, with a megawatt smile. "Where from? Where you from, Foffy?"

"Sweden." She dimpled. "You may call me Fufu, if you like."

"Foofoo! Cute, I like that. You look like a Foofoo."

"I hope that's complimentary," Faufi said.

"'Course it is, 'course it is." Smithers shifted his rifle to the other shoulder. "Sweden, ay? Staying 'ere long?"

"Not nearly long enough, Smithers." She took his hand. "In fact, I have to go now. 'Bye."

"'Bye." He looked at Mel. "All right, what are you hangin' 'round 'ere for? Be off about your business." To Ruth he said, "'Have a nice day, Miss."

"You too, sergeant," said Ruth. Smithers straightened visibly. "Bye-bye."

"At last," Mel said as they drew out of earshot.

"He was nice," said Ruth. "For a minute I thought we were in trouble."

"Lonely, boring duty up here," Mel said. "I can hardly blame him."

"Harmless flirting," said Faufi, looking around for their landmarks, "but a delay. Now about our business."

"We were facing away from the rest of them—" Ruth pointed north.

"Running away, actually," said Mel. He stood with the women atop the gallery over the Nicanor Gate in Herod's Temple early on a quiet spring morning of A.D. 67. A few minutes before, they had jumped from 1926 to the court below by the laver, and walked unmolested upstairs. The Temple seemed deserted.

"— but my impression was," Ruth continued, "Chazz was right behind us, about here, then Aulus slightly behind Baldy and to his right, just past the stairwell."

"I'll go for Aulus," proposed Faufi. "Mel, you grab Baldy, and Ruth Chazz. Okay?"

"Okay," Mel said. Ruth nodded.

Faufi stooped and printed an "F" on the floor by the balcony wall with a rod of soft luminous chalk. "Here, mark your positions." She snapped the rod in two and handed half to each of her companions. As they moved to initial the places they would occupy, she said, "Be ready. I'll scout now; when I find the right fibre I'll take us there, then we each jump to 6 B.C., grab our man, and return."

"Got it," said Ruth.

"As planned," Mel said impatiently. The sooner Chazz was rescued, the sooner Mel could clear his name—time travel would make that a piece of cake—marry Ruth, and resume his career. "Just rescue the ones in the white robes," he said unnecessarily again. "Roman soldiers were coming up the stairs."

"Yes, we know," said Faufi, and disappeared. They waited for her, motionless.

A few seconds later she was back. "Found it. Huddle." They joined arms. The morning daylight disappeared. "Stand on those chalk marks and go. The clock is running."

Faufi glanced down at her "F" and launched herself into the past.

The balcony felt nearly the same underfoot, the clagor of battle rose from below, but she was snowblind! What—

An enveloping white cloth struck her in the face, draping its voluminous folds over her like a furniture dust cover. Off balance, she stumbled and fell, her head striking the balcony wall a glancing blow. The gyroscope dropped from her hand and bounced on the floor.

"The screw!"

Mel, about to jump, looked in surprise through the gloom at Ruth, standing on her "R". "What's the matter?"

"My gyroscope—" There was a soft *tick.* "Phooey!"

Mel was at her side. In her cupped hands was a jumble of machined parts.

"It just fell apart in my hands, there was a screw loose." She sighed. "Then I had to go and drop that."

"We'll find it. Don't blame yourself. They don't make Kovalevskian Gyroscopes like they used to." He grinned into the dark. "It's still under warranty."

"It's down there somewhere," she said. "You go ahead without me."

"Not a chance. I'm not leaving you alone in a place like this."

As they stooped to grope, Mel asked, "I don't suppose you replaced the batteries in your penlight?"

"I will tomorrow, I promise," said Ruth.

Mel slid his hand cautiously along the floor. Time, surprisingly, was running out.

The auxiliary approached. "*Ave Caesar*," he saluted Aulus.

"Hail Caesar."

"Do you wish assist—What is here?" The soldier bent and whipped the white robe off the body huddled in the corner. He gasped.

Chazz stared at the girl from Uppsala slumped against the wall, looking dazed in her short blue dress, white cloche hat askew with its blue ribbon dangling, bare arms relaxed at her sides, loose-fitting pleated skirt showing a white-stockinged knee. Sophia! he thought. She…she's beautiful! Is she OK? A sudden realization struck him. She was here for him! She'd followed him here. How…She was *hurt* because of him! *No!*

With great presence of mind the garrison sergeant grasped the golden-haired girl's arm. "A…priestess?" he said. "The Jews do not—"

One of the guards made a sign to ward off evil. "Begging your reverence, sir! This may be the Goddess—"

"Nonsense!" Not relaxing his grip for an instant, the sergeant drew the girl to her feet. "Chain her up with the rest of them."

The other guard produced a length of stout chain, and manacles. Aulus looked an unspoken but obvious question at Chazz, glancing at the girl—Someone you know?—as the guards bade Balthasar stoop and submit to the hinged manacle's being placed around his neck.

It would not close. They settled for attaching it to his arm, where it latched with a solid clunk, fitting tightly.

The guard gingerly closed the next manacle about the girl's graceful neck. With Chazz he was not so solicitous. "Ow!" Chazz yelped as the guard snapped his collar smartly shut, catching a tiny fold of skin. The chain was passed through thick rings on all three manacles, then attached at each end to a guard's iron girdle, with more solid clicks.

"*Ite*," said Aulus, making his meaning clear with a wave of his dagger.

"You look familiar," whispered the girl chained to him, in Swedish. "Are you Caspar Lundquist?"

"Call me Chazz," he replied. "Are you Sophia Kovalevskaya?"

"Probably not the one you think." She staggered as Baldy reached for the banister with the arm connected to her neck. The chain rattled through the rings.

"*Lypemenos*," Baldy apologized.

They stumbled down the stairs to the Nicanor Gate. "You're the girl I saw with the paper!" said Chazz quietly. "You must know how to—"

"Yes," Faufi said. "And you're the boy who stole it....not such a boy anymore: I didn't recognize you at first. You can call me Faufi; I'm Sophia's daughter."

"Is that a relief," whispered Chazz. "I hate being chained by the neck to someone I've not properly met." He ducked a metal bar that flew spinning past his head to clang against the door of the music room, gouging marble chips. "How did you find me? And, by the way, am I ever sorry I got you into this. But say! Get us out of here! You can avoid chaos."

"Not without my gyroscope."

"I shall escort you to headquarters," the sergeant volunteered to Aulus. "These Jews have gotten out of hand."

Indeed, the Court of the Israelites was a battlefield, priests versus Romans. The original squad of palace guards was nowhere to be seen. Good thing, Chazz thought. They know we're wanted for murder. Including Aulus.

"Can you understand what they're saying?" whispered Faufi.

"A little," Chazz whispered back. "College Latin."

"Me too."

The noise ebbed slightly as Aulus pulled them through the Nicanor Gate and down the semicircular steps into the women's court. The fighting was just beginning to spread out here, but all the women had already fled, replaced by a maniple of Romans and auxiliaries.

Aulus spoke to the sergeant. "*Bonum nunc. Vale.*"

He's trying to split, thought Chazz. Will it work? Aulus veered off to the right, but the sergeant was persistent. "Please, sir," he urged. "My orders are to allow no one to leave before my commander has interrogated him."

"What is his name? And rank?"

"Centurion Antagonus, sir."

"As you see, I outrank the centurion. Consider his orders countermanded." Was that a sheen of sweat on Aulus's brow, Chazz wondered. Aulus must know that guy Antagonus. Trouble. "I am the legate Maximius, acting on a special mission for Caesar Augustus."

"*Ave Caesar.*"

"*Ave Caesar*. He insists on the immediate transportation of these suspected spies to Rome, incommunicado lest they divulge Imperial secrets. I command your assistance and a fast chariot to the port of Ascalon."

"Sir!" The sergeant saluted. "With all due respect, sir, I lack the authority to requisition chariots, or indeed to disobey orders from my immediate superior officer, be he only —" the sergeant tried to conceal a smile, not too successfully— "a centurion. And his field office is just a few *passui* away, right over there." He gestured toward the Eastern Gate, across the growing melee in the Court of the Gentiles. Chazz saw a plain blue pavilion staked out in a cleared space fifty yards away, amid wreckage of broken birdcages, overturned tables, and the pathetic, crushed bodies of trampled lambs. Under the awning sat a dark, stringy soldier in a crested helmet, shouting something at an attentive lieutenant.

Aulus glanced around at the struggling figures of zealots, auxiliaries, and panicked merchants.

Near Chazz two fresh corpses bled on the stone flags, a soldier and a priest locked in their last combat. Screams, whack of a staff on armor, sparks struck by a gladius that missed its stroke and clanged off stone, shouted commands and imprecations threatened to overload his sensorium. Still he saw Aulus straighten decisively, heard him mutter, "All right, let's get it over with." He swung into line behind the sergeant and they headed across the court toward the pavilion.

It looked like the trick wouldn't work this time.

Mel and Ruth finally found the screw, almost knocking it over the edge in the process, but reassembling Ruth's gyroscope was not an easy task in the starlight.

Fumbling, they lost minutes—"It's this spring. You need five hands."—before Ruth said, "Mel! What dopes! Your gyroscope can take both of us!"

"Oh! What dopes is right!" Dropping the useless parts, he stepped into Ruth's embrace. "But we've never tried more than three on one gyroscope."

"We can bring them out one at a time," she said. "At least we'll see why Faufi isn't back yet with Aulus."

"Hope she's not in trouble."

"Hope not. Jesus, watch over her! Take care of us all! Go."

The balcony was deserted, but there was plenty of light and noise coming from downstairs. They peered over the balustrade, then the wall opposite.

"I don't see her anywhere," Ruth said.

"She'd be easy to spot, in that flapper dress."

"And she'd draw a crowd, even in this mob." Ruth leaned over the balustrade, trying to see into the Nicanor Gate itself.

"Watch out, someone may take a pot shot at you."

"Mel, what can we do?"

"It sure wasn't as easy as we thought, was it?" He looked around again, but still saw no one he recognized. "I should have known. No battle plan ever survives contact with the enemy."

"What a mess!" Ruth sighed and turned toward the stairwell. "What's this?" She bent and picked up a white cloth from the corner.

"Aulus's robe," said Mel. "It's too big to belong to Chazz, but it certainly isn't Baldy's."

"Mel! Maybe Aulus got them out with his toga! He'd outrank anybody likely to be here." She dropped the robe on the floor. "Faufi must just be waiting for a quiet spot to use her gyroscope."

Mel considered this, found it plausible. "There's hope, then."

"Yes, but you know what we need?"

"CDF," he said. "Then we could scout back twenty minutes, see where they went."

"It's just a matter of a little practice, back at the hotel where our notes are. Then we can redeem the time."

It was so much better when she smiled, Mel thought. "Let's go."

"Your name is not Maximius."

The centurion had brought the party into his field tent. Faufi had been attracting too much attention outside.

Tight-lipped, Aulus glowered at Antagonus and shook his head meaningfully. "Centurion, a word in private."

Antagonus rolled his eyes to the ridgepole overhead, then reluctantly stepped off to the far corner of the tent. Aulus followed.

Chazz couldn't hear what they were saying, but the centurion was shaking his head. Finally they returned to the front, Aulus protesting, the centurion adamant. They stopped by the front corner of the table. Aulus was closer to Chazz's guard, the religious one, but he watched Antagonus, to his left, intensely.

"*Interficite omnes*!" said the centurion.

"Does that mean what I think it does?" whispered Faufi.

"No!" cried Chazz's guard. "I mean, your pardon, sir. But this woman—it was bad enough chaining her." He reached into his pouch. "To kill her, or try to kill her, will unleash on us the wrath of the gods!"

Aulus had taken advantage of this outburst to draw his poniard stealthily from its scabbard, hanging on his belt on the side away from Antagonus.

"Superstitious foolishness!" said the centurion. "Sergeant, you heard—"

The sergeant, standing in front of Faufi and facing left, started to draw his short sword.

"Wait!" cried Chazz's guard. "Superstitious, am I? Then how explain *this*?" He pulled Faufi's gyroscope, still spinning, out of his pouch. "From heaven it fell, the same time the Goddess appeared. Look, sir! It still lives!" He extended his hand toward his commander, offering the gyroscope like the holiest of icons. Then everything happened at once.

"Baldy, break the chain!" Chazz shouted, snatching the gyroscope and passing it to Faufi.

Faufi lashed out with one slender leg and kicked the sergeant in his bare knee. As he crumpled in pain, she grabbed the gyroscope and switched it to "F."

Aulus stabbed the centurion to the heart, then spun to menace Chazz's guard with the dagger.

Baldy flexed his bicep. The manacle's hinge screamed and *spanged!* open. Baldy slid it down the chain to its junction with his guard's belt. As the guard looked down in surprise, he met Baldy's almost casual uppercut; his head snapped back. He hung from the chain as Baldy rolled the broken manacle over it twice to securely engage it in the ring, and began to twist. The links between manacle and belt reached their turning limit. Baldy twisted the manacle with both hands.

A link snapped open, flew up and struck the ridgepole. Baldy released the manacle, which slid off the chain. His guard slumped to the floor, joining the sergeant. Baldy silenced the latter's cries with a kick, but already Chazz saw motion at the tent flap.

He shoved the superstitious guard. The man fell, dragging the chain out clattering through the two remaining manacles. *Free!*

Faufi hugged Chazz dearly, and they disappeared.

Epilogue

Mel and Ruth found Faufi, Aulus, Baldy and Chazz waiting in her room.

"It was easy once I had the gyroscope back," Faufi explained when they were settled in her spacious living room over refreshments.

"I was still on the same fibre, so I left Chazz by the Eastern Gate in '67, reparametrized, and returned to scout.

"But there was plenty of time. Only one soldier had come into the tent, and when he saw me slow to canonical arclength parametrization, appearing to him out of thin air, he scooted back out screaming.

"The guards in the tent were still on the ground when Aulus, Baldy and I left." She smiled. "I thought it was worth a try, to see if I could bring them all home at once. So we still don't know the upper limit."

Her smiled broadened. She sipped her drink, then concluded: "But Smithers will never be the same."

Mel didn't want to see anyone he knew until he'd cleared his name. Sneaking onto the Technion campus, he entered the same classroom where Morris and Schmuyle had taken him to make their accusation. He knew it had been deserted then, and he found it deserted now. With the door opened a crack, he had an unobstructed view of his own office down the hall.

He drew the small brass gadget out of his jacket pocket.

When Mel had first used his gyroscope he had felt a thrill of godlike power as never before. So simply, so precisely, so safely, he had the freedom of all time. Of course, there were snags, complications, dangers; but he knew he was about to solve his problem.

With a brief mental calculation and a spin of the gyroscope, he was back at the time of his last tutorial. Down the hall a murmur of voices—Shoshana's and his own—came through his open office door.

First question: Who was that he had seen in the hall? Once he knew that, Mel could get his testimony that the door was open. That would at least help persuade Morris—

His question was answered as the unknown colleague appeared around the corner at the far end of the hall and walked toward Mel, glancing into his office as he passed it.

It was Schmuyle Goldenberg.

No! No! Wrong answer! That did no good at all! Why did it have to be *him*, of all people? Now what could he do?

Schmuyle turned down the main corridor before reaching the classroom where Mel hid.

He might as well finish the program. Second question: Who shut the door?

The answer to this was soon forthcoming. Back around the corner from the main corridor came Schmuyle, treading silently this time. He edged down the hall to Mel's office and, keeping a steady watch inside (*so he can be sure we don't see him—and we didn't*), carefully swung the door along its painted arc on the hall floor and quietly latched it shut, turning the knob to prevent a click. Then he moved rapidly away around the far corner.

I might have known, Mel thought. Schmuyle set the whole thing up. Probably got the idea, when he went past the first time and saw us in there.

But I'll never prove it. Witness gone, last chance gone. That ends it. I've done all I can. And failed.

Oh *God* why did You let this happen? To me—to Shoshana. God! Jesus! Help me now! I'm at my wits end!

They'll be coming here, with *me*. I've got to leave.

Shutting the door, he reversed the gyroscope's polarity, wound the spring, and vanished.

The classroom was still empty when he returned to the present—as he knew it would be—but when he opened the door, Irv was passing and saw him.

"You here!"

Here it comes, Mel thought.

"Congratulations on your second bar, Captain Schwartz."

Mel was speechless.

"Don't tell me you haven't heard! Just get back?" Irv beamed. "Gee, it's great to be the first to tell someone good news for a change. Morris announced it yesterday. Of course, knowing the IDF, you won't get the official paperwork for months. But it was a foregone conclusion once you got tenure—you didn't know that either? My God!"

"Is good," Mel finished for him. *Thank You, Jesus.*

'"My congratulations again. I always knew Sammy wasn't even in the running. He must have known it too; he's gone."

Mel squeaked, tried again. "Gone?"

"Resigned. I heard a rumor he went to try some teacher's college. Frankly, it's good riddance, far as I'm concerned."

What had happened? "He'll survive," Mel managed. "Irv, thanks for your good wishes. We've got to get some celebrating done, and catching up. I have some news for you, too."

"Oh yeah, the chilly conference. Was it any good? I was a little surprised when you—"

"I'm getting married."

This time Irv was speechless. I've never seen a jaw actually drop before, Mel thought. Was I considered that ineligible?

"Best of luck, old buddy," Irv said at last. "You're gonna love it. Listen, this calls for a party. Where is she?"

"Right now she's in New York. Irv, I've got to talk to Morris. Hate to rush off."

Morris provided the answer. "I tried to reach you in Moscow, but they seem to be having some trouble there. It was my wife, Naomi."

"Naomi?" asked Mel faintly.

"I have no secrets from her, of course. When I expressed my regret that you were going to have to be dismissed since Schmuyle and I had turned up no one who could corroborate your story, she recalled something she had seen which had hardly registered at the time."

"What had she seen?"

"She was walking over to join me for tea, happened to glance through your office window, and saw Schmuyle closing your door."

Mel was struck dumb at the beauty of this arrangement, the precision of God's control. The only other person who knew the story "happened" to be the key witness.

"She remembered wondering a little at it at the time, because you and Shoshana didn't seem to know he was doing it. You were engrossed at the board."

She'd even seen their innocence!

"That cleared you completely, of course. I gave Schmuyle the choice of resigning quietly or being ruined."

"I can't express how relieved I am, sir. Thank you. And thank your wife."

"You ought to thank your lucky stars that it was she who saw you."

No, only one Star. "I thank God for it, sir. It's an answer to prayer."

"Mel! You never struck me as the religious type."

Mel and Ruth were married the following June in a beautiful Messianic Jewish double wedding in Haifa near the Technion, in the presence of their families, colleagues and other friends, and Jeshua the Messiah.

Many of Mel's colleagues had still not realized who their Messiah was. "But we're workin' on them," Mel told the other groom, a tall, handsome, twenty-five-year-old Swedish mathematician.

"Good," he said.

"We'll get them! Eventually. Won't we, Carl?" asked his beautiful, petite blonde Swedish bride.

The two best men agreed.

"I break heads if we don't," the bald tuxedoed giant threatened in his newly adopted English.

"If anyone can, you can," said the handsome, fortyish man with the Italian profile.

Baldy and Aulus had thrown themselves with enthusiasm into the new identities Faufi had arranged for them and "Carl."

Chazz, having spent some years getting to know Faufi in the nineteenth century, was no longer recognizable as the teenager who had hijacked a 747 the previous fall, a crime still marked "unsolved" in Interpol's files.

Faufi had found the way to his heart by taking him to the premiere of "Scheherazade" in 1897 Boston.

They had agreed to settle down in turn-of-the-century Sweden, with frequent excursions to the 1990's. The double wedding had been Faufi's idea. "Of course, we also need a wedding in 1903. Otherwise my people would be scandalized."

"The Naughty Oughties weren't that naughty," agreed Chazz.

Bart had a job as bodyguard for an elder Israeli statesman, and Ollie was ostensibly in real estate, but this was only cover for his real job as an agent for Shin Beth.

A little girl with golden hair approached Mel.

"It was a beautiful wedding, Professor Schwartz."

"Glad you could come, Shoshana."

"And you're the prettiest bride, Mrs. Schwartz."

"Shana! You're the first person to call me Mrs. Schwartz!" Ruth swung her off her feet and kissed her fondly on the cheek. "And it sounds great!" Mel watched her in a glow of pride.

Waiting for the wedding photographer to set up, he asked Chazz, "What are you two doing after the reception?"

"Paris,1911. The Russian Ballet is performing to guess what music?"

"Do you ever think about that little Parthian girl…what was her name?"

"Aletha?" Chazz supplied. "I'll never forget what's-her-name. Yes, she sure was cute. Did she really have a crush on me?"

"You never noticed, huh?"

"What a dummox I was. Ah, missed opportunities."

"What are you boys discussing?" asked Faufi, coming over to join the photo group.

"Nothing important," Mel said.

"Just a Parthian cutie who had a crush on Mel. Don't tell Ruth."

"Ruth knows all about Aletha, remember?" said Ruth, walking up behind Chazz. "You were the one she kissed."

"What's this?" Faufi asked.

"Special circumstances," pleaded Chazz. "As Ollie would say, you didn't have a need to know."

"Shhh!" Mel whispered. He looked around, but no one was anywhere near.

"I bet I can guess, though," said Faufi. She rose on tiptoe, clasped Chazz firmly in her arms, and planted a long, sweet kiss on his lips. His eyebrows rose; then he responded with zest.

A round of scattered applause came from a group of wedding guests ten yards away. The couple came up for air.

"Was it like that?" Faufi asked.

Chazz grinned. "No, more like this." He showed her. This time the applause was accompanied by hoots and whoops.

A light flashed. They smiled.

"Smile," said the photographer.

"That's backwards," called a guest. "Can't you guys control your time sequences?"

"Maybe not," Mel replied, "but we know Who can."

Author's Notes

Inconveniently, Herod did not die so soon, nor as described. He arranged to split his kingdom among three of his sons, and died, according to Josephus, in 4 B.C. He was buried in his summer palace at Herodium.

Also, sadly, Sophia Vladimirovna Kovalevskaya ("Faufi") grew up in Moscow, not Stockholm. She survived V. Lenin but died in 1952 under J. Stalin. She seldom saw her mother, except for one joyous summer; I have, I like to think, improved her childhood.

Zamaris (Zimri) and his son Jacimus are chronicled in Josephus. Their history is essentially as described here, except that I have probably foreshortened the time between their exile to Valatha and their relocation to Batanea. Also, I named Zimri's wife Bathyra after a city he founded, not the reverse, and invented his beautiful brown-eyed daughter Aletha. Her name, incidentally, arose from a desire to stay close to the home keys, so as not to further fatigue my wife Christine's pinkie, exhausted from all the Z's she encountered (NebuchadneZZar, ChaZZ, Zaran) in typing the manuscript, for which herewith my heartfelt thanks.

Biblical quotations are from the Authorized (King James) Version, with the italicized words left out to simulate the Hebrew original. Atuman and Orondes are invented names for the Kings of Epiphany, and their home is given here as Anatolia rather than "the east," transliterating the New Testament Greek. Professor Herbert M. Howe, Chairman of the Classics Department at the University of Wisconsin while I was there, read the manuscript and made many helpful suggestions, among them: "Why modern Greek?" To this I can only answer that, not a koinë scholar, I'm pleased that my struggles with dictionary and phrasebook resulted in something recognizable as Greek at all.

And now the mathematics. Interested readers will find Sophia Vasilievna's Bordin Prize paper, "*Sur la probleme de la rotation d' un corps solide autour d' un point fixe*" (On the problem of the rotation of a solid body around a fixed point), in the 1889 *Acta Mathematica*, where she indeed constructed the fourth first integral by regarding time as a complex variable—i.e., planar, not linear. Her "lost" paper is still lost, but here's what she wrote about it: "I tell (in the letter to Hermite) of some, as it seems to me, astonishing and interesting results, which I found relative to the general case."

The dialogue in the Baghdad coffee shop does not describe the displayed integral, but that can indeed be evaluated by the method of residues, provided one knows the polynomial

$$P_{mn}(z) = (z-(m+i))(z-(m+1+i))...(z-(n+i)).$$

The integrand has a simple pole with residue k+6 at each point k+i, where $m \leq k \leq n$ and $i^2 = -1$. In order for the integral to remotely resemble anything in Mme. Kovalevskaya's work, or anything hyperelliptic, the denominator would need a radical (square root) sign around it.

The Kovalevskian gyroscope was constructed by Delone and does exist. Its peculiarity is that the center of rotation is not at the center of mass.

The theory of time travel is quite simple. It can be explained by treating the case of

CLASSIFIED

to provide stability, as described in the text.

The city of Babylon and its points of interest are as described in some sources, contradicted by others. I chose the ones I liked best. The soap in Nebuchadnezzar's showers was poor in quality, in Georges Contenau's phrase, not unlike the soap in occupied Europe.

Expert chronologies (of all time) also contradict each other, and I haven't completely worked out one to my satisfaction yet. It does seem clear to me, at least, that "Good Friday" was really "Good Wednesday," the confusion arising from the presence of an extra Sabbath in Holy Week.

I'd like to thank Jacob Neusner for his *History of the Jews in Babylonia*. Just when I was ready to write "They saw a crocodile, and it ate them all up. The End" it called to my attention a means for getting my travelers to Bethlehem: namely, Zimri's caravan.

I made many discoveries in the course of researching and writing this book. One of the most exciting was reading in the Encyclopedia Judaica that the scripture sung at the festival of First Fruits in Herod's Temple was Psalm 30. Since this feast began three days after Passover, it was probably just at the time of Jesus' resurrection that the Jews were singing "O Lord, thou hast brought up my soul from the grave.... What profit is in my blood, when I go down to the pit?" I hope this blesses you as much as it does me.

In fact, I hope the same for the entire book—that reading it has blessed you as much as writing it did me.

D.R.B.

Multi-talented David R. Beaucage has a doctorate in mathematics, as does his wife, Christine, who aided in the extensive research for *The Shiloh Project*. While attending Rutgers University, David sang William Walton's *Belshazzar's Feast* with Eugene Ormandy and the Philadelphia Orchestra. He has worked as a computer scientist, a mathematician, a programming manager and a consultant. He is currently a staff member for The Potter's Hands Ministries, living in southern California. *The Shiloh Project* is his first novel.

Further Enhance Your Walk With The Lord With A Selection From America's Favorite Bible Studies

Further Enhance Your Walk With The Lord With A Selection From America's Favorite Bible Studies

[illegible] Bible Skills. [illegible] Paperback 328 pages, $[illegible].95. ISBN 1-56322-[illegible]

[illegible] the Faith. [illegible] Christianity [illegible] ISBN 1-56322-[illegible] [illegible]

[illegible] Relationships. [illegible] Paper 201 pages [illegible] Teacher's [illegible] Guide [illegible] ISBN 1-56322-[illegible]

[illegible] the [illegible] Testament. [illegible] Guide [illegible] cultural and political [illegible] Paper 126 pages $[illegible].95. [illegible] Guide [illegible] ISBN [illegible]

Faith [illegible] Understanding. [illegible] Paper [illegible] pages. $[illegible] ISBN [illegible]

[illegible] God's Way. [illegible] ISBN [illegible]

[illegible] Studies Turned [illegible] ISBN 1-56322-015-0

Becoming the Noble Woman. [illegible] ISBN [illegible]

Through the [illegible] Year. [illegible] ISBN 1-[illegible] ISBN [illegible]

Through [illegible] ISBN 1-56322-[illegible] ISBN [illegible]

Through the Bible in One Year. [illegible] principles of Christianity. [illegible] ISBN 1-56322-[illegible] ISBN 1-56322-[illegible]

All titles available through your local Christian bookstore